DEAD OF WINTER

TOM THREADGILL

Library of Congress Cataloging-in-Publication Data

Threadgill, Tom.

Dead of Winter / Tom Threadgill 1st ed.

Printed in the United States of America

for my dad
the best man I've ever known

ACKNOWLEDGEMENTS

I'll let you in on a little secret. Most writers are introverts. It's not that we don't like people (well, maybe sometimes it is, especially when we're out of coffee). It's just that being around others tends to sap our energy. We'd prefer to go days at a time without speaking to anyone. In fact, my wife asks me to do so quite frequently.

That said, writing a book that's worth reading is never a solo project. Sure, it's the author's name on the cover, but it takes the help of skilled professionals to really make the story shine. They polish the story, get it ready for publishing, market it, and handle all the details (like talking to people) that most authors would rather avoid.

My agent, Linda S. Glaz, has been there with me each step of the way. Her guidance and encouragement have been priceless. This book would not be here without her.

Darla Crass, my editor, has pushed me at every turn to make the story better. All authors cringe when the edits arrive in their inbox, but Darla's patience and knowledge have been invaluable. And to all the others at Lighthouse who helped make this book happen, I can't thank you enough. It's a pleasure to work with such outstanding people.

Finally, thanks to my wife, Janet, who supports me in every possible way. There's nobody else I'd rather travel through life with. Love you, babe. Always have. Always will.

1

J eremy Winter kneaded the evidence bag until the severed
finger pressed against the plastic. The top of the nail was bent
backward, nearly ripped from the flesh. She'd fought hard.

Three days since the finger had been sliced from her. The killer
had placed it in a Ziploc bag and mailed it. Same as all the others.
No odor, though the gases from decay had caused the sandwich
baggie to swell a bit.

Decomp was in full swing. The dry, brown skin had shrunk as it
lost moisture. A small arc of clear space grew between the chipped
red nail polish and the cuticle. The bone, a proximal phalanx the
doctors called it, jutted slightly beyond the clean cut. A tiny
splotch of blood, most likely the victim's, smeared the bottom
corner of the Ziploc.

He pointed to the evidence. "See how the skin has pulled back
from the cuticle? People used to think the fingernails kept growing
after death, but in reality—"

The postal inspector looked away and stifled a dry heave. "That
the one you're looking for?"

Jeremy tilted his head. "Why? You got more of these lying around somewhere?"

FBI Agent Maggie Keeley sighed and shook her head. "Ignore Mr. Winter. He's here in a consultant capacity only. Yes, that's the one we're looking for. We appreciate your help."

The inspector nodded and kept his focus on Maggie. "You made it easy for us. Told us where the envelope was coming from and who it'd be addressed to. Of course, we'd have caught it in the screening process even if we hadn't been given the information."

Jeremy arched his eyebrows. Three had been sent before this, and they'd only caught one, despite the enhanced procedures in place since 9/11. He was still trying to talk Maggie into letting him see the video of the Supreme Court clerks opening the mail and finding the fingers. She'd refused because she thought he would laugh at their reactions. He'd assured her he wouldn't. They both knew he was probably lying.

Maggie took the evidence bag and placed it in her briefcase. "Thank you for your help. We need to head back to the office and start working on this."

"So, um, the people these fingers come from ... I mean, are they, uh, dead?"

Maggie clicked her briefcase closed and headed for the door. "Have a nice day."

"Sure, sure," the man said. "Listen, uh, you think there will be more of these coming through?"

Jeremy paused. Four so far. Five more unless they caught the killer first. Based on what they had so far, he knew the answer. "Yeah," he said. "There's gonna be more."

2

She was under there.

Waiting for him.

He knew because he'd put her there, and bones hadn't moved on their own since Ezekiel prophesied in Old Testament days. Levi licked his lips and forced himself to wait. Let his adrenaline gorge on the anticipation.

The musty scent of the old house coated his mouth, and he worked up a good spit, then swallowed. Get it out, but not here. Not this room.

His thumbs rubbed circles on the other fingertips, and he closed his eyes, remembering.

Delighting.

Dem bones, dem bones, dem dry bones.

He hunched his shoulders forward and craned his neck, oozing the tension back to its hiding place. The west Texas wind swept under the house and up between the gaps in the floorboards. Dust fanned in every direction and spread the odor of worn-out dirt into the room. Lasers of light beamed through tiny holes in the tinfoil-covered window, scarcely illuminating the area. The bare bulb overhead had long ago given up hope of ever shining again. No matter. He knew his way around his bedroom.

The heavy oak dresser scratched the rotting floor as he dragged it away from the wall. He tugged his T-shirt's sleeve across his forehead, cleared his throat, and fixated on the floor where the bureau had been. His duffel bag held his necessaries, and he rooted through it, shoving rags and knives and duct tape and other essentials aside before finding the hammer. He wedged the claw between the floorboards and yanked on the handle, splintering the edges of the decaying wood.

Years had passed since he had last seen her, and there was no point in hurrying now. Lord knows she wasn't going anywhere. Not this time.

The daisy first, then we'll talk.

Moments later, the ritual ended. Flower petals died on the floor, insignificant ghosts lost in the next gust of wind.

He sat next to her, tilting the skull so he could look her in the eye sockets. They chatted briefly. She, quiet and contrite. He, forgiving but not forgetting.

A car horn interrupted his solitude, and his hands morphed into fists, daring her to honk again. Seconds later, she did. He ripped the foil from the window and glared at the vehicle.

A woman leaned out the passenger side and squinted, shading her face with her hand. Her shrill screams intensified his anger. "Cody, hurry up. I'm getting hot out here."

He exhaled a stream of torrid breath and ran a hand across his face before turning away. Time to go.

After exchanging goodbyes and shoving the dresser back into place, he hurried down the narrow hallway, careful to avert his eyes as he passed his mother's bedroom. Things happened in there. More things forgiven, but not forgotten.

His arm and shoulder scraped along the wall. Blood from his lip oozed onto his tongue. Warm, metallic, comforting. *Jesus loves me, this I know.* Safely in the living room, he paused to look at the faded yellow sign hanging on the open front door. *CONDEMNED BY THE SHERIFF'S OFFICE OF PECOS COUNTY, TEXAS.* The house didn't look much different than it had when they'd left about a year ago, but nobody cared about it back when the property taxes were being paid.

Outside, the stifling air blanketed the homestead. February shouldn't be this hot. The place hadn't changed, except for the rusted metal chair that no longer kept guard on the porch. The seat was now wedged against a mesquite tree halfway across the yard, a victim of the wind. A perfect picture painted for him by the Lord.

The tree represented Levi, planted and prospering. The chair signified the wicked and ungodly spoken of in Psalms: "The chaff which the wind driveth away."

Chaff. Tossed in the breeze and burned in the fire. Worthless. Like America.

But God had a plan. It was all right there if people would read and understand. The Lord had done it for Israel and, with Levi's help, He'd do it for America. The plan had worked once, and, with a few adjustments, it'd work again.

Warmth flashed through him, and he flexed his fingers, allowing the tingling sensation to overpower him. He'd wake them up. Show them their sins. Just as Israel had repented throughout its history, America would too. Jehovah's plan hinged on Levi's obedience, and he dared not fail Him. Not again.

The horn blasted once more, and he trudged toward the car, his jaw aching as he ground his teeth together. He tossed the duffel in the trunk and slid behind the wheel. "I told you, Mom. My name is Levi now. Call me Levi."

"I don't understand why. Cody was always good enough before. Why did we have to come back here anyway?" She pulled her woolen sweater tighter, clutching the thick fabric across her sagging breasts.

"For the thousandth time, the house is on the way, and I

wanted to check on the place. And if you're so hot, why don't you take off that sweater?"

"I get cold without it. And you know I don't like coming here."

And why is that, Mom? He started the car and watched the house grow smaller in his rearview mirror. "Okay, we're going. Tell you what. How about we swing into the first Whataburger we see? It's been a while since we had a shake from there. You used to love them, remember? What's it gonna be? Chocolate or strawberry?"

She patted him on the arm. "Chocolate, I think. But get me a small. You know what dairy does to my stomach. And you get a strawberry, in case I want to taste it."

"Sure, Mom."

She flipped down the visor and leaned close to the mirror. Her thin fingers tried in vain to poof the wispy strands of her sparse gray hair. "How long will it take us to get to Portland?"

"Another couple of days. But it's worth the drive. I'm pretty excited about this interview."

"Well, I certainly hope so. Rambling all over the country like some sort of hobo is no business for an old woman. Florida, Arizona, that horrible New York. I don't know how much more I can take."

Levi massaged his left temple. "We're not hobos. And it's not like I'm not trying."

"I wish you'd got that job in Nashville."

"Yeah, me too. You never know, though. If Oregon doesn't work out, I've got a feeling we may head back to Tennessee. But the human resources lady in Portland seems really nice. She said they're desperate for some help."

"I don't understand why you're having so much trouble finding a job. A nice boy like you with a good education."

"It's the economy. Everybody's looking for work. Even pharmacists. And it's only been six months since I graduated. Finding decent work takes time."

"All that money for college, and for what? I didn't scrimp and save my whole life so I could sleep in rundown motels. You know Cody, when your father left—"

He threw his hands in the air. "Mom, do we have to go through this again? I appreciate everything you did for me. *Everything.* But can you please let it go?"

His mother turned away and stared out the window, veiny hands clasped together in her lap. "You just don't know what it was like."

Don't I? He reached over and stroked her arm, resisting the urge to move his hand to her neck. "Mom, I'm sorry. It's been a long day."

She turned toward him and grinned, her yellowed teeth accented with red lipstick smears. "I forgive you. It's what Jesus would do. Now then, what's her name?"

"Who?"

"The woman you're interviewing with in Portland. I'll say a special prayer for her."

"Oh. I don't remember right off hand. Susie, Sally, something like that."

"Well, I'll pray for her anyway."

"That'd be great, Mom. I'm sure she'd appreciate it."

"You should pray for her too, you know. God answers prayers."

"Oh, I have been praying, Mom. I have been."

Soon I'll lay her down to sleep,

I pray the Lord her soul to keep,

And when she dies, she will not wake,

I pray the Lord her soul to take.

3

The Frothy Monkey teemed with people this morning, mostly college students by the look of them. Vanderbilt, Belmont, probably a few others mixed in. Young, hip, and gluten-free. Jeremy Winter would've preferred somewhere a bit less ... trendy. Someplace off Broadway, down near Nashville's famous honky-tonks and tourist shops, where they played real music and served real coffee in real old mugs. Not his call to make, though. The girl had insisted on meeting him here, no doubt because of the crowd. He couldn't blame her. Not after what she'd been through.

He kept an eye on the door while sipping his free-trade java. Not quite strong enough, but at least it smelled right. No free refills, though. This one would have to last until—

His left leg spasmed, and he squeezed the calf in a futile effort to dull the pain. More than sixteen years since Afghanistan and the knifelike aches still attacked without warning. The damage from the explosion at the Miller farm four months ago hadn't done him any favors either. His mental recovery had been fast, mostly thanks to his girlfriend, Maggie, and her six-year-old daughter, Rebecca. The physical recovery, not so much. Forty-seven years old, prime of his life, shouldn't take this long to get over bumps and bruises. At least that's what he wanted to believe.

His retirement from the Bureau had gone as planned. Smoother than he'd thought possible, considering the accommodations that'd been made. Full pension and insurance. Solid recommendations. Even some consulting work thrown his way now and then. Nothing big. Mostly background investigations, guest lecturing at Quantico, things like that.

Until this. FBI Deputy Director Bailey's call had been curt. Clearly, the man wasn't keen on using Jeremy. Their relationship had been coolly civil, especially toward the end of Jeremy's time with the Bureau. Going over Bailey's head to a senator probably had something to do with that. Jeremy had even considered turning down this contract just to spite him, but what would that accomplish? The money was good, and until he figured out what to do with his retirement, why not stay busy? Keep his name in the game. Besides, with Maggie still working at the FBI, upsetting the Director might not be his best move.

And so here he sat, waiting for a woman who may or may not have anything to do with a case that may or may not involve a serial killer. The Bureau felt there was no connection between this woman and the others. Couldn't be, for one simple reason. She was still alive. And yet, they'd wanted someone to take a second look at the files. Preferably, a person with extensive experience dealing with serial killers. A professional who'd spent the better part of a career identifying, chasing, and apprehending the worst society had to offer.

The Bureau wanted Jeremy.

He'd worked for the FBI long enough to know one thing for sure: nothing was as important as catching their prey. Nothing. The politics and infighting and bureaucracy were all there but could be set aside, albeit temporarily, when the situation demanded it. And Bailey must've figured this case had enough questions that it was worth putting up with Jeremy. Maggie had confirmed a small task force was being formed, but it was all hush-hush at this point. Didn't want word leaking to the public.

A gusty chill shot through the room as a young woman, bundled and scarfed against the frosty morning, slipped into the coffeehouse and scanned the patrons. Jeremy glanced at the photo on his phone. That had to be her. Late 20s, maybe five-three, hundred-twenty pounds. Hair was shorter and dyed a strawberry blonde. New glasses too. But that was definitely Claire Lawson. He stood and gave a half-wave to attract her attention, then put on his best smile—the one Maggie made him practice—when the woman made eye contact. Claire nodded and weaved his direction.

Jeremy motioned toward the chair across from him. "Miss Lawson? Jeremy Winter. Thank you for meeting me."

She pulled off her knitted gloves and shook his hand. "Certainly, Mr. Winter. Though I can't imagine I can tell you more than you already know."

"Can I get you some coffee? Maybe some hot tea? Bit brisk out there today."

She unwrapped the scarf from her neck and stashed the gloves in her coat pocket. "No, thank you. If it's all the same to you, I'd like to get this over with. I need to get back to work."

"You work from home, is that correct?"

"Yeah, I mean, I've moved since all that happened, but I still ..." She stared at him for a moment. "Um, do you have some ID I can see? It's not that I don't—"

"Please, Miss Lawson. You *should* be careful. Here's my badge and driver's license. You'll note, as I said on the phone, the badge has *retired* stamped on it. You're more than welcome to contact the FBI to verify I am who I say I am. I'd be happy to wait."

She passed the items back to him. "I don't think that'll be necessary. I called the local office before coming here this morning. They confirmed you were in town, though I still don't understand why you're here."

Jeremy rested his forearms on the table and clasped his hands together. "Of course. On occasion, the Bureau uses consultants to follow up on things that may not need the attention of a full-time agent. It saves taxpayer money, and if we do find something that requires the full force of the FBI, rest assured we turn everything over and let them handle it."

Claire scrunched her face and raised an eyebrow. "Uh-huh. And my case falls in that territory? Why is the FBI even looking at it? I thought the local police were handling the investigation."

How much to tell her? Always the tricky part. Unlike the FBI Director, Jeremy was convinced of a connection between Claire Lawson and murders in Tampa, Phoenix, Norfolk, and Binghamton. Barely two weeks ago, she'd been attacked in her home. The details had popped up in the Bureau's database due to some similarities with the other four crime scenes. Calls to the local detectives hadn't shed much light. They assumed it was a home robbery gone wrong. Probably a druggie. But they didn't know about the other women. By rights, Claire Lawson should be dead, and Jeremy needed to understand why she wasn't. It meant something. Something important.

"Yes, ma'am. The Nashville police do have jurisdiction. I'm looking into your, um, incident, because there may be similarities between it and a few other cases we're investigating. I've seen the detective's file, but I was hoping after some time had passed that you might remember a bit more. Maybe a detail you didn't mention in the prior interviews?"

Claire leaned forward. "Other cases? In Nashville? The police told me it was probably a guy looking to pawn stuff for drug money. That never made sense to me, considering nothing was taken even though he knocked me out. Plus the Propofol. I mean, drug addicts don't have that stuff, do they?"

Jeremy sipped his coffee and dragged the back of his hand across his mouth. The sound of ice being blended and crushed overpowered the room for a moment. Who buys an iced drink in February? "The other incidents aren't in Nashville. I'm sorry, but I really can't go into a lot of detail about those cases. We, the FBI I mean, just want to make sure there's no connection between what happened to you and what we're looking into elsewhere."

She crossed her arms and studied him for a moment. "You want me to go through it again? Agent Winter, I'm—"

"Just Jeremy, please. I'm technically not an agent anymore."

"Okay, Jeremy. I'm trying to forget everything about that day. I'm sure you understand why. But if it'll help, I'll tell you what I remember on two conditions. First, when I'm done, you'll tell me about the other cases."

He scratched the back of his neck and sighed. People always think they want to know. Most times, they don't. "I'll share what I can. No promises, though. And the second?"

"A White Monkey Mocha to go. Large."

"Now, that I can definitely manage."

Claire nodded and took a deep breath. "It was around nine-thirty on a Tuesday morning. I was working at my desk in the second bedroom and thought I heard a noise. The apartments were old, and you could hear everything through the walls. I figured it was just one of the neighbors going out. It wasn't."

"You work for an insurance company, correct?"

She stared down at the table. "Yeah, I do. Helping patients make appointments, that kind of stuff. Nothing too dramatic."

He turned his palms up and gave his best smile again. Training taught him victims needed encouragement and sympathy. His experience taught him there was usually something they forgot. Something vital. Juggling the emotions of the victim with his need for information was a skill he'd always struggled with. "You're doing great. So you heard a noise, and then what happened?"

"Well, I didn't think much of it. Then the door to my office squeaked. I kept it mostly closed because it was always cold, even in the summer. I had a heater next to my desk to keep the room warmer. But when the door creaked …"

She sniffled and rubbed her hands together as if washing them in an invisible sink.

His throat tightened. He repositioned himself, shifting his right hip away from the back of the seat. He let his elbow rest on the butt of the Glock holstered on his waist. Solid and lethal. "Take your time, Miss Lawson. I know this is difficult."

She brushed a hand under each eye. "Before I could turn around, he grabbed me. One hand on my shoulder pushing me down, and the other across my mouth. He told me not to scream."

"Left or right shoulder?"

"Left."

Probably right-handed. "Okay. What else?"

"That's it. I woke up on the floor and called 911. He was gone, and as far as I could tell, nothing was missing. He left white flower petals scattered around, though. No one could figure out what that was about. The police said he came in through the sliding door on my deck. I guess I forgot to lock it. They took me to the hospital, and I stayed overnight."

"No evidence of sexual assault, correct?"

"He didn't rape me."

"Yes, ma'am. According to the hospital report, they found Propofol in your system?"

"Uh-huh. It's a general anesthetic. Same thing that killed Michael Jackson. I was unconscious for almost an hour. But like I said, what kind of drug addict carries that around?"

Jeremy ignored the question. "Was there anything distinctive about his voice? An accent? Bad breath?"

"Nothing that stands out. Look, I've been through this a thousand times in my head. I don't remember anything else. I wish I did." She closed her eyes and massaged her forehead. "I really do."

"I know you do." He handed his business card to her. "Put my number in your speed dial. I think I've taken up enough of your time for now."

"We're not done here. We had a deal."

He leaned back in his chair. "Miss Lawson, are you sure you're up to this?"

"Yes. I think so. Please."

He rubbed his chin and sighed. "There've been four other attacks around the country. Yours was the fifth. In each case, we found flower petals. That's really all I can tell you." *Don't ask. Please don't ask.*

"What happened to the other girls?"

Jeremy swallowed hard. "They weren't as fortunate as you."

Her shoulders drooped. "Meaning?"

He scratched an imaginary itch on his arm. "Meaning they didn't survive their attacks."

Claire nodded and stared into his eyes. "Is he coming back?"

Jeremy cleared his throat and scrubbed a hand across his chest. "We don't know."

Wrinkles deepened on her forehead. "Do you have children?"

Heat flashed through him, and concealed emotions flooded his body. Does he have children? No. Had. At least was going to have before his wife and unborn daughter's murder back in 2002 when he was overseas defending his country instead of protecting his family. Holly and Miranda, his wife and dau—

"Mr. Winter?"

He drew his lips into his mouth and shook his head.

"Well, if you did have a daughter, what would you tell her to do if she was in my place?"

He squeezed the table's edge and locked eyes with the young woman. "Miss Lawson, do you own a gun?"

Her eyes widened, and a barely audible *no* crept from her mouth.

"Get one and learn to use it."

4

Levi squinted into the darkness before easing into the parking lot of the Portland Palace Motel and creeping to a stop in front of the office. The tail end of a rain shower spit a few final drops on his windshield. Distant rumbles threatened an angry return. A buzzing neon sign reflected its red *Vacancy* light on the wet pavement, creating a devilish pathway to the door. The lone streetlight flickered above a group of three women clustered near the curb, their meager apparel no match for the damp chill.

He climbed out of the car, careful not to wake his mother. Three hours of snoring had worn on him, but anything was better than her constant self-diagnosis of health problems, imagined or otherwise. One of the women shivering at the street headed his direction, and he stared for a moment, frozen as she approached. A dozen rapid heartbeats passed before he jutted his jaw and exhaled a steamy breath across his face. A quick flip of his hand in her direction to shoo her off, then he turned toward the motel's office.

A bell slammed against the glass door hard enough to explain the crack zagging from the top, but no one greeted him. Noise poured from a back room, and he leaned over the counter for a better view. A small TV sat on a coffee table and blared an infomercial while two stockinged feet wiggled next to it. The chirpy woman on the screen rubbed a grater across the soles of her feet, raving about how smooth they felt. As a bonus, her husband loved her more. Levi's fingernails dug into his palms.

He knocked on the countertop. "Hello?" No one responded. "HELLO?"

An overstated yawn echoed above the TV's volume, followed by a gaudy, wet snort. "Yeah, yeah. I'm coming."

The feet slid off the table, and the clerk shuffled to the front desk, never bothering to look at his customer. Red-and-black plaid shorts hung low on the man's waist, and a muscle shirt had abandoned its efforts to cover his belly. His ponytailed hair would have been better served obscuring the random tattoos and scars dotting his neck and face. A roach scurried from under the counter, and he stomped on the pest, using a magazine to scrape the bug parts off his sock. *Men's Health*. Of course.

He yawned and peered at Levi through half-closed eyes. "By the hour or day?"

"Actually," Levi said, "I'll be here for a week. Double beds please."

The clerk glanced up and shrugged. "Huh. Thirty dollars a day, cash up front. No refunds. Any fighting, I call the cops, and you're gone."

"No problem." Levi pulled the money from his wallet, allowing his fingertips to brush the wafer-thin fragments of white paper carefully tucked behind the twenties.

"Fill out this card. Name and address, in case we need to find your next of kin."

"Little bit of motel humor there, huh?" He tapped a foot and wrote the usual information on the form, twice stealing a glance at the clerk. Lots of roaches here.

The man held the registration at arm's length. "Aster Bellis. You a foreigner or something?" He tossed the card in a file cabinet and chose a key from the pegboard. "Room 12. I'm kinda busy, so if there's nothing else?"

"Nope, that's it. Thanks." Levi returned to the car, his mother's snoring perceptible from several yards away. He idled halfway down the parking lot, bouncing from pothole to pothole. The 2 from his door lay on the ground, and the 1 hung cockeyed, lonely and desperate. Lovely.

"Wake up, Mom. We're at the hotel. Let's get you inside."

He helped her to the room and slipped off her shoes. "You okay?"

She mumbled and crawled under the covers.

"I'll get our stuff." By the time he returned, his mother was snoring again.

He sat on the end of his bed and looked around the room. Old TV, dusty dresser, nightstand lamp shaped like a grizzly and stained blue carpet. Should've brought that condemned sign. He slumped backward and stared at the ceiling, welcoming the exhaustion as it slinked into his body, filling first his arms, then chest, before finally skulking toward his feet. A peaceful sleep blanketed him, and he dreamed of the bear lamp growling in a low, steady rhythm.

A few hours later, the hazy sunshine of an Oregon winter's morning pried open his eyelids. An apparently quart-sized hot water heater meant a two-minute shower, though, from the looks of the tub, Levi didn't mind. He'd seen crime scenes cleaner than that bathroom. Several of them. The less time in there, the better. He dressed and tapped his mother's shoulder.

"Time to get up, Mom. Got a lot to do today. I thought we'd take a drive and check out the sights."

His mother peeked from under the thin bedspread. "I don't know, Cody. I'm tired and don't feel good."

"Really?" He placed his hand on her forehead. "You do feel kind of warm. Tell you what. I'll swing by a drug store and pick up aspirin and a few other things. You rest today. I'll bring you something to eat too."

"Such a sweet boy. You go out and enjoy yourself. You've got a big interview tomorrow, so relax. Don't worry about me. Oh, and are there any of those white donuts left?"

He switched on the TV. "Yeah, Mom. I'll put them on the nightstand. Look, there's a *Murder, She Wrote* marathon on. You like that don't you?"

"I was so sad when she died. Such a good actress."

"Mom, she's not dea … forget it. I won't be gone long. You get some rest."

The Australian woman in his GPS directed him to the closest drug store, where he purchased aspirin, cold medicine, and junk food. After topping off his gas tank, he returned to the motel, provisions in hand. His mother dozed again, and he sat across from her on his bed, watching her heavy breaths gradually slow before accelerating again. Each time, his pulse quickened, hope and fear rising within. The process repeated itself several times before he bent over, brushed her hair back, and kissed her forehead.

"Wake up, Mom. Grabbed everything you need," he said. "It was slim pickings on the cold medicine, though."

"Any food?"

He shook his head and rustled through the bag. "Sorry. They were out of pretty much everything. I did find …" He jerked his hand out of the bag and showed off the treasure. "Powdered mini-donuts and dark chocolate M&Ms."

Her chuckle morphed into a harsh, phlegmy cough. "You spoil me, boy."

He handed her two green capsules and twisted open a bottled water. "Take two of these now, and two more in four hours if I'm not back. It'll take care of those symptoms and help you sleep too."

"I'll be fine. You go on and run around today. We might be living here soon, you know. Pick us out a nice area of town."

He kissed her on the cheek. "Love you, Mom. Get some rest. See you in a little while."

......

Levi cruised through downtown Portland until he found a café with a few wrought iron tables on the sidewalk. A chalkboard displayed a beaming sun sipping steaming coffee. A few people milled out front, chatting or sipping their drinks. An older couple held hands as two basset hounds sniffed the ground around their table, hoping to hit the crumb lottery. A cool breeze tossed puffy gray clouds across the sky, but the sun fought to spread its warmth on the customers. This would do.

He parked, chose a table away from other patrons, and eased onto the frigid metal seat. After ordering coffee and a croissant, he opened his laptop, accessed the free Wi-Fi, and established a secure connection. He grinned at the familiar multicolored logo on his screen. Yes, Mom, I do have "the Google" on my computer.

The waiter brought his order, and he sampled the roll. Buttery, flaky, and a touch of honey. Perfect. The coffee was a tad bland, a bit too mild for his taste, but not so much that it would ruin a pleasant day. A sporadic parade of people wandered past, window-shopping, jogging, or socializing. People watching, one of his favorite things. Not as nice as people-selecting, but still ... A young woman hurried along, pushing a stroller the size of a small car. He couldn't tell if there was an actual baby in there or just a pair of eyes surrounded by blankets. He shook his head and returned to his laptop.

The list of churches on his screen ran the gamut of organized religion. Methodist? Maybe. Baptist? Done that. Could do it again, though. Church of Christ? Catholic? Hmm ... kind of in the mood for Baptist again. He filtered his search results and clicked on a link near the top of the page. Big sanctuary, two services, people in suits, others in shorts, not televised. Worth a look.

He downed the last of his coffee and drove to the chosen church, stopping a short distance away from the building. Red brick covered the façade, with white columns supporting the roof over the entryway. Large clear windows along the side allowed light to stream into the sanctuary. Stained glass would be so much prettier.

The freshly paved and painted parking lot extended to the back of the church, and he caught whiffs of the new asphalt. Three men worked on the landscaping, two raking leaves and the other spreading mulch. Doing yard work in the dead of winter. Who'd have thought? On the outside at least, this church was beautiful.

A sign listed the hours for the services below the changeable message. "Come and meet God here this Sunday." Oooh … a special guest. Wonder if He'll be doing a book signing? Have to stop by tomorrow and see.

He pulled away from the curb and headed to the next stop, a Walmart superstore. Experience taught him their choice of flowers was more than adequate, and the individualized attention of a florist was definitely to be avoided. He idled through the lot, pleased with the crowds. People hustled in and out of the store, many of them returning unwanted Christmas gifts. He'd be one person among hundreds.

He found a spot near the back of the lot and wandered into the store. Customers with items to return ventured to the right, many toting crying children along with their bags. The employees there obviously lost their pasted smiles hours earlier, daring the hawkish supervisor to say something.

The floral department was in the back, and he slalomed through the shoppers to the display. Poinsettias lined both sides of the aisle, on their third markdown with no takers. Pretty, but sagging a bit and unwanted. Their competition, bouquets of roses and assorted spring flowers, stood proudly in the bright case, freshly misted and flaunting their wares. He brushed his fingers across a white daisy, the hairs on his arm rising as a wave of dizziness passed over him. So delicate and pure.

Only one thing missing now, but today was Saturday. He'd have to wait until tomorrow to find her. The day of rest. Sunday morning church. The Lord would provide. Levi would accept. Obedience demanded it.

He returned to the motel, observing the neighborhoods take on a darker persona as he drove. Run-down houses stood in stark contrast to the charming homes around the church. A few people sat on their porches, smoking, drinking, or simply staring. Women still gathered under the motel's streetlight, but he couldn't be sure whether they were the ones from the previous night.

His mother sat in the chair by the window and smiled as he entered the room. White flecks dotted her lips, remnants of the powdered donuts. Angela Lansbury worked a new case on TV, determined to serve justice again. That woman never quits.

"Hi, Mom. Feeling better?"

"Cody, look at those women out there. You know what they are, don't you?"

"Yeah, Mom, I do. I won't go near them, I promise."

"Such a good boy. We'll find the right girl for you. We just have to keep looking. She's out there somewhere."

Warmth spread through his body, giving him a prickly sensation on his scalp. "Sure she is. That's why I'm always on the lookout. You never know where you'll find her. Now, go get dressed. We'll grab dinner and be back here before dark. I want to get to bed early. Big day tomorrow."

His mother groaned and pushed herself out of the chair, pausing to catch her breath. "Sweetie, why are your interviews always on Sundays? It's such an odd day."

"Not sure, but I don't mind. People are nicer on weekends. More relaxed."

"Well, I hope so. Now, give me a few minutes to get ready. You watch and tell me if she solves the case." She planted her hands on her hips and looked out the window at the women huddled together beside the street. "It's a pity. But they'll get what they deserve."

He waited until she closed the bathroom door then increased the TV volume and stared outside. A car stopped in front of the women, and one of them leaned into the passenger side. Seconds later, she entered the vehicle, and the car drove away. A slow, steady stream of air flowed through his puckered lips, relieving the pain in his clenched jaw. Raspy coughing echoed through the bathroom door, distracting him. *Show's over.*

He closed the curtain and sprawled on the bed, belly down, feet at the headboard, and a pillow propped under his chin. Half a donut rested on the nightstand, a powdered white smile among the dust. He popped the treat into his mouth, licked his fingers, and focused on the TV. Okay, Angela. Let's see what you've got.

......

The crowd at the early service skewed younger, as he expected. The sanctuary, older but obviously remodeled, had three sections plus a closed off balcony. Levi sat on the end of a pew along the right aisle. Clusters of young adults gathered in their cliques around the church, but no one spoke to him. The old man who gave him a bulletin had at least nodded, so that counted for something.

A group of women settled on a pew across the aisle, giggling and showing each other pictures on their phones. Based on their makeup, they'd spent hours standing in front of a mirror. All wore different variations of the same outfit: a dress that ended somewhere around their knees, dark leggings, and furry boots. If they had swords, they'd be female musketeers.

The buzz in the sanctuary settled as the pastor took his seat. An older man shuffled to the pulpit, leaned into the microphone, and in a deep, shaky voice said, "Let us pray." The "Amen" came at last, and Levi wasn't sure if he'd heard the opening prayer or the sermon.

A man with spiky hair bounced up the steps to the stage, and with a quick "Are y'all ready to worship?" jumped into a song. Levi didn't know the tune, but the guitars and drums were loud enough to drown him out anyway. The musketeers still focused on their phones, glancing up occasionally to make sure they weren't missing anything.

Except the girl on the end.

He tilted forward and, careful to keep his face focused on the choir, used his peripheral vision to watch the young woman. Her eyes were closed, and she swayed ever so slightly in time with the music. She held her hands in front of her, palms up, and her lips moved, but she wasn't singing. Tension eased from Levi's body, and he grabbed the back of the pew to steady himself. God is good. Eyes closed. Head bowed. *Thank you, Lord.*

Three more unfamiliar songs later, the offering plate made its appointed rounds. On some rows the platter moved like a game of hot potato, on others, it halted as mothers dug coins from their purses, training and bribing their children at the same time. Levi placed a folded five-dollar bill in the plate and handed it off to a deacon, who did his best not to glance at those who didn't donate.

After a soloist performed a lilting version of "How Great Thou Art," the pastor took his spot at the podium. He wore a dark suit, but no tie. Bet he puts a tie on for the second service. The preacher glared at the congregation for a good ten seconds. Dramatic pause. Did they teach that in seminary? Finally, the minister cleared his throat and theatrically opened his Bible.

"Life, my friends, can be hard," he said. "Look at the world around us. Wars, disease, famine, poverty. Suffering is everywhere. But I'm here to tell you it doesn't have to be that way. That's not the world God designed for us. Folks, God wants better for you. He wants you to be happy. He wants you to be successful. Like a proud

Father watching over His children, God has promised to give you whatever you ask for."

And we're done. Levi reached for the Bible in the back of the pew and thumbed through the crisp pages, searching for the right passage. Here we go. Acts. "I will show him how much he must suffer for My name." Huh. Guess God didn't want *him* to be happy. Or Stephen or Job or pretty much all the apostles or even His own Son. If anyone knew suffering, it was Jesus.

He closed the Bible and contemplated the young woman again. Short brunette hair, dark-rimmed glasses, blue sweater over her gray dress. She chewed on the end of a pen for a moment, then wrote in her Bible.

The preacher rambled about God's ways and His plans. Levi listened long enough to hear the minister repeat "prosper" several times. A few "Amens" popped up around the sanctuary. Levi picked up his bulletin and read the events of the week. The pastor said something about having enough faith to ask for what we want. Levi scanned the rest of the bulletin. Oh, now he's talking about a mustard seed. Don't have it because you don't have enough faith. His nostrils flared. Sweat beaded on his forehead, and he sat on his hands, struggling not to scream. *Do you even know who God is?* Maybe He'll be here in time for the eleven o'clock service.

Mercifully, the preacher finished, and the congregation sang a closing hymn. A few people stayed to chat, but most hurried from the building, their Sunday obligation checked off their to-do lists. The young woman stood, and Levi glanced away, breathing hard. She walked out of the church alone, her friends still enraptured by their phones. He followed her outside and strolled to his car, maintaining a respectable distance. She stopped three rows before him and climbed into a small yellow Subaru.

Decals lined her car's bumper. Know Jesus, Know Peace. Do You Follow Jesus This Close? Save The Baby Humans. Levi grinned and scratched his chest. It wasn't the baby humans she should be worried about.

He allowed several cars to exit ahead of him, always keeping his gaze on Miss Subaru. She drove until the roads and houses got smaller and then pulled into a driveway. Levi stopped at the corner, his hands clutching the steering wheel. His tongue darted across dry lips, and the space between his shoulder blades grew tight.

There were no other cars at the home. Miss Subaru hurried to the door, one hand holding her keys and the other pulling her sweater tightly around her torso. She dropped her keys on the porch and glanced his way when she bent to retrieve them. He froze, but there was no indication he'd been spotted. She went inside, and he relaxed, surveying the future sacrifice site.

The small house had yellow siding with green shutters flanking the front windows. The landscaping was sparse but maintained. Two huge evergreens anchored the front yard, swaying in the wind. Brown branches hung from one of the trees, threatening to tumble to the ground with each gust. An ugly black scar curved around the trunk, a reminder of its battle with lightning. Small bushes dotted the perimeter of the house like round tombstones in a black mulch bed. Dead, brown ivy snaked up a trellis on the home's side. It'd probably recover in the spring. Unlike the home's owner.

Movement drew his attention. An elderly woman toddled out of a house two doors down from Miss Subaru. She shuffled along the sidewalk, heading Levi's direction. He placed his phone to his ear and held an imaginary conversation with an old friend from Texas. As the woman passed his vehicle, he looked away. After a moment, he stared into his rearview mirror and waited until the old lady turned the corner. Time to go.

......

His mother smiled when he opened the motel room door. "I was starting to worry you'd got lost."

Levi lowered the TV volume. "Watching *Matlock* now?"

"Oh, he's a wonderful actor. I was so sad when he died."

"Sure, Mom."

"How was your interview?"

"Great. She was really friendly. There might be other candidates, but I don't know. It just seemed like we made some sort of connection. It's hard to explain."

"Well, I hope this one works out." She coughed hard, and he placed his hand on her forehead.

"Still running a fever."

"Nonsense. I don't want to be cooped up in this room all day. Let's go get something to eat. Somewhere nice."

"Whatever you want, Mom. My treat. You get ready. I'm going to walk down to the ATM. I'll be right back."

He marched to the office, sneaking a few peeks toward the street on his way. Once inside, he slid his card into the machine and gave the okay for the added fee. *Criminals.* He counted the money and eased the bills into his wallet, careful not to damage the treasure he kept there. Better check the balance. A couple of button presses later, the ATM spit out his receipt. $448,937.63. Sounds about right, give or take a few pennies.

One of the ladies at the curb waved as he walked back. Levi ignored her, and she yelled something he couldn't understand. Fists clenched, he slowed. His chest slowly rose with each deep breath. The woman yelled again. *No.* He ran the rest of the way to his room.

"Ready, Mom?"

"Almost. So, what did she say?"

Levi's mouth dried, and he avoided his mother's gaze. "Who?"

"The lady who interviewed you. Who do you think?"

He licked his lips and rubbed his right temple. "Oh. I'll be seeing her again later this week." His finger dragged lines and loops through the dust on the nightstand. He stood back and admired his work, a lovely little flower. "I'm really looking forward to getting to know her better."

5

Levi hadn't seen Miss Subaru in three days and just as importantly, she hadn't seen him. A quick drive-by to confirm she came home for lunch daily was all he needed. Caring for his mother took up most of his time, but her naps gave him enough flexibility to work on his plan. Every detail had to be perfect. No more mistakes. The incident in Nashville couldn't be repeated. The Lord might not be so forgiving next time.

Tomorrow would be a special day for Miss Subaru. She'd be going home. Today, final preparations. Maybe take Mom to Multnomah Falls if she was up to it. First though, a stop for coffee and a chance to go over his schedule.

"Welcome to Jumpy Java. What'll it be?"

Levi half-smiled at the barista, a cheery young woman. "Good morning. Small coffee, please. Black."

"Bold choice."

"I'm sorry?"

"Bold choice. See, because it's just a black coffee. Bold. Get it?" She widened her eyes and flipped both palms upward.

He forced himself to maintain the grin. "Sure. Bold. Bet that's the first time you've told that one."

She chuckled and shook her head. "You're on to me. It's part of my regular rotation. The old guys who come in here like it, though. Not that you're an old guy. I mean, well ..." She rolled her eyes and sighed. "One black coffee coming right up."

Levi studied her as she pumped the handle on a silver urn. Young, early 20s, and pretty in a Goth sort of way. The dark makeup around her eyes and lips formed a stark contrast to her pale skin. Streaks of neon blue flowed through jet-black hair, a silver ring pierced her left eyebrow, and her shirt collar obscured most of a neck tattoo. What is that? A red-winged fairy with a black top hat maybe?

She slipped the cup into a cardboard sleeve and placed the drink on the counter. "This one's on the house. It'll be our secret."

Secrets? You have no idea. He mumbled his thanks, walked to a corner table, and flipped open his laptop. Password? D-A-I-S-Y-4. Need to remember to change that tomorrow. His virtual private network gave him a secure and almost untraceable connection to the Internet.

A search for thrift stores returned plenty of choices, and he ruled out the first few options. They were either too far away or specialized in vintage clothing. A Goodwill store was close and would be open by the time he finished at Walmart.

He took a sip of coffee, and the steam escaping from the hole in the lid soaked his upper lip, nearly scalding him. He dabbed at it with the back of his hand. No blood. If I had hurt myself ... He glared at the barista before turning back to his computer.

A quick Google search for "Cody Talbot" provided no relevant results. Still anonymous. "Serial killer" provided several million hits, though no recent news stories. Disappointing, but that'll change soon enough. He logged off and scooped up his laptop and coffee. Shopping time.

Goth-girl hollered to him. "Come back soon! Maybe next time I can talk you into a macchiato or something."

He turned around and nodded, half-heartedly waving when she tilted her head and grinned. His heart pounded, and he struggled to control his breathing. Her wanton behavior, so innocent on the surface, hid an implied message. One he should ignore. "I might take you up on that."

Walmart was not far and not quite as crowded as earlier, though the hordes still moved through the aisles, eager to find stuff they couldn't live without. He stopped by the office supplies and picked up a clipboard, legal pad, and pens. The floral section came next.

Exhausted poinsettias still pleaded for someone to take them, but their time was done. A time to be born, and a time to die. A vase of yellow roses, green chrysanthemums, and white daisies met his requirements, and he placed the flowers in his basket. Water droplets trickled onto his hand as he secured the bouquet among the other items. He turned his wrist and watched the liquid dribble one way, then another. After a moment, he rubbed his hand across his slightly parted lips. His tongue scraped his skin, and hot breath mingled with cold water.

A young woman walked past. She stared at her shopping list, unaware of her vulnerability. She selected a loaf of wheat bread, and he bit his cheek, savoring the metallic tinge of blood as it soaked into his tongue. This very night ... She turned into the produce section, passing within inches. A faint whiff of perfume wafted behind her, and he closed his eyes. Shook his head. Not now. Not her.

She wasn't chosen. Miss Subaru had the honor. God was clear about that, and He valued obedience above all else. For the plan to work, Levi couldn't stray. Not again. Not if he was going to point America back to the Lord.

He reviewed the items in his cart. Should be everything he

needed. Best not to linger too long. He moved to the cashiers, checked out, and drove to the next stop.

The Goodwill store was as empty of customers as Walmart was full. Rows of clothing filled most of the place, with stacks of old, dusty furniture toward the back. A few employees stood near the cash register chatting, but after a cursory wave, they turned back to their conversation.

Flannel shirts by the hundreds hung on racks near the front, and he found a red-and-black one with an L-shaped tear under the pocket. Someone had sewn the rip together using white thread, making it stand out like an old scar. Smelling faintly of cigarette smoke and at least one size too large, the shirt was the perfect choice.

Farther down the row, he selected a faded green T-shirt with a cartoon moose on the back. An assortment of hats hung at the end of an aisle, and he opted for a black baseball cap with a patch from the Rusty Rottweiler Brewing Company. A cardboard box held a mound of gloves, and Levi chose a pair of leather ones, stained with oil of some sort. A pair of jeans with a hole in the right knee and dirty brown steel-toed boots rounded out his new wardrobe.

He paid, took his goodies to the car, and pulled to the far side of the parking lot. Step-by-step, he went through his plan, trying to identify any possible threats. He knew he'd be protected, but God had given him a brain for a reason. Think. But obey.

The sunshine streamed through the windshield, warming him from the chest up. The musty smell of the Goodwill clothing mingled with the leather scent of the gloves, dragging him into a drowsy daydream. He closed his eyes and recited verse after verse, each drilled into him from a young age. Scripture about love and forgiveness and sacrifice and wrath. Especially wrath. God's anger. Only one way to quench the rage.

For the life of a creature is in the blood, and I have given it to you to make atonement for yourselves on the altar; it is the blood that makes atonement for one's life.

The Lord demanded satisfaction for America's sins, or the punishment would be swift. God used prophets to shake Israel from their disobedience, but that nation hadn't always heeded their warnings. Levi wouldn't let that happen to the United States. He was no prophet, just a dutiful servant. Sometimes the burden of being chosen was heavy, but not often.

Not often at all.

The girl resting under his Texas home had died to learn that lesson. He'd tried to explain. She was supposed to be with him. Had to be. He could protect her. It wasn't him she rejected. It was God. And when she ran, it was the Lord who demanded satisfaction. Atonement. How could he not obey his one true Father?

He pondered the flowers on the seat next to him. God's creation was beautiful. He selected a rose from the bouquet and held it at eye level, marveling at its fragility. Exquisite. His fist closed over the bloom, and he worked his fingers back and forth. Rose confetti floated to the floor. Beautiful. And so easily destroyed. The Lord giveth, and the Lord taketh away. Taking away. His appointed role.

He squinted at his reflection in the rearview mirror. Dark brown hair draped low, making his brown eyes seem menacing. He scrunched his forehead and pressed his lips together in a scowl. Terrifying. The look lasted almost three seconds before a smirk ended the exercise, and he laughed at himself. An average looking guy on a top-secret mission for an extraordinary God. Tomorrow, that duty would continue. Miss Subaru would probably thank him when he met her in heaven.

......

"Those flowers are beautiful, Cody," his mom said. "Are they for me?"

He held up the vase and nodded. "I thought they might brighten this place up a bit."

"Put them there by the TV, so I can see them. That's perfect."

He sat on the edge of his motel bed. "Got a call today. They want to interview me again tomorrow. Said it might take most of the day."

"Wonderful. Don't worry about me. You just focus on getting that job."

"I'm focused, Mom. Now, feel up to getting some dinner later?"

She coughed, drawing into a fetal position as she did. "I don't think so, honey. Another night's rest, and I'll be over this. You go on. I'll be fine."

He stretched out on the bed and kicked off his shoes. "Nah. I think I'll hang out here and watch a movie with my best girl."

An hour later, she was asleep. He channel-surfed for a while, occasionally prying open the curtains to peer toward the street. The women were still there, shadows under the flickering light. Sometimes one would be gone, only to be back the next time he peeked. His legs ached, the muscles tight, and he wiped his hands repeatedly on the bed. They shouldn't be out there. Just after midnight, he glanced outside one last time, looked over at his mother, and crawled under the covers.

He awoke early the next morning, tired after a restless night. His mother's cough was worse, and the raspy hacking had inter-rupted his dreams. She still slept, and he placed his hand on her forehead. Burning up. She needed antibiotics, but taking her to a hospital was too risky. Too many questions and forms. Being a pharmacist did have its advantages, though. Knowing what drugs were needed, and how to get them, was just one perk.

After a shower and shave, he checked the mirror. Big day. Got to look my best for coffee. *Coffee?* Why had he thought that? Miss Subaru. Got to look my best for Miss Subaru. He grabbed two of the daisies and headed for the Jumpy Java Coffeehouse.

He sat in the car before going in, watching the barista through the windows. Same black Goth makeup, a black top with some sort of sparkly Tim Burtonish design, and a bright red necklace. She worked by herself again, running the register and preparing the drinks.

The shop was more crowded than it had been yesterday, and several customers waited to place their order. An older man said something to her, and she laughed as she handed him his change. Her hand seemed to linger on his for an extra heartbeat, and the man dropped the change into the tip jar.

Rahab. The Jericho harlot who aided Israel and saved her family. The barista's red necklace radiated across the room. The scarlet cord in the book of Joshua. A sign to the Israelites. Was he supposed to save her? Was she supposed to save him?

He paused until no one waited in line, got out of the car, and walked to the shop window. His warm breath fogged up the glass until she noticed him and waved. He tilted his head and smiled back. Slowly, deliberately, he traced a flower in the condensation on the window. She pointed at herself and mouthed, "For me?"

He nodded and walked into the toasty coffeehouse.

She relaxed with her elbows on the counter, chin resting on the back of her hands. "Well, hey there. Come back to try something different?"

"Umm ... I'm not sure. I'm not really into all that fancy stuff."

"A simple guy, huh? Well then, let me be the one to broaden your horizons."

His heart raced, and he struggled against the urge to run his tongue over suddenly dry lips. He paused before speaking, fearful his voice would crack. "What do you suggest?"

"It's chilly out this morning, so you'll want a hot drink. None of that iced stuff for you. Let's see ... I know. We'll start with an Americano, double-shot."

"Americano?"

"Relax. It's just espresso with hot water added. A bit stronger than your regular coffee and a bolder taste. But nothing too far out there."

"Okay. Sure." New things can be good.

She glanced around before leaning closer and resting her hand on his arm. "It's on me."

Focus. "Great. Thanks."

"By the way, my name's Kat." She extended her hand, and Levi grasped it. Her palm was moist, warm, and inviting. He squeezed his free hand into a fist until she released him. *Thank you, Lord, for Rahab.*

"Nice to meet you, Kat. I'm Levi."

"Levi? Like the jeans?"

"Yeah, like the jeans. And you're Kat. Like the, umm, animal?"

She grinned, showing crooked white teeth under her ebony-tinged lips. "Short for Kathryn. Never felt much like a Kathryn, you know? Seems a little too high and mighty."

"Yeah. Sort of fancy, I suppose. Kat's nicer. It fits you."

The door opened, and two middle-aged women paraded to the counter. Kat winked at him. "No rest for the weary."

He took his Americano and chose a seat in one of the leather chairs tucked away in a corner. From there, he could watch her without being obvious. He logged on and found dozens of companies that would gladly ship antibiotics to him, legally or otherwise. He peeked up and stared as Kat washed a stack of mugs in the sink. The rhythmic motion of her hands hypnotized him. Allowed his mind to wander. She started to turn around, and he whipped his attention to the laptop, selected a pharmacy in Canada, and requested guaranteed overnight delivery to the motel.

A hand touched his shoulder. "So how is it?"

He jerked in surprise and looked up at her. "Scared me a little. But the coffee's good. Really good. Nice recommendation."

"Sorry I snuck up on you. Need some more?"

"Not right now. I've got to go to work. Don't want to be late."

She put a hand on her hip, arched an eyebrow, and squished her mouth to one side. "Yeah? What do you do? Make jeans?"

Levi closed his computer, stood, and forced himself to make eye contact. "Good guess. I work for a tree cutting service. Got a busy day today."

"So maybe I'll see you tomorrow? We can move up the ladder to a straight espresso. I mean, if you're feeling really brave."

He flexed his fingers and grinned. "Sounds good. See you tomorrow. I'll try to be brave." Rahab.

In the car, he relived the morning so far. Today would be glorious, and he was already being rewarded. A new girl, though he didn't know what to do with her yet. Miss Subaru on the schedule, and Mom's medicines on the way. Still, something about the antibiotics bothered him. Fake name. Charged to Mom's card. Motel address. All the usual precautions.

Except the private network. Traceable.

A distraction. That's what Kat was. She disrupted his routine, forced him to make a mistake. If anyone went looking, they could track the medication order back to this coffeehouse. Not that it would make much difference. Even if they did show up here, nothing and no one would point to him. He stared at Kat as she waited on another customer. That's not entirely accurate, is it? Oh, Rahab. What am I going to do with you?

First things first. Don't want to keep the Lord waiting.

He drove to a small city park and backed into a space near the restrooms. Another car was in the lot, but a flat rear tire and broken glass around the driver's door told its story. He stepped outside and leaned against his car. The wind gusted, died, gusted again. Dry brown leaves scratched across the ground. Empty swings clanked against each other in the abandoned playground. Beautiful day.

He walked to the restroom and changed into his newly bought clothing. The burnished metal door provided a hazy reflection. The flannel shirt swallowed him, making his six-foot frame appear even ganglier. Wiggling his toes in the boots proved difficult, but the jeans fit perfectly. The ball cap, lopsided to give a casual appearance, topped off his outfit. Ready for the cover of *GQ*.

Back at the car, he grabbed the black bag of supplies from the trunk and pitched it into the front passenger seat. He did a full three-sixty, scanning for any signs of activity. Satisfied, he sat behind the wheel and locked the doors.

The daisies lay beside him, and he licked his fingertips before lifting one in each hand. Nearly identical, yet at the same time, unique. Which one, Lord? He closed his eyes, waiting. His personal Urim and Thummim, used by Levite priests in the Old Testament to consult the Lord. No sound except the wind whistling past, chasing its own tail. His mouth dried, and he cleared his throat. His tongue poked his cheek. Left.

The flower in his right hand fell to the floor, and Levi twirled the remaining one, peering at the blossom from every angle. Good choice. He counted the petals twice. Won't make that mistake again. Thirty-five. Another test, Lord? He plucked one petal and rolled it between two fingers before flicking the discard to the floor.

The outside pocket of the bag held a rectangular black container, its paint worn around the edges. He bit his bottom lip, removed the box, and, barely breathing, posed the daisy in its felt lining. He replaced the lid and traced his fingers along the edges. Caressed it. More precious than rubies.

A cottony red bag tried to hide under a can of WD-40, but he recovered it and loosened the drawstring. A vial of Propofol saw daylight for the first time since Nashville, and two new syringes joined it. He drew a small amount into the first needle and double-checked the quantity. The second one got a full load. Recap the needles. Back in their bag. Back in the duffel. Work time.

He cruised past Miss Subaru's house and confirmed her car was in the driveway. Home for lunch. Right on schedule. A strip mall two blocks away provided the ideal parking spot, and he angled into a space near a sandwich shop.

He retrieved a flashlight from the glove box, hunched forward, and slid it into the back of his jeans. The red drawstring sack went into his shirt pocket, its top peeking over the edge. His tongue darted across his lips. Itchy fingers grabbed garden pruners from the bag. Thick, curved blades, still sharp. Dark crimson stains on the edges. Nicks in several spots. Used to be so shiny. No matter. The rubber yellow handles served their purpose. A steady grip was important.

He scanned his surroundings once more before stepping out of the vehicle and slipping the pruners into the back pocket of his jeans against the flashlight. His target was close now. No need to hurry. Several deep breaths to rein in his adrenaline. Slow, deliberate pace as he wandered down the street, clipboard tucked under his left arm.

Fake tree surgeon.

Genuine smile.

The flashlight's metal casing scraped against the pruners as he walked. A rhythmic scratching, urging him to join in.

He sang, his voice cracking and low.

When we walk with the Lord in the light of His Word,

What a glory He sheds on our way.

While we do His good will,

He abides with us still,

And with all who will trust and obey.

6

Jeremy focused on the clock's fuzzy red numerals and waited for his mind to rouse itself from a fitful night. Two minutes clicked by before he remembered he was back in Virginia. Home. His apartment was within a thirty-minute commute of DC and an hour from Maggie's home in Milford. She'd already be on the road headed into the office.

He'd assumed—hoped—retirement from the Bureau would mean less travel. More stability. A chance to spend more time on things a bit more ... personal. Maggie and Rebecca. Starting his own as-yet-to-be-determined business. And resolving the one case that mattered most to him.

None of that panned out, at least not yet. Retirement seemed a lot like a job.

He shoved back the covers and sat up, swinging his feet onto the cold wooden floor. His morning ritual began as it always did: with a notion he should exercise more, followed by a dismissal of the foolish idea. Life had caught up with him, or maybe he just gave up trying to stay ahead. His forty-eighth birthday barreled down, and short nights took their toll.

He stretched his legs and worked his left foot back and forth for a good three minutes. Got to keep that leg happy. The biggest scar meandered from his outer thigh to inner ankle, compliments of a grenade in Quli Khish, Afghanistan. A smaller crimson divot above the knee marked the damage from the explosion at the Miller farm. They'd never figured out what hit him. Too much debris. Not that it made any difference.

He grabbed his Glock from the bed holster, staggered to the kitchen, and flipped the switch on the coffeemaker before heading to the bathroom. A flimsy disposable razor scraped his face while the shower heated. Clouds of steam billowed toward the clicking exhaust fan, partially fogging the mirror. He turned sideways and ran a hand from his chest to navel. A slight bulge began below his sternum, so he pressed harder. Perfectly flat. *Lookin' good*. Wouldn't hurt to drop a few, though. Don't want the turkey neck. He reached behind the shower liner, pivoted the handle to its coldest setting, took a deep breath, and stepped in.

......

Just over an hour later, Jeremy sipped stone-cold coffee and glanced at the conference room clock. The Deputy Director of the FBI, Matthew Bailey, had scheduled the meeting for eight-thirty, ten minutes from now, but it would be at least twenty minutes before he arrived. Jeremy knew the drill. He'd sat through enough of these meetings when he was on the payroll. Bailey might really be busy. Then again, he might be setting the meeting's tone. Jeremy tried to give him the benefit of the doubt. Tried.

A few agents sat across from him, working on laptops and phones. They were polite enough, but conversation stayed to a minimum. An occasional head nod when someone arrived. Maybe a tap on the back as they moved to their seat. All of them worked multiple cases, and their load was too high to waste on idle chatter, at least when the DD would be present.

Jeremy squirmed in his chair and worked his back into a more comfortable position, then scrutinized the room, satisfied none of the agency's budget went toward decorating the area. A scratched plastic cover on the wall clock doubled as an echo chamber, elevating the tick ticks to an irritating level. Just a hint of cigarette odor hung in the air, whether from previous years or yesterday, he didn't know. The fake tree in the corner was droopy, dusty, and sad. A red and white nametag clutched one of the leaves, and Jeremy squinted to read the faded writing. *Hello. My name is Eeyore.*

Six people could sit comfortably in the room, but at least nine would attend. Officially, Jeremy was a guest, invited because of his experience, but he knew most of the attendees, either personally or through reputation. The agents in the room treated him as one of their own. Once an agent, always an agent.

His favorite FBI employee sat diagonally across the table from him. Maggie had chosen her seat intentionally. The relationship between Jeremy and her wasn't exactly a secret and violated no policies, but no sense making her job more difficult. Stay completely professional. A quick smile was the only greeting she offered. Jeremy understood completely. The FBI was no different than any other workplace when it came to rumors.

An irregular clicking bored into him, and he tracked the source to a young agent two seats away. Greg Simpson, three years with the agency, nicknamed Blondie because of his resemblance to that guy on all those food shows. Needs to touch up his roots. Got a little black showing. Jeremy stared at the pen in Blondie's hand for a moment and cleared his throat. The clicking continued. He cleared his throat again, louder, and Agent Simpson glanced up with a "who, me?" expression. Jeremy motioned toward the offending noise. The clicking accelerated. Guess who just moved to the top of my personal Most Wanted list?

The scheduled start time arrived, and Jeremy opened a folder on his laptop. He knew the details by heart, but no sense taking chances. He wanted the data nearby. The DD was notorious for asking tough questions that had no answer. He stretched his hands and traced a circle around the marginally paler area on his ring finger. 8:35. Fresh coffee would be good, but he didn't want to chance being out of the room when the DD showed up. The grittiness from the last sip would have to stay until they took a break.

Director Bailey barged into the room and took his seat. A large man, his suit jacket remained unbuttoned, and Jeremy doubted the two sides of the coat had met each other for years. Sitting behind a desk tended to do that to even the best of agents. 8:38. Impressive. Everyone quieted and waited for permission to begin. The DD checked his phone, frowned, and placed it on the table.

"Okay, people," he said. "I've got another meeting after this one, so let's get to it. Special Ag—Mr. Winter, thank you for attending."

"Yes, sir."

Bailey glanced around the room. "Somebody get us up to speed."

"As of now," Jeremy said, "we have —"

"I meant an FBI agent."

Ouch. Jeremy clenched his teeth and forced a smile.

The director pointed at Blondie. "Simpson, recap the case."

The man cleared his throat and shifted forward in his seat. "Yes, sir. So far, we have four known casualties, all female, ranging in age from twenty-one to thirty-four. One victim was Caucasian, two African-American, and one Hispanic. The attacks have taken place within the last year and a half, with gaps of anywhere from three weeks to eight months between them. At each crime scene, flower petals are left. Always daisies, always white."

"Locations?"

"Tampa, Phoenix, Norfolk, Binghamton, in that order. A fifth possible assault occurred in Nashville nearly three weeks ago. We're almost positive it's connected, but the victim survived."

"Agent Simpson, the FBI does not deal in 'almost positives'."

"Yes, sir. We have reason to believe the Nashville case is

connected to the others. The first round of DNA results was inconclusive, so they're running them again. We'll have an answer within the week."

"Database results?"

"No match to anyone in the system. The perpetrator doesn't attempt to clean the scene, but no fingerprints have been found at any of the sites. We're working under the presumption his prints are on file somewhere, and he knows it."

The DD's phone vibrated, and Blondie waited while he read the message.

"Okay. Go on."

"Yes, sir. In each incident, the victim was single and lived alone. Twice the perpetrator broke into the home, and twice the victim apparently let him inside. We have no indication the women knew their attacker. Once inside, he overpowers his target and injects her with Propofol. All four victims had two needle marks on their left arms. The flower petals are possibly part of a ritual, or maybe just his signature."

"Where's he getting the Propofol?"

"Internet probably. But we've got flags in the system for any thefts from hospitals or pharmacies."

The director grunted. "Other commonalities in the victims?"

"All of them were active members of a church. By active I mean—"

Bailey's buzzing smartphone stopped Blondie again. Jeremy frowned at his empty coffee cup and waited for the meeting to continue.

The DD muttered to himself and dropped his phone on the table. "Sorry. Instant communication also means constant interruption."

Blondie licked his lips. "Yes, sir. As I was saying, the victims were active members of churches, meaning they were more involved than just going to a Sunday morning service. Bible studies, fellowships, that kind of thing."

An agent across the table interrupted. "All the same denomination?"

"No. Two Methodists, Baptist, Church of Christ. The one in Nashville was also Baptist."

A few agents typed notes into their laptops, and Jeremy stretched his legs under the table. None of this information was new to him. He'd seen the files. Been over them several times. Of course, not everything ended up in the official reports.

Agent Simpson finished his summary. "In each of the four fatalities, the ring finger of the left hand was removed post-mortem. That's our biggest lead. He covers the finger with plastic wrap and mails it to the Supreme Court, always in a brown envelope and always via regular mail. The victims' towns match up to the birthplaces of the judges. The order of the assaults is random as best we can tell. It doesn't match up to the judges' ages, appointment dates, or anything else. If the pattern holds, and we have no reason to think it won't, he'll kill five more times."

Bailey turned to Jeremy. "Thoughts?"

"Oh, he'll keep going all right. I'd be surprised if these are the only four he's killed. Too clean. He's had practice. He'll hit the remaining five cities, if nothing else, to complete what he started. But he won't stop there."

"How can you be so sure?" Blondie asked.

Rookie question. He'd learn soon enough. "Because," Jeremy said, "they don't stop. Never. Slow down maybe. Take a break sometimes. But until they're caught, or they die, they don't stop."

Blondie frowned and scratched his cheek. "So we've still got Nashville, Sarasota, Chicago, Portland, and Brattleboro, Vermont. I'm thinking Nashville and Brattleboro are our best bets. There's a chance he could go after the same woman in Nashville. I'd like to put protective surveillance on her."

The DD shook his head. "I'd like to do it too, but it's not going to happen. Without more info than we've got now, I can't afford to lose an agent to babysitting duty. Get the local PD to increase their drive-bys. I'll reconsider if Nashville ends up being number eight or nine on his list."

Blondie's lips stretched into a thin line. "Yes, sir. Brattleboro is a small town. Strangers would be noticed, especially in churches. I'd like to … what I mean to say is, it might be beneficial to question some of the pastors there. Maybe let them in on this a little."

"Out of the question," Bailey said. "The last thing we need is for the media to get hold of this. Churches under attack by a serial killer. Makes for a good story on the evening news and a huge headache for me. It's too early to create that kind of alarm. Anything from the interviews you've done?"

"Nothing useful. No description. No one notices anything unusual, either at the victim's home or church. We've checked floral shops in the areas. No luck. No security cameras at the churches."

The fluorescent light above Jeremy flickered, and two of the bulbs went dark.

"Winter, anything new from your trip to Nashville?"

"Not much. Claire Lawson's moved. Changed her hairstyle. But she doesn't remember anything that might help. At this point, I'd recommend focusing on the flowers and the Propofol. Figure out what the daisies mean to him and where he's getting the drugs."

"Why a daisy?" Maggie asked. "Why not a rose or a carnation?"

"Good question," Jeremy said. "We talked to a couple of florists. A daisy represents innocence. When you put that with the amputation of the ring finger, I think it's significant. The Latin name is Bellis perennis, which translates as 'pretty everlasting.' According to the psych evaluation done by Doctor Andrews—"

"Sorry," Director Bailey said. "Got to make a quick call. Let's take a break, people. Ten minutes. Be back on time."

Jeremy stretched and headed for the break room. The coffee looked iffy. He touched the carafe and jerked his hand back. Still hot. He filled his cup partway and peered inside the pot. Coffee grounds with a hint of water. Enough to cover the bottom.

"You're going to make more, right?"

"Oh, sure," he said, turning to face his accuser. Late 30s, reddish-brown hair, five-six, one twenty, green eyes. Maggie looked great today.

She casually brushed against him as she grabbed a bottled water from the refrigerator. "Yeah. I bet."

Heat flashed through his face. "Honest. I was just about to brew a fresh pot."

"Uh-huh. I have a six-year-old at home, remember? I know suspicious behavior when I see it. Based on my observations, I'd have to say that wasn't your intention. In fact, I'd be willing to testify you didn't fill your cup all the way for the sole purpose of not having to make another pot."

"No more questions without my lawyer present."

"I see. Well, I'm sure I could pry the information out of you somehow, but don't worry. Your secret's safe with me. You'll never convince me to drink that stuff. Love the smell, hate the taste." She crinkled her nose to emphasize the point.

He shrugged and grinned. "More for the rest of us. You should know, though, it's a proven fact coffee has solved more cases than DNA and fingerprints combined."

"So, I suppose you're close to solving this case then?"

"On the record? I have every confidence the suspect will soon be in custody."

Maggie smiled and tilted her head upward. "And off the record?"

"I don't have a clue."

Her laugh was loud and deep. "Let's get back before the boss returns. Got to be on time so we can watch him walk in ten minutes late."

Jeremy told himself not to look as she strolled back to the room. He failed after her first few steps. The rest of the coffee found its way into his cup, and he switched off the burner before returning to the meeting.

The Deputy Director hurried in and took his seat, three minutes late. "Doctor Andrews, I believe you were about to give us your thoughts before we were interrupted?"

Jeremy turned to the FBI profiler and waited while he shuffled through his notes. Retired from private practice, the bearded septuagenarian did consulting work on occasion. His profiles on serial killers ran the gamut from scarily specific to uselessly generic. Jeremy already knew which way this one was going.

"Yes," Doctor Andrews said. "The religious commonality between the women makes this case a bit difficult to evaluate without background on the perpetrator. You have to figure out whether he was wronged by whichever god he serves, or whether he thinks he is doing his god's will. Or maybe it's both."

Wonderful insight. Very useful. Jeremy glanced at Maggie, and she rolled her eyes.

"In this case," the doctor continued, "we have someone who pursues unmarried Christian females. When you consider the meaning of the daisy, it's possible he believes the women are innocents, perhaps even virgins. Conceivably he thinks he is saving them from something, or someone."

"Uh-huh," Jeremy said. "Any guesses as to who or what he's saving them from?"

"Well, there's the rub now. It's just as likely he has some sort of vendetta in mind. These women may be the bad guys."

"Thanks for clearing that up, Doc. Anything else that might help us, you know, actually catch the guy?"

Several of the agents stifled a laugh, and Jeremy waited for a rebuke from the DD that never came.

The profiler's face maintained its bored façade. "In my professional opinion, you're looking for someone with a church background. He's seeking justice. For what, or whom, I don't know. Everything else is your standard serial killer stuff. Single white male, lives alone, late 20s to late 40s. Takes the fingers as his trophies."

Maggie cleared her throat. "Why would he get rid of his trophies? Don't serial killers keep them? Otherwise, they're not really trophies. Right?"

"Excellent question," the profiler said. "It plays into his appeal for justice. He is offering his most valuable asset to a judge. He wants someone to listen to him, and there's no higher judge in this country than the Supreme Court."

"What about God?" she said.

"I'm not sure I understand."

"I mean, Doctor Andrews, if he's so religious, wouldn't God be the highest judge for him?"

He shrugged. "Possibly. He may believe he's a messenger for his god and is simply following instructions. Or it could be that his god disappointed him, so he chooses human judges over deities. Or perhaps he doesn't believe in any god."

"He's giving the judges the finger," Blondie whispered. A glare from Director Bailey shut him down.

"Thank you, Doctor Andrews," the DD said. "Very helpful. I wonder if we're ignoring the elephant in the room, though."

"Excuse me, sir?" Jeremy asked.

"Terrorist? Muslim extremist targeting Christians?"

Jeremy paused a beat before answering. "There are no indications these assaults are related to terrorism. One-on-one killings with little publicity don't fit that profile. Still, it's a possibility to keep in mind."

"Do that. Now, if there's nothing else, I think we'll—"

"How many petals?" Maggie asked.

Interrupting the boss. Brave. Or suicidal. Jeremy scanned the file. "Let's see ... anywhere from twenty-six to forty. There doesn't seem to be any relationship between the number of petals and the victim."

"And in Nashville? How many there?"

"Thirty-three. Why?"

"None of the others were odd numbers, were they?"

"Umm … no. But we think he got scared off. He didn't have time to finish whatever he was doing."

Maggie's lips moved while she counted on her fingers. "Or he did have time and messed up. He couldn't finish because she loved him."

"Wait. What?" The DD turned to Jeremy. "I thought Lawson didn't know the attacker."

Maggie leaned back, arms crossed. "Oh, she probably doesn't, sir."

Confident or cocky? Either way works. Jeremy bowed slightly toward her. "Please continue, Agent Keeley."

"I have a daughter, Rebecca, and when she turned six we had a little party for—"

"I'm sure that's all very nice," Director Bailey said, "but get to the point."

"Yes, sir. My ex brought her some flowers. He held out a rose while she plucked off the petals one at a time."

Jeremy's shoulders drooped, and he swallowed hard. How had he missed that?

"He's playing a game," Maggie continued. "She loves me; she loves me not. He couldn't kill the victim in Nashville because she loved him." She turned back to Jeremy. "She only had one needle mark, right? Everybody else had two."

"Yeah."

"So he gives her enough to knock her out and does his thing. If she doesn't love him, he gives her a second shot, this one strong enough to kill her."

"Interesting theory," Bailey said. "But if it's true, shouldn't we have more survivors? I mean, it seems to me at least one of the others would have ended up with an odd number of petals."

Maggie raised her eyebrows and nodded toward Jeremy.

I owe you. "That would be true, sir, if he wasn't cheating. He counts before he goes in. Something went wrong in Nashville. He counted wrong, or a petal fell off somewhere."

Bailey checked his watch and scowled. "I've got to go. Agent Keeley, take charge of the meeting. You'll assume lead on this case. I want a recap in my email by the end of today. Any questions?"

"No, sir."

"You." The DD pointed at Jeremy. "You're on this full-time effective immediately. I want you training Agent Keeley."

Nice of you to ask if I'm available. "Thank you, sir."

Jeremy waited until Bailey walked out, then glanced at Maggie. This was going better than he could—

"Just so we're clear," she said, "I'm in charge."

7

Two days after the meeting, Jeremy sat in a Portland, Oregon home, pretending the plastic slipcover on the sofa didn't bother him. The homeowner, an elderly woman, had spent the last hour providing no useful information about her neighbor's murder. Jeremy had, however, learned the names of the local cats and that Doctor Oz could cure "Alltimers disease".

Maggie's phone rang, and she glanced at the number on the screen. "Gotta take this. Mr. Winter, can you keep Mrs. Ellenburg company for a moment?"

Jeremy knew the look. Whatever the call was about, Maggie wanted to make sure she wasn't overheard. "Sure," he said. "Ma'am, would you show me again where you saw the man?"

"Certainly, dear. Let me get my coat."

Jeremy escorted the older lady outside to the sidewalk. "Now then, you said he came from that direction and walked directly to Miss Bishop's front door?"

"Yes. I didn't recognize him. That's probably why I remember the day so clearly, Mr., uh …"

"Winter, ma'am." For the third time. He checked his notes.

"You saw a white male, around six feet tall, somewhere between one hundred eighty and two hundred ten pounds. He wore a baseball cap and old clothes, walked into Miss Bishop's yard, and looked at her trees. Then he knocked on her door, and that's the last you saw of him. Is all that correct?"

"Yes, I think so," Mrs. Ellenburg said. "But you know my memory isn't as good as it used to be."

"I understand. Is there anything else that might help us?"

"Just terrible, isn't it? All the police cars and sirens and newspeople. Such a shame about Nancy. Who could do such a thing?"

"We're working on it, ma'am. We'll find him." Eventually.

Maggie poked her head out the front door. "Don't get too cold out there."

"We were just heading back in, weren't we, Mrs. Ellenburg?"

The woman shuffled up the walkway. "Actually, dear, the weather's quite nice for Portland this time of year. It's good to have sunshine today. A hot cup of cocoa will warm you two right up."

"I appreciate the offer," Jeremy said, "but I think it's best if we don't take up any more of your time today."

"Nonsense. I've got nothing but time. Cocoa and some cookies, I think."

Maggie smiled. "Sounds wonderful."

The elderly lady hung her coat in the closet and headed for the kitchen. "Now then. Make yourselves comfortable. I'll be right back."

Jeremy sank back onto the sofa. "Who called?"

Maggie's lips turned down. "Postal Inspection Service. They've got it."

It. Nancy Bishop's ring finger. "Return address?"

"Sandy, Oregon. The Bureau's on their way to get the evidence now. Shouldn't take long to confirm it belongs to our victim."

"How far did this one get?" So far, none of the fingers had made it anywhere close to the Supreme Court judges. Like all mail addressed to the federal government since 9/11, intense screening caught virtually every possible threat. Between machines that sniffed the air for biological threats, X-rays, and heating all packages to kill anything that might be lurking inside, the USPS had become one of the worst ways to target a government official. Something their killer either didn't know or didn't care about.

"All the way to DC," Maggie said. "The woman who found it was pretty freaked out."

"I bet." Achill settled on Jeremy, and he wandered to the front windows. The sun's rays soaked him, though they did little to lift his mood. He didn't need confirmation to know whose finger it was. Who else could it belong to? Her body had been found by the police after a coworker called, concerned because Miss Bishop hadn't returned from lunch. As soon as the report hit the database, the Portland FBI office contacted Maggie.

A crash from the kitchen echoed into the room.

"Everything okay, Miss Ellenburg?" Maggie asked.

"Yes, dear. I'm afraid I dropped one of the cups."

Maggie stood. "I'd better go help her. When we're done here, we'll head back to the office."

Jeremy dropped onto the crinkly plastic encasing the couch and scrutinized the two women in the kitchen. Quite the couple. Maggie wore her usual dark suit and white shirt. Very FBI-ish. Mrs. Ellenburg had on a blue dress, now covered with a checkered apron, and a pair of tennis shoes. Very not-FBI-ish. He pulled out his phone to clear email.

Maggie yelled from the kitchen. "Cocoa or coffee?"

"Surprise me."

Whispered giggles trickled from the kitchen, and a moment later, the pair returned to the living room. The elderly lady handed him a shaking coffee cup and saucer, doing her best to avoid sloshing any of the steamy brown liquid. Probably her best china. She toddled to an old rocking chair across from him and eased onto the plaid pillow covering the seat. Maggie positioned a plate of chocolate chip cookies on the end table and stood in the sunshine, her hands clasped behind her back.

Jeremy cleared his throat. "Now, Mrs. Ellenburg, if we could just—"

"Have a cookie," Maggie said. "She made them herself."

He peeked at his partner from the corner of his eyes, hoping she received the message. We're going to have to set some ground rules. The toasty brown cookies looked fresh, and he chose a small one with a plethora of chips poking through the surface. The first bite sent shock waves to his brain. Raisins. Why did it have to be raisins?

"Delicious, isn't it?" Maggie asked.

Jeremy struggled to maintain a steady countenance. He nodded and worked his tongue across the gummy raisin bits stuck in his teeth. "Yes. It's wonderful. But I really think we should be going."

"Nonsense," Maggie said. "You've got time to finish your cookie."

He bit his lip. She knows I have a gun, doesn't she? "Maggie, we need to—"

She pointed to an oversize black-and-white photo on the mantle. "Is that your husband, Mrs. Ellenburg?"

The old woman's face gained new wrinkles as she grinned broadly. "Oh, yes. My George was really something. We were married for fifty-seven years before the cancer took him last year. He was a wonderful man. Just a wonderful man."

Jeremy wandered over and lifted the photo from its place of honor. Fingerprint smears dotted the glass, nearly blurring the image of the young couple standing in front of this same house. "Yes, ma'am, I'm sure he was."

"He had his own automobile repair business. That man could hear a car drive down the street and tell you what was wrong with it. He knew everything about them. Didn't matter what kind of vehicle, he could fix it."

"Good line of business to be in," Jeremy said.

"I didn't know anything about cars," Mrs. Ellenburg said. "He tried to teach me, but it was useless. We used to laugh about it all the time. He was such a patient man. We'd take walks around the neighborhood, and he'd test me. Point at a car and ask me questions about it. Got so I knew every vehicle on the block." She stared off into space, head tilted, and mouth open.

Jeremy looked at Maggie and tapped his watch. She held up her index finger.

"A car," the old woman said. "It's not usually there."

Jeremy leaned forward. "A car?"

"There was a car parked at the end of the street a few days before Nancy was killed. It's not from around here. I recognize most of the neighborhood cars. Of course, I suppose someone could have bought a new one. But I haven't seen it again. Isn't it funny how things just pop into your mind, Mr., uh …"

"Winter," Jeremy said. "Do you remember anything about the car? How many doors? What color? Anything that might help us?"

Mrs. Ellenburg smoothed her apron. "You don't live with an automobile repairman for all those years and not learn a few things. Even me."

Maggie scooted to the edge of her seat. "Can you describe the vehicle you saw?"

The woman stared blankly, forehead scrunched and lips pouted and gestured a path along the sidewalk. "A sedan, Malibu maybe, with beige paint. Oh, and the car had Texas plates on it."

Jeremy scribbled some notes before continuing, "That's excellent, Mrs. Ellenburg. Excellent. Was there anyone in the car? Any dents, bumper stickers, anything like that?"

"I'm sorry, but I didn't pay that much attention. I was out for my walk when I noticed the license plate wasn't Oregon. It was red, white, and blue. Just lovely. But I didn't think anything about it. This is such a quiet neighborhood. At least it used to be."

"Yes, ma'am. If I showed you some pictures, do you think you might be able to narrow down the car's year?" He typed on his smartphone.

"I'd be happy to try." She moved to the sofa and sat next to him.

"The pictures are kind of small, but if you see one that looks like a possibility, I can enlarge it," he said. "You just swipe your finger across the screen to go to the next picture." He handed her the phone and demonstrated the technique.

The older woman squinted for several seconds before moving to the next picture. On the fourth photo, she paused. "It was like this, but the front grill was smaller, and it didn't have this bar running through it."

Jeremy looked at the photo and typed in new information. "That's a 2005 model. Let's try the years around then." Moments later, a new picture popped onto his screen. "How about this one?"

"Yes, I think so," Mrs. Ellenburg said. "That looks like the one I saw."

"2006 Malibu. Are you sure?"

She chuckled. "Mr. Winter, at my age, I'm not sure of anything. But I believe that's the car that was parked on the street."

Jeremy nodded, stood, and handed her his business card. "Thank you, ma'am."

"Thank you for your time," Maggie said. "You've been very helpful. Please call if you think of anything else. Day or night."

"Oh, I will, dear. I hope you catch whoever did this, and soon. Feel free to stop by anytime you're out this way. I don't get many visitors."

"Yes, ma'am," Jeremy said. "And thank you for the coffee and cookie."

"My pleasure. Agent Keeley, I wonder if you'd help me with something in the kitchen before you go."

"Of course. Jeremy, do you mind warming up the car?"

After a few minutes, Maggie hustled out the front door and slid into the vehicle. The radio blasted a Miranda Lambert song about a woman, a shotgun, and her abusive ex.

"Ugh," she said. "You know there's more kinds of music than just country, right?"

He turned the volume down a notch. "No appreciation for true art. What did she want?"

"A present for you." Maggie handed him a brown paper sack.

He opened the bag and saw at least half a dozen cookies. "Maggie, I don't like raisins."

"Yeah, I figured that out. I wish I had a picture of you eating the one in the house. When you took the first bite … priceless."

"Glad you were amused. Nice work in there, by the way."

"Just doing my job," she said. "You know, it wouldn't hurt you to be less formal sometimes. Loosen up a bit. It helps people not feel so intimidated. They remember things easier when they're not scared."

"I'm not trying to scare people. And that *was* my soft side in there. I've done worse."

"You could do better, but I guess it's like that old saying. You can lead a horse to water, but you can't teach him new tricks."

"Make him drink."

Maggie tilted her head and scrunched her eyebrows together. "What?"

"You can't make him drink."

"Make who drink?"

"The … never mind. Let's head back by the office. I want to get started on the database search for that vehicle."

As they pulled away, Jeremy focused on the crime scene tape in Nancy Bishop's yard. The small house would be quaint were it not for the yellow and black strips draped everywhere. He stopped for a moment and tapped his finger on the steering wheel.

"Five down," Maggie said.

"Yeah."

"Think he'll go after the girl in Nashville again?"

"My gut tells me he will. But I don't know why. We're missing something, Maggie. Serial killers start with a pattern and a purpose. Sure, they evolve, change things up, even switch motives. Statistically speaking, no matter why they started, most of them end up killing for the sole reason they enjoy it. But this guy, there's something I don't understand."

"He does have a pattern. Christian girls, all single, living alone. We know the *who*, we need to figure out the *why*."

Jeremy scratched his cheek and rested an elbow on the armrest. "But why does he send his trophies to the Supreme Court? Doesn't make sense, no matter how deluded you are. The whole point of a trophy is to remind them, to remember what happened. Let them relive the moment. Even psychopaths have rules and habits."

"People are different. This guy makes his own rules. It happens. Makes our job a little tougher, that's all."

"I don't buy it. People aren't that different. Sure, this guy's got something screwed up in his head. But basically, people are the same. They like their routines. They fit in a group. And the serial killer group doesn't give away their trophies."

"Except for this guy."

He shook his head. "We're going back to Nancy Bishop's home. He took something else. We have to figure out what it was."

"We've been through the house twice already. Nothing missing according to her friends. All of whom have been cleared, I might add. But hey, you want to look again, then let's look again."

Jeremy stepped out of the vehicle. "We have to find it."

An hour and a half later, Maggie held her palms out and sighed. "Nothing," she said. "I don't know what I'm looking for. Or what I'm not looking for. How are we supposed to find something that's not here?"

Jeremy stood in the center of the small living room. The house was neat, at least for one kept by a young single woman. No ransacking, no mess other than a small bloodstain on the wood floor. Even that wasn't noticeable unless you knew where to look.

He shuffled through papers lying on a wooden rolltop desk, finding nothing of interest. A metal coffee table held a couple of magazines and a stack of tile coasters. Miss Bishop obviously had eclectic tastes. The walls were an off-red color with a splash of yellow in a few places. No paintings anywhere, but many photographs. Oceans and mountains. Cities and huts. Sunrises and thunderstorms. And people. Lots of photos of people. Is one of them the killer?

"What are you thinking?" Maggie asked.

"Why did he choose her? What was different? I mean, look around her home. Other than her taste in decorating, everything seems normal. But something has to be different. Our guy picks his targets for a reason. He's not random."

"Are you sure about that? There's nothing to indicate that he chooses them based on anything other than the fact they go to church."

"No. They mean something to him." He looked around again. "Crosses."

"What?"

"No crosses on the wall."

"So?"

"Don't religious people put crosses on their walls? Maybe that's what he's taking."

"Yeah, maybe," Maggie said. "But look at how everything's organized. There are no gaps. Unless the guy redecorated, where would you hang a cross?" She walked around the room and checked the walls. "Plus, no nail holes."

"Okay. Something else then, something religious. What would be important to him? And her?"

"Jeremy, did you ever go to church?"

He stepped back and crossed his arms. "My mom used to take me way back when I was a kid, but I don't see how—"

"Mom takes Rebecca every Sunday, and when you're not visiting, I go with them. There's a nice church not too far from our home. If the weather's nice, we walk."

"And?"

"And when I do go, I always bring my Bible. Habit from when Mom used to take me when I was a little girl. Don't really need to carry it since they put everything on the screen now. But I still do. It's, I don't know, comforting maybe?"

Comforting? Scary, more like it. "Her Bible's not missing. It's on the nightstand by her bed."

Maggie headed for the bedroom, and Jeremy tagged along behind her. She picked up the Bible, a red leather edition with "Nancy Bishop" inscribed in gold on the cover. She flipped open the book and read the dedication page.

"To Nancy on your 16th birthday.

Proverbs 31:10

With all my love, Mom."

Maggie thumbed through the pages quickly. "She's written notes all through this. Lots of stuff is highlighted too. Some pages are torn and dog-eared. She used this a lot."

Jeremy shrugged. "Sentimental value? Plus, you're missing the point. It's still here. Killers don't leave trophies behind."

"This Bible meant something to her. More than a trinket or a gift. She used it, wrote in it, and read it. I don't do that."

"I'm not following."

She patted the cover of the book. "I carry mine when I go to church. A lot of people do. But I don't write in mine. If it weren't for the dust, you'd think my Bible was brand new. Half the pages still stick together. Nancy Bishop was serious about hers."

He rubbed a hand over his chest. "So she bought into religion. Good for her."

Maggie's face flushed, and she cleared her throat. "It's not about buying into religion. It's about … never mind."

"Listen, Maggie; I didn't mean anything by that. Sorry. Didn't realize I was stepping on any toes."

She sighed and rubbed her hand over the grainy leather. "I overreacted. It's not that I'm religious, but I do think there's something to all this, you know? And obviously so did the victim. If this Bible was so important to her, maybe it's why he chose her. Maybe it's the thing that separates his victims from the others."

"But he wouldn't know she did all the writing and stuff unless he saw her do it, which means he had to be at the church. That's no surprise. But we did our interviews, and nobody remembers anything out of the ordinary."

Maggie kept flipping the pages, searching for anything that might offer a clue. Jeremy jingled the change in his pocket while he watched and waited. The rustling of the wafer-thin paper brought back buried memories. Sitting in a pew, hundreds of Bibles being used at the same time.

"Why do they make those pages so thin anyway?"

Maggie looked at him. "Because they can? Maybe so it won't be so heavy."

"I think Bibles would work better if they were heavier. You know, when people beat you over the head with it."

Maggie ignored his attempted humor. "Jeremy." She held the open Bible and pointed to the top. "This page is torn, and the name of the book is missing. Judges. That can't be a coincidence."

Jeremy scrubbed his hand across his face. "Maybe. Maybe not. Easy enough to find out, though. Bag it and bring it. We'll head back to the office. You dig into that and see if the other victims' Bibles are missing the same thing. I'll start working the automobile database. I bet there's more than a few 2006 beige Malibus floating around. Two decent leads in one day. Maybe we're actually making progress."

Progress. A woman dies, and he gets clues. Five dead so far. Maybe more. Progress came at a very steep price.

8

It got easier every time. *Practice makes perfect*. Levi had provided a low estimate for trimming Miss Subaru's damaged tree. Told her business was slow, and he needed the work. She'd hesitated, but when he dropped the price another fifty bucks, she jumped.

The true cost turned out to be much higher.

As he explained the details, she focused on the numbers written on his legal pad, not the syringe in his other hand. No struggle, only a look of confusion. Or maybe fear. It was hard to tell. That was the downside to the Propofol. Really no way to know what the girl thought as she drifted off to eternal sleep.

He'd grabbed her as she turned to run and stepped inside her home, closing the door with his foot. She slumped as the drug took effect, and he eased her to the floor. The daisy played its part perfectly, and the second dose of Propofol finished the job.

Miss Subaru kept a nice home. Nothing worse than seeing the mess that some of the girls lived in. Is it so hard to make up a bed once in a while? Put your shoes in the closet?

He wandered through the house to give her heart plenty of time to stop. Let the blood settle for a bit. Made less of a mess when he snipped off her finger. Learned that the hard way.

Lots of photos in her home. Decent furniture. None of that metal and fake wood IKEA stuff. Cold pizza in the fridge. Lots of veggies too. Organic milk? Isn't all milk organic? At least the stuff that comes from cows?

Clean bathroom. Still a lot of boxes piled in the guest bedroom, though. Moving somewhere? Or just moved here? Overall, a nice, tidy, cozy home. Perfect spot for a young woman with her whole life behind her. Good balance to everything.

He paused before stepping into her bedroom and traced a finger down the door jamb. She slept here. His heart raced, and he swallowed hard before moving into the room. A queen-size bed. Wooden dresser and full-length floor mirror. Matching nightstands with lamps. There. The Bible right beside her bed. Last thing she sees at night? First thing in the morning? Good girl. He took his reward, slipped it beside the others in his wallet, and returned to her body.

No pulse. He checked her pupils. Slightly dilated as the muscles of the iris relaxed. Skin still warm, but that'd change quickly. Yep, by now Miss Subaru was sitting at her feast in heaven. Her body, perfect. The empty shell before him no longer connected to whoever or whatever she used to be.

He pulled the garden pruners from his pocket. Good that she had hardwood floors. Not much work for the crime scene cleanup crew. Barely worth their time to stop by. A little spray of something. A quick wipe with a rag. Move on to the next project.

A quick snip later—he still closed his eyes at the last nanosecond—and her finger was in the Ziploc quart-size bag. A smaller sandwich bag would have been plenty big, but those didn't have the slider, and trying to seal them was a frustration he didn't need. The bubble wrap and envelope were back at the motel, and he'd prep everything for shipment there.

Two days since he'd sent Miss Subaru home. Life was good, and in another day or two, he would decide where to go next. The Portland Palace Motel remained safe, at least for now, and besides, he'd already paid through the end of the week. No sense wasting money.

The evening news covered the breaking story the night of her homegoing. The police spokeswoman wore her sternest expression. Her coworkers sniffled and wiped their eyes on cue. All so heart-wrenching to those who didn't understand her sacrifice. *His* sacrifice.

Last night, the pretty co-anchor smiled as she updated the story. A young woman, tragically killed in her home. Exterior shot of the house draped in crime scene tape. More details as they become available. Ten seconds of coverage, then a two-minute account of dachshund races somewhere in Minnesota. No update on this morning's news. The story was as dead as Nancy Bishop.

That problem needed to be rectified. His mission demanded the sacrifices stay front and center. People wouldn't wake up if they didn't get the message. Perhaps he'd underestimated the public's apathy toward killings. Not their fault, though. They didn't see the big picture. Not yet. Law enforcement's hesitation to provide information to the press infuriated him. How hard could it be to tie the murders together? The FBI was worthless. Sure, they'd probably made the connection, but failing to warn the public? Inexcusable.

He tapped his finger on his lips and stared at his mother. She'd been restless all night, and the fever clung to her. Beads of sweat covered her face in spite of the crisp air pumping from the rattling air conditioner. The antibiotics didn't help. He rubbed the back of his neck and frowned.

"How are you feeling this morning?" he said.

She opened her eyes and looked past him. "Is he still here, honey?"

"Who, Mom? Is who still here?"

"Your father, of course. He was just in here. Such a gentleman."

He sighed and shook his head. "Mom, nobody's been here. It's only you and me. Like always."

Her eyes closed, and her breathing slowed. She needed to go to the hospital, but that brought too many obstacles. Too many questions. If he didn't take her, she wouldn't live much longer.

The Lord giveth, and the Lord taketh away. Blessed be the name of the Lord.

Levi kissed her forehead. "Rest up, Mom. I'll be back in a little while. Got some thinking to do."

......

A hazy sun teased its warmth through the mid-morning cloud cover. Levi shoved his hands into his jacket pocket and hustled into the coffee shop. There was only one other customer, an older man reading the paper. He wore a heavy brown coat with the collar turned up. A crooked walking stick rested against the chair beside him, and a black beret balanced atop his bald head. A beret? Have some dignity, man.

Kat brushed her palms on her apron and beamed when she saw him. "Well, howdy, stranger. Isn't that what y'all say down in Texas?"

Levi stopped just inside the door. "Texas?"

"I saw your car's license plate. You know, I've always wanted to ask someone. Is it true?"

"Is what true?"

She arched her eyebrows slightly. "Is *everything* bigger in Texas?"

Oh, Rahab. Levi laughed. "How about something new today? What's this latte thing I've heard so much about?"

Kat wrinkled her nose. "Latte, huh? Living dangerously, aren't you? Well, I can't tell you. It's a top-secret mix of ingredients."

He rubbed his chin and wrinkled his eyebrows. "Top secret? I'm intrigued."

She motioned for him to come closer, and when he arrived at the counter, she whispered, "See, we make espresso, pour in steamed milk, then we triple the price."

"Outrageous," Levi said a bit too loudly. Beret-man glanced in their direction, scowled, and returned to his paper.

"But I'll cut you a deal," Kat said. "For you, I'll only double the price."

"Well, in that case, I'll take two. If you'll have one with me, I mean."

She leaned back and placed her hands on her hips, unable to conceal a grin. "Why, Levi, are you asking me out on a date?"

He swallowed hard as pinpricks of heat scattered across his face. "Can't really afford to take you on a date, what with the price of lattes and all. But I could use some company this morning. At least until you get another customer."

"Eh. There won't be much business until after lunch. This place is dead once the morning rush is over. Honestly, I don't know how much longer the owner will be able to hang on. But it's no big deal. I mean, it's not like I make a lot of money working here. No benefits either."

"So why stay? There must be a zillion coffee shops in Portland. You could easily find another job."

She placed both elbows on the counter and propped her head in her hands. "I get to meet some pretty nice people here."

He gestured toward her other customer. "Let me know if any of them show up. In the meantime, I'll be over at that corner table. Shouldn't be too hard to spot me. I'll be the guy without the beret."

She chuckled and bit her bottom lip. "Give me a couple of minutes, and I'll be right there. I need to clean up a few things before I can take a break. Want your latte now or later?"

"Now, if it's not too much trouble. I've got some thinking to do, and coffee helps."

"Ooh, sounds serious. I'll move you to the front of the line then."

Levi laughed and steadied himself against the counter as euphoria flooded his brain. *Been a long time.* "I'd appreciate that. See you in a minute."

He worked his fingers as he watched her go about the business of preparing his drink. She pulled a large ceramic mug from under the counter and poured the espresso into it. The steamed milk was next, and Kat drizzled it slowly, jiggling her hand back and forth. She grabbed a biscotti from a jar on the counter, placed the hard cookie just-so on a saucer next to the mug, and brought the order to him.

"Hope you like it. I'll be back in a few minutes. If you need any help with that thinking you've got to do, let me know. I've been told I'm a fairly smart girl." She winked and bounced back to the counter.

Levi nodded and picked up the mug, eyeing the design in the latte. A milky heart on a suntanned background. That could mean a lot of things. She liked him. That was obvious. But he didn't need complications. Distractions. Unless she was a sign? Rahab had saved the Israelite spies by hiding them. Was she there to help him? Or maybe God was offering him a reward?

It'd be nice to slow down, take a break from the travel, but the task wasn't finished. He looked at the heart again, now barely recognizable. A pale imitation of what it once was. Like Mom. He lowered his face over the latte and let the steam surround him. Wet heat soaked into his pores as the mist covered him. Calmed him.

Smothered him.

The sound of a breaking cup startled him, and he jerked his head toward Kat.

She smiled and waved. "Oops! I guess I'll be another minute here. Still doing your thinking?"

He slumped against the chair's back and blew out a long, slow breath. "Actually, I've got it figured out. Your latte did the trick."

"Works every time." Kat grabbed a broom and began sweeping up the glass shards.

"Listen, can I take a rain check on our chat this morning? Got something I need to take care of."

"Sure, I guess." Her shoulders drooped, and she kept her eyes toward the floor. "Tomorrow maybe?"

"Absolutely," he said. "Count on it."

......

After a stop at Walmart, he went into his room and perched on the edge of the bed. His mother still slept. Slow breathing with fits of coughing. Stale air, sickness, and sweat-soaked sheets. The stench of death-in-waiting.

He watched her for a few moments. Sporadic jerks. Low moans. Was she dreaming? "Mom."

No movement.

"Mom, wake up."

Still nothing.

He reached over and shook her. "Mom, time to get up."

Her breathing accelerated, and she moved a hand to her face. "Cody, is that you?" Her eyes remained closed.

"Yeah, Mom. It's me. How are you feeling? You look a little better today. The medicine must be working." He'd have to remember to ask forgiveness for lying.

Thank you, Lord, that Your mercies are new every day.

Another bout of her hacking cough ended in a whisper. "Baby, I'm so tired. Maybe we should go to the hospital."

Dirty hair stuck to her forehead like thin gray scars. He traced a finger across her temple. Filthy.

"Look, Mom. I brought you something to help you feel better."

She opened her right eye slightly and turned her head. "Oh, honey. Is that a flower? So sweet. Such a good boy."

Levi leaned over and placed the daisy on her pillow. Its petals brushed against her cheek. "I thought of you when I saw it. Mom?"

Her breathing was faster now, and she stirred slightly. The sheet fell off her left shoulder. The pink nightgown he'd given her for Christmas. How many years ago? Collarbone stretching pasty skin. Splotches of red.

Gently, Levi replaced the sheet over her shoulder.

"Mmm. Thank you, honey."

He kissed her on the cheek. "Sure, Mom. Go back to sleep."

Levi fluffed his pillow, stood beside the bed for a half-second, then leaned over his mother. Face flushed. Running a fever. He moved to the air conditioner and held the pillow over it. There. Good and cold. It'll feel better on her face.

As he returned to his mother, the hum of the air conditioner took on a rhythm of its own, inviting him to sing along.

Let us then be true and faithful,
Trusting, serving every day;
Just one glimpse of Him in glory
Will the toils of life repay.

He pushed harder.

When we all get to heaven,
What a day of rejoicing that will be!
When we all see Jesus,
We'll sing and shout the victory!

He lifted the pillow and looked at the daisy. Broken and crushed. A few petals held fast to the pillowcase, but most stuck to her cheek. Covered in innocence. How ironic.

"There. All better. Tell you what. I'm gonna take a nap, and then we're going to go check out Mount Hood. Haven't been up that way yet, but I'll bet we can find somewhere you'll be comfortable. Don't want to rush you, but you know how it is. Gotta hit the road soon. The Lord's work is never done."

He fell onto his bed and buried his face in the pillow. The scent of the flower petals mixed with old ... what? Just old. He inhaled deeply and held it, savoring the odor. A pleasing aroma before the Lord.

"Good night, Mom. Sleep well."

9

The FBI office in Portland was near the runways of the city's airport, and Jeremy's headache screamed for attention as another flight departed. The harsh lighting in the small office wasn't helping matters. Didn't matter which way he tilted the monitor. The glare burrowed its way from the screen to his brain. At least the building was warm. He leaned back in the chair and looked out the windows at the heavy gray clouds hanging low in the sky. The radio said the temperature hovered in the mid-40s, but it felt more like the low teens to him. The agents based here said on a clear day you could see Mount Hood. So far, he had been lucky to see the buildings across the street.

"What's that song?" Maggie asked.

He ran a hand through his hair. "Huh? What song?"

"The one you were humming. You do that a lot, you know."

"Something I heard on the radio I guess. Helps me think."

"Yeah? So what was it? Let me guess. Country. That's a given. Beer, tractor, women? All of the above?"

He frowned and shook his head. "Just a song I've heard a few times." No sense letting her know she was right.

"Uh-huh. If you don't want to tell me, just say so." Maggie laid a folder on the table next to his laptop, opened it, and pointed to her report. "Confirmed. All the victims had torn Bibles. Always Judges, but not always the same chapters."

She was inches from him, and Jeremy forced himself to keep his eyes on the folder. He swallowed and ran the back of his hand across his lips. "Okay, so we run with the theory that he takes those as his trophy. Makes sense. That's the link between the Supreme Court and his victims."

Maggie straightened up, gazing off into space. She scrunched her mouth and tapped her lips with an index finger.

"Unless," he said, "you have another theory?"

"No. Not yet anyway. Seems a little tenuous, though. Yeah, they're probably his trophies. But there's got to be more to it. I mean, I don't care how whacked you are, you don't cut off a finger and mail it just because you're bored. There's more to this guy."

"Sure there is. But at this point, I'll take whatever we can get. How about the girl in Nashville? Claire Lawson. Her Bible okay?"

"Don't know yet. We've got an agent swinging by her place later today. If I had to guess, our guy didn't touch Lawson's. No point, at least while she's still alive."

Her cell phone rang, and she looked at the caller ID. "Rebecca. Be right back."

Jeremy turned his attention to the monitor. The Texas Department of Motor Vehicles listed over four hundred 2006 Malibus registered in the state. Filtering by color was nearly impossible. There appeared to be no standardized method of inputting the data. Some dealers submitted the colors by their official names, others by whatever they happened to feel like using that day. His target could be brown, beige, tan, or any other shade of dirt.

He exported the file to a spreadsheet and sorted by color, then eliminated the obvious no-matches. Ninety-seven vehicles remained on the list. Brown, sandstone, tan, yellow, beige.

Maggie reentered the room. "Find anything?"

He shrugged. "Almost a hundred cars on the list. Of course, if he stole the license plate, we might not even be looking in the right state. But if there's a way to whittle the number down, I'm not seeing it. I'll fire the listing off to our guys in Texas. Maybe they can do some drive-bys, and we can cross a few off."

"The car could have been repainted."

"Yeah. I know. But we have to start somewhere. How's Rebecca?"

"Fine. Just wanted to talk. Seems the neighbor's boy pushed her down, and she got a little upset."

"You going to call the kid's parents?"

She sighed and smiled before sitting in front of her laptop. "Not likely. Apparently, she pushed him back. And then sat on him and pulled his ears. I'll be lucky if they don't call me. My mom said she's going to take her down to apologize to the boy after a nap."

"Your mom or Rebecca?"

"What?"

"Who's taking the nap?"

"Oh, both, I'm sure. Mom always says a good nap is the best thing since sliced cheese."

He grinned, his headache slinking to the far edges of his brain.

Maggie cocked an eyebrow. "What's so funny?"

"Your ability to turn a phrase is, um, endearing? I think you meant bread instead of cheese."

She scratched her cheek and shook her head. "Yeah, yeah. You ever stop to think that maybe it's you that got it wrong? You know, sometimes ... Jeremy. Did you see this?"

"Huh? See what?"

She turned her computer screen and scooted her chair closer to his. The breaking news scrolled across the top of the network's website. "Senator Diane Morgans (D-Pa) announces she will seek the nomination for President of the United States."

A chill ran along his spine. "Well, I guess we know what that means. Our friend'll be calling soon."

"You don't know that. Maybe he—"

"I know him, Maggie. Cronfeld's not the type to let go of things. And now that his wife's running for president ..."

She rubbed his arm. "Not a word from him since you got out of the hospital. Maybe the senator reined him in. When you met with her, she seemed agreeable, right?"

"Not sure I'd put it that way. More like, she didn't want to know what I was talking about but would handle it. Plausible deniability. She knows her war hero husband did some things in Afghanistan that need to stay buried. The question now is whether she thinks I'll still keep my mouth shut. Even if I do, Cronfeld's not going to leave any loose ends."

"Well, you made that sound ominous enough."

He clasped his hands behind his neck and stared at the ceiling. "He's dangerous. Not that he'd risk anything obvious. Listen, he tried to use you as a pawn before. If he does it again—"

"We'll deal with the situation if it happens. There's still the other option, you know."

"Sign the confidentiality agreement? Can't. It's all I've got. I sign that thing, and I lose any power I might have. And without the Bureau to protect me, I'm kind of on my own."

She crossed her arms and squinted her eyes. "Really? On your own, are you?"

"Sorry. I know you've got my back. It's just that I don't want to drag you and Rebecca into my mess."

"*Our* mess."

He glanced at the door before kissing her cheek. "My mistake. Our mess."

"You're putting the cart before the horse's mouth, anyway. Don't worry about Cronfeld. We've got enough problems trying to track down Nancy Bishop's killer. That's our focus. Oh, and remember the rules. No displays of affection on the job."

Jeremy grinned and saluted. "Yes, ma'am. Won't happen again."

She dropped her hand on his knee and tilted her chin upward.

"Fine. You can make it up to me by grabbing lunch for us. I'll keep working."

He bit his lip against the urge to kiss her again. "You make it hard, you know?" His heartbeat doubled as a wave of hot embarrassment flashed through his face.

She laughed and turned back to her laptop. "Good to know. Turkey on wheat, no mayo, extra sprouts, no chips. And hurry back. I'm starving."

......

Jeremy put the car in park. Today was "Kids Eat Free" day at the deli, and every child within a twenty-mile radius sat packed into the minivan ahead of him at the drive-thru window. The downtime allowed him to clear his mind and let his thoughts wander. That's usually when his best ideas showed up. Music helped, and the woman on the radio mournfully explained to anyone who would listen that they should plan on two burials if her husband ever leaves. It wasn't clear whether the second grave was for the other woman or the wife.

A flashing light in a window at the strip mall across the street caught his eye, and he surveyed the row of shops. Walgreen's. Women's Shelter Consignments. Mount Hood Sporting Goods. Christian Living Bookstore. Huh. He needed to read Judges, and trying to do it on his monitor would invite the headache to return. Could stop there and pick up a Bible.

Why did it bother him so much? There was a time when he might have enjoyed browsing in a religious bookstore, but not now. Not after Afghanistan, and the things he'd seen. He massaged his forehead and closed his eyes. The things he'd done. A short honk jolted him, and he pulled forward.

"Sorry for your wait," the young woman at the window said.

"No problem. Did all those kids get a free meal?"

She shook her head. "One free meal per adult. Two adults in the van. There must have been a dozen kids in there, so finding something they'd all eat took a while."

Jeremy arched his eyebrows. "I've got to know."

"PB&J. Same thing they could have got at home without the hassle and expense. Bunch of kids fighting over two sandwiches. I'd hate to be in that van." She handed his food out the window.

He gave her a twenty. "Thanks. Throw the rest in the tip jar. You'll earn it today."

She nodded and tried to work up a smile. "You have no idea. Have a great day."

He laid the food in the passenger seat and eased his vehicle across the street. Several cars and SUVs clustered around the entrance, most of them with bumper stickers. Fish eating other fish that had legs. Bible verses. Crosses. He skipped the open space by the door and parked in an empty area of the lot. After sitting for a moment, he took a deep breath and pushed himself toward the bookstore.

At the shop's entrance, he paused to look at the display in the window. Books on how to live a Christian life. Books on praying. And books on why bad things happen. He didn't need anyone to explain that to him. It was pretty simple. Bad people do bad things.

Once inside, he strolled past the angel figurines and Jesus T-shirts to the Bible section. Sorted by version, the variety overwhelmed him, and he stood there, staring at his options. Paperback or leather? Cheaper always looks better on the expense report.

"May I help you?"

He turned and saw a young man dressed in khakis and a button-down blue shirt. "I was looking for a Bible. Something I can understand. You know, easy to read."

The young man began pointing at different books. "Paraphrased or direct translation? The paraphrased is easy to follow. It's kind of like reading a novel, but you still get the gist of the Bible. Nothing wrong with them, but if you're looking for something truer to the original, go with a translation." He scanned the shelves for a moment before grabbing a brown leather Bible. As he reached for the book, his shirtsleeve slid up and revealed part of a tattoo.

Do they make him hide it?

The clerk handed the Bible to Jeremy. "See what you think about this one. It's a study Bible, so you get commentary included. Helps you understand some of the tougher parts."

"It's *all* tougher parts, isn't it?"

"Yeah, it can be. Not so tough to read, but sometimes it's tough to follow, you know?"

"Rules and regulations. I know all about them. Do this, but don't do that."

The young man shifted on his feet, opened his mouth but closed it without speaking.

"How much is this one?" Jeremy asked. "I'm not looking to spend a lot of money."

"On sale so it's $49.95, plus I'll imprint your name on the cover for free."

"That'll work, but I don't need my name on it."

The clerk hesitated. "We also have the same Bible in large print if you'd rather."

That would be easier to— "This'll do."

"Gotcha. Let's ring you up then."

The pair headed to the cash register and Jeremy pulled out his wallet. He handed over his credit card and caught sight of the tattoo again. "Nice tat."

The employee pulled up his sleeve to expose the whole image. "Thanks. Got it a couple of months ago."

Jeremy looked at the full-color image of the lion, covering most of the forearm. Inked under it in script were the words "Behold the Lamb."

"Isn't there something in the Bible about tattoos? I thought you weren't supposed to get them?"

"That's old school. In the Old Testament there's a warning

against tattoos, but if you read it in context, it's talking about the rituals pagans used to do for their dead. The point was to keep Israel from doing those same rituals. Still, we get a lot of folks in here that think it's wrong to get one, so I try to keep mine covered."

"Don't want to scare off any business, huh?"

"It's not that. To me, it's such a minor issue I don't even think about it when I see someone with a tattoo. But to others, tattoos are a big deal. Why risk it?" He handed back the credit card and gave Jeremy the Bible. "So long as we agree on the big stuff, why get bogged down with the little things? Sure you don't want your name on the Bible? Only take a couple of minutes."

Jeremy glanced toward his car, avoiding eye contact. Why did he feel like a twelve-year-old sneaking a peek at *Playboy*? "No thanks. Maybe next time."

"No problem. My name's Jonathan. Stop by anytime."

Jeremy waved and stepped into the dank air. He tucked the book under his coat and jogged to the car. Water puddles dotted his path, and he hopped over them, always timing his jumps so he landed on his right leg. In the car, he laid the Bible next to his lunch and peeked in the mirror.

Hints of crow's-feet around watery brown eyes. Stubbled midday cheeks. Red-tipped nose threatening to drip at any moment. Misty raindrops perched atop more-salt-than-pepper hair. *Still lookin' good.*

......

Jeremy handed the sandwich to Maggie. "Want me to grab you a drink from the break room?"

"Sounds good. You look cold. Better grab some coffee while you're in there. I made a fresh pot for you." Her grin got bigger.

What's she up to? "Will do. Then I'm going to plop down in the softest chair I can find and do some reading. Got a Bible while I was out. Figured I'd go through Judges. Maybe get some insight into our killer. My guess is it's a bunch of old guys walking around smiting people. Smite. There's a word we don't use much. I kind of like it. The world needs more smiting of bad guys. I'll be the first to sign up."

"Good luck with all that," Maggie said. "Let me know if you need any help. Not that I could provide much. Sunday school was a long time ago. New Testament, maybe. Old Testament, not a chance. I'll be in that cubicle over there. Still got lots of folders to go through, although I'm a little distracted by all the stuff on the walls. I don't know whose desk that is, but my powers of deduction tell me they like puppies and Star Wars. Oh, and the occasional vampire too."

"Sounds like the agency's screening process has slipped a bit. Back in my day, we would never hire anyone who liked vampires. Zombies, on the other hand ..."

Maggie chuckled and wandered back to her work while Jeremy headed to the break room. His scarred leg whined, protested, and punished each step.

He picked up the coffee pot and held it at eye level. So that's what she thought was so funny. Scarcely enough java to cover the bottom of the pot. He found a mug that might have been washed within the last day or two and poured in half the remaining coffee. After topping off the cup with hot water from the sink, he meandered through the office seeking a more comfortable chair he could requisition for the small office.

He scavenged a worn black leather manager's seat and dragged it back to his desk. The chair had a tall back, which almost made up for the thin padding. He settled in and took a deep breath. Clacking keyboards, an occasional sneeze, and muted conversations offered a soothing background serenade. His eyelids drooped, and he stretched his arms and legs. Gonna have to fight to stay awake. Just like church. He opened the Bible to the table of contents and ran his finger down the page. He found the introduction to Judges and read it twice. Israel messes up, God punishes them, then delivers them. Repeat again, and again, and again ...

By the end of the first chapter, Jeremy realized he was going to need more coffee. Much stronger coffee. The names of the people and the tribes became a blur. The high point came when he remembered an old joke from his childhood days at Sunday school. Who in the Bible didn't have any parents? Joshua, son of *None!* Sunday school. It was a lot easier to believe back then. Before choices were made that changed everything.

He stood and stretched, trying to keep his mouth closed as he yawned. Enough time had passed that someone, anyone, should have made a fresh pot. Just in case, he took the long route back to the break room.

His instincts were correct. A fresh cup of java at hand, he settled back into the chair, trying to focus on the pages before him. Ammonites. Amalekites. Benjaminites. *Wonder who made the coffee?* Stuck a sword in his belly so far he couldn't pull it out? Ouch. Drove a tent peg through his head? Tough girl. They sang a song about her? Won't hear that one on the radio. Dropped a rock on his head. Might hear that one on the radio.

The room brightened, and Jeremy gazed out the window. Sunshine. He walked over and let the warmth hit his face, easing the tightness of his dry skin. Mount Hood was barely visible, and Jeremy stared at it while sipping his coffee. The sunlight streamed across the Bible, making the pages appear almost luminescent. Half expecting to hear an angelic choir singing the Hallelujah chorus, he returned to his reading.

He reviewed several passages, seeking a connection to the killer. Nothing seemed to fit. Killed his virgin daughter as a burnt offering to God? He underlined the section and kept reading. Ahhh ... good old Samson. Was there ever a man as clueless about women? *I wish I'd gotten a cookie with lunch.* There was no king, and everyone did what he wanted. Not much has changed. Coffee's getting cold.

He flipped several pages to see how much more there was to read. Clouds filtered in front of the sun, darkening the room and sending a chill through him. He sipped the last of the coffee and let it sit on his tongue for a moment before swallowing.

Let's see; woman leaves man. Man goes after woman. Yadda yadda ya—

He read it four times, each time going slower. The leather chair banged against the wall when he jumped up. Probably dented the wall, but he didn't stop to look.

Mount Hood faded from view, but the aching in his leg was gone, pushed back for now. Maggie needed to know. They had one of their answers.

He knew why their target was killing.

10

The farther Levi drove up Mount Hood, the worse the weather became. Flurries morphed into a heavy, wet snow, often blown horizontally by the gusty mountain winds. Ice accumulated on the wiper blades, smearing the windshield and producing a *thump-thump* rhythm with each pass. The main road stayed clear thanks to an army of snowplows. But unblemished streets meant traffic, and his business demanded privacy.

He hunched over the steering wheel and willed his eyes to see farther. Barlow Pass lay just ahead, and he didn't want to go any higher. The last thing he needed was to get stuck or have an accident. Most of the surrounding vehicles had chains on their tires and snowboards or skis strapped to their roofs. Meadows Ski Resort would be busy today. In this weather, there was no other reason to be here. Except for what, or who, he had in his trunk.

He paced himself and calculated so no other traffic would be in view when he turned off onto Barlow Road. A quick right turn, and then the road veered, blocking the view from the main highway. The satellite view on Google Maps was spot on, though the trees were now snow-whitened, rather than glistening green. A ridge of powder ran along the shoulder, with only a couple of inches on the road. The plow had passed by within the last hour or so. He'd have to hurry in case the maintenance vehicle returned soon.

His attention darted between the street and the steep upward bank mere feet outside his window. His left knee bounced like a jackhammer, and his fingers squeezed the life from the steering wheel. What does an avalanche sound like? He'd spotted a tornado back in Texas when he was nine, but that was different. He could see the twister coming. An avalanche, though. Buried alive in a cold, dark tomb. Wondering if they'll ever find your body. Or even bother to look. No, that was no way for a person—

The car's rear tires slid, making the decision for him. This was the spot. Turning around would be a challenge, but so be it. Off to the right, a stand of evergreens opened to a small clearing. Room to do what had to be done.

He stepped out of the Malibu and searched for any signs of danger. Howling winds swayed huge Douglas firs, their creaky trunks and screechy branches protesting the snowfall's weight. Overhead, a hawk surfed the currents, ever watchful for its next meal. The frigid air numbed his face and hands. Wet flakes settled in his hair, melted in the warmth of his head, and trickled icy streams behind his ears.

He pulled the key fob from his pocket, rubbed his thumb over the trunk control several times, inhaled deeply, and pushed the button. A shiver ignited in his chest and exploded through his scalp, leaving his hair on end. He rubbed his palms together before looking into the trunk.

Cardboard boxes, filled with toiletries, clothes, and other necessities, sat on either side. In the center, a dirty spare tire, treads so worn that steel poked through. And under that, dead Mom.

He lifted the tire and balanced it against the bumper. The sheet from the Portland Palace Motel rippled as the wind dipped into the trunk. For half a second, his mother's face stared at him. Bruises around her nose and mouth. Glossy bright red lips shining like a beacon against ashen skin. He was glad he'd put the lipstick on her. She'd like that.

Boxes shoved to the side, he ran his arms under her body and lifted, careful to grasp the sheet in his hands so Mom stayed covered. She'd never been a big woman and was easy to carry. What was that he'd read once? Some doctors used to place people on a scale as they died to see how much their souls weighed. Mom's must have been pretty light.

He stepped off the road and wove through the trees to the clearing, forty feet or so away. The knee-deep snow was still fluffy enough to allow movement, but the surface already had an icy crust, soaking through his jeans. Three times he stumbled, unsure of his footsteps. Each time, adrenaline, or terror, shot through him, shocking his system. Falling in the snow with Mom's corpse was not a memory he'd cherish.

Finally at the glade, he inhaled the crisp air, filling his lungs with proof of life, and looked around. "This look okay, Mom? I bet there'll be wildflowers here in the spring. Probably some rabbits and squirrels too."

His right foot dragged back and forth in the snow, creating a subzero cavern. Would animals be able to smell her? He hoped not. As if laying a baby in a crib, he placed her on the uncovered ground. No time to prepare a eulogy. He bowed his head, leaving his eyes open and focused on the wrapped body, and prayed.

"God, thank you for my mom. She can be a pain sometimes, but please take care of her until I get there. Forgive her for her sins. All of them. And don't let the animals find her here. Amen."

He knelt and pulled back the sheet far enough to see her forehead. Pale. Bloodless. Cold. His eyes closed, he leaned forward and kissed her. "Good night, Mom. I love you."

He stood and piled snow on the body until it was concealed,

then moved toward the car. Halfway there, he glanced back at his path. A trench pointed to his mother like a one-way street sign. Dark clouds cautioned that the weather would be worsening. Try to cover the trail or leave before getting stranded?

The sound of a large truck headed his way provided the answer. A final look at the graveside and he shuffled quickly to his vehicle. He tossed the spare tire in the trunk and slammed it shut just as a snowplow rounded the curve, its flashing orange lights ricocheting off the trees. The huge vehicle slowed to a stop several feet behind Levi's car.

The driver swung his door open and stood on the step outside his cab. "Everything okay?"

Levi nodded and waved. "Fine. Thought I'd venture a little off the beaten path. You know, see what nature looks like without all the traffic."

"Probably not your best idea, what with the weather getting worse and all." He stared at the path in the snow, his head tilted and eyebrows cocked.

Levi swallowed hard and wiped his arm across his brow. "Thought I saw a deer or something over there. Wanted to see if I could get a better look."

The driver shook his head and pointed at Levi's license plate. "Won't be any deer this high unless Bigfoot drags them up here. Bet you don't get this kind of weather in Texas, huh?"

Levi forced a laugh. "Tumbleweeds and tornados. That's about it."

"No law against you being up here, but if I were you, I'd head back down. Going to get a lot worse soon."

He waved and opened the car door. "Good advice. I've seen enough snow to last me a lifetime."

The driver returned his wave. "I'll wait till you get turned around to make sure you don't get stuck."

"Appreciate it." Levi started his car and took a deep breath, holding it before slowly exhaling the tension. Turning around wasn't as difficult as expected, and he looked up and smiled at the snowplow operator as he passed him. Moments later, he was back on the main road, his mind racing.

Too many people knew his car and its Texas plates. That needed to change. Buy a new car? Paying in cash might raise questions. Steal one? He wasn't a thief, and stealing is a sin. Besides, police look for stolen cars. Other options? Rahab. Of course. Ask and you shall receive.

......

Back at the motel, Levi scanned his mother's bed. A few wilted flower petals still clung to the pillow. He plucked them off and tossed them out the door into the breeze. They rushed across the parking lot, barely touching the ground. A couple of them ended up in one of the potholes dotting the asphalt, but most blew into the street, past the three figures shivering on the corner.

A faded red minivan pulled up to the women and slowed to a stop. All three crowded around the passenger window, and after a moment, one of them hopped in and left with the driver. Levi kept an eye on the vehicle, staring at the decals on the back window. Dad, Mom, two kids, dog. He shook his head, spit, and jumped as the wind blew it back at him. In the room, he washed his hands under water so hot it nearly scalded him.

......

By the time Levi pulled into the coffeehouse's parking lot, it was late afternoon, and the sun decided to make a guest appearance, reminding everyone it still worked when it pleased. The snow changed over to rain, and from his car, he could see the lights in the shop were on. A few businessmen occupied the tables and killed time until their workday ended. Rahab wasn't working this late in the day. The middle-aged woman behind the counter yawned, making no attempt to hide her boredom. A large wet leaf smacked against his windshield and paused to look inside before slogging off to the next stop on its journey.

He turned up the collar on his jacket and hustled into the shop. One of the businessmen looked up but just as quickly returned to his laptop. The smell of burnt milk hovered in the air, no doubt the result of the barista's fine attention to detail.

"A small black coffee, please."

The woman sighed, spewing a cloud of cigarette-tinged breath at Levi. She held a cup under the urn's spigot, filled it two-thirds of the way, and handed it to him. "That's the last of the coffee," she said. "Not gonna make more since we'll be closing soon."

"No problem. Didn't need that much caffeine anyway." He dropped three dollars on the counter and took a sip. Burned and cold. "Busy day?"

"Too busy. You'd think people would have enough sense to stay in on a day like today. No offense."

"Yeah, none taken. You seen Kat around?"

"Huh? She works mornings."

"Sure, but I was supposed to meet her this afternoon. Kind of a date thing." He clenched his teeth as cold coffee grounds swept over his tongue.

"You don't look like her type. Then again, I'm not sure she has a type. I haven't seen her. You can wait here, but I'm closing up soon."

"I'll give her a call." He punched buttons on his phone for a moment, then stared at the ceiling. After a suitable pause, he frowned and drummed his fingers on the counter.

The barista folded her arms. "Everything okay?"

"Yeah. I've got a bunch of numbers in here. I'll find her, though."

"Stanton. Last name Stanton."

Levi dragged his finger across the phone's screen and grinned. "Got it. You're a lifesaver."

She flipped a switch, and the lights behind the counter went off. "Everybody out. We're closed."

Charming. He hurried back to his car and opened his computer. Kathryn Stanton. Over four hundred friends on Facebook and her photos available for the world to view. He skimmed through them, occasionally pausing. Right-click. Save image. Let's see what we can find out. Birthday. Favorite music and TV shows. And telephone number.

He shook his head and dialed, waiting as the call went to voicemail. "Hey there, Kat. It's Levi, you know, from the coffee shop. Got your number from the woman working this afternoon. Boy, she's a real charmer, huh? Anyway, just wondered if you wanted to get together sometime. Give me a call, you know, if you want. See ya."

He tossed the phone in the passenger seat and pulled onto the street. Less than a minute later, his phone rang. That didn't take long.

"Hey there," he said.

"Hey yourself. Glad you called. I was sitting around bored out of my mind. So, you get your heavy thinking all done?"

Bored? Where are your four hundred friends? "Yeah, I did. Business has been really slow, and I had to figure out what I wanted to do. Trimming trees isn't exactly my life's calling, you know?"

"You should work in a coffeehouse. We all get super rich and famous. Living the dream."

He chuckled. "So I've noticed. Listen, you want to grab dinner or something? My treat, of course. I've come to a decision and wanted to bounce it off someone." Oh, and I need your car. Sell it, give it, take it. Doesn't matter. Easy or hard, I need it for the Lord's work. And you'll need to keep your mouth shut about it. One way or another.

A few seconds of silence crept between them. "Sure. I know a great sushi place. It won't be too crowded. Sound okay?"

"Raw fish. That'll be a first for me. I prefer my food to be, umm, cooked?"

"You'll love it, trust me. I'll text over the address and meet you there in, say, thirty minutes? You do trust me, don't you?"

Oh, the irony. "I'll withhold judgment on that until I've tasted the sushi. See you in thirty."

......

The pungent odor of wasabi tangled with the salty smell of soy, clearing Levi's sinuses. He used a fork to poke at the concoction on his plate. "The rice I recognize. Everything else ... well, it looks pretty, but I think I'd like mine better battered and fried. Maybe a little gravy on it."

Kat's eyes narrowed, and her lips turned up at the corners. "Chopsticks are the best way to eat sushi. You really should at least try."

"Unless I whittle a point on the end and stab the food, it's not going to happen. Seriously, I'm like the most uncoordinated person on the planet."

"Uncoordinated? Sounds like you have the perfect job then. Climbing trees with chainsaws. It's a miracle you're still alive."

He poked his tongue into his cheek and rolled his eyes upward. "I think you're right. God's watching out for me. And I'm sure He doesn't want me to push my luck by jabbing wooden sticks at my face. Is it okay to use my fingers?"

"Perfectly fine. There really aren't any rules. Now, quit stalling and eat."

Levi picked up a piece of the fish, tilted his head upward, and wiggled the sushi over his mouth. He dropped it, swallowed loudly, and clutched his throat.

Kat covered her mouth and laughed. "Okay. I lied. There are rules, and I think you broke all of them."

"Sorry. Rookie mistake. Won't happen again. And shockingly, it tasted okay."

"Told you." She sighed and bit her bottom lip. "So, what's your big decision? About the tree trimming and stuff? Going to look for a new job?"

He glanced outside, watching drops of water race down the window, some of them spreading apart, others uniting. No lightning, no thunder. Just a steady rain declaring it was still wintertime in Oregon. Snow would be falling on Mount Hood. A pure blanket for Mom. A quick sniffle, a dab at the eyes, and the moment passed.

"It's time to move on," he said. "Looks like it's going to be a mild winter around here. Good for you, bad for me. I'll probably be heading out soon. That's why I called you. Wanted one last chance to thank you for expanding my coffee boundaries."

Kat focused on her plate and stirred the sushi from one side to the other. "So where you headed?"

He peeked out the window again. The neon *Sushi* sign reflected off the hood of her car, an old red Honda Civic. Red. For Rahab. "Someplace with more sun. Florida, I think. I'll pick up some landscaping work. Maybe go back to school, do something with computers."

"Sounds like you've got it all planned out."

He chuckled. "Yeah, maybe."

"Seems kind of lonely if you ask me. Driving all over the place by yourself."

"Got no choice. Can't stay here."

She laid her chopsticks on the table, placed her hands in her lap, and gazed at him. "I could go."

Levi's skin itched, and he scratched the back of his neck as a tingly hollowness flitted from his stomach into his chest. "What?"

"I could go with you. I mean, if you want me to."

He ran his hand over his arm, buying time. A reward for his obedience? Or a threat to his mission? Rahab *did* go with Israel. "Wow. Umm, are you sure? I've known you for what, a week or so?"

"You get to be a pretty good judge of character when you work in a coffee shop. I see lots of people and watch how they treat each other. You're one of the good guys. I can tell." She dipped some sushi in soy sauce, swirled it around, and held the raw morsel over the center of the table.

I'll bite. Levi leaned forward and slurped the fish into his mouth. "Yeah, but don't you have a life here? Friends, family, all of that?"

"No family, really. Haven't seen my parents in years. Got an older sister who went off to college in Colorado and never came back. I don't blame her. And I'm due to get some new friends."

He propped an elbow on the table and rested his chin on the back of his fist. "Sounds a lot like my story. No family either. Never had any brothers or sisters. Didn't know my dad, and my mom passed away not too long ago."

Kat touched his free hand. "I'm sorry, Levi."

His scalp burned as their fingers touched. He glanced out the window. Two water droplets meandered down until finally, right before the bottom, they joined. "Thanks, but I'm over it. Mom had a good life, and it was time."

"So what do you think? You up for a partner in crime?"

Several of the other patrons glanced over when they heard Levi's belly laugh. "Partner in crime, huh? Listen, Kat; I like you. I really do. But you need to think this through. I don't want to get a couple hundred miles down the road and have to bring you back."

"Seriously, I've been looking for an excuse to get out of here for a while." She tilted her head down, peeking up into his eyes. "And I think I've found one."

He stroked the back of her hand, brushing his finger against her skin, back and forth across the ridges. "Two conditions."

"Yeah?"

"First, no more sushi."

"I think I can manage that. And the second?"

He reached across the table and placed his hand under her chin, pressing her face upward so he could look directly into her eyes. "You have a red necklace. Wear it."

11

Jeremy scrubbed the back of his hand across his eyes, stifled a yawn, and looked around the office. Three FBI agents from Portland clustered together discussing the previous evening's Trail Blazers game. Based on the snippets he heard, the home team had a rough night. Basketball. Why didn't he think of that? It would put him right to sleep. Dribble dribble dribble. Shoot. Repeat. Hockey on the other hand ... His yawn returned with a vengeance, and this time he made no effort to hide his drowsiness.

"Will you please sit down?" Maggie said. "You're driving me crazy. This carpet's bad enough without you wearing a hole in it."

Jeremy sighed and sank onto the plastic chair he'd borrowed from the lunchroom. A throbbing beat pierced the top of his skull and waves of dizziness visited without notice. Sleep fled again last night, the third time this week. "Sorry. Trying to stay awake."

She moved closer and dropped her voice to a whisper. "The dreams again?"

"Yeah." The man in the chair had returned, pursuing him throughout the night. Never speaking. Only smiling. Accusing. He was quite dead, of course. Another Taliban member gone—sent—

to eternity. But the memory lived on. The doctors talked a good game. Tried to help. More than a dozen years had passed, and still, the terrorist remained.

The triangular gadget in the center of the table beeped, and everyone quieted. A monotone female voice announced FBI Deputy Director Matthew Bailey was now on the line. The sound of shuffling papers and muttered curses flowed from the speaker. Was the man ever in a good mood?

"Okay," Director Bailey said. "Let's get going. I've got another call coming up. Agent Keeley, Winter, you there?"

Jeremy cleared his throat. "Yes, sir. Did you get a chance to review the notes we sent?"

"I saw them. I'm not completely sold, but right now it's the best theory we've got. I still want to run this past a profiler."

"Yes, sir. In the meantime, with your approval, we're going to proceed as if this is his motivation. We need to fill in a lot of blanks, but I think this gives us an idea of why he's killing."

"Doesn't make any sense to me, but if there weren't lunatics running around, I'd be out of a job. This guy's not the first person to kill in the name of religion, and he won't be the last. Keeley, you there?"

Maggie leaned toward the phone. "I'm here, sir."

"You did the research on this Bible stuff, right?"

Maggie glanced at Jeremy. "It's a team effort, sir. Mr. Winter and—"

"I don't have time for that. Just give me the short version on what this story is about. I read it, and I'm not sure I understand why it's so important to this guy. A fairy tale from three or four thousand years ago doesn't seem relevant."

Maggie clenched her jaw and tapped her finger on the desk. "Sir, the story's significant to him. That makes it even more important—"

"What's that tapping noise?"

Jeremy nodded toward Maggie's fingers. She rolled her eyes and placed her hands in her lap.

"Okay, it stopped," Bailey said. "Go on."

"Yes, sir," Maggie said. "We knew the book of Judges was important to our perp when we discovered the torn pages in his victims' Bibles. Most likely, they're his trophies."

"Good work on that. Crime scene units should have caught it first."

"It's easy to miss," she said. "The Bibles are tattered, and unless you know what you're looking for—"

"Go on with your review."

"Yes, sir. Judges paints an unflattering picture of the tribes of Israel. They disobey God, are punished, repent, and God restores them. The key chapter as far as we're concerned is Judges 19. It's a rather sordid story, and to be honest, we're still trying to figure out what the whole thing means. What we do know, though, is a woman is killed, apparently during the course of multiple rapes. Her husband then cuts up parts of her body and sends a piece to each of the twelve tribes of Israel. We think that's the link with our guy as far as cutting off his victims' fingers."

"Uh-huh. But if I understand it, the dead woman in the Bible was a prostitute, correct?"

"Depends on how you translate it. She was his concubine, sort of a second-status wife. She left him and was unfaithful, whether as a prostitute or an adulteress, we're not sure."

"So then, Agent Keeley, why isn't your perpetrator killing prostitutes and adulteresses instead of innocent girls?"

Maggie's face flushed, and she moved closer to the phone. "Sir, if you're implying that prostitutes and adulteresses are somehow—"

Jeremy nudged her. "Sir, if I may. The man in the story is a Levite, which means he was from the priestly tribe of Israel. They were supposed to be the holiest men around. It's possible our suspect sees himself that way, and so he would avoid associating with prostitutes. We're still working on that, though."

The sound of shuffling papers echoed through the speaker again. "Give me a second."

The three Portland agents whispered again and compared notes. Their faces told Jeremy these guys were serious about their work. No smiles. Furrowed eyebrows. Clenched jaws. Good. They needed to be on their "A" game.

Maggie stood and stretched her arms overhead, standing on her tiptoes to get the full effect. The white shirt she wore under her dark suit jacket looked a little off, and Jeremy gazed, trying to figure out what was wrong.

She's got it buttoned crooked. He looked up, and she was staring straight at him, her eyebrows arched and head tilted. Oh, she thinks ... *oh, no.* It was suddenly very warm in the room. "You've got your shirt buttoned wrong."

The phone crackled. "What? Winter, what are you talking about?"

Maggie had a hand over her mouth, but he could see the upturned corners of her lips. He'd hear about this for weeks. Jeremy closed his eyes and massaged his forehead. "Oh, sorry, sir. Nothing."

"Okay. Keep going. She runs home to Daddy and becomes a prostitute. Then what?"

Jeremy nodded at Maggie to continue. "Then the Levite comes to take her home. He ends up staying at the father's house for a few days but then heads out. On the way home, they end up staying in a town called ... hold on ... Gibeah. And that's where things really go bad."

"A bit of an understatement, Agent Keeley. Hold on. Janice! Coffee! Okay."

"Yes, sir. The two of them are staying in some guy's home and a bunch of men from the town bang on his door. They want the guy to hand over the Levite. It's clear their intention is to rape him. But the homeowner offers his virgin daughter and the Levite's concubine instead."

The DD grunted. "Heck of a guy."

"Yes, sir. But the men don't listen, so the Levite grabs his concubine and throws her out to them. She's taken away, apparently raped repeatedly, then crawls back to the Levite's door and dies there."

"That's what's bothering me," Director Bailey said. "The Levite's no hero. Why would our killer pattern himself after someone who's a coward? I mean, what's the moral to this story? Who's the good guy?"

"Sir," Jeremy said, "not all stories have good guys." How well I know. "The Levite starts to go home the next morning and finds his concubine on the step, dead. Interestingly, the story doesn't say he went to look for her. He planned to leave without her, but there she was. So he throws her body on his mule, takes it to his house, and butchers the corpse into twelve pieces. One for each of the tribes of Israel."

"The point being?"

"The point being," Jeremy said, "when the tribes found out what happened in Gibeah, everyone was outraged. In fact, the act started a war. Kind of a wake-up call, I guess. They realized what depravity parts of the nation had fallen to and decided to do something."

Maggie cleared her throat. "We believe our killer may be trying to do the same thing. We don't have tribes, but we do have judges. He's sending a message. Wake up and look at the evil around us."

"So it's your belief he sees himself as a messenger? And his job is to wake us up to the evil in the world? Isn't he part of that evil? And I still don't understand why he's choosing innocent victims. And there's nothing in there about daisies or any other flowers."

Maggie frowned and shook her head, pointing at Jeremy.

"Sir," he said, "we don't understand either. Something triggered this. Or someone."

"Uh-huh. Well, get it figured out. We need to get this closed. One more question. Why didn't our killer cut up one body into nine pieces and send those to the Supreme Court? Seems to me it would have made more sense to do that if he's trying to play along with the story."

He sighed and bent toward the phone. "Yes, sir. But killing one person isn't going to get him the attention he wants. It might be news for a day or two, but then the story disappears. One murder—"

"What attention?" Director Bailey asked. "Nobody outside the FBI has linked these together. He's not getting any attention in the media."

Maggie frowned and bowed her head. "No sir, he's not. Not yet."

......

Another long night. Bouts of sleep interrupted by the need to review the case. Studying the details of each attack. Rereading the interviews. The dream didn't come, though. It didn't need to. Jeremy remembered. Might as well go into work.

The office was cold, part of the government's energy conservation program. The heat rarely cycled on during the night, so it was mid-morning before the room grew comfortable. White linoleum floors, fluorescent lights, and plastic furniture gave the break room a sterile aura, enhancing the chill. Still, it beat being outside.

A few agents and admins filtered in and out of the room, murmuring and nodding greetings in his direction. He answered with grunts, nods, and arched eyebrows. Getting good at the don't-wanna-talk-just-go-away smile.

He'd walked the mile and a half to the office, sending Maggie an early morning message to bring the car when she came. Jeremy hoped the brisk morning air would clear his mind as well as give him some energy. It hadn't.

"You look terrible," Maggie said. "No sleep again?"

"Coffee hasn't kicked in yet."

"Ever think maybe the coffee is why you can't sleep?"

"Nope. Got nothing to do with it." That was harsh.

Maggie turned to walk away. "Somebody got up on the wrong side of the bed."

His shoulders drooped, and he reached a hand out toward her, stopped, and let his arm fall back to his side. "Sorry, Maggie. Just getting a little frustrated. There's a part of me that wants this guy to ..." What? Kill again so we can get more clues?

She sat down across from him, pushing the sugar canister off to the side so nothing was between them. "Jeremy, we'll get this guy. We will. Maybe we'll get him before he kills again. I hope so. But maybe we won't. Either way, we'll get him."

"Yeah, I know. Look, at this point the best lead we've got is the car, right?"

Maggie nodded. "Assuming it's the killer's car."

"No choice. At this point, we have to presume it is. So we know he probably stayed at a hotel somewhere near Portland."

"He could be sleeping in his car."

"Possibly, but I doubt it. Too risky. Cops could see him and stop to check it out. No, if I'm him, I'm staying in a hotel. Someplace out of the way."

"Okay, I think I know where you're going, but there's no central database for hotel registrations. A search for Texas licenses would be great, but not going to happen. And there's over a hundred and fifty hotels around Portland. And that's supposing he didn't stay somewhere farther out."

"Uh-huh. But let's make a couple more assumptions."

Maggie grabbed his Styrofoam cup and carried it to the coffee pot. "Keep going."

"He's not going to stay close to where the murder happens. And probably not going to stay someplace expensive."

"Maybe." She pulled a pen from her jacket and wrote on his cup.

"So that rules out a lot of hotels."

Maggie refilled his coffee and poured a few drops in her cup before topping it off with hot water. "Yeah, it does. But it leaves a lot of them too. The local cops did their thing, and none of the hotels remembered any vehicles matching our description."

Jeremy took his cup and stared at the indentation of a *J* in the Styrofoam. "Out of ink?"

"Never could get a pen to write on those things." Maggie poured sugar into her cup, then took a sip.

"I thought you didn't drink coffee."

She shrugged. "Not enough in here to taste, especially with the sugar. I wanted something hot."

"Not going to stir it?"

She swirled the cup in her hand, then sat it on the table. The whirlpool continued for a couple of seconds. "There. Perfect. Plus, I'll get a sugar rush when I get to the bottom."

"Why the *J* on my cup?"

"Figured we'd be here for a while again today. I didn't want to get mine and yours mixed up."

He pointed to the red lipstick marks on the edges of Maggie's cup. "Good thinking. I'm wearing the same shade."

She threw her head back and laughed, ending with a snort. "Some detective, huh? Got up too early this morning. Three time zones away from Rebecca is tough. I try to talk to her every morning before Mom takes her off to kindergarten. Hard being away from the kid, you know?"

He stared at the table. "Yeah, I do."

Her eyes opened wide. "Oh, Jeremy, I didn't mean ... I'm so sorry."

Holly and Miranda. His wife and unborn daughter. Murdered while he was in Afghanistan. "It's okay. Really. Don't want you to be afraid to say anything around me. You and Rebecca, well, you know ..."

She rubbed her finger on his hand and smiled. "Yeah, I do."

He cleared his throat and straightened. "Let's get to work. I thought we'd get a map, divide it into sections, and start hitting hotels. Maybe we'll get lucky. It beats sitting around here all day waiting for something to happen."

"A map." Maggie tugged at her bottom lip.

"Yeah, a map. Those things with roads on them."

"He's coming from Memphis, right? Or maybe Texas."

"Yep. That's our best guess."

Maggie stood and paced, staring at the floor. "So if I'm driving all that way, I'm stopping at the first place I find that meets my criteria. Anything to get out of the car."

"I-84 comes in from the east. Texas or Tennessee, chances are he came in that way. There's bound to be some places to stay along there."

Maggie stood and picked up her hot, brown, sugar water. "Nice day for a ride."

12

Jeremy steered out of the grungy motel's parking lot and glanced at his partner. Her turned-down lips reflected his mood perfectly. "You okay?"

She shook her head. "Four hotels so far this morning and nothing. Nada. Zip. Maybe we're grasping at straws."

"Maybe. But for now, it's all we've got."

The GPS woman interrupted the conversation. "Turn left in one mile."

Jeremy lowered the radio's volume. "Want to stop for lunch or hit one more hotel first?"

She placed her hands on her stomach. "The rumbling that loud?"

"No. Not at all. I just thought a thunderstorm was moving in."

"Yeah, well, it's my body trying to protect itself by overpowering your music. And I use the term 'music' loosely. Very loosely. I can take a little country, but come on. Mix it up. Variety and spice and something. I don't remember the exact phrase, but you get the point."

He placed his palm on his chest and grimaced. "But this was a huge hit a couple of years ago. His girlfriend likes his John Deere. Tractors can be sexy, you know. At least to some women."

"Uh-huh. Not this woman. And have you ever even ridden on a tractor?"

"Tractor? No. But there's lots of sexy things I haven't ridden on." I can't believe I keep doing that. Heat rushed through his face, and he stared out the window, hoping she'd let the remark pass.

She didn't. "Wow. That's an interesting comment. Care to elaborate?"

The grin on her face wasn't helping. "I didn't mean it the way—"

The GPS barged in. "Arriving at destination."

Thank you. "Rough looking place," Jeremy said. "The Portland Palace. Let's check it; then you can buy my lunch. It's the price for insulting true American music."

He pulled up to the office, and they stepped out of the car. The wind had died down, but a gray sky and light mist dampened their mood even farther. The one-story motel was past its prime by at least three decades. Its twenty or so rooms all faced the street. Peeling paint on the doors exposed moldy wood underneath. Rusted pipes stood at intervals along the concrete path, relics of the awning that at one point had covered the walkway.

Beads of water formed on Jeremy's jacket, and he darted to the office. He grabbed the door handle and turned to speak to Maggie. What's she doing?

Still standing beside the vehicle, she gestured toward a meagerly clad group of women standing at the street. "You go on in. I think I'll go chat with those ladies out there."

"Good luck. Feds aren't exactly their favorite people, I'd imagine. I'll be inside."

The dim office was unoccupied, and the bell clanging against the door went either unheard or ignored. Jeremy could see feet propped on a coffee table in the back room. On the TV, a man worked to shove a turkey into a rotisserie oven.

Jeremy knocked on the counter. "Hello?"

"Yeah, yeah, yeah. I'm coming." The desk clerk shuffled to the counter, muttering as he moved. Orangey crumbs covered his too-small T-shirt. Cheetos maybe? His shoes were untied, and dark jeans hung low off his wide hips. The waistband of plaid boxers failed to fill the gap between pants and shirt.

"Hi there. I'm Jeremy Winter, working with the FBI. Just like to ask you a few questions."

"Whatever."

"We're looking for a car. Chevy Malibu, beige. Probably six or seven years old with Texas plates. One occupant, a man. Might have stayed here within the past week."

The clerk headed back to his TV. "Haven't seen it."

Jeremy's jaw muscles tightened. "Sir, I'm not finished."

"Well, Mister FBI, unless you know of another way for me to tell you I haven't seen your car, I think we *are* finished. Now, this man is about to tell me how fast that thing can cook a turkey. If you don't want to rent a room, I've got work to do."

The man returned to his previous position and propped his feet on the coffee table. Jeremy's pulse quickened, and he crossed his arms, exhaling loudly. Over the counter and in the room in less than two seconds. He'll never know what hit him.

The bell clanged, and cold air swept into the lobby. An old auto trading magazine on the counter flipped through several pages before the door closed. Maggie stood there, breathing hard. "Hey. Get out here. I think we've got something."

Twenty minutes later, three police cars and a mobile crime scene unit sat scattered around the parking lot. The few tenants at the motel left in a hurry, but not before being screened by the local cops. None stopped at the office and asked for a refund. In the back room, the desk clerk sat on a worn sofa, his jittery hands tapping chunky legs.

Jeremy stood in front of him, bent with his palms on his knees, staring into the man's twitchy eyes. "Sir. Do I have your full attention now?"

The clerk ran his hand through his hair. "Look. This is bad for business, okay? I've got paying customers. You understand, right? I mean, it's hard enough to stay open without you cops hassling me all the time."

"Uh-huh. What's an honest businessman to do? Yeah, I get it. But let me make this simple for you. I only care about one thing, and that's finding this car. Now, some of your customers out there at the street told us they saw a vehicle matching this description. It was here for a couple of weeks at least. Room 12 maybe. Any of this ringing a bell?"

The clerk rubbed a plump finger across his forehead. "There was this guy. Stayed for a while. Always paid cash up front, a week at a time. But he can't be the dude you're looking for."

"Why not?"

"You said he was alone. This guy had some old broad with him. She didn't get out much, but she was there."

Jeremy glanced at Maggie, and she cleared her throat. "Room 12? When did they leave?"

"Dunno. My job is to take their money, not keep track of them. See, we value our clients' privacy. Long as they've paid, they can do what they want." He pulled his shirt down and brushed a few crumbs off the ridge on top of his belly. He smiled, exposing a gap where a tooth should be. "Don't get many lady cops in here that look like you."

Jeremy's stomach hardened. "I've had just about all—"

"Aww, you're sweet," Maggie said. "Mind if we take a look at your registration database?"

"No problem, honey. See that stack of cards over there? That's my database. And you're welcome to look through it just as soon as you show me a court order."

Jeremy put his hands in his pockets and rocked on his feet. "It's on the way. You know, there's a lot to check into here. I'd say it's gonna take us a while. A few days at least. Could even be a week. Have to be thorough, you know?"

The clerk squinted and scratched the stubble on his cheeks. "Okay, okay. Maybe I can help speed things along?" He pushed himself up from the couch and grabbed the pile of registration cards.

Maggie grabbed his arm. "Put those down. There may be evidence on them."

"Sure thing, honey. Anytime you feel like grabbing me, you go right ahead."

"That's an attractive offer, but I think I'll pass." She tensed and held her grip but didn't stop smiling.

"Hey! That hurts." The clerk yanked his arm away and massaged the reddened area.

A police officer walked in and handed a piece of paper to Jeremy. "Got it."

Jeremy scanned the warrant before passing the document to the desk clerk. "Now, you sit there and don't move. What's the name on the registration card?"

"Funny name. Ashton or something like that. You know, like the young kid who married the older broad." He glanced at Maggie. "Nothing against older gals, though."

Maggie bit her bottom lip and looked at Jeremy. "A few minutes alone with him. That's all I need."

Jeremy stared at the clerk. "Maybe later. Let's get the crime scene guys in here first. They can start looking for the registration card. We need to get a peek at the room before it gets trampled by everyone."

"Okay." She glared at the clerk. "Hey, when was the last time the room was cleaned?"

He smacked his lips. "I run a tidy business. Every room gets a thorough cleaning every Tuesday, whether it needs it or not. So no, the place hasn't been cleaned since he left."

Jeremy shuddered. "Today's Sunday. Think the crime scene techs have a hazmat suit I can borrow?"

Maggie looked at the police officer and motioned toward the lump on the sofa. "If he moves, explain to him it's in his best interest to stay put. If he refuses, you may need to offer additional, umm, encouragement."

The cop nodded and grinned. "Be my pleasure."

They stepped outside and surveyed the area. Jeremy motioned toward the women from the curb, now clustered around one of the officers. One of the ladies waved in their direction, and Maggie returned the gesture.

"I'm surprised they're talking," he said.

Maggie grunted. "Take a look around. Cops everywhere. Can't be good for business. Besides, they wanted to help. Don't judge them based on their jobs."

How did she do that? See the good in everyone? "I wasn't judging. I was just ... here we go. Room 12."

A uniformed officer stood in the doorway to restrict entrance. Even from outside the room, the musty odors leeching out the door were powerful. Mildewed carpets, curtains, mattresses. The two flashed their identification, peered into the room, and snapped on a second pair of latex gloves.

Jeremy entered first, pausing to let his eyes adjust. The curtains were open, and all lights were on, but the room fought back, struggling to hide its secrets as long as possible. He nodded toward the beds, and Maggie stepped closer.

"Double beds, both slept in," she said. "Sheets missing from this one."

Jeremy moved to the bathroom to check for any personal effects that may have been left behind. "So who's the old woman with him?"

"Don't know," she said. "Anything in there?"

"Hair in the sink. From the looks of the tub, I'd have to say your friend in the office was being generous when he said they cleaned the rooms every week. CSI is going to have a field day in here." Back in the main room, he watched as Maggie knelt and shined her flashlight under the bed.

"Ugh," she said. "I hope the crime scene techs get paid overtime. They'll need it. I don't want to be in here when they bring in the black light."

He slid open the nightstand drawer and thumbed through the Gideon Bible. "No pages torn."

She stood, shifted the mattress, and looked under the headboard. "Hmm."

"Got something?" Jeremy asked.

She didn't respond.

"Maggie, got something?"

"Could be. Jeremy, look at this and tell me what you think it is."

He took the flashlight and leaned over, squinting into the crevice. The beam of light passed back and forth over a small white object hanging on the bed rail. His heartbeat echoed in his ears. "Maggie, that's a flower petal. Better get CSI in here now and get it bagged."

"On it. Secure the door. I'm calling our guys in for this one."

"Maybe we finally caught a break, huh?"

"Yeah. Maybe. I'll get a new APB out on the vehicle. Let them know there are possibly two occupants now. If he's headed out of town, he could be taking I-84 again. With some luck, a trooper will spot the car."

He rubbed a gloved hand across his chest. Luck? The killer had a two-day head start. Could be anywhere by now. Maybe even plotting his next attack. Identifying his next victim.

Luck? Wouldn't be enough.

They needed a miracle.

13

Willard Bay Reservoir stretched off to the right, partially obscured by towering power lines. On the left, a ridge of rusty cragged peaks pressed against a clear blue sky. Ahead, the pale gray pavement of I-84, spider-webbed with tar-filled cracks, flowed into infinity.

Levi leaned over the steering wheel of the Civic and strained to hear the engine better. The motor sounded like a tin can with a dozen pebbles rattling around inside. He slowed, and the noise stopped, then accelerated above seventy again. The pinging returned.

He looked over at Kat. Her bare feet tapped the dash, toenails painted black of course, and she looked bored. "Hey," he said. "Does the motor always do that?"

"Told you we should have kept your car and got rid of this one. Yours was in better shape. This thing's on life support. That noise is the car begging you to pull the plug."

Levi shrugged. "This old girl's not in too bad of shape. Besides, I was ready for something different."

"Me too, I guess. So, Florida, huh?"

"I hear Sarasota is nice this time of year. Lots of jobs too. All the rich old people go south for the winter. They call them snow-birds or something like that. We should be able to find jobs there."

She twisted a finger through her necklace and parted her lips slightly. "Wonder what people do for fun in Florida?"

"The same thing they do in Portland, I suppose. You know, eat sushi and stuff."

She giggled and slapped him on the arm. "You didn't give it a chance. Everyone loves sushi. Some people just need more convincing than others. And with the scene you made, we're lucky the owner didn't throw us out."

Levi winked and placed a hand on his belly. "I can still feel that fish swimming around. Poor Nemo. I think he's hungry. Ogden's about twenty miles farther. We'll swing in there and grab a bite. Maybe find a Long John Silver's so my little fishie will know what could have been. Besides, I need to drop a few things in the mail. Pay some bills."

Thirty-five minutes later, he pulled into a Denny's parking lot. "Grab us a table. There's a mailbox across the street. I'll run over there and be right back."

Kat slipped on her flip-flops, flicked down the visor, and straightened the blue streak in her hair. "Denny's, huh? You sure know how to impress a girl."

"Hmm. I see your point. I believe we passed a Taco Bell about a quarter-mile back. Maybe we'd be better off there."

"Denny's it is. Not sure I want to be locked in a car with you after Taco Bell. I'll grab us a booth." The door popped loudly when she pushed it open and cracked again after she stepped outside and closed it. She leaned against the car and poked her head inside the open window. Her faded T-shirt served as a fuzzy gray background to the red necklace as it swung freely.

Levi's eyes followed the movement of the jewelry. Left, right, left. Back and forth. Is this how people get hypnotized? His heart raced as a flashback roared to mind. A woman leaning in the passenger side. Now where had he seen that before?

"Seriously," Kat said. "I don't know if this thing will make it all the way to Florida. You sure there's not somewhere closer we should try?"

"It has to be Sarasota. That's where the job is."

"The job? You've already found one? When?"

His shoulders tightened. "No, of course not. But that's where our best chance to find one is. Like I said, lots of people in Florida this time of year. We'll find something."

Kat nodded and walked toward the restaurant, shouting back over her shoulder. "Yeah, if we make it there."

Levi waited until a waitress escorted her out of view, then reached into the back seat. He pulled the black duffel bag from under a laundry basket full of clothes and snapped latex gloves on his hands. Five envelopes. *New York Times. Chicago Tribune. San Francisco Chronicle. Dallas Morning News. Atlanta Journal-Constitution.*

A contest. Who could figure it out fastest? Which one would print the story first? Inside each envelope, a single sheet of paper. Five names. Five cities. Nancy Bishop of Portland, Oregon, was the newest addition. Under her name, four blank lines. That should get their attention.

An hour later, they were back on the road, heading south.

......

At the Portland FBI office, Jeremy laid his cell phone on the desk and pushed the speaker button. He and Maggie exchanged a glance before he spoke. "You're sure it's the car?"

Almost twenty-four hours after being issued, the APB paid off. A car matching the description of the killer's vehicle was found abandoned in a Portland suburb. Good news and bad. Another possible lead but no suspect.

"No, sir, I'm not sure," the voice on the phone said. "The plates are missing, and we're still running the Vehicle Identification Number. But it is a beige 2006 Malibu. Looks like it's been cleaned out. CSI's on the way, but I'm betting the car's been wiped down."

"Okay," Jeremy said. "Get the vehicle hooked up and inside somewhere as soon as possible. And let me have that VIN."

Maggie scribbled the numbers on a notepad and read them back for confirmation. She nodded to Jeremy. "Got it."

"Call me if the crime scene tech finds anything," he said. "We'll run the VIN too. I appreciate your help, officer." He disconnected the call and placed the phone back in his pocket. "Maggie, can you call—"

"Our office in Dallas. Got them on speed dial." She punched a button and placed the phone to her ear. Within a few minutes, she was reading the VIN to an agent in Texas. She covered the phone with her hand. "He said it would take a while."

Jeremy drummed his fingers on the table. "A while? Punch some numbers in a computer and tell us who the car belongs to. How long can that possibly take? We're, I mean, you're the federal government, aren't you?"

Maggie scrunched her face into a frown. "You want to talk to him? I'm sure with your sweet disposition he'd move much faster. Maybe you should try deep breathing exercises or yoga or something." She jerked slightly. "What? No, not you," she said into the phone. "Uh-huh ... okay. Where is that? Okay. Listen, thanks a lot. Hang by the phone. I'll probably be calling you back in a few minutes."

"What's the story?" Jeremy asked.

"The car is from Texas, registered to a Charlene Talbot in Pleasant View. That's a little bump in the road down in the southwest part of the state."

Jeremy scratched a spot on the table. "See if they'll send an agent out to Pleasant View. Find out why that car is here. Could be nothing."

"You don't think we should go?"

He shook his head. "Not yet. This could turn out be a wild goose chase. We need to keep working here for now. Figure out who's with this guy. You check the system. See if we've got anything on Charlene Talbot. Maybe she's the old woman the clerk at the motel saw. I'm going to check the stolen vehicle reports for the last couple of days. If that is his car they found, we need to figure out what he's driving now."

Maggie stood to leave the room. "What happens if this turns out to be a dead end?"

"Then we'll keep working until we get a new lead."

She nodded. "I guess we'll cross that bridge over troubled water when we get to it, huh?"

"You're doing that on purpose now, aren't you? But yeah, we'll deal with it. Until then—"

Maggie's phone rang, and she checked the display. "It's Rebecca."

"Take the call in here. I need to stretch anyway. And tell her I said hi." He rubbed the calf of his left leg, stood and walked toward the door. The pain had flared again last night, feeling like a rusty nail ripping from thigh to ankle. Aspirin didn't help. There was stronger medication in his toiletry bag, but he never opened it. Pain was a reminder.

"Hi, honey," Maggie said. "How are you this morning?"

Jeremy looked over his shoulder at her, now settled back in the chair, legs crossed.

She covered the phone. "You need to go back to the doctor?"

Jeremy turned, confused. "For what?"

"That leg. It's not supposed to keep hurting like that, is it?"

He shrugged. "Comes and goes. No big deal."

She frowned and returned to her phone conversation while he headed for the break room, hoping the snack machine still had something worth eating. His stomach regretted the decision to skip breakfast.

Multiple databases, two bags of barbecue potato chips, a Snickers, and a Diet Coke later, Jeremy had no useful information. Plenty of stolen cars reported, but nothing stood out. An hour slumped in a break room chair was fifty-five minutes too long. Maybe Maggie had better news. He wandered back to the office and sank into his chair. "You go first," Jeremy said.

"There's an agent on the way to Pleasant View. He's driving over from our office in El Paso and should be there in four hours or so."

"Four hours?"

"Ever been to Texas? It's a big state. I did manage to dig up some information on Charlene Talbot, though." She scrolled through her laptop screen. "Born in 1946 in Odessa, Texas, to Jimmy and Dinah Johnston. Lived there until she dropped out of high school and married Anthony Talbot. He was a local boy, played football, and worked for an oil company for a while after he graduated. Neither one has a criminal record."

"Children?"

"I'm getting to that. In 1968 they moved to Pleasant View. The oil company opened some new wells in the area and transferred him there. They emailed me a photo of the Talbots standing by one of their derricks."

"Print it out. Have the lab age both of them and see if we can get an ID back at the Portland Palace."

"Already in motion. My case, remember? After the job transfer, there's nothing until 1984 when Charlene gives birth to a son, Cody. And that's where it starts to get really interesting."

"How so?"

"I'm still waiting on information from the oil company, but apparently they have no record of Anthony Talbot after 1973. I figured he could've found another job, so I did some digging. Nothing with the IRS. Nothing with Social Security."

"Off the books, huh? Maybe he hit the lottery. Or he's a boot-legger or drug dealer. Close enough to Mexico to do it."

"That's a possibility." She swung her computer around so he

could see the screen. "But take a look at Cody's birth certificate."

He traced a finger down the display as he read. He paused and looked at Maggie. "No father listed?"

"Nope."

"So eleven years or thereabouts after the last record we have of Anthony Talbot, a baby is born to his wife. Interesting."

"Told you. Could be something."

Jeremy straightened and crossed his arms. "You're a woman. Why wouldn't you put the father's name on a birth certificate?"

She flicked a finger across her lips several times. "I think I should be offended by your phrasing, but we'll deal with that later. In most cases, you *would* put the dad's name on there. I mean, even if you didn't want anything to do with the father, you'd still want his name on the certificate. That way you could go after him for child support if you ever wanted to."

"What if your husband isn't the father?"

"Then you still put the husband's name on it. Assuming, of course, you want to keep your little secret. Nope. There are only two reasons I can think of to leave a birth certificate blank. Either you don't know who the father is, or you do know but want to make sure no one else does."

"So which do we have here? If Anthony Talbot were still with Charlene, his name would be on the certificate, father or not. That's what you're saying, isn't it?"

"That's my best guess. Until we talk to Charlene, we won't know for sure, but I don't think he was still in the picture when Cody was born. Maybe he's dead or possibly living in Mexico. Who knows?"

"No record of Charlene having a job?"

"I ran her Social Security Number, and nothing showed up. No income, no taxes. And no payments of death benefits for Anthony. She has one credit card, and we're trying to get a warrant to see if it's still being used."

"Could be she found herself a sugar daddy, and they never tied the knot. You should run a check on her address through the Postal Service. Find out if anyone else has been getting mail there."

Maggie grinned. "Sugar daddy? What are you … eighty years old? I don't think people say that anymore."

Don't smile. It'll only encourage her. Wait it out.

Her grin faded. "I'll check on their mail service."

"Great. What's the story on the kid? And don't tell me you're waiting on information."

"Don't know much so far. Graduated from high school. Worked at a local burger place for a while."

"And?"

"And … I'm waiting on more information."

"It's always like this. Hurry up and wait." He checked his watch. "Three and a half hours until our guy gets to Pleasant View. Keep digging."

"Aren't you forgetting something?"

"Don't think so."

"Oh. Well, care to share anything you might have found out about stolen cars?"

"Yeah. Sorry. In the last three days, there have been fifty-one cars reported stolen in the area. Six have been recovered. If we assume our guy wouldn't want anything too flashy, I can probably drop another twenty cars off the list. That still leaves us with a lot of possibilities."

"Too many for an APB."

"Yep. And at this point, I don't have any idea how to narrow down the list."

"Anything new on the recovered Malibu?"

Jeremy shook his head. "Not really. No fingerprints but plenty of hair. If anything turns up in Pleasant View, we'll have samples to match it against."

Maggie stood and walked over to the window. She slipped her hands into her pockets and rocked on her feet. "Beautiful day outside. Sun shining. Birds singing. Mountain on the horizon."

Jeremy stood next to her. She was right. It was a beautiful day. He looked through his reflection to Mount Hood, majestic and distant. "And a killer choosing his next victim."

Maggie took a deep breath and crossed her arms. "Yes, Jeremy. You know, it wouldn't hurt you to see the good things too. You might like them."

He cut his eyes toward her. "I see them, Maggie."

......

Three hours later, Jeremy sat alone in the office, fighting to stay awake. The adrenaline rush of the morning had worn off. The sleepless nights trapped him and pounded his energy level to zero. Trips to the restroom to splash cold water on his face helped, but only for a few minutes. The words on his computer screen blurred, and he squeezed his eyelids together trying to clear his vision. He should close the door. Take a power nap. That would—

"Got him," Maggie said.

He jerked and banged his knee on the table. "Geez, Maggie. Don't sneak up on me like that. You'll give me a stroke or something."

"Sorry, but I've got our agent in Pleasant View on the phone." She sat in the chair across from him and placed her cell phone on the desk. "You're on speaker. Go ahead."

"Mr. Winter, this is Special Agent Burleson. I'm at the location with the county sheriff. This place looks like it's been abandoned for quite a while."

Jeremy leaned toward the phone. "Any idea how long?"

"Couple of years at least. The house was condemned. It's pretty isolated from the rest of the town if you can call Pleasant View a town. We checked inside, and nothing too unusual. Whoever lived here left some of their stuff behind. From the looks of the place, I don't blame them."

"Does the sheriff know anything about the family who lived

there?" Maggie asked.

"Not much. Says he never had any call to come out here. I figured when we were done at the house we might spend a little time asking around town. I'm not sure what you were hoping to find here, but I don't see anything that makes me suspicious."

A second voice spoke in the background, and the agents strained to understand what was being said.

"Hold on a sec," Agent Burleson said.

Jeremy's shoulders sagged, pressing his arms onto the table. He cleared his throat and kept his eyes on the phone.

"You guys still there?" Agent Burleson asked.

"Yeah," Maggie said. "What's going on?"

"We're in one of the bedrooms. The sheriff thinks some of the scratches on the floor are new. Most of the wood is pretty rotten, but you can see lighter marks where something's been dragged. I'm gonna put the phone down for a second."

Jeremy glanced at Maggie. She bit her lower lip and stared at the phone. She caught him looking and held up both hands, displaying her crossed fingers.

They heard a scraping sound, and Agent Burleson picked up the phone. "We moved an old dresser that was left here. There's got to be a foot of dust on the thing. There's scattered wood chips underneath. Looks like someone's been prying the boards. Sheriff, you got a screwdriver or crowbar in your car?"

Jeremy stood and twisted his head, stretching his neck and shoulders. His heart rate accelerated, and he scrubbed a hand across his face. "Agent Burleson, be very careful. If there's evidence there, I don't want it disturbed."

"No problem. We see this a lot down around the border. Hiding spots for drugs or illegals. Okay. Yeah. Just pry up that board there. Careful … okay. Stop. Don't touch anything. Back away. That's good. Hey, Agent Keeley?"

"Yeah?"

"You guys better get down here."

14

The ramshackle house in Pleasant View, Texas, swarmed with law enforcement, most of them FBI. Jeremy and Maggie stood in the entry room of the small home while the forensics team did their work in the smaller bedroom. A portable generator fed power to floodlights, revealing every dust speck and cobweb. A dirty, dry scent permeated the home. Decay and abandonment.

Jeremy was alert in spite of the lengthy travel time from Oregon. Almost robotically, he scanned the living room for at least the fourth time, left to right, top to bottom. "Still nothing on the boy?"

Maggie shook her head. "Went off to college and pharmacy school. Got through an eight-year program, then just disappeared. Seems to be a habit with this family."

He nodded toward a bookcase leaning against the wall, its shelves sagging as gravity and age did their work. Several thick Bibles stood proudly as a dozen or so figurines held court. "Religious family."

"Guess that depends on your definition of religious," Maggie said. "I mean, I'd guess most homes have at least one Bible in them, but that doesn't mean they're spiritual."

"Five Bibles on the top shelf, and a Nativity on the one underneath. And from the looks of the thing, baby Jesus and his friends stayed out year-round. Know many people who do that?"

She moved closer to the bookshelf. "No, I don't. All of the Bibles are King James."

Jeremy shrugged. "So?"

"Nowadays, most people opt for a translation like you got at the bookstore. You have to be hardcore to stick to the King James. Tough to read, tougher to understand."

"Okay, so she's strict, wants to stick with the original. Why?"

"Beats me. As far as I know, unless you're going to read the Bible in the original Greek and Hebrew, one translation's as good as another. The techs check them yet?"

"Yeah. All clean. No torn pages."

Maggie squatted and took a closer look at the Nativity. Wood, ceramic, and plastic figures mingled together in an ancient Israeli melting pot. "Kind of weird, huh? You've got at least three different sets mixed here. Looks like there's an extra Mary hanging out with the shepherds. And I'm fairly certain there weren't any pigs around the manger."

"Too messy?"

"Not kosher. A Jewish family would have never allowed pigs anywhere near them."

"So why have a pig in your Nativity scene?"

"It's probably just a toy that got mixed in. Maybe the kid played with them, you know, like action figures. Spiderman, Captain America, all those guys."

Jeremy grunted. "You seem to know a lot more than I do about this stuff."

She stood and chuckled. "Nice that you're finally admitting I'm smarter. You know, they say the first step toward recovery is to acknowledge you have a problem. I think you've taken—"

A forensic technician interrupted them. "We're done with the bedrooms. You can go in if you want."

"Any idea about the bones?" Jeremy asked.

"Don't know much yet. Female, young, likely somewhere between eighteen and twenty-five. She's bagged and on the way to the lab. We'll run the DNA and try to get a match with missing persons reports. Maybe we'll get lucky."

"That rules out the mother and the son," Jeremy said. "Find anything else?"

The technician nodded. "A few hair samples in the bathroom and on the mattresses, but honestly, I don't know that they'll be any good. DNA won't last long in this environment."

"Prioritize anything found in the kid's bedroom," Maggie said. "Whoever put the body there came back, hopefully not too long ago. What's your best guess on processing time?"

"We already got a call from Washington to move this to the front of the line. Twenty-four hours to get the body and evidence to the lab, another forty-eight hours or so to process."

Jeremy massaged his forehead. "Three days before we know if there's anything here. Too long." He turned to Maggie. "Let's check out the bedrooms."

Their blue shoe covers kicked up dust as the two moved past the mother's room into the smaller area. An old mattress was on the floor, and the dresser sat in the middle of the room, a gaping hole in the floor behind it. He squatted and peered into the opening, grateful the bones had been removed. Whoever she was, she didn't need to stay here.

"Check out the walls," Maggie said.

He leaned to his right, planted his hand on the floor, and grunted as he stood. Most of the room was painted in what once might have been a dark tan but was now simply brown. Beside the window in large, shaky letters, running nearly ceiling to floor, dingy yellow paint relayed its timeworn message.

But thou, when thou prayest, enter into thy closet, and when thou hast shut thy door, pray to thy Father which is in secret; and thy Father which seeth in secret shall reward thee openly.

Above the mattress, the same scrawling had been repeated.

But every man is tempted, when he is drawn away of his own lust, and enticed. Then when lust hath conceived, it bringeth forth sin: and sin, when it is finished, bringeth forth death.

"Not the cheeriest place I've ever been," Jeremy said. "Did you notice the door? Painted black with a lock on the outside. A deadbolt lock. Window's nailed shut too."

Maggie dragged her gloved hand over the latch, twisting the knob and watching the deadbolt pop out of the door. "I guess Mom didn't want him coming out of the room. Think she knew about the body?"

Jeremy held up both hands, palms facing her. "Don't jump to any conclusions. We don't know the boy is the one who put the bones in there. Could have been the mother or anyone else."

Maggie shrugged and moved to look outside. "I suppose. Did you notice this window's mostly clean on the inside? Not covered with dust like everything else in this place."

Jeremy scanned the perimeter of the window, pausing at each of the top two corners. "Something was tacked here. Either to block the sun or the view or both. Can you track down Agent Burleson? We need to know what else he saw in this room."

She leaned out the doorway. "Hey, you. Do me a favor. Find Agent Burleson and tell him we need him." She turned back to Jeremy. "He'll be right here."

"Thanks. Does Rebecca follow directions as well as you do?"

She hears her daughter's name, she smiles. Every time.

Maggie grinned. "Afraid not. She's a little bit stubborn sometimes."

"Huh. Wonder where she learned that?"

"I'm sure I wouldn't know." She poked her head around the doorway again and lurched back as Agent Burleson entered the room.

"You wanted to see me?" he asked.

"When you and the sheriff came in here," Jeremy said, "was there anything in the room besides the mattress and dresser?"

The agent looked around the area, pointing with his finger as he did. "Right there," he said. "On the floor against that wall. A piece of wadded up aluminum foil. I bagged it."

"Off the window," Jeremy said. "Check with forensics. That's our number one priority for DNA evidence. Got it?"

Special Agent Burleson scowled. "Yeah, I got it. I'll tell them, and then I'm heading back to El Paso. This is your case, not mine. I've got enough headaches of my own to deal with." He pivoted and left the room, his footsteps echoing through the wall.

Maggie glared at him, one corner of her mouth dipped into a frown.

"What's that look for?" he asked.

"You can catch more flies with honey than vinegar."

Jeremy smiled. "Wow, that's right."

"Of course it's right."

"No, I mean that's the actual saying. You got it right."

Maggie crinkled her eyebrows. "What are you talking about?"

He glanced around the bedroom. "Nothing important. I've seen enough here. If you're ready, let's head down to the mother's room."

She nodded and led the way down the short hall, stopping just inside the second bedroom. The space was much larger than the boy's room. A king-size bed filled most of the area. A mirrored dresser lined one wall, brass handles on each drawer. Floral wallpaper covered all four sides, peeling badly in several places. Washed-out scarlet paint peeked from behind the torn wall covering. Two nightstands flanked the bed. Each had a brass lamp with an ornate lace shade that had faded to a stale yellow. A slight burning odor filled the room as spider silk and dust settled onto the portable floodlight.

Jeremy focused on the bed. "Four poster. Don't see those much these days. Seems kind of fancy compared to the rest of the house, doesn't it?"

A large painting of an Italian landscape, complete with vineyard and villa, hung over the headboard. "Maybe," Maggie said. "Look at the paintings. Cheap, but colorful. And the linens are all still on the bed. I can see leaving the stuff in the kid's room, but why wouldn't you take all this with you if you moved?"

"What if she didn't move?" He walked to the bed, knelt, and looked underneath.

"Seriously," Maggie said. "You think forensics wouldn't check under the bed?"

He stood and brushed the dust off his pants, grunting as he bent. "Old habit. Always check under the bed."

"And did you find anything?"

"Besides the pain in my leg? Nope."

Maggie turned and opened the dresser drawers. "All empty. So she took her clothes, but not her furniture." She pulled the dresser away from the wall, checking the back of the mirror. "Nothing here either."

He perused the room again, letting his mind absorb every detail. "Let me ask you a question. Let's say it was just you and Rebecca, living alone out in the middle of nowhere. Little bit of money maybe, but nothing extravagant. If you're going to decorate one of the rooms, which one? Yours or Rebecca's?"

"Easy. Rebecca's room. And I wouldn't put a lock on the outside of the door either." She tapped her lips for a moment, then peered at Jeremy. "Unless there was something going on I didn't want her to see."

"So the kid's locked away in his hellhole doing who knows what while mom's ... what? The fancy bedroom in an otherwise dismal house. Her son confined out of sight, either so he can't see, or he can't be seen. Maybe both. If I were the type to jump to conclusions, I'd say this is where she was earning her income. But how would that jibe with all her religious stuff?"

Maggie shrugged. "I can't help you there. Never heard a preacher talk about prostitution. But if that is what she was doing, I imagine the kid would've figured it out. Could really mess with his head."

"Yeah, but people can overlook things they don't want to know. Especially a kid. Look at the research on sexual abuse cases involving children. Lots of times they convince themselves nothing happened. But it doesn't go away. Just sits there in the back of their brain, waiting to claw its way out. Even if you do have a stack of Bibles in your living room."

Maggie's stance widened, and she drew her lips into a thin line. "You do what you have to do to take care of your family. If she was, um, working here, and at this point, it's still *if*, she may not have had a choice. Bible-believing or not, we've all done things we're not proud of."

Yeah, we have. He nodded. "Point taken. Let's head into Pleasant View and talk to some of the locals. See what they remember about the family."

Maggie's phone rang, and she glanced up at him as she brushed past. "Don't judge her until you have the facts. You have no idea how hard it is to be a single mom."

He held up both hands and started to speak, but she was already heading out the door. Anyone else, and he wouldn't bother. But Maggie mattered. He cared what she thought, especially about him. He shook his head and took one last look around the room before following her.

She stood beside their car, staring off into the distance. Her expression hadn't changed.

He run-walked to her, leaned against the vehicle, and sighed. "Hey, there. I didn't mean—"

"That was Director Bailey on the phone."

"Yeah? What's up?"

She cleared her throat and dabbed under her eyes. "Jeremy, you're fired."

15

The drive to Pleasant View would take thirty-five minutes, most spent on dusty back roads, and the conversation was as sparse as the view. Moonscape barren scenery peppered with clusters of scrub brush and mesquite trees pushed the mood even lower. Maggie drove while Jeremy stared out his window and tried to focus.

Who was the girl under the house? Were the mother and son the killers they pursued? If so, where were they now? And, mixed somewhere in there, why had Bailey fired him?

"Nothing," he said. "Bailey didn't say anything other than he was canceling my contract?"

"I told you everything he told me. Said to tell you today was your last day, and the Bureau would be handling the case on their own."

"Think this is Cronfeld's work?"

Her shoulders slumped. "Who knows? If it is, you can bet he'll be contacting you soon to make sure you know he's responsible. Don't get fixated on him, Jeremy. It could just as easily be budget concerns."

"Yeah."

"Oh, come on. You're not going to pout, are you? Look at the bright side. This'll give you a chance to figure out what you want to do with the rest of your life. Take some time off. Relax. Clear your mind."

He crossed his arms and frowned. "I'm not pouting."

She rolled her eyes and squished her mouth to one side. "Fine. You're not pouting. But if you'll be good, maybe we'll go get ice cream later. Okay?"

He chuckled, opened his eyes wide, and leaned forward in the seat. "Two scoops?"

"Don't push it."

"Sorry. I'll get over my pity party soon enough. Hate to leave something half-finished, though. Wanted to see this case through."

"Yeah. I'll keep you in the loop as much as I can, but you know how that works."

"Not your job. Don't do anything that might get Bailey worked up. It's not worth—"

She pointed out the windshield. "Finally."

A dilapidated wooden sign teetered beside the road, welcoming them to Pleasant View. Several of the letters had faded away, leaving a ghostly outline as their own version of a chalk-marked body. Bullet holes pitted the "P," most of them clustered inside the loop.

They crested a small rise and caught their first glimpse of the town. Larger than he expected, with storefronts on either side of the main thoroughfare, many of them with vehicles parked outside. A hill on the left supported an abandoned drive-in movie theater, half the screen gone, its marquis holding desperately to three letters from the last double feature.

"Huh," Jeremy said. "Guess they were playing *Gone with the Wind.*"

Maggie grimaced. "Nice try."

The shuttered shops on the outskirts of town showed signs of long-term deterioration. Peeling paint, missing wallboards, weedy parking areas. The remaining businesses toward the center of Pleasant View fared marginally better. Small side roads snaked off into the distance, homes and trailers getting farther apart as they fell away from town. A few people moved about, getting gas at the mini-market or lumber at the hardware store.

"I can see why they named this place Pleasant View," Jeremy said.

"Sarcasm is not your strong suit."

He rubbed the back of his neck. "No? Maybe I need more practice. Now that I've got some free time coming up ..."

They cruised past a building with large windows, benches out front, and a flashing neon "OPEN" sign. A chicken was hand painted on the wall, either by a master abstract artist or a second-grader, and above the fowl, "The Side Porch Restaurant." A dozen pickup trucks filled the lot, their drivers parking wherever the mood hit.

Maggie gestured toward the diner. "Let's stop there. Twenty bucks says there's a bunch of old guys sitting around inside, playing dominoes or cards and solving the world's problems."

"Stereotype much?"

She glanced at him. "Care to put some money on it?"

Jeremy nodded. "Loser buys lunch." *Hope they take MasterCard.*

Inside, mismatched booths and tables filled the main room, with roosters being the owner's decoration of choice. A chalkboard announced the day's special: chicken fried steak and gravy. It didn't appear the board had ever been erased. The aroma was fattening and delicious.

Most of the patrons paused their activity and turned to stare at the strangers. The room grew silent except for the whirring of a vent hood in the kitchen.

"Good afternoon," Jeremy said, nodding in their direction. A few customers returned his nod and refocused on the business of eating. In the front, a group of elderly men sat around two tables. Their canes and walkers formed a barricade against any intruders.

Maggie motioned in their direction. "Looks like you're buying."

The lone waitress hollered from across the room. "Welcome to the Side Porch. Sit anywhere you like."

They chose a booth along the wall and looked over the short menu. The server brought two glasses of ice water. "What can I get you?"

Jeremy slid the menu back behind the napkin holder and ordered without looking at the server. "Burger and fries for me."

"Same here," Maggie said.

"Y'all must be in that group working up at the Talbot place. They say the Feds are all over it."

"Yes, ma'am," Jeremy said. He looked at the waitress. Late thirties, old enough to have known the family. She wore jeans and a black T-shirt with a rooster logo, and her smile seemed genuine, not the plastered-on-so-I'll-get-a-bigger-tip look he usually got. He propped an arm across the back of his seat. "You happen to know any of the Talbots?"

She cast a glance at Jeremy's ring finger and placed her hand on his shoulder. "Honey, everybody around here knows everybody else. I know who they are but don't really know much about them. Except what I hear, of course."

"And what have you heard?" Maggie asked.

The waitress kept her hand on Jeremy. "Oh, this and that. You know how rumors go. Town like this, not much to do except talk."

Maggie cleared her throat, and Jeremy glanced at her. She shifted her eyes to the waitress's hand, still resting on his shoulder. Jeremy pressed his lips into a frown and slid over in the booth.

"Why don't you have a seat for a second?" he said. "Rumor or not, we'd be interested in listening to what you've heard."

"Sure thing. Let me run and turn in your order. Be right back."

Maggie openly grinned. "Flies with honey. You're learning."

"Doesn't mean I have to like it."

"Okay," the server said as she slid next to Jeremy. The torn vinyl bench seat was big enough to easily accommodate both of them, but she scooted over far enough for her hip to brush against him. "I'm Shirley, but most everybody calls me Shirl. Now, what do you want to know?"

"For starters," he said, "have you seen any of the Talbots lately?"

"Honey, nobody's seen them for, what, going on a year now probably. Used to come to town to pick up groceries and stuff. Big churchgoers too. If the sanctuary doors were open, they'd be there. At least that's what I heard."

Jeremy sipped his water. "What church?"

"Biggest one in town. Second Baptist, down the street on the left."

"Did the mother or son have any close friends?" Maggie asked.

Shirley peeked across the table before directing her answer to Jeremy. "None that I know of. Word is her boy went off to college to be a doctor or something. He must've been pretty smart, 'cause nobody around here has that kind of money. I figured he was on some sort of scholarship."

"What about before then?" Jeremy asked. "When the boy was younger? The father around much?"

"I've lived here my whole life and never saw or heard of the father." She leaned in closer. "Now, lots of folks around here spend their time gossipin', but I don't go in for that. The Good Book says if you don't have something nice to say, then keep your mouth shut." She looked around the room. "But I did hear tell the daddy run off a long time ago. Found himself somebody else."

"Interesting," he said. "So how did the mother support the two of them? It couldn't have been easy. Small town like this, not a lot of jobs to be had, I'd guess."

The waitress laughed and patted his shoulder. "Oh, honey. If I were the kind to spread rumors, then I'd tell you she found a way to bring in money. A few of the ladies from the church used to get together to discuss the situation. You know, see if they could figure out a way to help. At least that's what they said. More likely they were sharing stories."

"Anyone ever go out to her house? Get to know her?" Maggie asked, her eyes narrowed.

The waitress shook her head. "Don't remember anybody doing that. I don't go to Second Baptist anymore since my divorce and all."

"Right," Maggie said. "Tell you what, here's my card. If you think of anything else, call me."

Shirley leaned closer to Jeremy. "You got a card too?"

"Fresh out," he said. "Maybe you could go check on those burgers?"

Her shoulders sagged, but she kept smiling. "Sure, honey. Whatever you want."

Maggie waited until Shirley was out of earshot. "Nothing we didn't already know, or at least suspect. Want to talk to anyone else here?"

Jeremy looked around the restaurant. "I get the feeling if we need to talk to any of these people, we can find them here most any day. If it's okay with you, after lunch we'll swing by the church."

Shirley returned and carefully set his plate on the table, aligning it in front of him, hamburger on the left, fries on the right. Maggie's plate thunked on the table in her general direction.

"Y'all enjoy your lunch. Let me know if you need anything."

"We're fine. Thanks," Jeremy said. She wandered off, and he bit half a crinkle-cut fry, pointing the steamy remnant toward Maggie. "I could be wrong, but I don't think Shirley likes you very much."

Maggie lifted the bun on her hamburger and inspected underneath. "Don't see how the FBI's gonna survive without you. Your powers of observation are incredible."

Burger grease tried to escape to Jeremy's chin, and he dabbed at it with a napkin. "Sarcasm is not your strong suit."

......

The Second Baptist Church of Pleasant View stood less than half a mile from the diner. Flaky white paint peeled from most of the exterior. Tiny dust tornadoes spun through the gravel parking area. A steeple stood atop the roof, proud of its status as the tallest structure in town. Out front, a small bell hung from a rusty metal stand, its clapper teasing the sides in the near-constant breeze. Stained glass windows contrasted with the blandness of their surroundings, fresh colors in a black-and-white movie. Against the wall, scraggly brown weeds surrounded a tattered yellow sign promoting Vacation Bible School.

"Think anybody's home?" Maggie asked.

"One way to find out. News travels fast around here, so I'd be surprised if we weren't expected."

They climbed the three wooden steps, pulled open the heavy door, and stood at the back of the sanctuary to allow their eyes to adjust to the dimness. A center aisle divided the church, with wooden pews on either side. Bibles and hymnals sat stacked at the end of each row, readily available for any soul who would use them. No carpet, no frills, not much in the way of decoration. An elevated platform, with a wooden pulpit in the center, rose at the front of the room. The choir's plastic chairs fanned out in front of a tiny baptistery, an American flag standing at attention on one side. Opposite was a white flag, its corner displaying a red cross on a blue background.

An elderly man, dressed in worn coveralls and a black T-shirt, leaned against a broom near a door at the front. His scratchy voice echoed through the room. "Can I help you folks?"

Jeremy half-waved toward him. Is he holding up the broom or the other way around? "Yes, sir. We were hoping someone could direct us to the pastor."

"Don't need to be directed," the man said. "You found him.

And I suspect y'all are here to ask me some questions about that big to-do you've got going on out at the Talbot place."

"We are," Maggie said. "If you could spare us a few moments of your time, we'd be grateful."

The pastor shuffled toward them and motioned to a pew in the middle of the room. "Young lady, at my age time is a precious commodity. But you know what the Bible says, don't you? The Psalms tell us to number our days. The clock is a priceless treasure at your age too. So I figure if you're willing to spend time with me, the least I can do is return the favor."

Jeremy extended his hand. "Jeremy Winter. And this is FBI Special Agent Maggie Keeley."

The preacher clasped both hands around Jeremy's and held them there. His grip was weak, and the fingers bent at odd angles. The oversize knuckles made his hands look like the gnarled roots of an old tree. "Grayson Wynford. I'm the pastor of this little outpost. It's my pleasure to meet you folks."

The two sat in the pew in front of the preacher, twisting around to talk to him. "Pastor Wynford," Jeremy said, "we have—"

"Grayson, young man. Call me Grayson."

"Yes, sir. As you know, we're investigating a situation at a house outside Pleasant View. The home belonged to Charlene Talbot, and we were hoping you might be able to give us some information about her."

"I'd be glad to, as much as I can, at least. Only been pastor here a few years, and there may be things I heard in confidence I won't go into. I'm sure you understand."

Maggie handed him her business card and nodded. "Of course. Can you tell us when you last saw Mrs. Talbot or her son?"

The pastor rubbed his whiskers with a bony finger. "As near as I can recollect, it's been a year or so since I saw Charlene. Even longer since Cody was around."

"Do you know where they went?" Jeremy asked. "It's urgent we locate them as soon as possible."

The old man shook his head. "No, I don't, son. Cody went off to college a long time back. I haven't seen him since. Charlene, well, Charlene just stopped coming around."

"Any idea why?" Maggie asked.

Grayson focused on the stained-glass windows, avoiding Maggie's gaze. Three times he opened his mouth to speak but remained silent.

Jeremy squeezed the back of the pew. "Sir, people's lives are in danger. We're trying to help them. If you know something, anything, that might give us answers, you need to tell us." He reached and touched the pastor's hand. "Now."

The old man's head drooped, and he picked up a Bible from the pew. "Son, some things are between a person and their Creator." He squeezed Jeremy's hand and stared intently at him. "I'm sure we've all done things we wish we could undo."

Why did people keep saying that? Jeremy pulled his hand away and cleared his throat. "Of course we have. But we're trying to stop some very bad things from happening. This is about the future, not the past."

Grayson smiled and pointed a finger at Jeremy. "Exactly."

"Okay," Maggie said. "How about I tell you what we already know? That way you don't have to feel like you're breaking a confidence. For starters, Charlene lived in the house with Cody. We have a suspicion, a strong one, that she survived by becoming a prostitute."

"Go on," the old man said.

"We also know Charlene was a member of this church. A very active member. If we can find out why she left, that may give us insight into our investigation."

"Miss Keeley, bear with me for a moment." The pastor opened the Bible, licked the tip of his finger, and rustled through the pages. "Ah, here we are. Are either of you familiar with a young woman named Rahab?"

The two exchanged a blank look.

"Well, then. Allow me to enlighten you. In the book of Joshua, the tribes of Israel are finally going to enter the land God promised them. In preparation for that, they sent two spies ahead to scout out the area. Now, the king of the city got word they were there, so he sent people to get them. You can guess what he would have done if he found them."

Maggie smiled at the pastor. "Sir, I'm really not sure what all—"

"Let him finish, Maggie."

Grayson tapped Jeremy's arm. "Thank you, son. Now, these spies were in real danger. But a woman named Rahab had heard all about the things the Lord had done for Israel. She knew there was no way the king would be able to win a battle against them. So she hid the spies, saving them from certain death."

He licked his shaking finger again and turned the page. "Look, right here in this verse, what does the Bible say about Rahab?" The preacher turned the book so Maggie could read it.

"She was a prostitute."

Grayson nodded vigorously. "Exactly. And yet, she had faith in the Lord. In the end, that faith saved her and her family. When the Israelites attacked, she hung a red cord out her window as a signal to them so they wouldn't kill her or her family. Red, the color of blood. Sounds an awful lot like the lamb's blood on the Jews' doors at the first Passover, doesn't it? Didn't matter that Rahab was a prostitute. Her past didn't destroy her future."

"I get that everybody makes mistakes," Maggie said. "Desperate times call for desperate measures. But the pressure on Charlene Talbot must have been immense when she came here. People talk in a small town, church or not."

The preacher arched an eyebrow and inclined his head. "And people don't talk in a big city, Miss Keeley?"

"What? No. I mean yes, of course they do. I meant to say that she couldn't hide here. Everyone probably knew what she was doing."

The old man patted Maggie's shoulder. "And is that why you think people come to church, Miss Keeley? To hide?"

Maggie pinched her lips together and turned to Jeremy. "Feel free to jump in here anytime."

Why did he feel like they were the ones being questioned? "Sir, did Charlene Talbot leave because of her lifestyle?"

"No, she didn't." The pastor closed his eyes and brushed the back of his shaking, age-spotted hand across them. "She left because of me."

16

Jeremy rubbed his forehead and turned so both hands gripped the back of the pew. He studied the old man's face, drawn to his dark eyes set deep under bushy gray brows. "I'm not sure I understand."

The preacher stood and, using the broom as a cane, shambled to the front of the church. Wood floors and old bones creaked as he knelt at the base of the platform and tilted his head forward. The wind gusted enough for the bell outside to clang twice, then died back down, becoming white noise among the groans of the aged church. The pastor let the broom fall to the floor and buried his face in his hands. After an eternal minute, he nodded his head, straightened his back, and grabbed the broom for assistance.

His voice was soft and urgent. "You say that lives are in danger?"

"Yes, sir," Jeremy said. "Several lives."

Grayson nodded again. "Then there are things you need to know." He looked back over his shoulder. "But first, would one of you be so kind as to help an old man get up off the floor?"

Maggie escorted him back to the pew and sat next to him. She took his hand in hers and held it there. "I know this must be difficult for you, and we wouldn't ask if it wasn't important."

"Things are not always what they seem," the preacher said. "In fact, in my experience, things are rarely what they seem. Everyone has their secrets. The important thing"—he leaned closer to Maggie—"is what they do with them. Love them, hate them, bury them … or give them away."

Jeremy swallowed dry air and resisted the urge to turn away from the pastor's gaze. "What are you saying?"

"Charlene Talbot was not a prostitute."

Maggie's lips parted and turned up at the corners.

Jeremy's stomach fluttered. "What? Are you sure?"

"Oh, yes," Grayson said. "Quite sure."

"And you know this how?" Maggie asked. "Everyone in town seems to be certain she was, um, working at home."

"I know Miss Keeley because one night I went to her house and confronted her. I'm as guilty as everyone else around here, believing the stories. A single mother, living in a rickety house in the middle of nowhere. Desperate to take care of her son, provide for him at any cost. What else was she supposed to do?"

"Go on," Jeremy said.

"Charlene is a smart woman. Once the rumors started, she did nothing to discourage them. As a pastor, my job is to take care of my flock. When one strays, I have a duty to do everything I can to bring them back. Finally, one night I decided I had to talk to her. Go to her home and explain that if she wouldn't break her lifestyle, I would have to bring her before the church."

"Bring her before the church?" Maggie said. "What exactly does that mean?"

"It means she would be confronted with her sin in front of the other members. Harsh sounding, I know, but it's not meant as punishment. The purpose is to point her to repentance."

Jeremy squeezed his lips together. "So much for the whole love-one-another thing, huh?"

"Mr. Winter, I understand how this looks to an outsider. But I assure you, it is biblical and is done in a spirit of love. The church considers it a last resort. It's only done when someone's sin is so egregious that the church's reputation, and by extension, Jesus', is at stake."

"Right. A room full of perfect people telling a desperate woman to change her life or else. Sounds more like a witch trial to me."

Grayson shook his head. "Your sarcasm isn't lost on me, Mr. Winter. My only concerns were Charlene's well-being and the church's character. I'd never done anything like that before and spent many hours asking the Lord to change her so I wouldn't have to do it this time. Turns out, I was praying for the wrong thing. Should've been asking Him to change me."

Maggie lifted the old man's hand and squeezed. "What happened at her house that night?"

He scratched his whiskers again and cleared his throat. "There was a car there I didn't recognize. Cody was off at college so you can imagine my concern. She wasn't alone and I feared ..."

"Afraid another church member was with her," Jeremy said.

The preacher nodded. "I knocked on the door, but no one answered. So I sat on the porch and waited. I figured whoever was in there would have to go home eventually. After a while, the door opened, and Charlene stuck her head out. I asked if I could speak with her. Told her I wasn't leaving until I did. And then I heard a man's voice telling her it was okay. That I could come in."

Jeremy ran a hand through his hair. "Who was the man?"

"Don't know. He got in his car and left when I came in. Don't think I'd ever seen him before, and I didn't ask Charlene who he was."

"Can you describe him?" Maggie asked.

"About her age, I guess, although I only got a quick look at him. Dark hair, average height. I'm sorry I can't be more specific. And I can tell you even less about his car."

"Okay," Jeremy said. "So after he left, what happened?"

"Charlene and I talked about my concerns with her, shall we say, occupation. She told me not to worry about it. That it was all just rumors."

"And did you believe her?" Maggie asked.

"I'm sorry to say I didn't. At least not at first. A strange man there at night. All the rumors. What was I supposed to believe?"

Maggie patted him on the arm. "So what changed your mind?"

"A bank statement, Miss Keeley. Charlene showed me a bank statement. She's been making one deposit a month for years. Each exactly six thousand dollars. That's more than enough to live on around here."

"How does that prove anything?" Maggie asked. "I mean, she's depositing a load of cash every month and—"

"Slow down," the preacher said. "Not cash. A check. She showed me one she'd just received in the mail. Made out to her for six grand from some oil company."

Jeremy shifted in the pew. "Can't be legit. We ran her taxes and didn't find anything. Even if she didn't report it, whoever was paying would have."

"Can't help you there. All I know is what I saw, and Charlene wasn't hurting for money. That being the case, why would she need to, um, work? Desperate people do desperate things, but Charlene wasn't desperate. She was way better off than most folks around here."

"We'll subpoena the bank for the records," Jeremy said. "Most likely going to be some sort of shell company set up to launder money, but we might get lucky and trace it back somewhere. Did you talk about anything else that night?"

"I was too embarrassed. More like ashamed, I guess. I saw her face, the hurt on it. I'll never forget the way she looked at me."

"So why didn't she stop the rumors?" Maggie asked. "Why let people keep thinking she's something she's not?"

"Miss Keeley, how do you stop a rumor? People are going to believe what they want to believe. Listen, in spite of what you may think about Charlene, she tried to do the right thing. She cared more about her boy than anything else. She was determined he would be in church and learn the Bible. Homeschooled him so she could control what he was taught. Strict, yes, but that's no sin. Wouldn't be a bad thing if there was a little more strictness in the world."

"And is that when she stopped coming to church?" Maggie asked.

The old man gave a half-nod, his chin hanging near his chest. "Never came back. I'd see her around town, tried to visit her a couple of times. But I'd hurt her. I was supposed to be her shepherd, not her accuser."

"Pastor, you need to know," Jeremy said. "We found something in Cody's room."

Maggie scooted closer to the old man, keeping a grip on his hand. "Grayson," she said, "we found some bones."

The preacher's free hand began shaking, and he sniffled several times. His face morphed from old to ancient in an instant, tears welling, eyelids drooping.

"It's a girl," Jeremy said. "She was in her early twenties. We're doing tests, but do you have any idea who she might be?"

A lone tear made it through the wrinkles and whiskers of Grayson's face. "We all figured she just left town. To start over."

"Who?" Maggie asked. "You thought who left town?"

"Sondra Kesson. Cody's girlfriend. They'd only been together a few months, not really dating even. She was his first girl. Charlene wouldn't allow him to date until he was eighteen. By then he was ready to go off to college, and Sondra wanted out of Pleasant View. You can understand. Not much to do around here. Most young people move on as soon as they can."

"Sure," Jeremy said. "So what happened?"

"Sondra enrolled at the same college as Cody. I guess it didn't work out, though, since a couple of months later she was back here. And then, about a week later, she disappeared. Never saw her again. Her folks called the sheriff, but they wouldn't even file a report. Said she was over eighteen and no reason to suspect anything."

"That gives us something to go on," Jeremy said. "We'll check dental records and DNA against Sondra Kesson. Pastor, if by any chance you hear from either Charlene or Cody, or think of anything else, please call us right away."

"Of course."

"One more thing," Jeremy said. "Any photos of Charlene or Cody here? Church directory or anything like that? The only picture we have is pretty old."

The preacher shook his head. "I'm sorry."

Maggie pulled the black-and-white photo from a folder. "We can have our lab do some work on the photo we have and get an idea of what she looks like now. Can you confirm the woman in this picture is Charlene Talbot?"

Grayson held the photo and squinted, his face inches from the image. "Yes. I believe that's Charlene when she was younger."

"Thank you, Grayson." Maggie reached for the photograph, but the old man gripped it, staring intently.

"Miss Keeley, I can't be sure, but the man with her looks an awful lot like the man I saw at Charlene's house that night."

Maggie frowned and looked at Jeremy. "Anthony Talbot. Her husband."

17

Levi didn't miss Oregon, except for the time he'd spent with Miss Subaru. At least he'd finally settled the dilemma with Mom. He half-jogged toward the water and kicked a small seashell into the ocean. The brown-striped cone tumbled and spun before disappearing into the foam. "So what do you think? Does the Gulf of Mexico look any different than the Pacific Ocean?"

Kat shrugged. "Water's water. But it's a lot prettier in Oregon. Florida is sort of flat all over."

Levi laughed. "The scenery may not be as nice, but I'll take this weather. Stuff grows year-round here. Plenty of chances for land-scaping work."

"What about going back to school? You said you might want to learn computers and stuff."

"Still considering taking a few classes, but I've got to make some money first. I need to get us out of that dumpy motel into something a little nicer. An apartment or maybe even a rental home."

"Cool. That motel gives me the creeps." She looked at the pink tinge spreading across her pale arms. "I can't stay out here too long. Don't want to ruin my Goth image. I'd have to buy all new makeup."

"Tell you what. Let's check out coffee shops near the beach and see if we can find you a job. We'll swing by an ATM, and I'll grab some cash. You got any money left in your account?"

She grabbed Levi's hand in hers and swung them as they wandered along the beach. "Less than a hundred. Not much to start a new life on." She scrunched her nose and glanced up. "Is that what we're doing here? Starting a new life?"

The beginning pangs of a headache crawled from the back of his skull toward his forehead. He stopped, clasped Kat's free hand, and stared into her eyes. He tilted his head from side to side, squinting, trying to see inside her. "You know, Kat, I've spent a lot of time looking for the right girl. And I think I've found her."

"Really?" She threw her arms around his neck. "I feel the same way about you." She released him and slipped her arm around his waist. "Take me job hunting. I'm ready to get this new life started."

He rubbed his chest and clenched his teeth together. His headache stood, stretched, and sprinted to the front of his brain.

Half an hour later they cruised the area, checking out coffeehouses and restaurants. Kat had already turned down one job offer after seeing the clientele was mostly young people. Terrible tippers, she said. He turned into a bank parking lot and hopped out.

"Wait here. I'm gonna grab some cash. Be right back."

At the ATM he punched in his code and opted for the fast cash dispersal of two hundred dollars. He folded the twenties and put them in his front pocket before hitting the "Balance Inquiry" button. As he pressed it, a reflection appeared on the screen. He jerked his head around and nearly knocked Kat to the ground.

"I thought I told you to stay in the car." His pulse drumbeat in his ears, blurring his vision.

Kat blinked rapidly. "I wanted to make a withdrawal from my account too. What's the big deal?"

"No big deal. You scared me, that's all." He closed his eyes and forced himself to slow his breathing.

"Yeah, well, you scared me too. So I guess we're even." She poked him in the stomach and twisted her finger. "Okay?"

"Yeah." He pulled her finger to his lips and kissed it. "Okay."

He walked toward the car and tried to shake off the incident. Something nagged at him. Something important. *Think.* He patted his front pocket where the twenties rested. He turned slowly and looked back toward the ATM. Kat stood there, mouth and eyes wide open, holding his balance inquiry in her hand.

Oh, Rahab. Just when things were going so well.

"Levi, what is this?"

Lie or the truth? Would she believe either? Didn't matter, really. "What's what, babe?"

She extended her arms toward him, one hand holding the receipt, the other palm up. "Your balance is almost half a million dollars."

He frowned and scratched his cheek. "What? That has to be a mistake. I wish I had that kind of money."

"Check your balance again. See if it's still there. We could use the money to ... to do anything we wanted." She shifted her weight from leg to leg.

Levi walked toward her, nodding and furrowing his eyebrows. "We could. But baby, Kat, it's some sort of bank error."

She crossed her arms, head cocked, right eye squinting. "Mistake or not, it's in your account. I say we get what we can before they figure it out."

He planted his arm around her waist and guided her to the car. His heart raced, the seed of anticipation planted. "Let's go somewhere and talk about this. Figure out if that's what we should do."

"What's to talk about? Who knows how long the money will be there?"

Exactly. Levi brushed the back of his hand across his mouth, the taste of sweat lingering on his tongue, reminding him. Salt of the earth. Disciple. Was he losing his saltiness?

Kat unwrapped herself from his arm. "Levi, I'm serious. That's enough money to go anywhere. Do anything. Just you and me." She pulled him close, shoving her hands into his back jean pockets and tucking her head under his chin. "We can disappear."

Not we. *You.* He tilted her face upward and brushed her forehead with his lips. The lavender scent of her shampoo mixed with the beach odors. He sighed. Time to get my saltiness back.

"Okay," he said. "You wait in the car while I figure out how to do this."

She pecked him on the cheek. "I love you." She walked, almost skipped really, to their vehicle and clambered into the passenger seat.

After a wave and a smile, Levi turned and headed toward the bank. He took a few steps, paused, and hustled back to the car, opening the rear driver's side door.

"Everything okay?" Kat asked.

Levi unburied his black duffel bag. "Yeah. Thought I might need extra ID. I think my Social Security card is in here."

Kat patted her hands on her thighs and stared at the bank. "I am soooo excited. It's like God wants us to be happy or something."

He filled a syringe and glanced at her exposed neck, the blue streak of hair pointing to his target. The red-winged fairy tattoo. What's one more needle mark there? Less than three seconds later, the Propofol began its work.

She spun around, a finger pressed on the injection site, her lips parted and eyes unfocused.

"Oh, Rahab," he said. "God doesn't want us to be happy."

Kat slumped forward, slamming her head against the dash.

Levi exited the back seat and walked to the passenger door, pausing to watch seagulls fight over French fry scraps several parking spots away. Stupid birds. Always fighting. He opened the door, tilted Kat upright, and fastened the seat belt. Her breathing was shallow and slowing.

He swept the back of his fingers across her cheek and looped her hair behind her ear. Leaning close enough to nuzzle his nose against the side of her head, he waited as long as he dared. "My headache's gone, Kat. Thank you. And God doesn't want us to be happy. Obedient. God wants us to be obedient."

18

Jeremy paced the floor of his El Paso hotel room, phone in one hand, Diet Coke in the other. Three days he'd been cooped up here waiting for Maggie to finish her investigation in Pleasant View. The pressure of doing nothing had swelled until he decided to take action and contact the man responsible for his current situation. And after an appropriate delay, Colonel Ramsey Cronfeld had finally returned his call.

"I thought we had an understanding."

A snort from the other end of the line. "That what you thought? An understanding? Must've missed the memo. Don't know why you have to make this so difficult, Winter. Honestly, after all I've done for you."

"Done for me?"

"Of course. Early retirement from the FBI with full benefits? Think something like that comes easy?"

Jeremy downed the last of his drink and crushed the can. "I suppose it does if your wife's a senator and presidential candidate."

"Maybe. Remember that what's given can easily be taken away.

We—I ask so little in return. A signature on a form. Think of it as an insurance policy for both of us."

"Yeah. I keep my mouth shut about Afghanistan and you ... what? Quit interfering in my life? Restore my contractor status at the Bureau?"

Cronfeld sighed. "You think too small, Mr. Winter. The future's full of possibilities. Some, greater than you can imagine. Others, well, not as nice. And I'm going to let you choose. I think you've got an idea what I'm capable of either way."

Jeremy glanced at his open briefcase. Three pieces of paper, folded and tucked in a manila envelope. Delivered to him at the hospital while he recovered from the incident at the Mason farm. An official government report on his interrogations in Afghanistan. Every name redacted except his. And all true, save one detail. In spite of what the document said, he'd never killed any prisoners.

He squeezed the phone and clenched his teeth. "Don't threaten me again. The truth finds a way, Cronfeld. And we both know the facts are on my side."

"The facts are what I make them. You'd do well to think about that. But why dwell on the negative? Change is in the wind, my friend. Just think what a man in my position could offer someone like you once I'm in the White House."

"A long time between now and the election. Twenty, twenty-one months. I imagine your wife's considering her options. Thinking if she dumps her baggage now, there's plenty of time to deal with any fallout."

The colonel chuckled. "Now who's threatening? Be careful you don't misread the situation. You have no idea how simple it is to ruin someone's life."

"Just takes a bullet, right?"

"Goodbye, Mr. Winter. Our little dance has become tedious. Sign the confidentiality agreement by tomorrow morning. Or not. It's your future."

Jeremy threw his phone onto the hotel bed and shoved his

hands in his pockets. Anger boiled in his chest and threatened to erupt. Why now? Just when they'd started to make progress on the case. He had to get out of the room. Burn off the rage before the long flight home. Calm down before he talked to Maggie. Chase the thoughts that told him to end this once and for all. Only one problem.

He couldn't decide whether to race away from the thoughts or rush toward them.

......

Jeremy sank onto the edge of Maggie's hotel bed while she sat at the desk and used her laptop to access the conference call. She could see the other attendees but had left her camera turned off after warning him to stay quiet. Fortunately, Director Bailey couldn't attend, so there'd be no one to question whether Jeremy was present. It'd have to be a short call. Their flight departed in less than two hours.

"Cody Talbot graduated from the University of Texas College of Pharmacy in Austin," Maggie said. "By all accounts, he was an above-average student. Stayed off-campus in a two-bedroom apartment, no roommates. Crime techs are going through his old place now.

"As near as we can tell," she continued, "his tuition, books, apartment—everything was paid for by his mother. Her bank records show regular deposits, always in cash. Sporadic larger amounts seem to indicate that when she needed more money, she got it. Our assumption is the funds were coming from her husband, Anthony Talbot."

Agent Greg Simpson, a.k.a. Blondie, spoke. "Federal regulations require all pharmacists be fingerprinted. Cody Talbot's prints are on file, but as you know, we've never recovered any from a crime scene. Nothing to match them to. We do, however, have this."

He held up a plastic evidence bag with a white index card

inside. "This is the motel registration form from Portland, completed by a gentleman named Aster Bellis from Chicago. Interesting name. Turns out it's one of the scientific designations for daisies. Even more interesting is the fact that Cody Talbot's fingerprints are on this card. We're checking motels in the cities where the other girls were killed to see if he used the same alias there."

An agent in a paisley tie and blue shirt interrupted. "Scale of one to ten, is Cody Talbot our guy?" The question would not have been asked if the director was present.

Paisley? Is that back again? Jeremy leaned over and scribbled a number on the notepad beside Maggie. She frowned and brushed him away.

"Nine point nine," she answered. "Everything points his way. DNA confirmed the body found at his home is Sondra Kesson, his old girlfriend. Cause of death is undetermined still. We think she's the trigger to all of this. The concubine who ran away. There's a lot we don't know, but all indications are he's our perpetrator. We're open to other possibilities, but right now our number one priority is finding Cody Talbot."

Blondie pointed at the screen. "Any luck tracking the financials?"

"His mother has one credit card," Maggie said, "and we're getting a warrant to access the charges. Witnesses at the motel in Portland could not positively identify the older woman, but we're confident she was Charlene Talbot. She may be involved, or she may be completely unaware of what's going on."

An agent in the back spoke up. "Is Anthony Talbot providing their living expenses?"

Maggie shook her head. "Not as far as we can tell. There have been no unusual deposits into her account. In fact, her money hasn't been accessed for months, which means there's another source of funds. It's possible Cody has money we haven't found yet, probably under an assumed name."

"If this is our guy," Blondie asked, "why now? Assuming he

killed the girl at his house right after he started college, what triggered him to begin killing again? I mean, he was in school for what, seven or eight years? That's a long time to lay low and then suddenly start murdering people."

"He may not have stopped," Maggie said. "Austin PD and the Texas Rangers are reviewing cold cases for anything that might fit Talbot's style. By now he's left Oregon and is headed to find his next target. Did you get the *Tribune*?"

Paisley Tie tossed a newspaper on the table. "The Chicago office has the letter Talbot or whoever sent. Didn't take the *Trib* long to figure it out. 'Serial Killer Stalking Supreme Court.' Nice headline."

"Any luck finding a photo of Cody Talbot?" Maggie asked. "Now that the story's gone public, why not plaster his picture everywhere?"

Another agent shuffled through some papers and held up a color copy of a University of Texas identification card. "That picture look familiar to anyone?"

"Looks like a young George Clooney," Maggie said.

The agent nodded. "That's because it is a young George Clooney. Someone hacked into their system and changed his photo. Talbot altered the school's database, or he paid someone else to do it."

"Driver's license?" Blondie asked.

"Doesn't have one," the agent said. "Either never bothered to get a license or most likely has a fake. He was homeschooled, so no yearbook photos. Not on any social networks either. The bottom line is we do not have a reliable photo of him. We're holding off on doing sketches for now. Too vague."

"What we do have is a photo of Charlene Talbot," Maggie said. "The picture's old, but the lab says they can enhance the image. They're aging her, and we should have a good idea of what she looks like now. We can have the Chicago news run the photo and call her a person of interest in the case."

"What if Chicago's not his next target?" Agent Paisley said. "Shouldn't we distribute the picture in the other four cities too?"

"I'll bounce it off the Director but wouldn't be surprised if he doesn't want to go nationwide with the story or photo yet." Maggie shrugged. "Won't make much difference. The *Tribune*'s article will be picked up by most major news outlets. The story will be all over the country soon enough."

A young agent raised his hand. "Anything on the car?"

Maggie shook her head. "Nothing. The auto they abandoned in Portland was clean. The elderly woman who spotted the car near the scene confirmed it was the same one. So far, running the list of stolen vehicles hasn't turned up anything."

Paisley Tie clicked his pen. "So if I can summarize, we know who we're looking for, but we don't know where he is, what he looks like, or what he's driving."

"But we do know who he's with," Jeremy said.

Maggie swatted at him and frowned.

Blondie smiled and craned toward the camera. "Well, hello there, Mr. Winter. Must've been killing you to keep quiet, huh? I'll let you in on a secret. We had a betting pool going on whether you'd be on the call. In the background, of course. Problem is, no one wanted to bet against you joining. Now that we've confirmed you're here, anything you'd like to add?"

Jeremy cleared his throat. "We know who he's with. That's a start. Once we—you—get access to her credit card, hopefully later today, you may get more information. In the meantime, there's another avenue of investigation you need to pursue. Maggie can fill you in."

She turned on the laptop's camera and held up the old photo. "That's Anthony Talbot standing next to Charlene. The lab's aging him as well. We need to know where he's been and what he's been up to. Nobody drops off the grid this long without something to hide. He's got money, and no one except the Talbots seems to know he's alive. Southwest Texas and easy access to Mexico. I'm no rocket surgeon, but my money's on drugs."

"Right," Jeremy said. "Once you get the updated image, run it through facial recognition software. Maybe we'll get lucky. Maggie's also sending the photo to the DEA and Border Patrol."

The agent in the back cleared his throat. "I don't understand what the father's agenda is. Everybody thinks you're dead, you've got wads of cash from somewhere, and you let your kid run around the country killing people? Doesn't make sense. If it was me, the last thing I'd want is to bring any attention in my direction."

Jeremy nodded. "Agreed. I'd be surprised if Anthony knew what Cody was doing. Far too risky for everyone involved. Nope, either Cody's doing this on his own, or his mother's working with him. That doesn't mean Anthony can't be useful to us. There may be regular communication between them. We can't find any records of cell phones but didn't expect we would. They're probably using prepaid phones and trashing them when the minutes expire."

Maggie's cell phone pinged, and she glanced at the screen. "Got the warrant for Charlene's credit card. Let's go ahead and break. I'm heading to the airport, and I'll recap for Director Bailey there. Blon— Agent Simpson, when we get Anthony Talbot's updated photo, I'd like you to run point with the DEA and Border Patrol."

Agent Simpson nodded. "All over it."

"Thank you, gentlemen." She shut down the laptop and shoved it into her carry-on bag. "Let's head to the airport. With any luck, I'll have the credit card records before the flight leaves, and we can review them on the plane."

"Sorry about that, Maggie. Jumping on the call, I mean."

She half-smiled. "Don't worry about it."

He placed his hands on her shoulders. "No. I mean it. This is your case now. I'm not sure what I'm going to do next, but I won't put you in that situation again. Promise."

"Thanks. I know how hard this must be for you, especially now that Cronfeld's breathing down your neck. And like I said, I'll keep you in the loop as much as I can. Don't want all your experience to be wasted."

"Experience? That's just a nice way of saying I'm old, isn't it?"

She kissed him, grabbed her luggage, and headed for the door. "Let's go, old man. If you want a peek at those credit card records, you're going to have to keep up."

19

Jeremy stared out the airplane window at the vast, open flatlands below. Such an easy place to hide. Not too hospitable maybe, but if you didn't want to be found, there's the place to do it. "Anything interesting?"

Maggie skimmed Charlene Talbot's credit card statements a third time, highlighting any charges that might be useful. Almost all of the items listed came from online stores like Amazon, Urban Outfitters, and eBay. "Lots of Internet orders. I'll start the paperwork for the warrants. What they're buying and where it was shipped. Anything that will help us tie them to the cities where the murders happened. It'll take weeks before we get any answers, though."

He tensed his leg muscles, stretching as much as possible in the confined space of the plane's seat. After the layover in Dallas, still two-and-a-half hours to landing. Long flights sucked, but his seatmate eased the pain considerably. "Tired of being one step behind this guy all the time."

Maggie covered her mouth and yawned. "Seems to me when we

started we were a lot more than one step behind him. At least we're gaining."

"Always the optimist, huh? You know the problem with tracking serial killers, don't you? They operate on a bell curve."

"I really want to agree with you, but since I have no idea what you're talking about, I'll wait for an explanation."

Jeremy grabbed the SkyMall catalog and sketched a bell next to a photo of a Bigfoot tree sculpture. "See, the first killing or two are over here at the bottom left of the bell. He's new at it, and no matter how much he plans, he makes mistakes. But the more he kills"—he traced his finger along the bell, heading upward—"the better he gets. The killing becomes a rhythm. A pattern. He's focused."

Maggie nodded. "So when he reaches the top of the bell?"

"He becomes overconfident. Starts to think he's invincible, that he'll never be caught." He tracked the downward side of the bell. "He makes mistakes. Gets lazy. That's when most of them are caught."

He pointed back at the bottom left of the bell. "If you don't catch them right when they begin killing, then you're not going to catch them until they start to slide down. Unless you're lucky. Very lucky."

"So where do you figure Talbot is on your curve?"

"No idea. Nine Supreme Court judges, and if I thought he'd stop then, I'd say he had to be somewhere near the top."

"He's not, is he? Sticking to nine girls."

"Serial killers don't stop. They may go quiet for a while, but they start again. Sondra Kesson didn't count for him. All her finger bones were there. Maybe she was his first, maybe not. But I wouldn't be surprised if he's already in double digits."

"Then this whole thing about Judges is just a ruse? Some sort of game to him?"

Jeremy half-frowned. "I don't think so. He wouldn't be the first person to think he was God's personal avenging angel."

"Yeah," Maggie said, "like God needs the help."

Jeremy held up his plastic cup and motioned to the flight attendant. "Meaning?"

"Meaning God can take care of himself. Why would he need you or me or Cody Talbot to do his dirty work?"

"And you believe that?"

She nodded. "I do. I have to. This guy we're after ... when we catch him, what happens? Maybe he dies, or maybe he spends the rest of his life in prison. Either way, it doesn't seem like it's enough. All the lives he's taken. All the families left behind to deal with loss. I've seen enough to believe, or maybe hope, that people will pay for what they've done. Haven't you?"

He waited while the flight attendant refilled his water. "It's a nice thought. I suppose, one way or another, we all pay for what we've done."

"For better or worse."

He nudged his shoulder against hers. "I'll take 'for better,' please."

She grinned and slid the laptop onto his tray. "You look at these for a while. My eyes could use a break."

He dragged his finger down the list of credit card charges, pausing when one caught his attention. "Here. What's this?"

"Yeah, I saw that one. A Canadian pharmacy. No other charges from there in the past couple of months. I've got a friend up that way who may be able to help us out. Sometimes regulations can be a little, shall we say, 'looser,' north of the border."

"I'd focus on that one. We know Talbot's a pharmacist. Could be that's where he's getting the Propofol."

"Possibly. I'll shoot off an email. See if I can have the info before we land." She fired off a message, grabbed the blanket from the seat back, and spread the thin cover over her. "In the meantime, I'm going to take a nap. Got a long drive ahead of me when we land."

"You could move closer to DC, you know. Rent's not bad in my neighborhood."

She snuggled into the seat. "What, and leave my home in Milford? No way. And even if I wanted to, I'd never get Mom to agree. We like it there. If anyone's moving, it's you."

He kissed the top of her head. "Get some sleep. You're going to need it if any of these credit card charges pan out."

......

Two hours later, Maggie had the information. "Antibiotics. And guess where they were shipped?"

"Portland?"

"Yep. That's not all, though. Turns out the pharmacy was also able to provide the IP address of the computer that ordered the drugs. The tech lab already tracked it to a coffee shop in Portland."

Jeremy nodded. "Free Wi-Fi. Makes sense."

"Maybe," she said. "Seems like he's smarter than that, though. Every kid under the age of thirty knows about secured networks. Most people don't care, but Talbot would."

He shrugged. "Could be he's on the downside of the bell curve."

She closed her laptop in preparation for landing. "Whatever. It's a break, and God knows we need one. I'll call the Portland office after we land, then a quick trip home to see Rebecca, and I imagine I'll be in Bailey's office first thing tomorrow morning. You figure out your plan?"

"Track down Cronfeld. Put this thing to bed once and for all."

She tightened her lips and patted his leg. "Won't be that easy, you know. Anything I can do to help?"

"You've got your hands full already. I'll take care of it."

"And by take care of it, you mean—"

"I won't do anything stupid. Unless he gets me going, then I reserve the right—"

"Uh-huh. Play nice. We'll figure this out."

The ground grew closer, and he shook his head. "Yeah. Wish I had more leverage, though. Something to call his bluff on the bogus report."

"Look at it this way. The last thing Cronfeld wants is for any of this to become public. He can't win. The media would be all over it, no matter what some government document says. Too many questions. Too much negative publicity. No way Senator Morgans wants that."

"Probably. Unless she's playing both of us."

"What do you mean?"

"Think about it," he said. "If this goes public now, no matter what happens, she's got time to deal with it before the primaries start. If Cronfeld takes a hit, she becomes the sympathetic wife. If I go down for it, her husband's still the war hero, standing proudly by her side. And if we both get burned ..."

"She's killed two birds in the hand with one stone."

He chuckled and rubbed her knee. "Exactly."

......

The posh cafe buzzed with the swarm of government workers filing in and out. DC in February could be miserable, but this morning tested even those limits. Not much wind, but icy cold. Jeremy stamped his feet before jogging across the street and stopping in front of the man seated at the lone outdoor table.

"Beautiful morning," Colonel Ramsey Cronfeld said. He motioned to the seat opposite.

"No thanks. I won't be staying."

"Pity. Nothing like hot coffee on a freezing morning to remind a man what it's like to be alive. None of that fancy oversaturated sugar water, mind you. The real stuff."

Jeremy glanced around. "No escort?"

"I wasn't aware I needed one."

"With your wife running for president, I assumed—"

Cronfeld flicked his hand in the air. "Too early for that nonsense. I trust we'll—she'll have your vote, though? Never too soon to start politicking, you know."

"Like I said before, long time between now and the election. I'll keep my options open."

"Now why doesn't that surprise me?"

Jeremy stepped closer to the table and lowered his voice. "You want a surprise? I'm not signing the form. Not today. Not ever. Back off, and I keep my mouth shut."

The colonel dabbed at a corner of his mouth with a napkin. "I see. Nonetheless, your decision changes nothing. We won't discuss this again. Take a look around you, *Mr.* Winter. What do you see? Power. DC reeks of it. There are only two types of people here: those who have power and those who want it. How do you suppose you and I fit into that equation?"

Tension squeezed Jeremy's neck muscles. "You said it yourself —what's given can just as easily be taken away."

Cronfeld laughed. "By you? I don't think so. Oh, I know all about your escapades. Digging through old files, trying to find someone to substantiate your story. Honestly, Mr. Winter. What did you expect to discover? My men are intensely loyal to me, as I am to them."

"Uh-huh. So loyal that you forced them to sign the confidentiality agreement or get stuck in Afghanistan."

The colonel stood and inclined his head toward Jeremy. "Have a pleasant day, Mr. Winter. And know that when things happen, as they must, you'll think back to this moment and regret your decision."

"Oh, I know all about regret, *Ramsey*. Had more than enough for one lifetime. You want to come at me? Bring it on." He jabbed a finger in Cronfeld's chest. "But if you go near Maggie or her family, I promise you, we *will* meet again. On my terms."

A black Lincoln Town Car pulled to the curb and stopped. The bullnecked driver hustled around the vehicle, opened the rear passenger door, and made eye contact with the colonel.

Cronfeld downed the last of his coffee, dropped the cup in the trash, and wiped his palms with a napkin. "You still don't understand, do you? You have no terms. No leverage. Things happen because I choose for them to be that way. You'll learn. It's simply a matter of how much you're willing to endure before you admit what you already know."

Jeremy moved within inches of the colonel. "Go to hell."

The colonel slid into his vehicle and winked. "Been there, Mr. Winter. Things seemed to have turned out all right."

20

Maggie picked at her chicken salad croissant, pulling out any large pieces of celery and shoving them to the side. The late lunch offered a few minutes of peace since most of the deli's customers had long since returned to work. "Doesn't sound like you played nice."

"He started it," Jeremy said.

"I swear, you're just—"

He laughed. "I said that to get you going. How'd your meeting with Bailey go?"

"Okay, I guess. The Portland office is interviewing employees and customers at that coffeehouse today. They're supposed to call me if anything turns up. No security cameras in the restaurant or parking lot, though, so no help there."

"What's your plan? Gonna hang out in DC until something else breaks?"

She arched her eyebrows and frowned. "Don't see as I've got much choice. Could go back to Portland, but Talbot's long gone from there. Nothing in Pleasant View to see. Chicago's our best bet, but that's a roll of the dice. Might as well stay close to home until we get something solid."

Good. "How's Rebecca?"

"Oh. Glad you asked. I almost forgot." She reached into her purse and handed him a folded sheet of green construction paper. "Another one to add to your zoo collection."

A light tingling sensation filled his chest as he opened the rough paper. A grayish blob with four thick legs filled most of the page's bottom area. Red dots speckled the animal's feet, and its huge, open mouth revealed monstrous teeth. In the background, a blue band flowed from side to side under a bright yellow sun. "Hippo, right? She's getting a lot better."

"Right. She's got my artistic ability, sadly. I think we can rule out a career as a sketch artist. But yeah, that's a hippo."

He pointed at the feet. "These red dots are ...?"

She rolled her eyes. "Nail polish. She thought the hippo needed to look nicer."

"Love it, Maggie. This one goes to the top of the refrigerator. Tell her I said thanks."

"Tell her yourself. I told Mom you'd be calling after Rebecca gets home from school."

He dabbed a French fry in ketchup. "First grade. Three toughest years of my life."

"That explains a lot. Figure out what your next move is?"

"Yeah. Cronfeld made a comment that got me thinking. Said his men are loyal to him. Reminded me of something. I've got to make a few phone calls. Track down whatever information I can. But if it leads where—"

Maggie's phone vibrated, and she held up her index finger as she answered the call. "Hold on a sec. Agent Keeley. Okay ... okay. Got a name? Kathryn Stanton ... with a K? Okay ... how long? Four days? Could be a coincidence. You check with family? Uh-huh ... okay ... someone on the way to her ... why not? How long before you get the warrant? Uh-uh ... too long. Kick in the door if you have to. She could be in danger … okay. Let me know as soon as you do. Good work."

"What's going on?" Jeremy asked.

She stood and put on her coat. "Sorry. Got to get back to the office."

"No problem. Go get 'em. I'm gonna hang out here for a while. Maybe finish off that chicken salad for you."

"I'll check in with you later. Don't forget to call Rebecca." She bent down and kissed him before hurrying out the door.

He opened his laptop and searched through several spellings of Catherine before locating her. Surprising how little he missed the FBI database. Ten dollars a month bought him unlimited access to nearly the same amount of information on every person in the country. Kathryn Stanton, Portland, Oregon. No Facebook or Twitter. Parents in Seattle and older sister Sarah in Colorado.

He clicked over to Facebook and located Sarah Stanton's profile. Messages, photos, friends, and … there. Her phone number. Barely finished the first ring before she answered.

"Hello?"

"Sarah Stanton?"

"Um, yes. Who's calling?"

"Hello, Miss Stanton. My name is Jeremy Winter. I'm trying to get in touch with your sister. Have you spoken to Kathryn lately?"

"Are you a bill collector? The law says you can't call me for my sister's debts. If you call me again—"

This could be risky, especially if Maggie finds out. Still … "No, ma'am. I'm working with the FBI on a case. It's important we speak to your sister as soon as possible."

"Why? Is she in some kind of trouble?"

"We're not sure. That's why we'd like to talk to her. Have you spoken with Kathryn in the last several days?"

"No. No I haven't. That's not unusual, though. We aren't real close, but we do kind of keep up with each other. Mostly on Facebook and text messages."

"She's on Facebook? Are you near a computer now? Could you log on and check for any recent entries on her account?"

"Uh, okay. Hold on." A few seconds passed. "That's weird. She's not on there anymore. What's going on? Where's my sister?"

"Miss Stanton, we're working on that. Her apartment is being checked now. If they find anything, they'll let you know."

"She already got an apartment?"

"I'm sorry?" Jeremy said. "You didn't know she had her own place?"

"Well, I figured she'd get one, but I didn't know it would be so soon. The last post I saw on Facebook, she'd just got there."

Jeremy's heart stopped. "Got where, Miss Stanton?"

"Florida. Sarasota, Florida."

21

Levi hopped off the bus two blocks from his destination and watched as the Sarasota County Area Transport vehicle drove away. SCAT. Well, that was poor planning.

Only nine-thirty in the morning and sweat already darkened his T-shirt. A breeze rustled the palm trees, their dry fronds scratching against each other. Little brown-green lizards scurried across the concrete sidewalk chasing invisible gnats. The Gulf of Mexico's odor filtered through occasionally, a not-so-delicate mixture of seaweed, fish, salt, and sand. Eau de Ocean. Wintertime in Florida. The snowbirds might be on to something.

He walked past an abandoned gas station and several vacant warehouses surrounded by rusty chain-link fences. Up ahead, a string of colored flags circled the perimeter of the car lot, waving desperately at anyone who ventured out this far. The sign out front proudly proclaimed that good credit, bad credit, or no credit, all customers were welcome.

A couple dozen vehicles, shiny and fresh, waited eagerly. Like puppies at the pound, none wanted to spend another day here. An old construction trailer served as the worldwide headquarters of

Bennie's Used Cars, and its door flew open as the CEO stepped out to attend to the day's business.

"Beautiful morning, isn't it?" the man said. He dressed impeccably, from a button-down oxford shirt to spit-shined shoes.

"Too hot to be walking, though," Levi said.

The man laughed and stuck out his hand. "Well, you've come to the right place. I'm Bennie, and our motto is, 'We're the walking man's friend.' Planning to add that to our sign out front as soon as we get the chance."

Levi shook his hand. "Sounds great. I was hoping to find something with low miles. A good road car, you know."

Bennie nodded energetically. "Mmm hmm. What you need is an SUV. Extra weight, rides better, sits up high so you can see what's coming. You do a lot of traveling, do you?"

Levi ignored the question and walked to a vehicle with deflated balloons hanging from its outside mirrors. "This one looks nice."

The salesman ran his hand over the hood of the black SUV. "Yep. She's a beauty all right. Toyota FJ Cruiser. She's got a couple of years on her, but the miles are low."

Levi grinned. "Don't tell me. Only driven by a little old lady to church on Sundays."

Bennie's fake laugh echoed across the lot. "You're on to me, aren't you? I can give you a good deal on it. What do you say? Want to take her out for a spin?"

Levi put his hand on the salesman's shoulder. "Tell you what, Bennie. I'll take the SUV around the block. When I get back, you're going to give me a price. I'll pay in cash, and there'll be no paperwork."

Bennie shuffled his feet and avoided eye contact. "Oh, no, sir. We can't do that. There are all sorts of laws that—"

"Sure thing. I understand. Thanks for your time." Levi turned to walk away.

A hand tapped his arm. "Now hold on there. We might be able

to work something out. I assume you'll want a title and registration as well?"

Levi smiled at Bennie. "Uh-huh. Pick a nice name to put on them."

"Will you be trading in a vehicle?"

Levi squeezed the salesman's shoulder. "Now, Bennie, what do you think?"

An hour later and thirty-three thousand dollars lighter, Levi sat in Starbucks sipping an iced coffee. *Kat should have made me one of these.* He didn't want to spend so much on a vehicle, but the paperwork fees jacked up the price, not to mention the extra three thousand to make sure he had anything except Florida tags. Buying from an individual would have been cheaper, but more dangerous. If by some miracle the Feds did talk to Bennie, he couldn't connect Levi to the vehicle without incriminating himself. He'd have to remember to replenish his emergency fund, withdrawing various amounts daily as he traveled. A few hundred here, a thousand there.

His pulse quickened as he surfed the Internet. Virtually every news site had his story on the front page. He leaned closer to the screen, trying to read the articles faster. Seeing the old photo of his mother had shocked him, but the FBI wasn't stupid.

The sparse details in the stories didn't give much away, but it seemed clear Sondra had been found. Good. She deserved a decent burial now that she'd come around to seeing things his way. They probably knew about Kat too. His mistake in ordering the medicine on an unsecured network had turned out to be a blessing. Good luck finding her or her car, though. They'd need scuba gear to locate either one. Poetic justice in a way. With her love of sushi, she'd feel right at home. Still, the FBI likely assumed he was in Florida. Facebook did come in handy sometimes. You just have to toss out a few breadcrumbs now and then to get them on the right trail.

He finished his coffee and paid for a refill. The adrenaline rush would wear off soon, and he needed to stay awake for the long drive. The road conditions were good now, but snow was predicted in the next few days. No problem. He'd always wanted to see Vermont in the winter.

......

Tampa's FBI office was a modern facility, built with security in mind. Armed guards protected the gated entrance and searched all vehicles before allowing them access to the parking garage. Once they verified Jeremy's ID, they waved him through, though he got the impression they were looking for any reason to keep him out.

A receptionist directed him to a temporary office, and he paused to look at the name on the door. Printed, laminated, and centered at eye level. Special Agent Margaret Keeley. He tapped on the door and paused before cracking it open and poking his head inside. "Can I come in?"

Maggie tapped a finger on her lips and pondered for a moment before nodding and grinning. "Yes. But leave the door open."

"What's that about?"

"Trying to keep rumors from starting. It was all I could do to get you in here to begin with. Director Bailey wasn't too thrilled, but I told him you clued us in on Sarasota and might have additional info that could help us out. All as a concerned private citizen, of course."

Jeremy dragged a chair closer to her desk and sat. "Of course. Starting to like it that way. Good flight?"

"Guy next to me got a little handsy. I dealt with it."

He laughed and shook his head. "I'll bet. Anybody notify his next of kin?"

She straightened the papers on her desk and frowned. "Two hundred and seven churches in Sarasota. No way to cover all of them."

All business. He cleared his throat and uncrossed his legs. "Local PD got Kathryn Stanton's photo?"

"Yeah, that, details of her car, and the updated picture of Charlene Talbot. Stanton's credit card hasn't been used since Oregon."

"Not surprising. Too risky."

"We're considering leaking some details about Stanton to the press," she said. "Haven't decided yet."

"Could put her in danger, assuming she's not an accomplice."

Maggie squished her lips to the side. "You think she's not in danger otherwise?"

"Don't know. Maybe. Probably. She doesn't fit his target profile. Could be she's merely a convenience. Of course, it's just as likely she's already dead."

"Thought of that. Three people in the car would get awful crowded on a long drive. Until we have evidence to the contrary, though ..."

He stretched his left leg and massaged the calf. "We assume she's alive. Something else occurred to me this morning. Could be overthinking this, but is it possible Talbot's playing us?"

Wrinkles appeared on her forehead. "How so?"

"His story's all over the news now. He wanted publicity, and he's got it. No one's tying the killings to anything religious yet, but they will. Sooner or later, word will leak out. And once the public gets hold of his punishment-from-God motive, there's going to be a feeding frenzy at the networks. The pressure's already building, but it's on law enforcement, not on him."

"Yeah," Maggie said, "but I don't think he cares much about that. And even if he does, so what? Doesn't change how we operate or, at least this point, how he does. Talbot's sticking to his pattern. Sondra Kesson is still a question mark, but as far as we know, his other victims fall into place. He's following a process. He's a believer."

Jeremy tapped his fingertips together and stared at the ceiling. "Okay. Say you're Talbot. Your story's all over the country now.

Maybe not the whole thing, but enough. What do you do to avoid being caught?"

She exhaled loudly. "Ditch the car first thing. Too easy to track."

"Right. The VIN's in the system, so if he tries to swap the car for a new one, you'll get notified."

"Plus, we've got cops stopping by every dealer in west Florida spreading the word. I'd stay on top of the media too. I want to know what they know. Then I'd assume the FBI has a lot more information than the press does. He's got to figure we're closing in."

"Exactly. So what does the FBI know?"

"Well, we know his name and who he's with. Oh, and where he's been and where he's going."

"You'd think that would be enough, wouldn't you? So why isn't it?"

"Because he's got options. Four cities to be exact. And we don't know what he looks like."

Jeremy scratched his cheek. "But we do know what Charlene and Kathryn look like. And that's a threat to him."

"You think he would harm them?"

"You think he wouldn't?"

She rested her chin on her fist and focused on the desk. "No. Not if he's on some sort of mission. But no bodies so far."

He rubbed his eyes and blinked several times. "Something's bothering me, Maggie."

"Besides a lack of sleep?"

"Yeah. Why are we here?"

She scrunched her eyebrows. "That's kind of a deep question isn't it?"

"No, I mean why are we in Sarasota?"

She shrugged. "It's one of the four cities left, and Kathryn Stanton posted that she was here."

He nodded. "And do you think Talbot knows she put that information on the Internet?"

"Probably. That's why there haven't been any more posts on Facebook. He shut off her access."

"And?"

Maggie drummed her fingers on the desk. "And … he would assume we saw the post. Which means Talbot would take for granted the FBI is looking for him in Florida." She shook her head. "If I was him, I'd be anywhere but here right now."

"Me too. If you look at the locations that are left, where would you go?"

"Easy. Brattleboro. Smallest town, and it's going to be tough for him to hide. I'd make a beeline for Vermont and cross it off the list while—"

"While the FBI's on the other side of the country."

She glanced at her watch. "I've got to make a call."

He motioned toward the door. "Want me to wait outside?"

"Yeah. And close the door on your way out."

He smiled and saluted. "Yes, ma'am."

Her lips formed a thin line. "And ask the receptionist to check flights to Vermont."

22

Levi perched on the edge of the bed. Eyes closed. Slow deep breaths. After a few minutes, his heart rate returned to normal, and he walked to the window. His second-floor room offered a scenic view of the side parking lot. Piles of icy early-March snow barricaded the perimeters, but the entrance remained clear. The Brattleboro plow drivers would earn their overtime this week.

Lodging choices were limited but tolerable. A bit too upscale for his taste. On the drive in, he'd spotted a couple of dairy farms and a few homes scattered about, but no motels. As a result, he ended up in the middle of town. Not his favorite spot.

But he did have a good view of the comings and goings on that side of the hotel. The streets teemed with people eager to spend time browsing the art galleries and antique shops. Anyone with common sense would be holed up in their homes with weather this bad, but not here. Not in Vermont. Good for them. Enjoy the day. Life's too fragile to worry. Cast your cares upon the Lord, and I'll take it from there.

He closed the curtains and shuffled back to the bed, stooping to pick up the local newspaper on the way. He'd read all four pages last night. For sheer entertainment value, the local writing couldn't be beat. The lead story gave updates about the mysterious serial killer stalking the country, possibly even headed to Brattleboro. Oooohhhh. Spooky. He'd have to remember to put the chain lock on the door tonight. Still, no sense taking chances. He needed to finish his task on Sunday and move on to somewhere with more opportunity. More places to … hide? No, of course not. Blend in. Prepare. Maybe even take a few months off and relax. If that's what God wanted, of course.

Two days. Get it done and move on.

He rolled up the paper and dropped it in the trashcan on his way to the shower. The sight of the snow brought back memories of Oregon. Mom. Kat. Miss Subaru. Cold reflections from his past. Three women waiting to thank him when he went home, though it was iffy as to whether Kat would be there. What a reunion it'll be.

The hot shower relaxed his muscles and mood. He dried off and hung his towel on the rack so housekeeping would leave it. Doing his part to save the planet. Might be a small gesture, but wasn't that how big change started? Sondra Kesson would agree.

Important day today. Learn the town, get a sense of the roads, shops, and churches. Got to find the right place, but Brattleboro had barely two dozen houses of worship, and most of them were of the tiny tourist-picture variety. He scanned the list on his laptop again and ruled out several immediately. Nothing more than glorified cults, not worthy of his time. Best to let Him decide.

He closed his eyes, pointed at the computer screen, and moved his hand in circles. Riiiiggghhhttt … here. He peeked and clicked on the link for the chosen church. Small white building, looks like a one-room schoolhouse. A new pastor. Visitors welcome, members expected. How quaint.

He sprang off the bed and paced the floor, his fingers jittery. Laughter from the hallway crept into the room, and he pressed his eye against the peephole, both palms flat against the cool metal door. Two women passed by, their jeans tucked in suede boots and white ski coats enveloping everything from the thighs up. Hoods lined with faux-fur flopped against their backs, bouncing in tandem. Levi's hands slid inches down the door. One of the women whispered to the other, both giggled, and they were gone.

Time stopped. Levi stood motionless. Stared out the peephole. Hot, painful breath streamed across the raised hairs of his left arm. A coppery drop of blood from his lip dissolved on his tongue. Warmth tremored through his body.

Finally, he straightened, arched his back, and sighed. Wet handprints remained on the metal door, mementos of what could be. He grabbed his coat and headed out. Time to see who else Brattleboro had to offer.

......

Jeremy phoned from his Tampa hotel room. "You touch base with the local police yet?"

"I told you," Maggie said. "I just got here. They put me on a flight routed through Detroit. It was delayed for four hours. You ever spend any time in the Detroit airport?"

He turned down the volume on his cell phone. "No, Maggie. I don't believe I have."

"Yeah, well, don't. They tried to bump me off the next flight, but I flashed my ID and told them it was a matter of life or death."

"Uh-huh. I'm sure the ticket agent didn't take that as a threat."

"I'm not in the mood, Jeremy."

No kidding. "Sorry. Look, get settled in and then give me a call, okay?"

She sighed. "No, it's all right. I get a little cranky after a long travel day."

"Really? Hadn't noticed."

A half-laugh came through the phone. "Whatever. As soon as I hang up, I'll get with the Brattleboro cops and let them know I'm in town. Maybe stop by and visit the chief to find out if they've taken any precautions."

"Sounds like a good start. Be careful, though. Don't want to set off any alarms. We can't be sure Talbot is there, and you don't want the locals putting the churches on lockdown. 'FBI closes churches.' That's a headline you don't want Bailey to see."

"I'll be subtle. Figured I'd spend tomorrow checking out Talbot's options. The town's not that big, but there seem to be a lot of tourists around. The desk clerk said there was some sort of music and arts festival this weekend. Just our luck."

Jeremy paused before responding. "I'm not sure that'll be an issue."

"Really? More strangers in town translate to more possible suspects."

"Think about what we know, Maggie. Talbot picks his victims from churches, most likely after observing them there."

"Sure, but it's not like I can ask every church to get photo ID from any visitors. Actually, I could, but I like my job. Wait. I'll get the local cops involved. Put a plainclothes officer in every Christian church in town, even if they have to call in people from half the state to cover it. Make sure they have a description of the women with Talbot and the car. Tell them the FBI will pay for everything."

"How are you going to get that approved?"

"I'm not, but by the time they figure that out, I hope to be gone."

He chuckled. "Fast learner."

"Yeah. I figure ninety-nine percent of the tourists won't be going to church, especially with the weather. Should narrow down the search quite a bit."

"Ninety-nine percent? You're probably still low."

"I'll have the officers phone in as soon as the service is over. If there were visitors, we want to know. Tell them to be subtle, but any information they can get will help. License plates, that sort of thing."

Jeremy grinned and pressed the phone closer to his mouth. "I've gotta say it, Maggie. I'm proud of you."

"Yeah, well, I learned a lot from this old guy that used to work here. And, thanks. Really. So what's your plan? Hang out at the beach?"

"Not likely. Still finding sand in places I'd rather not. Beats the snow you've got, though. I'll stay here a few more days. See if anything turns up."

"And pray it's before they find a body."

......

Levi awakened early. His stomach churned, but whether from butterflies or the hotel room coffee, he couldn't be sure. Sleep had come easily and, other than the occasional door slamming somewhere in the hotel, been peaceful. Sunday morning. Time to be about the Lord's business.

First things first. A good meal to get the day started right. The hotel offered a free continental breakfast, whatever that meant. English muffins with jelly most likely. Still, the price was right. He passed the elevator and took the stairs down the two flights to the lobby.

The buffet meandered along a counter with steam rising from several spots. An older man wearing black pajama pants and a sleeveless T-shirt poked at the sausages, checking each one closely before dropping half a dozen on his plate. The waffle iron had batter dripping from every side. Ugh. Looks like drool from an overweight bulldog. A mother held her young daughter high so the tot could see the scrambled eggs. Levi looked away when the girl sneezed directly in them. The only untouched item was a stainless-steel pot at the end of the counter. He glanced in and saw four or five gallons of oatmeal, mixed with what he assumed were raisins.

He placed a hand on his stomach and turned to go. Got to be a coffee shop in an artsy town like this. Three men sat at a table near the door, apparently not concerned about the buffet's health code violations. As he passed them, a snippet of conversation floated by.

"So which church did they stick you with?"

Levi didn't slow, but his mind and heart sprinted. It could be nothing, just a precaution. After all, law enforcement would know Brattleboro was on his list. Or it might be more than that. The men didn't look like FBI. Not unless their standards had loosened.

He forced himself not to look back. A young woman at the front desk smiled and wished him a good morning. He nodded but was afraid to speak. He had to find someplace to think. God would tell him what to do.

A cluster of shops lined the street, and he headed toward them. Twice he slipped on patches of ice but righted himself. Other people strolled the sidewalks, and he watched them in his peripheral vision. His leg muscles were tense, ready to spring if needed. He paused at a shop window and stared into the reflection. Works in the movies. No one following as far as he could tell.

A cafe across the street advertised an all-organic breakfast. He walked to the corner and strolled over, wondering when he'd started humming "Jesus Loves Me." The wind blustered in his face. Tears trickled down his cheeks. It's the cold. That's it.

The restaurant was small and uncrowded. He checked the menu and ordered bacon, eggs, and coffee. "All-organic" appeared to be code for "double the price." The coffee arrived, and he wrapped his hands around the mug, allowing the heat to soak through his palms. He focused on the rising wisps of steam and tried to clear his mind.

Joseph. Samson. Job. Paul. All suffered, yet persevered. And in the end, hadn't they won the battle? But was he worthy to be included in that list? He tried to obey. Sometimes it was hard, but that's why God forgives. If He is for me, who can be against me? The FBI? God's bigger. He takes care of his children.

Snow began to fall and pile along the window ledge. Miserable day to be out. Attendance at the churches would be down and that would … of course. His feet tingled, and he tapped them on the floor. Heat radiated through his chest as his heart pumped life through his body. Tension faded. He blinked several times and took a couple of deep breaths, burying his face in warm, steamy palms.

"Thank you, Lord, for this food I'm about to eat. And thank you for Your mercy that's new every day." Someone's going to need it.

Three hours later, he cruised past the one-room church and counted the vehicles in the parking lot. Twelve. With only minutes before the service started, he doubted anyone else would show up. The snow continued, and ice pellets ricocheted off his windshield. If the police were there, they were already inside the church. Good for them. Best place to be on Sunday morning. Might even learn something.

He turned his SUV around and stopped half a block away. Leaving the engine running was a risk, but he had no choice if he wanted to see anything. Ice would overwhelm the windshield if the defroster didn't keep running. Already, a pure white blanket formed on top of the old snow, removing any trace of footprints. Light streamed from the church's windows and bounced off the bleached ivory ground, creating an image worthy of a postcard. Hi, Mom. Wish you were here.

The flurries increased, and visibility shrank. No worry. It reinforced his confidence. Anyone who would go to church in this kind of weather must be a true believer. And the Bible says believers are blameless and pure. Only clean, unblemished sheep make acceptable sacrifices. When the service ended, he would choose from the flock as they paraded past.

Moments later, the sanctuary door opened, and a man stepped out, quickly closing the door behind him. Levi recognized him from the hotel lobby. A flame flashed, and the man lit a cigarette. Hello, officer. No visitors today? After a few puffs, the cop flicked the still-burning butt toward the street and hustled back inside.

Twenty minutes later, the sanctuary door swung open, and a young man stood there, shaking hands with each person as they left. He didn't have to stand in the cold long. The building emptied as twenty or so people ducked their heads and hurried to their vehicles. The officer exited last and paused to speak to the pastor. Both men shook their heads.

The decision turned out to be simple. Other than the cop, only one person attended the service by herself. A middle-aged woman stepped toward a minivan, planting each foot firmly before taking the next step. She sat in the vehicle while the engine warmed and the windshield defrosted.

The undercover officer trudged to his car, and Levi scrunched lower in his seat. He peered through the steering wheel and watched the cop drive away. His chosen sacrifice left shortly after, and he eased the SUV down the street, maintaining ample distance between them.

The woman steered out of town and into the rolling hills of the Vermont countryside. The main streets were recently plowed, making travel easier. They drove a few miles before she turned off onto a smaller road. Her minivan slowed to a crawl as she followed the mostly invisible path. Too risky.

He stayed on the main road and kept his speed before cresting a hill and losing sight of her in his rearview mirror. At the bottom of the slope, he turned around and headed back to town. The taillights of the woman's vehicle were still visible, and he slowed to mark the location in his memory. Interesting. The sheep lives on a dairy farm.

Don't get too comfortable. Got to stop by the hotel and check out, but we'll get acquainted soon. He dabbed at a drop of sweat trickling through his eyebrow.

Real soon.

23

"I'd like to go ahead and check out," Levi said. "Trying to get out of here before the weather gets any worse."

The desk clerk nodded. "Certainly, sir. Let me check your account." He printed a summary of the charges and reviewed the list before passing it over. "You're all set, Mr. White. Paid in full. I didn't charge you for today even though checkout time was three hours ago. I must say we don't get many people who pay in cash anymore."

"Never trusted credit cards. Too many friends got in trouble with them."

"I understand completely," the clerk said. "I do hope you'll stay with us again the next time you're in Brattleboro."

"Thank you. I'm sure I will." He faced the door and turned up the collar of his coat. A group of men gathered around the tables in the dining area, sipping coffee and laughing. The cigarette-smoking officer from the church sat with them.

A female voice settled the group. "All right, let's get started."

Levi fidgeted with his coat's zipper and tilted his head to get a view of the speaker. The woman had reddish hair and a decent figure. Not unattractive for a woman her age.

"My name is Margaret Keeley. I'm your FBI contact for this case."

Levi picked up his suitcase and moved toward the exit. Margaret Keeley. Pleased to meet you. The temperature had risen, and freezing rain fell, creating a thin sheet of ice on top of the snow. A salt concoction kept the sidewalks clear, but his footsteps crunched as he moved through the parking lot. After tossing his bag in the back of the SUV, he pulled away without waiting for the vehicle to warm.

He drove to a public parking lot and popped open the rear hatch. No one walked the streets now. The rain kept them huddled indoors, away from the elements. He unzipped the suitcase and moved aside a T-shirt. A daisy from the lobby display perched atop his dirty laundry. A plastic flower, not ideal, but beggars can't be choosers. Turned out there's not a lot of demand for fresh daisies this time of year in Vermont. At least it's white. He placed the flower in his duffel bag and moved it to the front seat. The genesis of a plan floated through his mind, but there were too many variables. She probably didn't live alone. The dairy farm looked small, but it was too much for one person. A husband and children were definite possibilities.

The broken-down car routine was always an option, but it seemed too ... predictable? Cliché? Plus, if there were others in the house, he'd still have to deal with them. Tiny droplets of sweat beaded above his lip. He wiggled his fingers to speed adrenaline to his mind. Or maybe he could cut the communication lines like they do in the movies. Nope. Cell phones ruined everything. He flexed his toes and cracked his knuckles. What if he got a cow costume and sneaked up on her? But doesn't that take two people? Half a cow. She'd *have* to come outside to see that. His scalp tingled, and he scratched at it with both hands.

Get serious. Focus. He closed his eyes, took a deep breath, and held it, waiting for his heart rate to stabilize. No time to plan. Improvise. Have faith. He put the SUV in gear and drove toward the dairy farm. When God wanted a sacrifice, he provided one. Hadn't Abraham found a ram in time to save Isaac? The Lord would furnish one for him as well.

He drove to where he had last seen Miss Minivan and pulled off the main road. Her vehicle's tracks were still there, though somewhat reduced by the mixed freezing precipitation. He crept along until he could get a better view of the farm. A large red building dwarfed the white one-story house. The front of the barn structure stretched toward him, a rectangular space covered with a metal roof. A huge white door took up most of the front, and windows lined the sides. The back of the rectangle fed into a much taller barn with openings on either side. A silo stood next to the building, a towering sentinel watching over the farm. Looks like the cows live better than the people.

Smoke drifted from a chimney at the house. People inside. Two four-wheelers sat parked by a side door, and trails ran in all directions. Kids. Movement caught his eye. A man in overalls grabbed logs from a woodpile and tramped into the home.

He backed the SUV down the road until the house was no longer visible. Thoughts scurried through his mind. Sacrifice them all? Too many people in the house. And no escape route. Has to be a way. Otherwise, he'd have to wait. And then what? Can't go back to town. Police are everywhere. Can't go back to Florida. Maybe God was telling him not today. Take some time off. But why? Did He not understand what needed to be done?

He pressed his forehead against the steering wheel. Screamed. Frustrated. His ears pounded in time with his pulse. Failure. It wasn't his fault. Couldn't be. He'd done everything right. But God allows bad things to happen to good people. The prophet Job lost everything, didn't he? But God gave it all back with extra. Satan tested Job. Satan tries to destroy everything that's good.

Levi sat up straight and twisted the mirror to see himself. The steering wheel imprint arced above his eyebrows, a red frown showing its disapproval. He brushed away tears. Ran his sleeve under his nose. God's plans were delayed, not canceled. This was another test, that's all. He would show himself worthy of the task and strike back at Satan. Force him to retreat. But how? There had to be a way to ... Levi's lips turned up at the corners as he received his instructions. The Lord giveth and the Lord taketh away. He took away this sacrifice for something—someone—better.

The Lord giveth him Margaret Keeley.

......

Jeremy sat on the Sarasota restaurant's patio, watching seagulls swoop in the ocean breeze. A young boy tossed Cheetos in the air, laughing as the birds snatched them. His parents stretched on blankets near him and roasted in the midday sun.

"What's going on there?" Maggie said. "I hear a lot of noise."

Jeremy held the phone closer to his face. "Sorry. Got the TV turned up too loud."

"Uh-huh. You're at the beach, aren't you? I don't believe it. I'm freezing my you-know-what off, and you're on vacation."

"Sorry, Maggie. I go where the job takes me. I mean, if I had a job. Still got to eat though, right? Walked down to this little beach-side café. I'm telling you, this is about the best chicken salad and mango iced tea I've ever had." He slurped his drink, making as much noise as possible. "That tea is so good. Now, where were we?"

"You were digging a hole. And I'm getting nowhere. Dead end yesterday. Only two churches in Brattleboro had visitors, and both of them checked out. No Aster Bellis at any of the hotels either."

"Unless you know something I don't, still quiet in Sarasota too. There was a murder Sunday night, but it was a domestic issue. If Talbot's here, he's biding his time. Chicago and Nashville didn't have anything unusual either."

"Speaking of Nashville, you talk to Claire Lawson lately?"

Jeremy motioned to the waitress to refill his drink. "Yeah. Poor kid. She sounded okay, though. She's taking handgun classes. Says she's a pretty good shot too. Talbot might be better off if we find him first."

"Not much more I can do here. I'm heading home. See if I can light a fire under someone and find Talbot's father. You headed back to DC?"

Two seagulls tangled in midair, fighting for the last Cheeto. "Not just yet. Think I'm going to do some more poking around back in Texas."

"Right. While you're there, lay off the chicken fried steak. That stuff will clog your arteries; it builds a brick wall inside them. And tell Shirley I said hello."

"Jealous?"

She chuckled. "Mom keeps telling me I could do better."

"I thought she liked—"

"You can be so dense sometimes. Yes, she likes you. A lot."

"As much as Shirl does?"

"Idiot. Call me tonight. Early, before Rebecca goes to bed. She's taking requests now on what animal to draw next. Better come up with a good one."

"On it. Love you guys." Why was it so hard to put the *I* at the beginning?

She sighed. "We love you too, though for the life of me, I can't figure out why."

......

Jeremy waited just inside the entrance of the Side Porch Restaurant, out of view of most diners. The daily special hadn't changed. Neither had the employees. The waitress made eye contact, and a grin spread across her face as she hurried toward him.

"Welcome back, honey," Shirley said. "Where's your girlfriend?"

"Hi, Shirley," he said. "Just me this time. Wonder if you could do me a favor?"

She wiped her hands on her apron. "Business or pleasure?"

"Uh, business." Jeremy reached into his shirt pocket and pulled out a photograph. The FBI photo lab had aged Anthony Talbot but left the picture black and white. "I was hoping you could show this around. See if anyone recognizes this man."

Shirley held the picture at eye level, squinting and moving the photo closer and farther from her face. "Doesn't look familiar. Why don't we walk through the restaurant and ask some of the regulars?"

"That's a good idea, Shirley," he said, "but—"

The waitress scooted closer. "Shirl."

"Shirl. But I'm afraid my presence might make people afraid to speak openly. It's probably best if you go by yourself. They're more likely to talk to someone they know."

"Like your official deputy, huh?" She arched her back, then snapped her hand to her forehead and gave a salute. "Aye-aye, sir."

"Thanks, Shirl. I'll stop by later. See if you had any luck."

"Make sure you're hungry. I'll fix you something extra special."

Can't wait. He forced a smile. "Sounds great. Got to make another stop down the road, but I should be back in an hour or so."

Jeremy sat in his car outside the Second Baptist Church of Pleasant View. It didn't look like anyone was there, but he couldn't be sure. His fingers drummed on the dash. Stalling? His stomach churned. Why was he so nervous? Something about churches ...

He stepped out of the car and walked to the building, hoping the door was locked. It wasn't. He inhaled deeply and stepped into the sanctuary. Pastor Grayson Wynford sat in the back pew.

"I wondered how long you were going to sit out there," the preacher said.

"Hello, Pastor. Good to see you again." Jeremy shook the old man's hand, careful not to squeeze too hard. "I just wanted to ask a few follow-up questions."

"Certainly, son." He patted his hand on the pew. "Have a seat."

"We're trying to find Anthony Talbot and have hit a dead end. He may be involved in all of this, or he might not be. Either way, we need to find him. I was hoping you might have remembered something that could help."

The old man shook his head. "Don't believe I ever saw him before that night, and I'm sure I haven't seen him since. But, everyone has their secrets. Some of them I know, some I don't. I didn't know Charlene's."

"Okay, then. Well, thanks for your time." Jeremy brushed his hand across his forehead and stood to leave.

"Sit down, son."

"Sir?"

"You didn't come here to talk about the Talbots. I'm no FBI agent, but I do know you have a telephone. You could've called. And you aren't the first person that's sat in their car, debating whether or not to come in. Truth be told, most of the time they drive away. It makes me sad when they leave, like they think they can drive away from God."

Jeremy shook his head and eased onto the pew. "God? This isn't about religion."

"God and religion are two different things. Most folks never figure that out. Carry their pain their whole life."

Jeremy rubbed his leg, imagining he could feel the scar under his pants. "They teach you that in seminary?"

The pastor scratched his whiskers. "Never went to seminary. Got most of my Bible learning the old-fashioned way. By studying it."

"That must have taken a while."

"Oh, it did. Or I should say it does. Not finished yet, and don't figure I ever will be. But when you're sitting behind bars for nearly twenty years, you've got the time."

Jeremy straightened in the pew. "Really? I'd have never guessed you were in prison. Can I ask why?"

"You can ask. But first, answer this for me. Does it make any difference?"

He frowned and stared at his lap. "No, I don't suppose it does."

"We've all got a past, Mr. Winter."

Jeremy scanned the sanctuary. Left to right. Top to bottom. Dusty wood. Worn hymnals. Pulpit and pews and stained glass. "Yeah, we do."

Grayson placed his hand on Jeremy's shoulder. "Want to talk about it?"

"I think we already did."

24

Darkness settled on the landscape as Jeremy headed to the diner. The main road through town had old streetlights that illuminated basketball-sized circles on the sidewalks. A few folks sat on the curb, the orange dots of their cigarettes flaring when they took a puff. The cool breeze carried an earthy scent of sage. Far on the horizon, heat lightning teased rain that wasn't coming.

A dozen pickup trucks were scattered around the restaurant's parking lot, some of them the same ones he'd seen earlier in the day. A quick call to Maggie confirmed nothing new had turned up on any of the Talbots. In other news, Rebecca had drawn an octopus on the living room wall.

"All eight legs?" he asked.

"Yep. Mom's scrubbed three of them off so far. The rest are going to have to wait until tomorrow. We're praying they don't grow back overnight."

Jeremy laughed until Maggie reminded him Shirley was waiting, and he was headed in without backup. He grunted an acknowledgment and promised to call when he got back to his hotel in Fort Stockton.

......

Shirley stood just inside the door, holding her index finger to her lips. She motioned him to a booth away from other customers.

He slid into the red vinyl seat and was relieved when she sat across from him. "So," he said, "any luck?"

She scanned the room before lowering her voice. "I showed the picture to everybody who came in here. Nobody said they recognized the fella."

Jeremy exhaled and leaned back. "Okay, then. I appreciate your help. You can hang onto that and keep showing it—"

"Jeremy. I can call you Jeremy, right? Or would Jer be better?"

He gritted his teeth. "Jeremy would be fine."

"Well, Jeremy. Everybody said they didn't know who the man in the picture was. But it's a funny thing. Most folks took a good hard look at that photo. But this one guy, he just glanced at the picture and gave it back. Seemed kind of jittery. As soon as I walked away, he got in his truck and left. Didn't order any lunch or say anything."

"And you think this gentleman knows more than he's letting on?"

She flopped her hand on top of his. "Honey, I know men. He comes in here real regular and gets himself a double cheeseburger with onion rings. Every time. A man doesn't suddenly up and decide he's not hungry without a good reason."

Jeremy eased his hand from under hers and pulled a notepad from his pocket. "I'll check him out. Got a name?"

"Clay McGraw. His ranch is about twenty miles outside town."

"Know anything about him?"

"Not much. Raises Angus cattle and mostly keeps to himself. Got a pretty little Mexican wife, they say, but I've never seen her. He always comes in here alone."

"Okay. I'll make some calls and maybe take a drive out to see him."

"You gonna do one of those stakeout things? Bet it gets awful lonely sitting out there by yourself all night." She twirled her fingers through her hair.

He stood, shook his head, and extended his hand. "Not tonight. I appreciate your help, Shirley. Please call me if you hear anything else. Oh, and this is just between us, okay?"

She stood and took his hand, holding it too long and too softly. "Sure thing, Jer. That's what deputies are for, isn't it?"

......

Jeremy hit the speaker button on his phone and laid it on the nightstand. "Still there?"

"Still here. Nothing solid on McGraw," Maggie said. "Looks like the DEA's had some interest in him, but he's never been charged with anything. I talked to Agent Burleson down in El Paso. Said they suspect McGraw's smuggling drugs into the area. Mostly small-time stuff."

Jeremy propped another pillow against the headboard and rested his back. "You take a look at the place?"

"Yeah, on Google, same as you. No telling how old that image is, though."

Jeremy zoomed in on the satellite view of Clay McGraw's ranch. "No sneaking up on the place, is there?"

"I'll see if I can get the boss to approve someone from El Paso coming up to question the guy. You hold off. Too dangerous."

"This is my lead, Maggie. I'm sharing the information to keep you guys in the loop. You want to send someone out there, go ahead. In the meantime—"

"You'll wait. Too late to do anything today anyway. Let me make some calls. I'll update you in the morning. Promise me you won't do anything until we talk then."

He kicked his shoes off and stretched his legs. "Promise. Got a big night planned anyhow. Thinking about heading back to Pleasant View. Maybe interrogate Shirl a bit more."

She chuckled. "Uh-huh. Just stay away from McGraw."

......

The three-plus hour drive to El Paso late the next morning had been tolerable only because Jeremy knew who would be waiting at the airport. Maggie had managed to convince Director Bailey that she needed to interrogate Clay McGraw personally. After all, no one understood the Talbot case better than she did, and this could be the biggest break they'd had.

Or it could be nothing. Jeremy didn't miss that part of the Bureau. Plenty of freedom to do what you needed to do, as long as you made progress. If you didn't, expect to have your leash shortened. For Maggie's sake, he hoped the McGraw lead panned out.

"Got your badge handy?" he asked. "I need to pick up the pace if we're going to get there by dark."

"Go for it. The last twenty-five miles are dirt road, so better hit it now. You're sure he doesn't know we're coming?"

"Positive. Nobody knows except Shirley, and she won't tell anyone."

Maggie tilted her head down and arched her eyebrows. "Yeah. She's not much of a talker."

"Not about this. Told her it was our secret."

"Oh, I'll bet she was all over that."

He grinned and patted the steering wheel. "I'm telling you, Maggie. This whole sex appeal thing I've got going on ... it's a curse."

She rolled her eyes and stared out the windshield. "Yeah, I don't know how you do it."

The drive took longer than expected. Even at high speeds, low traffic volume and vast open land made it seem as if they were hardly moving. A cold front blew in, and the wind gusted thick clouds of dust across the road in several locations. Finally, they located the turnoff to the McGraw homestead and stopped. The entrance was marked with two steer skulls mounted on poles, one on each side of the road.

"That supposed to be some sort of warning?" Maggie asked.

"Yeah, to the other cows. Probably to remind them to look both ways before crossing the street."

Maggie tried but failed, to stifle her laugh. "Time to get serious. Got a bad feeling about this, and backup's a long way from here."

Jeremy turned down the road toward McGraw's place. The SUV bounced through a deep hole, and he focused on the road, trying to stay in the ruts. There were no cattle in sight as the sun sank below the horizon, leaving an orange-brown glow. Soon, the lights of the house came into view, and he slowed the vehicle. They pulled in front of the home and stopped next to an old pickup truck. Once the dust settled, they exited the SUV and assessed the layout.

In the distance, a hundred fifty feet or so, a single light reflected off a large metal building. A semi-truck with a cattle trailer sat next to the structure. The outlines of three smaller sheds were barely visible.

At the house, porch lights flanked the steps, illuminating the immediate area. The home was smaller than he expected but decorated pure Texas-style. A metal star surrounded by barbed wire hung on the wall by the front door. The porch railing appeared to be handmade and looked as if horses should be tied to the post while their owners had a beer. Off to the side, a flagpole clanged in the breeze. A single spotlight pointed skyward and lit the flags. Texas on top, America underneath.

The front door opened, and a man stepped onto the wooden porch, cradling a shotgun in his arms. He looked to be in his mid-40s, shorter than average, a good fifty pounds overweight and wore the biggest cowboy hat Jeremy had ever seen.

The man stared for a moment and tapped his fingers on the shotgun. "Can I help you?"

"Yes, sir," Jeremy said. "We're with the FBI and wondered if we could ask you a few questions." He gestured toward Maggie, and the man swung the rifle into firing position. Jeremy stopped moving. Maggie's pistol was drawn, and she stood in a firing stance.

"Easy, everybody," she said. "Sir, you'll want to lower your weapon now."

The man looked at her and shifted nervously from foot to foot.

"Sir," Maggie said, "do it now."

He placed the shotgun on the porch and stepped back, holding both hands out. "I didn't mean nothing by it. Don't know you folks, and out here, we pretty much take care of ourselves. A man would be a fool not to tote a gun when strangers show up. It's loaded with birdshot anyway. Wouldn't hardly scratch you."

Maggie lowered her handgun. "Interesting. I'm loaded with 9mm hollow-points. The first one would hurt pretty bad, but at least it would take your mind off the next one. Now, let's start over. Are you Clay McGraw?"

"Yeah. So?"

She nodded toward Jeremy. "That's Mr. Winter. I'm Agent Keeley. We're investigating the incident at the Talbot house, and your name came to our attention. We just want to ask you a few questions; then we'll be on our way."

McGraw spat on the porch. "You got a warrant or something?"

Jeremy picked up the shotgun and moved it away from McGraw. "We don't need a warrant to talk. Unless there's some reason we need to get one?"

"I've got nothing to hide," he said.

"Can we come inside?" Maggie asked.

McGraw motioned toward the door and walked into the house. The two followed behind him, stopping just inside to scan the room. A deer antler chandelier lighted the area and cast irregular shadows along the floor and walls. On the left was an open seating section that led to a dark hallway. On the right, a dining area with an entrance to the kitchen. The smell of cornbread saturated the room, and Jeremy inhaled deeply.

"Smells good," he said. "Who's the cook?"

"That one of your questions?" McGraw asked.

Maggie sidled toward the kitchen, keeping a hand on her weapon.

"I didn't give you permission to search my house. You can stand by the door."

Maggie stopped and angled herself so the kitchen doorway was in her direct line of sight.

"Sir," Jeremy said, "for our safety, and yours, we need to make sure we know who's around."

"Well, I certainly understand that. So I guess the best thing would be for you to get back in your vehicle and head on out of here."

Jeremy sighed. "We'll leave, but before we go, I'd like you to take a look at this photo and tell me if you recognize this man." He handed the picture of the aged Anthony Talbot to him.

McGraw glanced at the picture and passed it back. "Never seen him."

"Really? Are you sure? You barely looked at it."

"Yeah, I'm sure. Now if there's nothing else, you two can—"

A loud clang from the kitchen reverberated through the room, followed by a voice yelling in Spanish. Seconds later, a young Hispanic woman darted from the kitchen into the dining area. Fresh brown and red stains covered the front of her blouse.

"Are you okay?" Maggie asked.

"She's fine," McGraw said. "Honey, can you wait in the kitchen for a minute? These folks were just about to leave."

The woman threw a dishtowel at McGraw, nearly knocking the hat off his head. "*You* wait in the kitchen. I'm done cooking."

Jeremy walked toward her, holding the photo in his hand. "Ma'am, do you recognize the man in this picture?"

McGraw moved toward them, and Maggie stepped in front of him.

"Far enough," she said.

"That's my wife. She can't incriminate me. I do not give you permission to speak to her."

The Hispanic woman darted toward McGraw. "Oh? So now I need your permission to speak?" Jeremy stepped in front of her, moving left and right to block her progress.

"Please, take a look at this." He handed her the photo.

She stared at the picture for a moment. "*Si*. It's my papa."

Jeremy's heart jumped. "Are you sure?"

The woman handed the photo back to him. "The hair doesn't match, and there aren't enough wrinkles, but that's him. Why? What did he do now?"

"Well Mrs. McGraw, we just—"

"Don't call me that." She glared at her husband. "My name is Lena."

Jeremy glanced at Maggie and nodded toward Lena. "Would you mind talking to Agent Keeley for a few minutes? I'd like to have a word with your hus ... with Mr. McGraw."

"Call me Maggie," she said. "It's a nice night. How about we get some fresh air?" The two women walked outside, leaving the men to themselves.

"Mind if I sit?" Jeremy asked.

"Make yourself at home. Always happy to have guests." McGraw motioned to a rocking chair while he settled onto a leather sofa, its frame fashioned from hand-hewn logs. An ashtray and a pack of White Owl cigars sat on the end table. "Mind if I smoke?"

"Not at all," Jeremy said. He walked over to the end table. "Mind if I check the drawer first?"

The man frowned and watched as Jeremy inspected the table,

lifting a few magazines and removing a revolver. "I'll keep this with me for now. Wouldn't want you to be tempted."

"Suit yourself," McGraw said. "A man can't be too careful nowadays."

Jeremy settled into the rocker. "Real nice place you've got here. Must be kind of tough to keep it maintained with no income."

"Look, buddy. I don't know where you're getting your information, but I sell cattle. It's a good business. People like to eat."

Jeremy held his palms out. "Sure. And Lena?"

"What about her?"

"How'd you meet her? I mean, don't take this the wrong way, but she's quite a bit younger. Nothing wrong with that, of course. But she didn't seem real happy to be Mrs. McGraw."

The man grinned. "She got what she wanted. Now I get what I want."

"Ah. So she gets a shot at permanent residency as long as she sticks with you for two years. How much longer on her sentence?"

McGraw tapped his chest. "That hurts. Don't you recognize true love when you see it?"

Jeremy rocked for a moment before speaking. "Honestly? No, I don't suppose I do. But I'll tell you what I do recognize. A man who's about to have his world turned upside down. There are two ways we can do this. You can give me permission to search your property. If I don't find anything, I go away."

"Not gonna happen."

Jeremy shrugged and stood. "Option B it is then. We'll leave your property and park on the main road. We'll make a call and have a search warrant by morning. That works for me. Gives us time to wake up the rest of the team. We'll bring the dogs too. They're itching for a good run."

McGraw leaned forward. "You do what you gotta do."

Jeremy opened the door. "Have a good evening, Mr. McGraw. I'll see you in a few hours. Oh, and don't go anywhere." He lowered his voice. "Agent Keeley doesn't like you very much.

Between you and me, I think she'd welcome the chance to hunt you down. I could be wrong, though. You seem to know a lot more about women than I do."

Maggie and Lena reclined against the hood of the old pickup truck, their arms crossed. Their voices drifted toward him but were too low to understand. The moon was just a sliver among the stars. In the distance, a coyote yelped, and cattle responded. Like being in a John Wayne movie.

"Time to go, Maggie."

Lena walked toward him. "You can look around. I don't care." She pointed toward the house. "That man, he needs to go away. It's too much."

"Sorry," Jeremy said. "He told us we couldn't search. We'll be back in the morning with a warrant."

"What if you didn't have to search?"

"I'm not sure I understand. Unless there's something in plain view, we have no legal basis to take action without a warrant."

Clay McGraw stepped onto the porch. "That's enough, Lena. Time for you to come inside and let these folks be on their way."

Spanish phrases flew in his direction.

McGraw chuckled. "Hot-blooded Latinas. What's a man supposed to do?" His eyes narrowed. "Come in the house, Lena. Now."

The woman turned to Maggie. "Do you have a flashlight?"

Maggie nodded. "Yeah, in the car. I'll grab it."

McGraw started down the steps. "I've had about enough from you—"

Jeremy grabbed the man's arm and twisted it behind his back. "Did you just threaten my partner?"

"What? No. I was talking to my wife."

"Uh-huh. So you threatened your wife in front of the FBI. Real smart."

"It's a figure of speech. I wasn't gonna do anything."

Jeremy jerked McGraw's arm upward before releasing it. "Your lucky day, my friend. As it turns out, Agent Keeley is an expert on figures of speech. Isn't that right?"

Maggie grinned. "Sure is. Maybe I should have a chat with Mr. McGraw? Just to make sure we're all on the same page here. Wouldn't want any misunderstandings."

Jeremy smiled. "Excellent idea, Agent Keeley. I'm going to grab the flashlight from the car. Would you be so kind as to stand beside Mr. McGraw here in case there are any more questionable comments?"

She glared at the man. "It would be my pleasure."

McGraw shifted on his feet. "Look, I see what's going on here. I want you people off my property right now."

Maggie stood inches from his face. "Sir, you threatened this woman. You think I'm going to walk away from that? I'm not going anywhere until I'm confident she's safe. It's my duty to inform you that you need to calm down so no one gets hurt." She moved closer. "There's only one person here in any danger. You figure it out."

Jeremy shrugged. "Hot-blooded redheads. What's a man supposed to do?" He retrieved the flashlight and handed it to Lena.

"Wait here," the woman said. "I'll be right back."

She walked toward the metal building, stopping at the semi-truck parked beside it. She opened the cab, leaned inside, then jumped down. Her voice echoed toward them. "Such a clever hiding spot. I've got the keys."

McGraw squirmed and yelled. "Lena, baby, please don't. We can talk about this. I'll make it right. I promise."

The flashlight shined on a side door to the structure, and she unlocked it. McGraw jumped down the steps and moved toward her. Half a second later, he landed face-first on the ground, gasping for air.

"You got my suit dirty," Maggie said. "Dust washes out. Blood doesn't. You move again, and I'm going to have to buy a new suit. Do we understand each other?"

McGraw grunted.

Jeremy stood above them. "You got this?"

"Yeah. I got this." She inclined her head toward the building. "Check on Lena. Make sure she's okay."

"Right. I'll be ... " He stared toward the building, his mouth slightly open. Oh, my God.

Lena walked toward them, her flashlight moving back and forth across the ground. A cluster of people shuffled behind her, with more straggling out of the building. Several of them supported or carried others.

"You think I didn't know?" she screamed. *"Que Dios me ayude.* God help me. I knew. I knew."

25

Clay McGraw slumped in his chair in the interrogation room of the FBI's El Paso office. His lawyer sat beside him with a blank legal pad and pen carefully aligned on the table before him. The men were a study in contrasts. One a short, overweight rancher, the other a high-priced attorney who could easily grace the cover of *GQ*.

"As I have stated numerous times," the lawyer said, "my client is not going to answer any questions. He is innocent of these spurious charges. His wife is the one you need to be interrogating."

Maggie tapped a finger on the table. "We have questioned her. As you're aware, she's also being detained." She glanced toward McGraw. "She's in isolation for her own protection. And we don't need your client to answer anything. Honestly, we have all the evidence we need."

The lawyer examined his manicured nails. "Mr. McGraw was completely unaware of his wife's activities. He is shocked and dismayed that someone he loved and trusted would be involved in human smuggling. Isn't that right, Mr. McGraw?"

The man nodded. "Shocked. And dismayed too. I guess you just can't trust some women."

Maggie placed her palms on the table and spread her fingers apart. "I don't get it. I try. I really do."

The attorney shrugged. "Agent Keeley, was it? Don't be too hard on yourself. I'm sure you did the best you could. You simply arrested the wrong person. I'm confident it's not the first time."

She tilted her head. "What? Oh, no. You misunderstood. Your client is going to prison for a very, very long time." She held up her hands. "My nails. I can't keep them looking good. I really need to get the name of your manicurist."

The lawyer's nostrils flared. "I think we're done here."

"No, we're not," Jeremy said. Maggie shot him a look, and he quieted.

"You can just sit there and listen," she said to McGraw. "I'm going to tell you a story. It's a tale of a man who makes a lot of bad decisions. The thing is, I'm not sure how the story ends." She pointed to the rancher. "He's going to tell me."

The attorney whispered to his client, and McGraw frowned.

"At some point in the past," Maggie said, "Mr. McGraw met a man named Anthony Talbot, and they made a business arrangement. Each had something the other wanted. Mr. McGraw wanted money. Mr. Talbot wanted a partner on this side of the border. And a friendship was born."

"Speculation," the attorney said.

Jeremy scratched his chin. "Uh-huh."

Maggie used her foot to tap his leg. "Business was good. Lots of people from all over South and Central America gave everything they had for a chance to come to the States. Getting them over the border was risky, but most of the time they made it. And if they didn't"—she shrugged—"these gentlemen still had their money."

The suspect licked his lips and leaned forward. "Listen, you don't—"

"Mr. McGraw. Please," the attorney said.

Maggie continued, "But Texas is a big state. They couldn't just drop off all these people in the middle of nowhere. Might attract unwanted attention. Can't have that. No, population centers are the way to go. So how to get them to the cities with as little risk as possible?" She opened a manila folder and slid a photograph across the table.

McGraw looked at the picture. "It's a steer. So what?"

She nodded. "That is indeed a steer, although I'd probably just call it a cow. I'm not a rancher. But I have seen some old Westerns, and they always had to get their cows, and steers, somewhere they could sell them. I mean, no one comes to your ranch to pick them up. Am I right?"

"Is this going to take much longer?" the attorney asked.

"I think we're almost finished," she said. "Now, your client there has a livestock trailer he uses to haul his cows all over the state. San Antonio, Fort Worth, Amarillo, you name it. Funny thing, though. He doesn't sell most of the cattle he takes there."

"If the price isn't right, I'm taking them home until it is."

"Fair enough. But why would a man go all that way, spend all that money, and go home empty-handed? Because of this." She slid another photo across the table.

The attorney glanced at the picture. "An empty water bottle?"

Jeremy inhaled and squeezed his fingers into fists. The pressure of his clenched jaw shot lightning bolts into his brain.

Maggie retrieved the photos and closed the folder. "An empty water bottle found in a compartment built under your client's live-stock trailer. Six feet wide, twelve feet long, and barely a foot high. The crime lab says it will take a while to go through the whole compartment. Human waste, blood, hair, all kinds of evidence there. Tell me something, Mr. McGraw. Did it bother you even the least bit that your cattle lived better than these people?"

The attorney stood. "All right. That's enough. Mr. McGraw, don't say another word. We're through."

"Yep," Maggie said, "you're done. Your client's prints are on that water bottle. Circumstantial? Maybe, but do you think a jury will care? Assuming it gets that far, of course. I hear the Latino gangs in the prisons get pretty upset about this kind of stuff. I suppose I can understand why. Anyway, thanks for your time. I'll see that Mr. McGraw gets transferred back to his cell as soon as possible. You gentlemen have a nice day."

The lawyer glared at the agents. "Are you implying that my client is in danger? I demand he be placed in isolation. No contact with the other inmates."

Maggie shook her head and frowned. "Afraid we can't do that. We'll keep him in the general population until the charges are formally submitted. Rules and everything. I'm sure he'll be fine."

McGraw crossed his arms. "You put Lena in isolation."

"Sure did," Maggie said. "She gave us information. We have reason to believe she could be in danger. Certain people might be interested in seeing your wife dead. You, on the other hand, well, we just don't know. Best to play by the rules for now. Who knows? Maybe you'll make some new friends?"

McGraw slammed his fist on the table. "Wait. What do you people want?"

The attorney placed his hand on the rancher's shoulder. "Clay, it'd be best if you kept your mouth—"

"Just asking a question," McGraw said. "I didn't do anything, but if I did, what kind of deal is on the table?"

"Deal?" Maggie said. "Here's your deal. You can either take the heat for the whole operation, or you can drag Anthony Talbot down with you. Lena's already given us his alias. We'll find him with or without your help. And we're not offering anything in return."

"Then why would I help you?"

She stared at him until he looked away. "Because Mr. McGraw, you're a coward. You need to be able to point the finger at someone else. This is your only chance."

"And," Jeremy said, "a murder conviction in Texas puts you in the express lane for lethal injection. Might be good to have a clear conscience when that happens."

"Now wait a minute," the lawyer said. "Nobody said anything about murder charges."

Maggie stood, breathing hard. "Tell you what. You climb in that box and ride for hours. We'll even let you have the space to yourself. But let's wait for a nice summer day. Temperatures around one-thirty or so in there. Murder charges? They're coming just as soon as we find the bodies."

McGraw shifted in his chair and glanced at his lawyer. The attorney nodded and returned to his seat.

The rancher drummed his fingers on the table. "If I give you Talbot, I want immunity from prosecution."

"Gentlemen," Maggie said, "you give me Talbot, a guilty plea, and all the details including the location of any bodies. In return, I'll give you solitary confinement. Death sentence is up to a judge. Non-negotiable. And if I find out you've held anything back, deal's off. You go in the general prison population."

"May I have a few moments with my client?" the lawyer asked.

She stood and shook hands with the attorney. "You have my number. And don't forget. I really need to know who does your nails."

......

Jeremy sipped his Shiner Bock and scanned the menu for the third time. Dinner alone. Again. Maggie had gone home three days ago. Clay McGraw had agreed to assist, but the FBI was still trying to figure out how to handle the new information. With nothing to do except wait for Cody Talbot or his father to turn up, no point in her staying in west Texas.

Jeremy decided to remain in El Paso. Could work just as easily here, and if something did break loose, there was a good chance it'd be somewhere close. The downside was being alone. Never used to bother him. In fact, he preferred the solitude. But that was before Maggie.

His phone dinged, and he checked the text message. The word "onearm" followed by seven digits. Maddix Kimbel. An old friend from his Afghanistan days. And his CIA contact.

He motioned to the waitress and asked if there was a phone nearby. She handed over hers with a warning not to look at the pictures. He replaced "onearm" with "202" and dialed the phone number. "Hey, Maddix. Got any news for me?"

"I could get in a lot of trouble for this, you know."

Jeremy chuckled. "Are you required by some sort of code to say that at least once in every conversation?"

"I'm serious, Jeremy. This could get real ugly, real fast."

He pressed the phone closer and scanned the area near his table. "Understood."

"Whose phone are you on?"

"Waitress's at a restaurant in El Paso."

"Make sure you delete this number from the call log."

Jeremy scrubbed his hand across his mouth. "Will do. You find a name?"

"Yeah. And a last known location."

"And?"

"Not over the phone. Could be NSA flagged."

"Do you want me to—"

"Go old school. Be careful, Jeremy. And don't forget to delete this number."

He hung up and erased the phone's call log. Maddix was always security conscious, but this took things to a new level. Not surprising, considering the risk if certain people found out. No, Cronfeld wouldn't be happy and, worse, could put an end to Jeremy's plan before it even started. The fewer people who knew, the better.

Old school. Regular mail. His PO Box was half a country away. Not so far to go for a piece of paper that could protect his future.

And destroy Cronfeld's.

26

Levi cruised the Magnificent Mile, sickened by the ostentatious display of wealth. Four days since Brattleboro. Dairy farms gave way to Burberry, Tiffany, Prada, and untold more like them. Even in the frigid wind from Lake Michigan, window-shoppers sauntered about, lusting after the golden trinkets inside the stores. The rich of Chicago no doubt sat inside the boutiques and waited for their personal assistants to bring drinks and appetizers. Only in America would so much abundance go to waste. Pearls before swine.

His riches waited in another world. Obedient children received rewards, and he was nothing if not dutiful. Still, he hadn't gone before God and presented an offering since Portland. Kat didn't count. She was in the way. His own personal Judas. True, she hadn't actually betrayed him, but he knew. He could see it in her eyes, even at the end. Especially at the end. Same thing with Mom. Her interference wasn't intentional, but did that really matter? The Lord's work would not be stopped.

A sense of unease had enveloped him since leaving Sarasota. The FBI was grasping at straws, and yet he detected the need to hurry. Not for his own sake, of course. The Lord would protect him. But America had not changed. A day or two in the news and now nada. Zilch. Serial killings were nothing special. A death here and there, scattered around the country, wasn't waking anyone up. Life continued as normal in spite of his efforts. He needed to rethink his—God's—strategy.

Traffic slowed as a limo pulled to the curb, its rear blocking a lane. The driver hopped out and ran around, opening the back-passenger door. A woman bundled in a fur coat sauntered out of Gucci. She carried a tiny dog dressed in pink and whispered to the animal as she walked. A salesman followed with two enormous bags. She slid into the car without acknowledging the chauffeur. He closed the door, placed the purchased goods into the trunk, and hustled back to his assigned seat. The limo pulled away and drove two stores down before stopping. The driver hurried around to open the door again, consciously avoiding eye contact with his employer. Such arrogance.

Of course. The message was clear. The wealthy, powerful people of the world were front-page news every day. He needed to choose higher value targets. America's attention span was short, except when it came to the famous. Movie stars, politicians, athletes were all fodder for the headlines. Normal people were killed every day, but not the rich. The dirt of daily life never touched them.

If one of the elite of society was the next sacrifice, the media would take notice. They would latch onto the death, and like a wildfire feeding on itself, the story would grow out of control. The public would demand it. After all, if the wealthy could be taken, was anyone safe?

He had to find someone who was both pure and rich. Was that even possible? Jesus said it was easier for a camel to pass through the eye of a needle than for a rich man to enter heaven. But his own bank account was overflowing, wasn't it? So it could be done. He just needed to do a little research.

Back at the motel, he scanned the Internet, searching for information on Chicago's upper-class citizens. He needed to get close, gain an understanding. A poor sacrifice was worse than none at all. Just ask Cain.

Levi's choice reflected on him, and when the day came that he stood before the Lord, he wanted a clean conscience. Offering the wrong person, well, that might be hard to explain.

Several events were scheduled over the next day or two. A benefit for the humane society. A bake sale to raise money for women's shelters. An auction for the preservation of historic homes. An interfaith meeting of local churches to discuss ways to reduce gang violence. Interfaith. Sort of a religious buffet. That one has possibilities.

Mayor Whelan and his wife would attend, so plenty of hangers-on would be there too. A photo-op for everyone involved, with the added benefit of making themselves feel better about doing nothing substantive. Still, someone may stand out. Tomorrow morning, ten o'clock. Felt good to be working again.

......

A hushed reverence hung inside Old Saint Patrick's Church. The venue was beautiful. Much nicer than those ginormous churches that swallowed everybody. With its marble floors, flickering candles, and ornate statues, the sanctuary emitted an aura of calmness and peace.

A hundred or so people were dispersed about the room. None of them looked like gang members. A row of chairs sat near the altar, and people began to filter into them. The mayor sat next to a stunning brunette—wife, maybe?—but Levi recognized no one else. At the scheduled time, a man in a black robe approached the microphone.

"Good morning, everyone, and thank you for coming. It's our hope this meeting will come up with real policies that can make a difference in our communities. Young people are dying on our streets, and it's going to take all of us to change that. Now, will you join me in prayer?"

The next forty-five minutes consisted of the men on the platform extolling each other's virtues. Hearty rounds of applause followed as they had their say at the microphone. We need to pray more. We need to get rid of the guns. We need to build community centers. We need a curfew.

A few moments later, the mayor glanced at his watch and whispered to the man in the black robe, who nodded and approached the microphone.

"Folks, that's about all the time we have for today. I think we've made some real progress here. I'd like to thank our distinguished guests for coming, and especially our mayor and his lovely wife." He led the attendees in applause while Whelan did his best to look embarrassed. "Now, if you'd join me in a closing prayer."

So that *was* the mayor's trophy wife, no doubt chosen because she'd look good on the society page. Still, unlike most of the others on the platform, she didn't fidget during the prayer. Head bowed, wrinkled forehead, lips moving. Levi squinted and massaged his chin. Maybe.

Have to do a bit more digging. Make sure he chose wisely. But if the mayor's wife turned out to be the one … well, praise God for the publicity that would follow. The whole country would know who'd done it. Maybe not why. Not yet. But a phone call or two to the press could fix that easy enough.

The prayer ended, and he licked his lips, watching as she shook hands with a few people in the audience. Her beauty-pageant looks attracted the attention of most of the men in the crowd, and she smiled dutifully as several took selfies with her. On the outside at least, she certainly appeared unblemished. After a moment, Mayor Whelan placed his hand on her back and guided her out of the building.

Levi hesitated to give the multitude time to thin, then sauntered outside. The mayor and his wife slid into the back seat of their oversize SUV. The driver and another man filled the front seats. Bodyguards? We'll see. Even if they are, so what? Hadn't the Lord slain entire armies with a single angel?

No rush, though. After Chicago, only three cities left. Nashville, Sarasota, and Brattleboro. Have to bend the rules a bit for that last one, but who God wants, God gets. For now, scout out Mrs. Whelan. Make sure she's worthy. Wrap it up here, then back to Pleasant View to get everything ready for the big day.

......

The two-story house didn't seem opulent, at least on the outside. It was a simple blue-and-white home, blending in well with the old neighborhood. The only sign that the mayor of Chicago lived there was the permanent presence of a police car parked at the curb. The auto's blue stripe matched the house color.

Levi drove past without looking at the home. Four days since the interfaith meeting, and as far as he could tell, gang violence hadn't slowed much. Imagine that. But his time hadn't been wasted. He'd learned things that would be ... useful? No. Providential. That's the word.

Researching the mayor had been neither difficult nor interesting. A lifelong politician who'd worked his way up the ranks. His early years as an alderman were full of promise. New daycares, parks, and rec centers for youth in his ward. Job training programs. A women's shelter and drug counseling program.

As time passed, his focus shifted to a bigger agenda. Defying the party on property tax increases. Marching arm-in-arm with civil rights leaders. Declaring to anyone who would listen that this was Chicago's time to put the politics of old behind them. His picture was in the *Tribune* almost weekly. A man who wanted to make a difference became a man who wanted to keep his power. Just another politician in a country already teeming with them. Overwhelmingly elected mayor for his first term, not so much his second.

Mrs. Whelan, the mayor's wife, spent much of her time being the dutiful politician's spouse. Meetings, fashion shows, ribbon cuttings, anything to stay in the public eye. Her personal life was nearly as open.

A regular church-attender, once a week she hosted an in-home Bible study. A Google search turned up dozens of photos of her working with the homeless and chatting with at-risk kids. Always in a crowd, though. Hard to do what needed to be done with so many others near.

If she weren't the mayor's wife, now that would make life, and death, simpler for everyone, wouldn't it? If something were to happen to her husband, the grieving widow would have plenty of time alone. And killing the head of Chicago's political machine would be a delicious appetizer to the main course. He had run it past the Lord, of course, and received immediate approval. No surprise.

It had been surprisingly easy to follow Mayor Whelan and learn his routine. Levi had hoped to hone his surveillance skills, but the man's routine never varied. Every morning, the same thing. Disappointing, really. His Honor stopped for coffee and an oat bran bagel on the way to his office. At least one bodyguard, and more often than not, two, accompanied him everywhere. Well, not *everywhere*. Certain things demanded privacy and a newspaper. The mayor was nothing if not regular.

Levi had a plan and was confident, even excited. It would be simple, but he'd have to wait for his chance. No hurry, though. Timing was everything. Not knowing when it would happen heightened the thrill. Tomorrow? The next day? That was in the Lord's hands.

......

Two mornings later, Levi relaxed at a side table in Beans & Bagels and read the *Tribune*. The rustle of the newspaper, the hum of chatting commuters, and the smell of java floating through the room all combined to soothe him. The toasted sweet onion bagel was delicious, and a special morning java washed it down perfectly. He kept the collar of his Chicago Bulls jacket turned up, a buffer against the wind. A matching black ball cap obscured his vision, but if he couldn't see out, they couldn't see in.

The noise intensified as the mayor walked in with two security personnel. Mingle with the commoners, then ride the Brown Line into the office. Show everyone you're just like them. Shake a few hands. Listen to a few complaints and nod seriously. A regular, down-to-earth guy.

Levi folded his paper, tucked it under his arm, and strolled down the hallway to the men's room. It was a one-seater, and he locked the door behind him, then pulled blue latex gloves from his jeans pocket and snapped them on his hands, wiggling his fingers to work them to the ends. After using an alcohol swab to clean the door handle, he pulled the syringe from his shirt pocket and removed the orange cap. Mayor Whelan was a good-sized man, but Propofol didn't discriminate. The bigger they are, the—

The door handle jiggled, and he checked his grip on the syringe. Confirm the target, then left hand opens the door, right hand does the dirty work. Showtime.

He swung the door open, keeping his right hand behind his back. Mayor Whelan stood there, alone. Noise from the shop filtered through the empty hallway.

"It's all yours, buddy," Levi said. He stood in the entry, bracing the door open.

"Thanks." The mayor brushed past him, and Levi pivoted quickly, plunging the syringe into the politician's neck while using a foot to push the door closed. His left hand clamped around the mayor's mouth.

"You know, Mayor, your wife seems like a fine Christian

woman. She deserves better than you, and I'm going to make sure she gets it."

Whelan slumped to the floor, and Levi grabbed the man's wrist, waiting as the mayor's pulse slowed, then stopped. He stood, removed his gloves, and tucked them into his jeans pocket. A last glance at the once-powerful man sprawled on the floor. No camel through the needle's eye for him. Looks like Chicago will be having an election soon.

The hallway was empty, and a brisk walk later, he was a block and a half away. The mayor's body would be discovered any moment now. Best to not be near when that happened. Surveillance cameras surely had Levi's image, but there was nothing he could do about that. The jacket and cap blocked most of his face, but technology could do wonders. Oh, they would know who had done it soon enough. But not until he finished his—the Lord's—work in Chicago.

......

Levi stretched out on the motel bed, the TV remote in his hand. Most major channels covered the news conference, which had lasted over two hours so far. Everyone needed their moment in the spotlight. The good ones even whipped up some tears for the cameras. An autopsy was scheduled, but a heart attack was suspected. A public memorial was in the planning stages, followed by a private graveside service for the family. In the meantime, government business would continue as normal. They said it was the best way to honor the legacy of the great man.

Step one completed. The preliminaries over. Now then, widow Whelan. When shall we meet?

27

The cell phone interrupted Jeremy's deep knee bends. Thankfully. He snatched it off the nightstand and smiled. "Mornin', sunshine."

"Good morning," Maggie said. "Wake you up?"

"Nah. Just getting ready to hop in the shower."

"Big day today, huh? Call me as soon as you're done."

He emptied the tiny coffeepot's contents into a paper cup and took a sip. "Will do. What's on your agenda?"

"Got some big news late last night. Might've caught a break on the Talbot case."

He scrubbed a towel across his face and plopped onto the bed. "Yeah?"

"Yeah. Yesterday morning some tourists on Mount Hood found a body. No confirmation yet, but we're reasonably certain it's Charlene Talbot."

"His mother? What makes you think it's her?"

"The body was wrapped in a sheet matching the ones from the Portland Palace Motel. DNA won't be back until tomorrow, and we're still trying to find a dentist that might have her records."

"Cause of death?"

"Might be difficult to determine, but we're guessing asphyxiation. The snow kept her body chilled, and the coroner found something interesting in her trachea. A flower petal. It's being tested, but we all know what it is."

He nodded. "A daisy. Mom must've become a burden or a threat. Any indication of assault?"

"Hard to say. The body's not exactly in pristine condition."

"How so?"

"A couple of tourists were out driving around, taking pictures and stuff. They spotted a hawk plucking at something and pulled over to snap some photos of the bird. Figured it was eating a squirrel or rabbit. It wasn't."

"Nice."

"Gets worse. Too much damage for just a bird or two. Coroner thinks a coyote got there first. Said they usually don't go up so high on the mountain, but who knows. Maybe a wolf or black bear."

He finished off the coffee and tossed the cup toward the trashcan, missing badly. "How's the couple?"

"Shook up, but not so much they couldn't tweet about it. We've got the photos and deleted the pictures from their cell phones."

"Find anything that might help us locate Talbot?"

"Nothing so far. It's just a body, nightgown, and sheet. Nothing else around the area."

"Not surprised. You'll keep me in the loop?"

"Much as I can. You take care of your own business, though. Don't worry about Talbot. I'll get him."

"Don't doubt it for a second."

"Call me later, okay? Now get a shower. I can smell you from here."

He raised his arm and sniffed. "Eh, I've been worse."

She laughed and kissed the phone. "Don't doubt it for a second. Don't forget to call me."

He tossed the cell phone on the bed and moved into the bathroom. No time for the steam this morning. After a quick shave and downing a couple of aspirin, he stepped into the icy shower. The scar on his leg, already irritated by his plan for the day, screamed at the frigid stream flowing along its crooked path.

He gritted his teeth and focused on the pain by tracing the wound as it twisted from his outer thigh, across the kneecap, eventually finding its way to just above the inside of his ankle. The doctors had told him how lucky he was. That by all rights he should have lost the leg. If not in the first incident, definitely in the second.

He squeezed his thigh until the throbbing slowed and the ache eddied down the drain. Not today. Not now.

Too much depended on his upcoming encounter.

......

Jeremy stood beside his rental car, arms crossed against the chill of an early May Colorado morning, and savored the view. He'd have to bring Maggie and Rebecca out for a visit one day. Sunlight awakened the mountaintops to the west. Weekend traffic on the Denver-Boulder Turnpike sped past, and vehicles' headlights caught wisps of fog creeping across the open field alongside his hotel. If the rest of the state was as beautiful as this—

An 18-wheeler's horn broke the spell. He placed his hands on his hips and arched his back, stretching out the hotel bed's firmness. After three days in Superior, he knew his way around pretty well. No hurry today. Best not to rush anything.

It'd been more than a month since the FBI had theorized Cody Talbot killed Chicago's mayor. The combination of Propofol and one of Talbot's target cities was all they had, though. Video footage from the crime scene hadn't been helpful beyond providing partial facial images. Not enough to even go public with. Since then, nothing. State and federal investigations continued. If Talbot had murdered Whelan, he sure wasn't taking credit for it.

Jeremy had spent his time working on a more personal matter. The letter from his CIA contact gave him the information he needed. Homa Nezam. Superior, Colorado. Today he'd meet the sister of the man who'd tried to kill him in Afghanistan.

......

Jeremy made a quick left turn followed by a right, then pulled to the curb and waited until he was confident no one followed. Paranoia was becoming his way of life. A short drive later, he arrived at the small complex and parked beside a beat-up Honda Civic. He knocked on the door of Homa's second-floor apartment and stood back from the peephole. Should've called. Told her who he was and why he was coming. Couldn't take that chance, though. Without knowing her and understanding how she'd react, too risky. She might refuse to see him or, worse, run.

A voice filtered through the door. "Yes?"

"Miss Nezam? My name is Jeremy Winter. I wonder if I might have a moment of your time?"

"Check the apartment rules. No soliciting."

Her fourteen years in America had weeded out most of her accent. "Yes, ma'am. I'm not selling anything. This is more of a, um, personal nature. About your brother."

No response for nearly a minute.

"Miss Nezam?"

The door cracked open, the chain lock on, a butcher knife visible in her hand. The thirty-year-old woman squinted and breathed rapidly. "I don't have a brother."

Jeremy stepped back and held his palms out. "Not anymore. But you did have one. Nezam. You even took his name when you came here. I knew him in Afghanistan."

"Lots of people knew him. What do you want?"

"I was hoping I could ask you a few questions. It'd really help me out."

She bit her bottom lip, exposing the small gap between her pearlescent front teeth. "Questions about what?"

He cleared his throat, clasped his hands behind his back, and raised his chin. "About your time at the military base in Afghanistan."

"I don't think so, Mr. Winter. Please, don't contact me again." She shut the door and clicked the deadbolt.

Jeremy moved closer and dropped his voice. "Miss Nezam, I was with your brother when he died."

A soft thud, the rattling of a chain, and the click of a deadbolt. The door opened, and Homa stepped back, the knife still clutched in her hand. "Please, come in."

He nodded and entered the apartment. "Thank you. I understand how difficult this must be for you."

She motioned to a threadbare sofa, its beige foam peeking through the cushions' dark green fabric. "Information on Nezam's death has been hard for me to obtain. I would be grateful for anything you can tell me."

"Of course. I'll share what I know."

"And in return ...?"

Jeremy sighed and let his head hang. "Miss Nezam, I—"

"Homa, please."

"Homa. And I'm Jeremy."

"May I offer you some water? Perhaps chai?"

"I'm fine, thanks."

She laid the knife on an end table, sank into a flowery over-stuffed chair, and tucked her feet under her. "What exactly do you want from me?"

"As much as you're willing to give," he said. "No secrets here. I'll answer any questions I can. About me, your brother, Afghanistan, whatever. In return, all I ask is for you to hear what I have to say. I'm confident you can help me, but I won't force you.

When we're done, you can tell me to disappear, and you'll never hear from me again. I promise."

She rubbed her hands on her jeans and exhaled loudly. "Tell me about my brother."

"I was in Afghanistan shortly after 9/11. Back then, I worked for the FBI, and they sent me to interrogate some prisoners. An American soldier had been taken by the Taliban, and we were trying to find him. Your brother was my translator. A good one."

"He used to watch American TV shows. Picked up your language so quickly."

"Told me *Dallas* was his favorite."

The hint of a smile crossed her lips. "It was."

Jeremy scooted to the edge of the sofa. "He also told me about you, Homa. How he agreed to work with the CIA if they helped get you to Pakistan, then to America. That was all he cared about. His family. Making sure you were safe."

She stared at her lap and dabbed a finger under her eyes. "You said you were there when he died?"

He swallowed hard. "I was. What he did … he had no choice. The Taliban had your mother, and if he hadn't …"

"Tell me everything. I've waited long enough."

Yeah, you have. "It was a grenade. He smuggled it into camp. We were interrogating a Taliban chief, and it wasn't going well. Things were starting to get out of hand, and the prisoner signaled to Nezam. When I turned to your brother, he already had the grenade out and pulled the pin. He told me he was sorry. I believed him. I ran, ended up in the hospital for a long time. Homa, I don't blame your brother. He was a very brave man."

She looked up, and wrinkles appeared on her forehead. "You said things were getting out of hand. What did you mean?"

His chest hollowed, and his shoulders sagged. "My fault. I got angry. Let the prisoner get to me. I shot the man. Didn't kill him, but I wanted to. Would've done it if your brother hadn't beat me to it. He didn't have a choice, Homa. Not if he was going to protect his family."

She squeezed the chair's arm and glared at him. "You should have killed him. You should have killed all of them."

"Homa—"

"What they did to my country. My family. You can't know what that feels like. If I had the chance, I'd cut their throats."

He brushed the back of his hand under his eyes.

She leapt to her feet. "Did you know they killed my mother after Nezam died? Did the government tell you?"

"No. I'm sorry, Homa."

"Ask your questions. Then leave. Do not come back." She crossed her arms and fell back into the chair.

"I do know. What it feels like to lose your family. I lost mine too. While I was over there for the FBI. My wife and baby girl …" He took a deep breath and tapped a fist on his knee. "No one ever caught. No one. I do know, Homa."

She studied her fingers for several dozen heartbeats before nodding and looking up. "Ask your questions."

"Has anyone else been in contact with you about Afghanistan? In the last year or so, I mean."

"No. When the CIA brought me here, they asked if I wanted to be around other Afghans. Why would I? What does that life, that religion, have for me? I chose Colorado because there were enough other immigrants around that I could learn from, but not so many I would be surrounded by Afghanis. The government paid six months on an apartment, scheduled me for English classes, and disappeared. I have spoken to no one about Afghanistan in over thirteen years."

Good. "Okay, I need to share some information with you before I ask questions. In Afghanistan, the commanding officer was a man named Colonel Ramsey Cronfeld. Do you remember him?"

Her brownish-green eyes darkened, and she drew her mouth

into a thin line. "I remember. He is the husband of that woman running for President."

"Exactly, and he's worried. I imagine his wife is too. Worried about some things that happened overseas and how they could affect her campaign. Do you know the things I'm talking about, Homa? Did you see anything while you were at the Marine camp?"

"I saw things, as did many others."

"Yes, but you and I are the only people who can talk about what happened, and I don't think he knows you exist. If he does, he's forgotten, or he would've already been here. Everyone else—the other soldiers—will go to prison if they say anything. Cronfeld's made sure he's protected from them. Now he's after me. Wants me to sign a document agreeing never to disclose what I know. Won't do it because that's the only leverage I have against him. I don't trust him. Still, if it was just me ..."

Homa tilted her head. "You said only you and I knew."

He pulled a photo from his jacket pocket and handed it to her. "We're the only ones with firsthand knowledge. We're not the only ones Cronfeld will use to get what he wants."

She studied the picture of the red-haired woman with the little girl in her lap. "Tell me about them."

28

Levi shined the flashlight over the area and surveyed his work. It had to be perfect. Every detail exactly as instructed. Four months from now, the final sacrifice would take place here. The culmination of his work. The end of the race. Finish strong.

He'd never been good with his hands. Construction didn't come naturally, but he couldn't exactly buy the finished product. Some lumber, curtains and bedsheets, and bleach. Spray paint. Lots of spray paint. Angels and a big plastic cooler. The room was ready. Good.

Very good.

He moved about the space and lit the candles, then turned off the flashlight. He'd debated using battery-powered candles but opted for the real thing at the last minute. The flickery scent of smoke added to the ambiance and realism. The curtains and bedsheets hung from the ceiling behind him, sealing off the area from unwelcome light. A wooden table, the work of his own hands, sat to the left, a golden pail beside it. In the center of the room, the cooler, also spray-painted gold, sat atop a smaller table.

Stuffed angels, made in China and bought at Hallmark, perched atop the ice chest.

His new clothes remained in the shopping bag. He wouldn't wear them today. Not allowed. Had to wait until it was time.

The only things missing were the sacrifices. One to set free. One to die. The first was easy. He'd volunteered. The second? Already chosen. He closed his eyes and pictured her. The purest sacrifice yet.

His break from the mission had done more than give him time to make the final preparations. He'd been able to plan. To lay everything out on a schedule. Do the research. No mistakes. Chicago, Nashville, Sarasota.

He dragged a finger back and forth across a candle's flame. Slower.

Slower.

The faintest odor of burning flesh tickled his nose. He jerked his hand back and popped the finger into his mouth.

And Brattleboro.

God had spoken clearly. FBI Agent Margaret Keeley would face her sins. Interfering with the Lord's work could not—would not—go unpunished. She would suffer. Understand pain and holy wrath. Know what it is to weep for all that is lost.

Rebecca Keeley would never finish second grade.

29

Jeremy pressed the binoculars against his face and panned the horizon. He lay on top of one of several small hills and looked over the barren landscape. A few mesquite trees provided cover from the midday sun, although the southerly breeze forced in dust and heat. This section of McGraw's ranch wasn't fit for anything except scorpions, and twice he'd imagined one creeping up his pants. His training allowed him to casually reach back and brush his leg to confirm nothing was there. His training and the thought of Maggie making fun of him. A scorpion sting or showing fear in front of her. He knew which would be worse.

"Think he'll show?" Maggie asked.

"Yeah. Been months since we let McGraw out on bail. Talbot will figure enough time's passed that it's probably safe."

McGraw stood beside his pickup truck, three hundred yards from Jeremy and the FBI team. The man's huge cowboy hat shaded most of his body, and he alternated between puffing on a cigar and sipping a beer.

Maggie flicked a strand of hair off her forehead. "Maybe.

Talbot's got to figure something's going on. If it were me, I'd suspect a trap."

"Still don't think we should have let Lena come too?"

She shook her head. "Too dangerous. She's done enough. Telling her papa she needed to see him might be what gets him back on this side of the border. As long as McGraw holds up his end of the deal, we'll be okay."

"He will. Got no choice if he doesn't want to meet the Latino prison gangs."

"Uh-huh. You just remember our agreement, or you'll be dealing with worse than that."

He grinned. "Trust me. This is your operation. I'm only here as an observer. I don't know how you talked your boss into it."

"By assuring him you'd behave or have me to deal with."

"Big talk from such—"

She glared at him. "I'm serious, Jeremy. I stepped out on a limb for you. Don't make me regret it."

He frowned and scratched his leg. "I won't, Maggie. I'd never do anything like that. I'm sorry if—"

She chuckled and peered at the distant pickup truck. "Good to know I've still got it. Seriously, though. Behave." She clicked the radio twice, receiving one click in response. "SWAT's still good to go."

Jeremy wiped sweat from his forehead. "Got to be over a hundred degrees in that truck. Lying on the floorboard's got to be making him miserable."

She tilted her head toward the man next to her. The sniper's splayed body melded with his menacing weapon. "Agent Sanchez here seems to be doing fine."

"Yeah. He asked if he could cut McGraw's cigar in half, just for fun. Said he needed to check the alignment on his rifle's scope."

"Uh-huh. Some guys get to have all the ..." She pointed off to the left. "Dust trail. Here they come."

Jeremy wiggled himself flatter against the desolate earth.

Maggie whispered into the radio. "Target acquired. ETA less than three minutes." One click responded.

The sun glinted off the windshield of the oncoming vehicle. A late model green pickup truck shimmered through heat waves and approached at high speed. Jeremy eyed the small bales of hay packed in the bed and the two occupants in the front seat. "At least two, maybe more in the back."

"Yeah. That straw in the bed makes me nervous." Maggie relayed the information to the SWAT agent hidden in the rancher's truck.

McGraw stepped away from his pickup and waved his arms over his head. The approaching vehicle slowed and stopped twenty yards away from him. For a moment, no one moved. Both doors swung open, and the men stepped out, weapons trained on McGraw.

Maggie pressed against the binoculars, her mouth slightly open. "Neither one looks like Talbot. Driver has an Uzi. Passenger has a short-barreled shotgun. Uzi is Target One. Call it in for me."

Jeremy whispered in the radio, sharing the information.

Target One moved sideways and increased the space from his companion. The three men stalked toward each other. The human triangle shrunk until they met in the center. McGraw talked while Target Two frisked him.

"Good thing he didn't wear a wire," Jeremy said.

Target One motioned to McGraw's truck and moved toward it, his finger on the trigger of the submachine gun.

"Sanchez, you got him?" Maggie asked.

"Say the word," the sniper said.

"Jeremy, let SWAT know. If that guy gets to the cab, we'll take him out from here."

The man sidled up to the opposite side of the truck, checked the bed, and nodded to his partner.

Sanchez grunted. "If he gets to the cab, I won't have a clean shot."

"Stand by," Maggie said.

The man stared at McGraw for a moment, then began moving toward the front of the pickup. As he closed on the cab, he craned his neck to see through the back window.

The man suddenly yelled, jumped back, and swung the Uzi into firing position, its stock pressed against his shoulder.

Maggie didn't hesitate. "Drop Target One."

A shot reverberated, and the man disappeared in a spray of red. His partner swung his shotgun toward McGraw's truck, scanning the surroundings. The driver door opened, and the SWAT agent rolled out and maneuvered to the back, his Heckler & Koch MP5 submachine gun aimed at the men.

All three shouted, and Target Two grabbed McGraw, using him as a shield against the SWAT agent.

"Permission to engage Target Two?" the sniper asked.

Maggie paused for a heartbeat. "Clear shot?"

"Clear enough."

"We may need him to get to Talbot," Jeremy said.

"McGraw's our responsibility. We have a hostage situation on our hands. Doesn't matter that we don't like the hostage."

Target Two wrapped his left arm around McGraw's throat and drew him closer, shoving his weapon into his back. The two of them walked backward to the green pickup truck.

Maggie shifted on her elbows. "Situation?"

The sniper grunted.

"Engage Target Two when clear."

McGraw was shorter than his captor, but his hat obscured most of the other man's head. Jeremy stared through the glasses, knowing what the sniper planned to do. "Make sure you aim high enough."

A second shot cracked, and both men went down. The SWAT agent moved forward in a half-crouch, sweeping his weapon between the men and the other vehicle. McGraw rolled away from his captor and crawled toward his truck.

The agent kicked the shotgun away from the body and sidled to the suspects' vehicle. His movement slowed as he neared the truck. He peeked through the driver window, then crept to the bed, pausing after each footstep. His weapon pointed at each bundle of stacked hay. Suddenly he moved back and shouted. Slowly, one of the bales moved, and a man stood, his hands raised.

"Can't see him," Maggie said.

Jeremy spoke into the radio. "Tell him to turn around."

The man pivoted and stared in their direction. Old, thin, dark tanned. Almost bald.

Maggie lowered the binoculars. "Hello, Mr. Talbot."

30

L evi pulled into the Chicago Ridge Mall's parking lot and
stopped among the smattering of vehicles in front of Sears.
He'd used his time wisely in the month and half since Whelan's
death. Everything was ready back in Texas.

He scanned the talk stations on his SUV's radio again. The
mayor's killing was still a prime topic of conversation. The official
autopsy report had leaked in spite of law enforcement's desire to
keep the memo hush-hush. Acute Propofol intoxication. He
wanted attention, and now he had it. No doubt the FBI had
cranked up their search for him. Propofol was rare enough they'd
throw his name in the suspect pool and, combined with the fact
the murder happened in Chicago, a task force might already be in
the city.

No sign of his photo anywhere online, which could only mean
the security cameras had failed to capture an adequate image. If
they had, his face would be plastered all over this town by now.
God had protected him. No surprise there.

Today he'd track down the widow Whelan. The interim mayor
had gone on record as stating Mrs. Whelan was welcome to stay in

the official residence until she felt up to moving. Like he was going to kick her out or something. Not if he wanted to drop the "interim" from his title.

Made life simpler for Levi. Assuming she hadn't relocated, the grieving widow would be easy to find. He'd have to do it soon, though. Too many people in the city, all seemingly looking at him. Made it hard to sleep sometimes. Best to reduce the population by one and move on.

......

Levi idled past the house, careful to keep his vision focused forward. A Chicago PD car still sat parked out front. The police no longer stayed in the vehicle but now stood at the front door. Even from the street, he could make out the black strips across the cops' badges. He gripped the steering wheel until his knuckles whitened. Why did everything have to be so hard?

Of course, he could always choose another sacrifice. If that's what God wanted. But without Mrs. Whelan's death, the mayor's demise meant nothing. The Lord might hold that against him. Best not to take that chance. Not with eternity on the line.

He accelerated away from the home. Have to find a place to stay tonight. He'd come prepared to resolve his business. Duffel bag in the back. Fresh flower, counted three times. Syringes full. Didn't look like anything was going to happen today. Congratulations, Mrs. Whelan. You get to spend one more day on this—

The white blur in his peripheral vision slammed into his back passenger door. The SUV spun into oncoming traffic, and Levi fought to maintain control as his view whirled and blurred. A blue minivan swerved and dodged, the kids in the back wide-eyed. Honking somewhere off to the right, now left. An impact just behind his door caused the side airbag to deploy. His head snapped to the side. The SUV stopped, and he listened to his breathing. Slow and distant like it came from somewhere else. The smell of burnt rubber and gunpowder drifted through. Fragments of glass plinked somewhere behind him.

He worked his eyes open and shut repeatedly, trying to focus on something, anything. His left arm and shoulder were numb. Side airbag. He shook his head, trying to understand what had just happened. Pain flared through his neck, and bits of glass from the shattered rear window fell from his hair. Bright red splotches appeared on his hands and shirt as blood dripped from somewhere on his face. He looked in the mirror and tried to concentrate. A haze surrounded him, and he pressed his eyes closed again.

Why, God?

His vision morphed from double to hazy to normal. He pushed the back of his hand against the cut on his chin and forced the door open, waiting to build the strength to stand.

"You okay, buddy?"

A bus driver.

"Just sit there," the man said. "I'll call an ambulance. Man, you blew right through that stop sign. It wasn't my fault, right?"

Levi pulled himself out of the SUV and braced against a light post. Pain flared around his body as the adrenaline faded. He looked at his vehicle, then at the bus. Passengers were getting off, and several moved in his direction. Other cars slowed to look. He had to leave. Get out of there.

The bus driver leaned in closer. "Not my fault, right?"

"What? Yes. I mean no, not your fault."

The driver wiped his brow. "Good. You tell them that, okay? Tell them it wasn't my fault. Man, you scared me good."

Levi pulled his hand away from his chin and looked at the dried blood. "Nothing a Band-Aid won't fix." He pulled his phone from his pocket. "I guess I should call my insurance agent. Everybody on the bus okay?"

The man looked back. "I think so. I'll check."

Levi waited until the driver climbed in his bus, then held the phone to his ear and turned away. He took a few steps, moving away from the accident. The onlookers stared and pointed at the crushed back of the SUV, ignoring him. A police car crawled toward the accident, its horn and siren failing to move the traffic any faster.

The duffel bag was in there among the debris. No time. Within moments, he was around the corner and in a taxi, headed ... where? Widow Whelan would have to wait, but not long. God had sent a warning. The Lord was impatient and angry. Full of wrath. But Levi could fix everything. Had to. Get back on track. Buy some time. And he knew how.

Finish his business in Nashville. Do it right this time.

And do it now.

31

"I didn't do anything," Anthony Talbot said.

"Could you please stop saying that?" Maggie said. "I've heard it for two days now. I get it."

Clay McGraw's lawyer sat next to Talbot and conspicuously kept his hands below the table. "My client has told you everything he knows. If you have evidence to the contrary, present it and charge him. Otherwise, I'll ask a judge to release him this afternoon."

Jeremy rubbed his eyes and stared from the other side of the one-way mirror. "Come on, Maggie. Ask him again why he was hiding in the back of that truck."

Maggie straightened the papers on the table. "Your time's running out to cooperate, Mr. Talbot."

The man leaned forward. "I didn't do anything."

"Fine. We'll have you transferred to a cell. There'll be enough charges filed by the end of the day to hold you for a while. Your daughter's told us enough to take you to a federal grand jury. At least one of your kids has a conscience."

Talbot tilted his head. "What's that supposed to mean?"

"Good call, Maggie," Jeremy whispered.

She folded her hands together. "Your son, Mr. Talbot, is a serial killer. But you already knew that, didn't you?"

Talbot's mouth opened, and he placed a hand on his chest. "What?"

"Yep. Quite the family you've got there. Dad's a smuggler. Mom's a ... well, we haven't got that figured out yet. Son's a murderer. Looks to me like Lena's the only one halfway normal."

"Cody's not like that," Talbot said. "He's a pharmacist. His mother told me he was looking for a job."

"Mr. Talbot," his lawyer said, "perhaps it's best you not say anything. We'll listen to what they want to tell us, but you need to keep your mouth closed. They're looking for ways to twist your words."

"Your son didn't tell you himself?" Maggie asked.

Talbot's tongue darted through his lips, and he ran a palm across the stubble on his leathery face. "If I talk, what's in it for me?"

"Talk?" his lawyer said. "There will be no talking. As your attorney, it's my duty to remind you—"

The look he received from his client kept him from continuing.

"What's in it for you?" Maggie said. "Nothing. I promise to do everything I can to make sure you never see the outside of a federal penitentiary. But for Lena, maybe I can do something."

"Uh-huh," Talbot said. "She got me into this mess. Let her take care of herself."

"She's your daughter. Don't you care what happens to her?"

The wrinkles on Talbot's face doubled. "I gave her everything, and this is how she repays me? Falsely accusing me of her own crimes? She'll get what she deserves."

Maggie leapt to her feet, upending her chair in the process. "Mr. Talbot, you have the opportunity to do something decent. Probably for the first time in a very long time. But that doesn't matter to you, does it? So let me make this simple. Your buddy McGraw already cut his deal. He's prepared to tell us everything he knows."

Talbot shrugged. "Good for him. Your problem is he doesn't know much. I'm good at reading people. If I was doing anything illegal, and I'm not saying I was, I'm not stupid enough to tell that idiot anything he didn't need to know."

She nodded. "No, Mr. Talbot. I don't think you're stupid. You're a businessman, right? Anything to make money. People, cattle, no difference."

"I didn't do anything."

Heat flashed through Jeremy, and he squeezed his fists, fighting the urge to bang them against the glass.

Maggie slid a black-and-white photograph to Talbot. "Long time ago."

The man stared at the picture, placed it face down on the table and slid the photo back. "Everything was easier then. Just me and Charlene against the world."

She flipped the image over. "Was it? So how did life get complicated?"

"Things happen."

"Yeah, they do. What things have you done, Mr. Talbot?"

"I think I'm finished here."

"You didn't know about your son, did you?"

Talbot looked at the table and tapped a finger on his temple. "Cody? Hardly know him, except what his mother tells me."

"Bet it was hard, not being there while he grew up. But of course, you had to make the money to support them. We have your wife's bank account records. We know you were providing for them."

"Family's important."

Jeremy grinned. So it *was* him.

"Sure is," Maggie said. She replaced her chair and sat. "Look at the way you sacrificed for them. Living in Mexico all these years.

Suffering for them. A good Christian woman like Charlene's got to appreciate that. Even if what you're doing is illegal."

Talbot jerked his head. "Leave her out of it."

"She doesn't know, does she? What do you tell her, Anthony? That you're still working for the oil company? Maybe she'd like to meet Lena?"

Talbot banged the table. "I want to talk to my lawyer alone. I'm not saying another word."

"No problem. Want a priest too? They say confession is good for the soul. I'll have an officer escort you two to another room. You know where to find me when you're ready to talk. Oh, one more thing, Mr. Talbot."

Jeremy's breath fogged the glass. Get him, Maggie.

She scrunched her forehead and sighed. "If you could give your attorney the details on how you'd like us to handle Charlene's remains, that'd be great."

The man's eyes widened, and his mouth fell open. "What?"

Maggie tilted her head. "I'm so sorry to be the one to tell you. Your wife is dead, Mr. Talbot. Murdered by your son. Crazy world, huh?" She turned to leave the room. "Again, you know where to find me. Help us. Don't help us. Your call. Either way, you're done. The only question is what you think should happen to your wife's murderer. Have a nice day, Mr. Talbot."

Jeremy met her in the hallway. "You okay?"

She leaned against the wall. "Yeah, fine. When he said he didn't care about his daughter, I wanted to reach across the table and rip his throat out."

He chuckled. "You hid it well."

"Uh-huh. I'll get a team digging into Talbot's finances. He's got to have money holed up somewhere, probably in Mexico. Most banks there wouldn't ask questions."

"You think he gave his kid money too?"

She shrugged. "It fits. We've been wondering where Cody gets his cash. Maybe dear old dad is helping him out."

"It may fit, but it doesn't make sense. As far as we're aware, Cody doesn't know his father exists."

"Yeah, well, maybe Charlene passes the money on to him. Let's at least rule out the possibility." Her phone vibrated, and she pulled it from her jacket pocket. "Yeah. Uh-huh ... uh-huh ... okay, and you're sure about this? Right ... got it. We'll be on the next flight."

"What's up?"

"Heading to Chicago. They've got Talbot's car. His kill bag, GPS, all of it."

"And him?"

"No. Not yet."

He tapped his finger on his leg. "Why would he hang out there? And where's he been? I mean, he kills the mayor, God knows why, and then stays in the one place he knows we're looking? Doesn't add up."

She headed for the elevator. "You staying here or coming to Chicago?"

He trotted after her. "Is that an official FBI invitation?"

"Dutch. You pay your own way, and I'll let you sit in."

He pushed the elevator button for the building's lobby. "I've had worse dates."

......

At Chicago's downtown FBI office, Maggie shuffled through the reports, scrutinizing each page before handing it over to Jeremy. The information from the crime lab provided enough evidence to convict Cody Talbot if they could find him.

His duffel bag contained Propofol and syringes. That was good. There was also a box holding a white daisy. That was better. Talbot was planning to kill again. A city bus had stopped him. For now. Divine intervention? He'd take it.

"Maggie, he might have been there."

She glanced at him, keeping her head tilted toward the paper in her hands. "Been where?"

"Brattleboro. His GPS had a hotel there stored in its memory."

She reached for the paper, but Jeremy held it away from her.

"Hold on," he said. "The GPS didn't store route information. The lab says it's a privacy thing. It doesn't keep that data unless you tell it to. But the GPS does hold onto addresses you key in unless you manually delete them. He didn't."

"Are you going to tell me what addresses were in there, or do I have to guess?"

He took a deep breath. "The hotel in Vermont was the same one you held your meetings at."

Maggie's eyes widened. "The lobby has three security cameras. If he's already been there, we'll get a clean photo."

He nodded. "Assuming the hotel saves their security tapes long enough."

"What else is in there?"

"Chicago mayor's residence. No surprise there, but it does confirm our suspicions. Kill the mayor to get the publicity. He doesn't fit the requirements, though, so he has to find a real victim. The daisy wouldn't have lasted much longer, and he had to know the autopsy would point us to him. He was ready to kill again."

"Some girl has no idea how lucky she is. Mrs. Whelan?"

He shrugged. "Probably never know for sure. Better make certain they tighten her security, just in case. Talbot's most likely moved on to another target in another city. Too much visibility around here right now."

"Nashville maybe. I've got to talk Bailey into a protective detail on Claire Lawson. Anything else on the GPS?"

"Nothing useful."

She riffled through the stack of papers. "Local cops are checking the traffic cameras for possible photos. The police chief is holding a press conference in a couple of hours to confirm Talbot as a person of interest in the mayor's murder. The plan is to ask the public if anyone got video or pictures of the accident scene."

"Thank goodness for cell phones. What about the SUV?"

"Tracked back to a car dealer outside of Sarasota. Registered to a woman who died almost twenty years ago. The dealer's in a world of trouble, but it doesn't look like he's going to be much help to us."

"And Kathryn Stanton?"

Maggie sighed. "Multiple hair samples were collected from his vehicle. None of them match her."

Jeremy shook his head. "It never stops."

"We don't know for sure that Stanton is dead."

Yeah, we do. "You're right. Until there's evidence to the contrary."

She closed her eyes and tilted her head back. "You ever get tired of this? Dealing with death all the time?"

He stared into space. "They tell you to focus on the positive. The deaths you're preventing. Doesn't always work that way."

Maggie intertwined her fingers, focusing on them as if nothing else mattered. "I look at Rebecca and see so much happiness. And I think that one day she'll understand what the world's really like, and that joy will go away. And there's not a thing I can do about it."

Jeremy placed his fingers on her hand, not squeezing or stroking, just … there. "You're a great mom. You'll do the right thing. I know you will."

"Charlene Talbot might have been a great mother to Cody. Look where it got the two of them."

Jeremy sat straighter. "Hey, none of that. You're talking about a psychopath in a completely dysfunctional family. That has nothing to do with you and Rebecca."

"Yeah, I know. But do you think Charlene Talbot ever looked at her son and thought he would become a serial killer? I doubt it. I don't want to get into the environment versus genetics discussion, but you've got to believe that some people are just plain evil. Maybe from birth, maybe something changes them."

"You remember the room he grew up in? There was no joy there, Maggie. Maybe it didn't have anything to do with the way he turned out. But somehow I don't picture drawings of pippapotamuses on their refrigerator."

Maggie chuckled and shook her head several times. "Okay. Enough psychoanalysis and pity for one day. Let's get back to work. If we don't pick up the pace, we'll have to burn the midnight oil at both ends."

"I've got to start writing these down."

"What?"

"I said we need to start right now."

Her cell phone vibrated. "Uh-huh. Oh. Anthony Talbot wants to talk to me. Says he's prepared to share information."

"Back to Texas?"

She frowned and slipped the phone back into her jacket. "Not if I can help it. I'll set a video call up from here. Want to sit in?"

He crossed his arms and gave his best now-what-do-you-think look.

"Okay, but one word, and you're out of there. Clear?"

"Not a peep."

She paused and arched an eyebrow. "And no writing questions on my notepad either."

32

The drive to Evansville drained Levi. Every car an unmarked state trooper. Every stop a game of cat and mouse. At a gas station outside Effingham, a woman with two young children stared at him while he filled up. She knew. He could see it in her eyes. Would've been quicker to go through Louisville, but they might be covering that route. Watching for him.

He perched on the end of the motel bed, his knees almost touching the cracked old dresser. An ancient TV sat bolted onto the top, its remote control glued to the nightstand.

Nearly one o'clock in the morning. The top news stories would cycle back through in a moment. No more secrets. Everyone knew now. His name. The girls. The Supreme Court. Finally.

A weather map filled the screen, colored lines swooping across the nation. Unseasonably cool in the eastern states, mild in the Southwest, and rainy in the Pacific Northwest. His stomach shot an eruption of queasiness through his torso, and he swallowed hard, forcing the bile down.

The news ditty played, and the camera zoomed in on the anchorwoman, her normally cheery smile replaced by a "serious news" sternness. An image of the former mayor of Chicago hovered in the corner of the screen.

"Here's the latest on this breaking story out of Illinois," she said. "A man the police are referring to as a "person of interest" in the death of Chicago Mayor Whelan is apparently on the run after a vehicle accident."

The view on the television shifted to a video of Levi's SUV being loaded onto the back of a tow truck. Barriers had been set up to keep the public at a distance, but there were at least two dozen people working the scene. The image shifted to an older man with multiple microphones held inches from his face. The caption on the screen identified him as Chicago's Chief of Police.

"What we know at this time," he said, "leads us to believe the operator of this vehicle, Cody Talbot, has information on Mayor Whelan's homicide. We just want to talk to him. Surveillance cameras provided an image which we will supply to the media."

Levi's photo filled the screen, a black-and-white image with the cut on his chin clearly visible. He leaned until his eyes were inches from the television, squinting to reduce the brightness. The picture was grainy but passable. Anyone looking close enough might recognize him.

The Police Chief reappeared, and Levi jerked back, startled by the transition.

"Sir," one of the reporters asked, "is it true Talbot is the prime suspect in a series of killings across the country?"

The officer shook his head. "I don't know where you're getting your information, but at this time we simply want to talk to him."

Another reporter jumped in. "Sources tell us his vehicle had a bag with Propofol. Can you confirm that?"

"Look," the Chief said, "I'm not going to get into the details of an ongoing investigation. When we have more information to share, I'll let you know."

The serious anchorwoman was back, holding papers in her hand as she read from the teleprompter. "Since that press conference, we've learned Cody Talbot is indeed the prime suspect in a string of murders across the country. We've got our own expert, former FBI Special Agent Richard Halls, here with us to explain the situation."

The camera pulled back to show a well-dressed man sitting at the anchor's desk, nodding gravely at the viewers. "Young women across the country slain. Theories this is some sort of vendetta against Christians. The Supreme Court receiving body parts in the mail. The mayor of Chicago brutally murdered. All textbook serial killer actions, escalating to gain the publicity he craves. In the end, most of these psychotics want the same thing. Attention."

The anchorwoman wrinkled her forehead and nodded. "These theories that for some reason he's targeting young women in churches, why?"

The man intertwined his fingers and leaned toward the camera. "Perhaps they weren't worthy enough. Maybe God told him to do it. Possibly a traumatic experience at a church at some point in his life. We won't know for sure until we catch him, and maybe not even then. I mean, we're obviously dealing with a very depraved individual here."

"So why does he want attention? Wouldn't it be better to lay low, protect himself?"

"Oh, some serial killers do. But most need the limelight. Look at the Unabomber. We'd have probably never caught him if it wasn't for his manifesto. The Daisy Killer is no different. An egomaniac who knows he'll eventually be caught, and when he is, his picture will be splashed all over the news. That's what he wants. His moment of glory."

"No!" Levi screamed. "Not me. Never me. Open your eyes. They're sacrifices, not victims. Don't you see? Why can't you understand?"

He dove for the remote control and turned off the TV before sliding onto the floor. He knelt beside the hotel bed. Interlocked his fingers. Here's the church, and here's the steeple. Fingers throbbing. Squeeze tighter. Things were happening too fast. Spinning out of control. Questions, but no answers.

A day and a half since the accident. Finding a new car on the Internet had been easy enough, but buying from an individual was dangerous. People look at the cash, but they remember the person too. His photo all over the media. Everyone searching for him. Answers? No. A miracle. That's what he needed.

Lord. Please. Safety to Nashville. I'll clean this up. Fix it. You know I will. Just get me there. Please, God. Let me finish what I started. What You started. I can do it. I want to do it.

For You.

......

A tapping sound disturbed him, and he willed his eyes to open. He lifted his head and wiped dried drool off his cheek, gathering himself. Sunshine streamed through the worn curtains. His spirit was willing, but his flesh was weak. He pushed himself up from the floor. Stiff muscles complained about the car accident. Or sleeping on the ground. The knocking came again, and he staggered to his feet, brushing the sleep from his eyelids.

"Yes?"

A muffled voice on the other side of the door. "Housekeeping."

He glanced at the clock. Almost noon. The maid or a SWAT team?

He peeked out the curtain at the woman standing there. Anyone could be hiding in her linen cart. A sniper under her sheets and towels. "I'm good. Thanks."

He listened as she walked to the next room and repeated the ritual. At the sink, he splashed icy water on his face. No time for a shower. About three hours to Nashville. He'd have to hurry.

Claire Lawson was his first mistake. One that needed to be corrected. Erased.

......

Jeremy crossed his arms and pressed his back against the chair. Keeping his mouth shut was as hard as he'd expected it to be.

Maggie adjusted the laptop's angle and activated the camera. Anthony Talbot and his lawyer fidgeted on her screen. "I'm here," she said. "You said you wanted to talk, so talk."

Talbot leaned forward, a smirk across his face. "What's the matter? Afraid to be in the same room with me? Can't control your temper?"

"You're not worth the plane ticket. I know your type, Mr. Talbot. I was married to one. Napoleon complex. Little guy. Acts tough around women. Got to control them, right? Like your daughter and wife. But not the boy. No, Cody's different. Going to carry on the family name. Nice plan except for one thing. Lethal injection. Ever hear of it?"

Talbot rubbed the thick gray whiskers sprouting from his chin. "Look, I don't care what you think of me. I provide a service that customers are willing to pay for. Quite handsomely as it turns out. It's the American way, except south of the border. But my son, that's different. If he did what you say he did to Charlene, I've got a problem with him."

Maggie exhaled, propped both elbows on the table, and tapped her thumbs together. "So you're claiming you don't know anything about the murders?"

"Listen, Maggie—"

"Agent Keeley."

"Sure, Maggie. The boy doesn't even know I'm alive."

She tilted her head, narrowed her eyes, and pointed at Talbot. "We know that's not true. You went to the house on numerous occasions."

"Yep. His mother didn't want him to know so she kept him locked in his room. I haven't seen the kid since he was a few months old. Things got a little too messy, so I spent some time in

Mexico building up my business. Charlene pretended she didn't know what I was doing, but she knew. Didn't want the boy to have anything to do with me. She didn't have any problem taking my money, though."

"Things got messy? How so?"

He shrugged. "You saw the place. She started to get real strict about religious stuff after Cody was born. Said she wanted the boy brought up right. No beer, no cussin', that kind of thing. A couple of months later, she found out I was visiting someone who didn't mind my bad habits. I did the right thing and left her."

Maggie's lips drew into a tight, straight line. "So leaving a mother and baby is the right thing?"

Talbot scratched his whiskers again. "Didn't want the boy to hear us fighting all the time. What was I supposed to do?"

Maggie shook her head. "Oh, I don't know. Maybe put your family ahead of yourself? But that's me. If it was so bad, why'd you keep coming back?"

"At first, just to make sure she had enough money to take care of herself and the boy. But later, I figured out I missed her. Maybe even still loved her. Funny, huh? Sometimes the cash was just an excuse to see her. I'd take her gifts too. Jewelry, candy, flowers, stuff girls like. Plus, she was lonely, and we were still husband and wife after all." He winked at Maggie.

"Did she know about Lena?"

He glanced away from the camera. "No. I didn't want to hurt her."

"Awfully big of you."

"Maggie, Agent Keeley, I knew Charlene. She might turn a blind eye to me, but not to the boy. I guarantee you she didn't know what he's doing."

Maggie's voice deepened. "So you're not concerned about all the other murders. Or the girls he's going to kill if we don't catch him."

"You think I'm a monster. You got kids, Agent Keeley?"

"Yeah, a daughter."

"You'd do anything for her, wouldn't you?"

"Of course."

Talbot rubbed his hands together. "Well, Cody's my boy. In spite of what he's done—allegedly—he's still my son. I know I'm not in any position to ask, but—"

"If you think I'm going to treat him—"

He held his palms up. "I'm not asking for anything for him. Lena. Go easy on her."

Maggie narrowed her eyes. "Why the sudden change of heart?"

"She's the only piece of me I've got left."

"So you'll help us?"

Talbot glanced at his attorney before continuing, "I gave Cody the money."

Maggie rolled her eyes. "That's all you've got? We already suspected you supplied the funds. The FBI's digging through the quagmire Mexico calls a banking system now. We'll find the money."

Talbot looped his hands behind his head and leaned back. "Cody doesn't know where it came from. No idea his long-lost daddy gave the money to him. Kind of a graduation present."

"How much?"

"Half a million."

Jeremy grunted and shifted in his seat.

Maggie's eyes opened wide. "I'm supposed to believe someone gets that kind of money and doesn't question where it came from?"

The old man grinned. "His mother always told him the Good Lord would provide. The kid finally gets out of college, and one day, an envelope shows up with an ATM card and a congratulations note. He uses it a few times. Finds out the card's legit. Several months go by, and nobody comes looking for it. You know many people who would walk away from that? Would you?"

Maggie leaned forward. "An ATM card?"

Talbot crossed his arms over his chest. "Yep. Furnished by a bank in Mexico. Of course, that means he has to pay transaction fees when he makes a withdrawal, but I don't suppose the boy minds too much."

"You're offering access to Cody's account?"

"I'll give you the banking information. You do what you want with it. In return, you agree not to prosecute Lena."

Maggie shook her head. "I can't make that deal. She knew what was going on and didn't report it. There's some culpability there. I'll talk to the DA. We'll work something out."

Talbot frowned. "Suit yourself. Give my condolences to the next girl's family."

Jeremy tapped her shoulder, and Maggie muted the laptop and angled it away.

"Don't say it," she said.

"You've got to cut a deal. Don't gamble another girl's life. If we can catch Cody Talbot before he kills again, it'll be worth whatever you have to give up. You don't want to prosecute Lena anyway."

"What was the deal, Jeremy?"

"That you wouldn't press charges against—"

She wrinkled her forehead. "What was *our* deal?"

"Um, that I'd keep my mouth shut."

"Dinner's on you. A fancy one. Now, if I could finish my call ..."

He motioned toward the laptop and drew his hand across his mouth, zipping his lips shut.

She cleared her throat before continuing. "Here's my offer, Mr. Talbot. I want everything. Bank accounts, testimony against McGraw, points of entry across the border, contacts in Mexico. All of it. Nothing and I mean nothing, held back."

Talbot nodded. "And Lena walks?"

"I'll talk to the DA. Get my boss in DC to make some calls if I have to. If you're straight with us, bottom line is that yeah, she walks."

33

Levi stopped at a Walmart in Bowling Green, Kentucky, and hustled in from the cold. He turned up his shirt collar and kept his chin tucked, telling himself it was enough disguise. Stealth had to take a back seat to speed. He dropped a duffel bag, pruning shears, and flowers in the cart then hurried to the electronics counter.

He needed a new GPS. Using the maps function on his phone meant he had to keep it turned on, which made the device trackable through cell towers. A prepaid phone was a possibility, but it could be traced just as easily.

An older woman stood behind the counter. "Help you?"

Levi hunched over the glass and pointed downward. "I'd like to buy that GPS."

"You'll have to pay for it back here."

"Okay. Can I—" *That's the third time that man has walked past.* "Can I pay for everything here?"

The employee nodded, and Levi waited as she scanned each item. He declined the additional warranty on the GPS, paid, and paced out of the store with his purchases. Half a dozen steps into the parking lot, he stopped. His SUV was gone. Stolen? Chest pounding, he scanned the lot. A loud metallic clang behind him. Gun? He jerked his head around. Shopping cart. Had to find his car. Not where he left it parked, right over ...

His arms fell to his side, and he exhaled into the afternoon breeze. Sweat chilled on his face as he remembered his SUV from Florida was sacrificed to the Chicago Transit Authority. His new auto, a forest green Jeep Cherokee, waited where he left it, beeping cheerfully when he pushed the unlock button on his key fob.

Inside, he hit the door locks and used his phone to search for local veterinary clinics. There were dozens in the area, and it took time to find one that would work. Time he didn't have. No, no, no, this one. Their office closed at noon today. Levi punched the address in his GPS and waited for the new maps to load. His fingers drummed on the dash, and he peered in his rearview mirror. That man again. Go. Now.

Thirty-five minutes later, on an isolated back road, he arrived at the clinic. As far as he could tell, no one had followed him. The veterinarian used an old house as her office. No cars sat in the parking lot, which had spent its previous life as the front yard of the tiny home. Perfect. He pulled his Jeep around back, blocking it from view as much as possible. No signs of an alarm system, but that didn't mean much. Out here, a shotgun was all they needed.

He left the engine running and kicked the back door four times before it splintered. No noise or flashing lights. Just a mudroom, appropriately named. A door off to his right was locked, and he kicked it open, pain shooting from heel to knee.

The office area. A desk, chair, files, and ... there. Drugs. A glass cabinet on the wall contained medications, and he threw a stapler, sending shards of glass and white pill containers flying around the room.

He searched bottle after bottle, tossing them until he found one he could use. Ketamine. A general anesthetic, not as powerful as Propofol, but it would have to do. Just need to use more of it. He grabbed some syringes on the way to his car and tossed everything in the bag on the back seat floorboard.

A little over an hour later, he was in Nashville, parked outside Claire Lawson's apartment. Love the new place. Internet access and a credit card. That's all it took to find you.

A few vehicles sat outside her building, but no one in sight. That'd change soon as people arrived home from work. He reached behind the seat, grabbed his supplies, and prepped three syringes. Work time. Knock this out and head for Florida. His right leg still ached and throbbed, the door at the vet clinic having done its damage. He limped up the stairs to the second floor and scanned the hallway. Nice and quiet.

"Hey, man. What's the deal with that girl?"

Levi jerked his hand back and spun around. A man holding a garbage bag stood a few doors down. "Excuse me?"

"She's pretty popular, huh?"

Levi moved away from the door. "I'm not sure what you mean."

The man grinned. "You're the third guy there today. I know her boyfriend." He winked. "But I won't say anything. The guy in the suit, new to me. And now you. Busy day."

"Yeah. Maybe I'll come back later." He turned to leave.

"Hey. You looking to score some stuff?"

"Um, no."

The man walked toward Levi. "You sure? Got good weed down in my van."

Levi moved toward the steps. "I told you I didn't want anything."

Claire's door opened slightly, the chain still visible. "Everything okay out there?"

He froze, his back to the door.

"Yeah, girl," the man said. "That dude's looking for you, though."

"Oh. The other agent told me someone else would be by this evening to introduce himself. Can I see your FBI ID?"

The man in the hall backed toward his apartment; his hands extended toward Levi. "Hey. Just kidding about the weed, you know?"

Levi listened as the man locked his door. He looked at the stairwell and gripped his duffel, debating. Might never get another chance. Dangerous, though. But God would protect him.

His thumb tapped against his pants leg, and he turned toward Claire, wondering if he looked FBI-ish enough. "You've got some interesting neighbors."

"Tell me about it. Looks like you guys get a lot more casual at night, huh?"

Something about her was different. Oh. New hair color. Looks good. "Sorry, been a long day. Undercover."

"Your identification?"

He walked toward her. "Sure. Got it right here." He moved his hand to the back pocket of his jeans, turned sideways, and threw his body against the door. The chain snapped easier than he expected, and the momentum carried him into the apartment. He caught himself on a sofa's armrest and looked back at the door.

Claire was on her right side on the ground, moaning, but not moving. He shoved the door closed with his foot and opened the duffel bag. He found the three syringes and popped the caps off, taking his eyes off her long enough to ensure he didn't stick himself. Even from this vantage point, he could see the blood starting to pool on the carpet. Broken nose probably. She won't feel it much longer.

He crept to her and squatted, electricity shooting up his leg to his hip. He planted a hand on the floor to steady himself and brushed away her hair to expose a patch of skin. That color looks good on you. He laid two needles on the carpet and pressed a third into her neck, slowly shoving the plunger toward his sacrifice.

The daisy. Careless.

He yanked the syringe out. Half gone. He shuffled to his bag and found the white daisy. She loves me. She loves me not. She loves … faster. Yes. No. Yes. No.

Claire stirred, and he snatched most of the petals off the flower and threw them on the ground. "Yes. No. Yes. No. Sorry about that, but I counted five times. You don't love me. You're no better than Sondra. See, God saves those who love. That's why He picked me to fix things."

He tossed the flower stem in the direction of the bag and spun back around. She was trying to push herself to a sitting position.

"No, no, no. You just sleep."

She turned her head, and he saw the trail of blood running from her nose, across her lips, and dripping off her chin. He picked up the partially used syringe and grabbed her left arm. "Shh. It's okay."

Her right arm twitched, and he glanced in time to see it swinging toward him. He leaned back, anticipating the blow heading toward his skull. Her arm stopped short of his head, and he turned to—

A blast sent him reeling backward. His ears rang, and the acrid odor of gunpowder filled the room.

She was on her knees now, squeezing her eyes open and shut. The weapon swung closer, and he crawled out of sight behind the couch. Another explosion blew a piece of the sofa across the room. He looked at the exit, seemingly so far away now. She moaned again, and he ran.

He yanked on the door as the wall beside him erupted, blasting specks of drywall in his face. The humid air in the hallway slapped him, and he jumped down the steps to his car. A woman in the parking lot yelled something, but his ears still battled the gunshot.

Once in his vehicle, a quick once-over confirmed no major injuries. Specks of blood on his face from the drywall and his leg burned and pulsated, but nothing required immediate attention. He sped from the apartments, then slowed, careful to maintain an even speed and obey traffic lights.

Why, God? Was she not an acceptable sacrifice?

Find the interstate and get out of Nashville. Ditch the Jeep. Spend some time thinking. Planning. Praying. The gunshots had been another warning from God. No question about it. The coppery taste of blood soaked into his lips, and he—

Headlights lit up the interior of his car as another vehicle pulled close to his back bumper. Police? He glanced in the rearview mirror as an old van pulled around him and sped past, its back windows blocked with trash bags. Just a nut with road rage.

He drove toward the setting sun until he hit Arkansas, passing the truck stops and motels of West Memphis before turning north. Tonight, he'd find another car, get some sleep, and do more research. Rethink his strategy. Move on to the final phase.

Traffic on the interstate thinned, and the night surrounded him, his headlights poking through the blackness. The ringing in his ears was gone, the ache in his leg a memory. His battle scars were healing, preparing him for the next skirmish. This time, he'd be ready. Changes had to be made to his schedule, but atonement couldn't wait.

His problems had started with her, and they'd end with her. Margaret Keeley would learn. We all have to make sacrifices for our nation.

Onward, Christian soldiers, marching as to war,
With the cross of Jesus going on before!
Christ, the royal Master, leads against the foe;
Forward into battle see His banners go!

34

Jeremy checked the time before answering his cell phone. Two-fifteen. Nothing good happens at two-fifteen in the morning. "Hey, Maggie. Everything okay?"

"I'm booked on a flight to Nashville in a couple of hours. Won't be here when you get up."

He sat up and rubbed his eyes. "Nashville? Something happen?"

"Yeah. Got a call about twenty minutes back. An attempt was made on Claire Lawson's life a few hours ago. We're sure it was Talbot."

His heart leapt. "Is she okay?

"Busted nose, bruised, and a little bit of a hangover, but otherwise fine. I'd say she got the best end of the deal."

Jeremy swung to a sitting position. "Talbot?"

"Gone. We've alerted law enforcement in all surrounding states, and we've got a half-decent description of what he's driving. He'll be looking to dump the car as soon as he can, so we're giving priority to stolen vehicle calls."

He walked to the window and pulled open the curtain. The orange glow of the hotel's parking lot lights illuminated the room. "What happened? I thought she was supposed to be under protection."

"Tomorrow. Or today, I suppose. One agent had already stopped by to introduce himself. The other came after the incident. Just bad luck."

Jeremy took several breaths before responding. "Yeah. Bad luck. How'd she get away?"

"She didn't. He did. The short version is she was dazed but alert enough to get off three shots."

"Maggie, she—"

"I know. We've got round the clock coverage on her now."

He flipped on the bathroom light. "What time's your flight?"

"Meet me in the lobby in thirty. Already reserved you a seat on the plane. Assuming you want to go?"

"Will do."

He hung up the phone and leaned on the counter. The harsh glare of the lights over the vanity made him look pale. Dark circles puffed under his eyes. His abs were asleep, tucked under a midsection that enjoyed its recent surge in fast food and late nights. Every woman's dream.

The net was closing, and it was only a matter of time. Cody Talbot was definitely on the downside of the bell curve, making mistakes, becoming desperate. They'd get him. Jeremy was sure of that now. The question was, would anyone else die? Claire Lawson wouldn't. For today, that'd be enough.

......

In the eighteen hours since the attack, FBI agents from Memphis and Knoxville had created a temporary command center in the Secret Service offices near the state's capitol building. Police departments across the Mid-South were on alert, and helicopters scouted outlying areas of Nashville for any green SUVs. Jeremy listened to the radio chatter and watched the commotion. Would this organized chaos be happening if Chicago's mayor hadn't been killed? He knew the answer but wished he didn't.

The door opened, and Claire Lawson was escorted into the room. Jeremy stood, extended his hand, and nodded. "Miss Lawson."

She walked past his hand and wrapped her arms around him. "Thank you, Mr. Winter."

He patted her on the back. "Yes, ma'am. For what?"

She pulled away and dabbed her eye. "Telling me to protect myself. If you hadn't ..."

Maggie introduced herself and motioned Claire to a seat at the conference table. "I understand you're in the market for a new sofa."

Claire grinned, sniffling and running a hand under her nose. "Yeah. That's one couch that won't be bothering me again."

The tension seeped from Jeremy's shoulders. *Good. She's handling it well.*

"Miss Lawson," Maggie said, "I'm not going to ask you to go over the attack again. I can get all the information I need from the other agents. I wanted to make sure you were okay."

"I am," she said. "I'll probably take a few days off. Maybe get a cabin in the mountains while they repair my apartment. Get away for a little bit."

"Sure. Of course, we'll keep protection on you until we get Talbot."

Claire scooted to the edge of her seat. "Agent Keeley, why me? Why did he pick me? The news said he's choosing women who go to church. Why does he hate God so much?"

Jeremy clamped his teeth together. *She doesn't see this as an attack on herself. Brave young woman.*

Maggie cleared her throat. "We think we know, but I really can't share that information. I'm sorry. You may have to testify at some point. I hope you understand."

She dipped her head and clasped her hands together. "I do. I just hope ..."

He reached and grabbed Claire's hand, holding it firmly. "The FBI *will* get him, Miss Lawson. They're close."

......

The early morning adrenaline faded to late afternoon weariness. Jeremy's stomach churned from a cold coffee overdose. "Long day. Anything new on the information Anthony Talbot provided?"

Maggie stifled a yawn. "The account number checks out, and we've got some people in Mexico working with the bank now. We'll keep the account open and track the ATM card. If it gets used, we'll get notified. Only question is how quickly we'll get the updates. Things don't work as fast south of the border."

"Yeah. Hey, thanks again, Maggie."

"For what?"

"Keeping me in the loop. Letting me sit in on the case."

She smiled and shrugged. "No problem. We can use all the help we can get."

He shifted forward and placed his hands on his knees. "I've been thinking about that. I'm going home tomorrow."

Her lips parted slightly. "Home? Why?"

"Maggie, this is your case, not mine. I don't want anyone here thinking you need my help. You don't. But as long as they see me here, there'll be the possibility that—"

"Don't be an idiot. Nobody thinks that."

"I would. I mean, if I didn't know you so well."

She bit her bottom lip. "I don't care what others think."

"I do. If there's even the slightest chance that my presence here might jeopardize—"

Her phone dinged, and she held up a finger as she scanned the message. "You might want to hang around for another few hours."

"What's up?"

"They found Talbot."

35

Jeremy and Maggie stood in the motel's office, away from the windows. The green Jeep Cherokee had been spotted almost thirteen hours earlier by a Buckhannon, West Virginia, police officer. The vehicle had been under constant observation since then. The Illinois plates were tracked to a man outside Chicago, who confirmed selling the Jeep to a man resembling Cody Talbot.

A SWAT team from Pittsburgh had arrived forty-five minutes earlier and now waited two blocks away. A second squad from Columbus was on the way, and the decision had been made to hold off until they arrived. Six-thirty now, and by seven o'clock this morning, everyone would be in place.

Parker's Motel sat fifteen miles from Interstate 79 and had the appearance of a once-proud facility now struggling to stay in business. A picnic table, swing set, and free HBO no longer enticed weary travelers. The L-shaped building's rooms all faced a central parking lot. The motel backed up to a residential area, a fact that added an exponential amount of risk to the planned forcible entry.

An auto parts store across the street opened thirty minutes ago and already did a steady business. Two agents would put the shop on lockdown just before the assault began. The white storage building next to it was unoccupied, save for the FBI sniper. Local police were in position to block all traffic. The homes immediately behind the motel had been emptied, their occupants taken to a church after being searched for cell phones. The last thing the FBI needed was someone getting word out to the press too early.

"How many are left?" Maggie asked.

"Two more rooms," the motel's manager said. "Not counting the one he's in."

"Make the next call."

The two listened as the manager informed the guest in Room 6 he needed to come to the office. So far, only one person had hesitated to come, but once the manager explained he had overcharged the customer, any reluctance evaporated.

A sketch of the motel lay on the counter. Arrows and letters swooped in from two directions and converged on Room 12. Maggie traced a finger on the paper, her lips moving slightly. "I wish we knew whether or not he was in there," she said.

Jeremy checked his watch. "In less than thirty minutes, we'll know. All we can do—"

The office door opened, and the guest from Room 6 entered. Maggie showed her badge and escorted him to a back room where other lodgers waited. Once the last customers arrived, they would all be loaded into a van and driven a safe distance away. She returned to the lobby as the manager was making the last call.

"Room 14," Jeremy said. "Right next to Talbot's room. It's a couple from Michigan. That's their minivan parked next to his vehicle."

"There's a car seat in it," Maggie said. "Might have a kid with them."

"No answer," the manager said as he hung up the phone.

She tapped her finger on the counter in time with the clock on the wall. "Can't go in until we get those people out of there. Too early for housekeeping. No room service."

"Want me to go knock on the door?" the manager asked.

Maggie shook her head and gave him a quick scan. "What size shoes do you wear?"

"Maggie," Jeremy said, "you can't—"

"Can and will." Minutes later, she exited the restroom wearing sagging blue jeans, an oversized plaid shirt, and tennis shoes. She splashed cold water on her face and tousled her hair before heading out the door.

She shuffled toward Room 14, stopping twice to yawn and look over the parking lot. The tennis shoes were several sizes too big, and her pants threatened to give in to gravity at any moment. A handful of white towels concealed her service weapon. In any other situation, it would've been funny. But not this.

She passed Talbot's room, stopped at the next door, and positioned herself so she faced the entrance to the fugitive's room. She knocked on Room 14's door and yawned again.

Jeremy had his Glock in hand and strained to see what was happening. From his vantage point, he could see her talking, but the room's door remained closed. This was taking too long. His finger danced around his weapon's trigger, and he stared at the clock's second hand. Too long.

Finally, a trio exited the room and run-walked to the office, the father in his sleep pants, the mother in her robe, and their son in a diaper, his head bobbing on mom's shoulder. Maggie waited until they were almost inside before following. By the time she was back in the office, Jeremy had ushered the family into the back room. He looked at his watch.

7:06.

It would all be over within minutes if Talbot were in there. Jeremy closed his eyes in a long blink, unsure if that counted as a prayer or not.

A voice on Maggie's radio confirmed both SWAT teams were in position and ready to move. "Shut down traffic, and get everyone out of here," she said.

The hotel manager, clad in a too-tight T-shirt, boxers, and a robe tapped her shoulder. "Can I get my clothes back first?"

She stared out the front windows. "Jeremy?"

"On it." He turned to the manager. "Sir, you need to go. Now."

"Listen here," the man said, "I can't go out there dressed like this."

Maggie turned to glare at him.

"Right, I'll just get my clothes later then."

A moment of silence after he left and Maggie keyed the radio mike. "SWAT One, stand by."

"Copy."

Jeremy pointed at a white van driving out of the parking lot. "They're gone. Building should be clear." Two agents entered the auto parts store across the street. On the building next to it, he could barely make out the sniper on the roof. The SWAT team from Pittsburgh would take the lead on making entry, with the crew from Columbus acting as backup. A stun grenade would disorient Talbot while the team stormed in. With no rear windows in the room, he'd have nowhere to run.

7:10.

Maggie scooted closer to Jeremy, took a deep breath, and closed her eyes for a moment. "SWAT One," she said, "you are clear to execute."

Four SWAT members rounded the corner of the building nearest Talbot's room, with two others approaching from the opposite side. In less than a minute, the team was in position.

The squad leader stood next to Room 12's door with his back to the wall. With a black metal battering ram in his hands, the leader nodded. One of his men counted down with his gloved fingers. Three. Two. One.

A stun grenade broke the front window. Flash of light and explosion. Battering ram against the door. Yelling. The team disappeared into the room. Smoke filtered out the broken window, and seconds later, the SWAT leader keyed his mike.

"Suspect in custody."

Jeremy and Maggie ran to Room 12, her tennis shoes slapping the ground with each step. A man lay on the floor, his hands bound behind his back with plastic ties. Jeremy knelt beside him and rolled him over. A middle-aged man with a graying mustache.

"What's going on?" the suspect asked. "Who are you people?"

Maggie rubbed her hand across her face. "Sir, where'd you get the vehicle?"

"Traded a guy for it yesterday. Gave him my Buick for his Jeep. Did I do something wrong?"

"Where did you trade?"

"Over in Charleston. Listen, if he wants the Jeep back, all he has to do is ask. No need for all this excitement."

Maggie squeezed her hands into fists and spoke tersely to the lead SWAT agent. "Call it in. Have them check him out and get the details on his Buick. Get the APB broadcast as soon as possible. I'll call Director Bailey. Talbot's probably changed vehicles again by now."

"Yeah, but at least we know where he's headed," Jeremy said. "Got to be Brattleboro again. Nothing else up this way."

"Maybe," she said. "No new ATM transactions since we got the account information, so he's got to be running low on money. Never withdraws more than a few hundred at a time unless he's making a big purchase. He's due. We'll hang here until this is cleaned up, then head to D.C. until something else breaks loose."

Jeremy nodded. "Time for me to go home."

......

Two-hundred fifty miles away, Levi parked outside a Richmond, Virginia, coffee shop and logged onto their wireless network. He already had the information he needed but looking at her picture brightened his day. Margaret Keeley had been a bit more challenging to track down than most people. FBI agents must take extra precautions online.

Too bad her mother didn't. And how that woman loves to post on Facebook. Pictures, locations, it's all there. No home address, but that's no problem. Tomorrow she'll be taking her grand-daughter to school. He'd watch. Learn. He ran his fingers over her picture. Rebecca. Such a sweet little girl. So innocent and pure.

Levi closed the laptop, but he could still see her. Clear green eyes, freckles dotting her nose, frizzy red hair. He shut his eyes, imagining. She smiled at him, and he grinned back. He picked her up, spun in a circle as she giggled, and sang to her, squeezing tighter with each line.

Jesus loves the little children,
All the children of the world;
Red and yellow, black and white,
They are precious in his sight,
Jesus loves the little children of the world.

He opened his eyes and stretched his fingers. The hairs on his arms stood on end. He resisted the urge to run his hands across them. Enjoy. Savor. Taste and see.

He was doing the girl a favor, really. She'd never have to experience the sadness and depravity of the world. In a way, he was her … what? Rescuer? Yes, but so much more. Deliverer? Of course, sending her on to a peaceful eternity. He was saving her from a life that would end in sin, frustration, and death. Saving her. That's what he was doing.

And in two or three days, Rebecca's salvation would begin.

36

Jeremy eyed the two men through his apartment door's peephole. Dark windbreakers, darker sunglasses. FBI.

Surprised it took this long. He removed his pistol and laid the weapon on a table before opening the door, careful to keep his hands in plain view.

"Gentlemen," he said. "How can I help you?"

The one in front showed his identification and frowned. "Jeremy Winter?"

"Yeah, that's me."

"Mind if we make sure you're not armed?"

Jeremy raised his hands to shoulder height and smiled. "Was about to remind you to do that. My Glock is inside the apartment."

The silent agent frisked Jeremy and shook his head.

"Sir, we have a federal warrant for your arrest."

Jeremy arched his eyebrows. "Really? On what charge?"

The agent read his Miranda card and confirmed Jeremy's understanding before continuing. "Can't get into that. You'll get all the information from the US Attorney shortly."

Jeremy spun around and touched his wrists together behind his back. "Oh, I'm sure I will."

......

"Can I offer you anything?"

Jeremy clasped his hands on the table. It was the third time the woman had popped in to ask the same question. "I'm fine, thank you."

"Someone will be with you in a few minutes." She pulled the door closed and clicked the lock, leaving him alone again.

He stood, stretched, and moved about the room to work the tightness out of his legs. The space had no windows, no mirror, and no cameras he could detect. Definitely not an interrogation room, though no doubt everything said in here could be recorded. Not that he cared. He'd expected to—

The door opened, and Colonel Ramsey Cronfeld, dressed in his Marine dress blues, strode in and extended his hand. "Sorry to keep you waiting, Mr. Winter."

Jeremy shrugged and ignored the man's gesture. "No, you're not. And you don't look like a US Attorney."

Cronfeld glanced at his uniform. "No, I look like a man who will be moving into the White House soon. Campaign event this morning, another one this afternoon. Got to look good for the photos."

"Take more than that to get my vote."

"My wife tells me that every vote counts, but I think we'll make an exception in your case. And the way things are looking for you, the election should be the least of your concerns."

Jeremy sat and rested his elbows on the table. "And just how are things looking for me?"

Cronfeld remained standing and turned down the corners of his mouth. "Not good, I'm afraid. Certain people are looking into your past. Ugly phrases are being batted about. War crimes and the like. Not good at all."

"I see. Then I guess we have nothing to discuss."

"My offer is still on the table, Mr. Winter, but when I leave this room, everything is out of my hands. You're on your own."

Jeremy chuckled. "Out of your hands, huh? Somehow, I doubt that. Tell you what. I'll counter your offer. You talk to your friends. Tell them what really happened in Afghanistan. Let them know how you changed the official reports. Do that, and I might agree to go my way and not make your life even more miserable than it's gonna be."

"Your word against mine, Mr. Winter. And, unfortunately for you, I have the facts on my side."

"You want to talk facts? Fine. You killed those people, Colonel. Word *will* get out when all this starts to go public. Someone will talk, regardless of any agreement they may have signed."

Cronfeld grinned and reached for the doorknob. "Go public? Tell me, Mr. Winter, do you really expect the United States government to air their dirty laundry? A rogue FBI agent murdering Afghani civilians? Now, please enjoy your stay at one of our fine federal establishments. We won't see each other again."

"Finally, some good news. Please, give my best to your wife."

......

Sitting on the wrong side of the bars was worse than he'd imagined. A TV mounted in a far corner provided a little distraction, but the boredom overwhelmed Jeremy. How did long-term prisoners deal with this? Second day in this cell. No reading material. No personal effects. Food wasn't bad, though.

He'd thought about all those prison movies where the innocent person spends all their time working out. Getting in shape. Ready to exact their revenge when they were free again. He'd decided against it. Wouldn't be here long enough. Not if his plan played out as he expected.

The US Attorney had visited twice, each time being rather vague on the situation. Jeremy had the distinct impression they were making this up as they went. If he were still here tomorrow, he'd have to get his own lawyer. At least get someone new to talk to.

Maggie had come right away. Who else was he going to phone with his one call? She wanted to take vacation time. Talk to her boss and convince him to speak on Jeremy's behalf. Whom Director Bailey was supposed to speak to hadn't exactly been decided.

At this point, they'd have to presumably outrank Cronfeld's wife, Senator Diane Morgans, or at least want to tangle with her. With only five months left until the election, she easily outpaced all other candidates. Barring a major stumble, she'd be the next POTUS. No one in DC would want to risk her wrath.

Jeremy had talked Maggie into waiting. Give his plan a chance, and if the strategy didn't work, then she could start her phone calls. Talk to Bailey and the media and whomever else would listen. Get the truth out there front and center for the world to see.

Wouldn't matter. He understood what Maggie didn't. The forces in play would never allow the story to get out. His hope—their hope—rested with a frightened Afghani immigrant.

If Homa Nezam didn't follow through, he was finished.

37

Levi pulled into the bank's ATM lane, fidgeting while waiting his turn. He checked his mirror and practiced looking friendly. Broad smile, eyes open wide. She'd like him. He was sure of it.

The car ahead left, and he idled forward. He'd need to get some extra cash. Little girls looked like they were expensive. Not that she'd be around long, but still, a new dress might be nice. Eight hundred dollars was the limit here, but this was the third bank he'd been to this morning.

He pulled away and turned toward Milford, propping a pink teddy bear in the passenger seat. Girls like pink things. Next to the stuffed animal lay a colorful bouquet of spring flowers. A lovely gift for someone he'd never know.

He switched on his wipers as a light mist sprinkled the windshield. Gray clouds hurried across the sky. Low, rumbling thunder nipped at their heels. A dreary day. He grabbed the bear and held the plush animal next to his face, moving his finger so the bear's pink arm waved at him. Who could be sad with a toy like this?

School got out at four o'clock, but he wanted to be there by three. Make sure he got a good spot to watch from. Nobody would be walking today. Not in this weather. Grandma would be in her white Mercury Marquis, and he needed to be in position.

He drove past the school, turned left at the next street, and stopped halfway down the block. Across from the school was a small cemetery, well-kept by the church behind it. Ashen tombstones planted in neat rows. Plastic flowers, most faded, struggled to bring a dash of cheeriness to the graveyard. A lone metal bench hunkered under a large oak. Exactly the place to avoid if lightning was around. He sighed, grabbed the bouquet, and crossed the street toward the massive tree.

The mist settled on his hair, with drops randomly chasing each other down his neck or across his forehead. Like rain on the window of a sushi restaurant. He shuddered and walked on, queasy at the thought of raw fish.

The bench was cold, hard, and wet. Water soaked through the seat of his pants, but the tree blocked most of the sprinkles. At a price, though, the huge oak saved up the smaller drops and combined them, randomly dropping giant spheres of liquid. Within minutes, two had found him, soaking a shoulder blade and knee. Small fee to pay for such a perfect view of the school entrance.

A line of vehicles began to form in front of the building, and at precisely three-fifty, Levi stood and paced directly to a tombstone several rows away. He bowed his head and scanned the marker. Who'd won the flower lottery? Elsie Mae Rollins. Died at less than a year old. A lamb carved in the granite symbolized her tender age. Such a sad thing, to die so young, without purpose.

He placed the bouquet against the stone, observing for a moment as the rain dripped from the flower petals to the grave. Anyone watching would have seen a man paying his respects to a baby. Perhaps a relative or family friend. He nodded as if finishing a prayer and returned to his bench. Grandma needs to hurry.

The downpour chilled him despite the June heat, and he bounced his knees to keep warm. The tightness in his chest led to several deep breaths. It took increasing effort to avoid scowling. What was taking her so long? How could she make him wait like this? Rage floated from his torso to his brain until his head couldn't hold any more. He wanted to scream. To tell her she'd pay for making him—

Grandma slowed to a stop in the line of cars, her wipers going full blast. Levi stood and walked to his car, careful not to look toward the school. He moved slowly, keeping his head bowed and hands in his pockets. Once inside his vehicle, he cranked the engine and turned on the heat. Soaking wet and chilled, he needed to hurry. Dry clothes and a hot shower would feel wonderful. But first things first.

He kept an eye on his mirror, waiting for them to come. It didn't take long. Several teachers stood under the awning as the line of cars crept along collecting their precious cargo. Finally, Grandma's turn came, and the six-year-old walked toward the vehicle, pausing to hop in a puddle on her way. The splash must've been a disappointment since she ran back for a bigger jump. This time, water reached as high as her face, and she looked up, laughing.

He smiled and rubbed a hand across his chest.

Hello, Rebecca.

......

Maggie pulled a compact from her purse and stared into the mirror. "Should've brought an umbrella."

Jeremy chuckled. "You look beautiful, as always. But I think you know that. And if you don't, you should."

"Ugh. My hair's a frizzy mess."

He reached across the table and closed the compact. "Looks great to me."

She laughed and brushed a strand of hair off her forehead.

"Yeah, well, I suppose a man who's been locked up can afford to drop his standards."

"Better watch yourself. You don't know what the joint does to a person."

"The joint? Showing your age again, Mr. Winter. Not sure I can wait another twenty or thirty …" She dabbed her eyes. "How much longer, Jeremy? I can't stand this. Let me make some calls. Please."

He grabbed her hand. "Give it time, Maggie. Not much longer. I promise. Talk to me. Tell me what's going on with the Talbot case. Give me something to think about so I don't go crazy in here. Who knew it'd be so boring in the slammer?"

She rolled her eyes. "The slammer? Wow. If you don't get out soon, I may have to—" Her phone dinged, and she scanned the incoming message. "Got to go."

"You just got here. Everything okay?"

"Sorry, babe. Got a hit on Talbot's ATM card. Three of them, early this afternoon. All clustered around … Hanover, Virginia." She blinked rapidly, and her breathing accelerated. Her normally red cheeks had paled. She placed a trembling hand on the table and stared at the jittery fingers. "Jeremy, Hanover is twenty minutes from my house."

For half a heartbeat, he froze as a wave of dizziness smashed into him. All energy flooded from his arms and legs, and he struggled to form words. A freight train roared through his brain as the adrenaline did its job. "Give me the phone, Maggie."

She stared into space, her mouth open and shoulders beginning to shake. "The guard said—"

He snatched her phone and dialed the FBI. Director Bailey's secretary answered on the first ring. "Janice," he said, "this is Jeremy Winter. I need to speak with Bailey. It's urgent."

"Oh, hi, Jeremy. Sorry, but he's in a meeting now. I can give him a message if you want."

Jeremy gripped the phone, pressing it against his face. "Listen to me, Janice. Get him on the phone right now. I don't care who's in the meeting. I'll take the heat."

"Mmm hmm," Janice said. "Can I at least tell him what this is about?"

Jeremy slammed his fist on the table. "Janice, get him. *Now.*"

"Sheesh. Okay, hold on."

A guard entered the room and tapped Jeremy's shoulder. "You can't make calls. I told her that when she came in here."

Maggie stood, braced herself on the table, and addressed the guard. "I need to borrow your phone. Please."

"I'm sorry, ma'am. I'm not allowed—"

Jeremy glanced up and forced himself to maintain a steady tone. "You're FBI too, right? She just wants to make sure her family's okay. Please give her your phone. Now."

The guard handed his cell to Maggie. "I could get in trouble for this, you know."

She grabbed the phone, jabbed the buttons, and held it to her ear before running a shaky hand under her eyes. "There's no answer on Mom's phone."

Jeremy dipped his head and listened as Director Bailey grumbled and cursed his way to his secretary's phone.

"What is it, Winter?" he said. "You're not supposed to have phone access. This had better be—"

"Sir, Maggie—Agent Keeley—got a hit on Cody Talbot's ATM card. Three hits, actually. All of them this afternoon, and all of them in Virginia. And sir, they're all about twenty minutes from Agent Keeley's home."

"Is she with you?"

"Yes, sir. And she's unable to establish contact with her mother at the residence."

"Anyone else at her house?"

Jeremy leaned his head into his palm. "Yes, sir. Her six-year-old daughter. Rebecca."

"Stay by the phone. Don't either of you move. Give me a few minutes." Click.

Maggie buried her face in her hands. Jeremy could hear sniffling. She was on the verge of losing it completely. "Maggie," he said.

She looked up, her eyes red and puffy. Her chin quivered, and he knew. If she tried to talk, she'd break down. He swallowed hard, afraid to speak, not knowing what to say. So he said the only thing he could.

"Maggie." He slid his hand toward her, palm up.

She grabbed his fingers and ran her free hand under her nose, sniffling again. "Jeremy, what if—"

"Shhh," he said. "I'm sure it's a coincidence." He didn't believe that, but it had to be said. Problem was, she wouldn't believe it either. "Maggie, look at me."

Her knee bounced rapidly, and she rocked back and forth, but she held his gaze. Her lips were drawn into her mouth, her nose now bright red, but she kept looking. A solitary tear dripped from her face.

Jeremy knew fear when he saw it. He'd seen it before. He wanted to tell her everything would be all right. That her family was okay. But he couldn't. They might be safe, but he didn't know that.

The phone rang, and he grabbed it, not wasting time on a "hello."

"First helicopter with a team will leave here in ten minutes," Director Bailey said. "ETA is fifty minutes. Second helicopter is on standby for you and Keeley. I'll get you released on my authority. That's not going to sit well with certain people, so move fast. The local cops will be at her house any minute, and an emergency response unit from Richmond is being assembled and deployed."

"Thank you, sir," Jeremy said.

"We need photos. Get pictures of Keeley's family so we can get them out and issue an AMBER Alert if needed. Why her?"

"Maggie—Agent Keeley was at the same hotel in Brattleboro that Talbot had in his GPS. He probably found out who she was and decided to come after her. Us."

"Us?" Director Bailey asked.

"Yes, sir. The FBI." He glanced at Maggie. *Us.*

"Hold on … I've got an update from the Milford PD."

Jeremy waited and forced an optimistic smile at Maggie. An expletive from Director Bailey erased his hopefulness.

"Winter, we only need her daughter's photo."

Jeremy bit his lip. His heart plummeted to the floor. Afraid to speak, he cleared his throat and squeezed Maggie's hand tighter. "Sir?"

"They found her mother's body. The girl is missing. Winter, listen very closely. Agent Keeley needs to hold it together. I'm pulling her off the Talbot case, but we may need information about her daughter."

Agent Keeley needs to hold it together? What about him? "Yes, sir. We'll head to the chopper in a few minutes. Thank you, sir."

"You don't mess with family, Winter. Not our family. Give the phone to whoever's in charge there."

Jeremy handed the cell phone to the guard and stretched his other hand across the desk. He could feel the pool of water forming under his eyelids but made no effort to brush them away.

"Maggie," he said.

That was all it took. She collapsed into tears. He walked around the desk and knelt beside her chair, placing a hand on her back. "Maggie, I'm sorry. They found your mom."

"Rebecca?" was all she choked out.

"Gone. A manhunt's already in progress. There's a helicopter waiting for us, whenever you feel up to it."

She shook her head violently and took a deep breath before standing. "Now. We go now."

Jeremy stood and placed a hand on each of her shoulders before drawing her into his chest. He'd do anything to take it from her.

Pile it on himself. The fear, the anger, the frustration. And most of all, the desperation. He closed his eyes and offered a silent, two-word prayer. *God, please.*

He leaned closer, brushing his cheek against her hair, and mouthed words so quietly he wasn't sure she heard. "I'll find her, Maggie. I swear it."

38

The dark blue helicopter landed hard on the Caroline County High School's football field. Its landing skids squished into the mud, and the spinning blades blew a fine mist. Jeremy was the first out. The other copter sat at the opposite end, the FBI logo clearly visible on its tail. A crowd of onlookers gathered on the running track that circled the field. Sheriff's deputies stood near the perimeter of the playing surface and kept people away. Maggie jumped out, and the two moved toward a black SUV parked at the entrance, its blue lights flashing through darkened windows.

As they neared the vehicle, a man in a police uniform stepped out of the driver's side and motioned them toward him. Noise overhead caught Jeremy's attention, and he looked up. Two more helicopters circled the area. One, a white chopper with blue and red stripes had "Virginia State Police" painted above the doors. The other was a news helicopter from DC, circling and filming. No doubt other television stations would be joining soon enough.

"Agent Keeley?" the man asked. "I'm Sergeant Scanton, Richmond PD."

Maggie nodded. "This is Jeremy Winter. He's with me."

Jeremy motioned to the crowd. "Sergeant, do those deputies know what our suspect looks like? I want to make sure they're checking the crowd."

"They do. The first team took care of that. I'm to get you to Agent Keeley's home."

Maggie opened the rear door and hopped inside. "Let's go."

Four minutes later, the SUV pulled up to the crime scene. Two vans sat out front, each with a satellite dish raised high above the roof of the vehicle. Reporters stared into cameras and gestured toward Maggie's house. Jeremy expected the national news feeds would pick them up soon if they hadn't already.

The red brick home was a ranch style with a metal carport anchored to the side. Black shutters gave the house a somber look, though the crime scene tape draped across the yard probably contributed to that. Large trees spread their canopies and provided slight shelter from the drizzle. Maggie ducked under the yellow tape and hurried to the front door. Jeremy caught up with her and stepped in front.

"Maggie, why don't you wait here? I'll go in and evaluate the scene."

She shook her head. "No chance. This is my house. I might see something you wouldn't notice."

He understood. She needed to see what Talbot had done. "Maggie, at least let them get your mother out first. Please."

Her lips formed a straight, tense line, and her eyes narrowed. "Jeremy, I'm going in there."

He nodded. The unknown could be worse than the known. "Okay. But I'm going in first."

He walked up the two steps, showed his identification to the officer on the porch, and waited while their names were recorded in the entry log. The front door was open, providing Jeremy a view of the living room. After donning shoe covers, they stepped inside. A rocking chair lay on its side next to a broken coffee table. Pieces of pottery and figurines lay scattered across the wood floor. A bent metal lamp dangled across the back of the sofa. Good for her. She'd fought hard to save her granddaughter.

A flash of light off to the left grabbed his focus. The photographer was in there, which meant the body probably was too. Jeremy stepped into the house, careful to stay close to the perimeter of the room. Maggie brushed past him, and he held out his arm.

"This is as far as you go, Maggie."

"What? No, my mother's in there. I need to see Mom."

Her shoulders hunched forward, and she wrung her hands together. Jeremy clenched his teeth. Whatever it took, he'd make her hurt stop. But he wouldn't, couldn't, let her see the body. It was a memory she didn't need. She might not know that now, but she would later. Hopefully.

He shook his head and kept eye contact, steeling himself for her outburst. "No, Maggie. For your own good, no."

The eruption didn't come, but what did was far worse. Her head tilted forward, and she stared at the floor. Her voice broke, and he leaned in to hear better.

"Please, Jeremy?"

Her grief poured through him, emptying his chest, and pulling his head down. "I'm sorry, Maggie. I'm so sorry."

She leaned into him, and he wrapped his arms around her. Anguish overwhelmed him. Thoughts of revenge gave way to shared grief. After a moment, she straightened, sniffled, and brushed her hand under her nose.

"You might need to get that shirt cleaned," she said.

"Wait here. I won't be long."

The eat-in kitchen was surprisingly orderly, considering the chaos in the living room. A small movable island sat askew against the refrigerator, and one cabinet drawer was open, but otherwise, nothing seemed out of place. Nothing except the body on the floor.

Maggie's mother lay face-up on the linoleum, one arm across her chest, the other stretched above her head. Plastic bags already covered each hand to preserve any DNA evidence that might be under her nails. A small scratch on her forehead and massive bruising around her neck were the only visible signs of trauma. This was one of the cleanest murder scenes he'd been to, and he was grateful for it.

"Got much longer?" Jeremy asked the photographer.

"Wrapping things up now. The coroner's outside unless you need him to wait?"

"No. Let him in."

Jeremy returned to the living room, not surprised to discover Maggie wasn't there. He trudged down the hallway, stopping to look at the photos hanging on the wall. Maggie and Rebecca in front of the giraffes at a zoo somewhere. Grandma pushing a much younger Rebecca in a stroller. A teenage version of Rebecca, dressed in stonewashed jeans and a baggy flannel shirt. Grunge, Maggie?

He moved down the hall and stopped at the entrance to Rebecca's room. A pink wooden *R*, dotted with large white polka dots, hung on the door. Stuffed animals perched in their assigned seats around a small table, waiting for their best friend to start the tea party. Coloring books filled a shelf, and a plastic Dora the Explorer toy box overflowed its contents in a wide arc. Maggie sat on the bed, clutching a Disney princess pillow to her chest.

"Hey there," he said. "You doing okay?"

She glanced up. "Was it bad?"

He dragged his hand across the back of his neck and sighed. "Strangulation probably. Your mom fought hard, Maggie."

She nodded slowly. "Not surprised."

"Listen, Maggie. Is there someone you can stay with for a while?"

"Um, I need to be here. In case they need me."

Jeremy moved over and sat beside her. "Sure you do. But you can't stay in the house. Maybe a friend or a neighbor?"

Her head jerked up. She reached into her pocket and pulled out a cell phone. "I need to call Rebecca's father. Let him know what's going on."

"Uh-huh. He needs to know." He hesitated before continuing, "Maybe you can stay with him for a few days?"

Maggie shook her head. "He lives in Roanoke. Too far away. And I wouldn't do it even if he lived next door. Look, I'll just get a hotel room. No problem."

Jeremy placed his hand on her back. "I'm going to work, Maggie. I'll head to DC and talk to Bailey. Get in on the investigation. Keep your phone charged. You need anything, you call me."

"All I need is Rebecca," she said. "Bring her home, Jeremy."

He stood, not sure what to say. The thought of Maggie losing her daughter was more than he could take. He knew that pain. And he'd deal with Talbot for inflicting this agony on Maggie. He had experience dealing with people like that, didn't he? Cody Talbot was an animal who needed to be put down. He turned to leave, and she grabbed his hand.

"Jeremy," she said, "when I said all I needed was Rebecca ..."

His hand wrapped around hers, swallowing it in his clasp. His fingers stroked the back of her hand. Electricity shot up his arm, reviving his heart. He looked at her and lifted their hands to his face. He kissed hers before releasing it. After nodding once, he strode from the room.

He'd find the man responsible for all of this, and when he did, Talbot would learn the meaning of true fear.

39

Levi swung into the driveway of the house outside Rogersville, Tennessee, tired after the nearly seven-hour drive from Virginia. The weeds around the "For Sale" sign nearly obscured the realtor's phone number. The home sat on several acres, its nearest neighbor out of sight. Most likely a foreclosure. It'd do.

The little girl still slept on the back seat floorboard. It had been over an hour since she'd moved. The antihistamine-laced chocolate milk had done its job quickly. Better she slept and didn't see what was about to happen.

He glanced at Rebecca before exiting the vehicle and walking to the home's back door. The windows were bare, and he could make out a laundry room leading into the kitchen. With any luck, the electricity and water might still be turned on.

A rusty chair sat on the patio, white paint flaking from its metal frame. Levi grabbed it and rammed the seat's legs against the door's window. The glass shattered on the third attempt. No more kicking in doors. He reached through the window remnants, careful not to cut himself, and turned the lock. After opening the door, he checked the frame for any security system connections. None.

No lights were on, but a low hum emanated from the refrigerator. Electricity. Excellent. Pieces of old furniture remained strewn about, signs of owners who'd most likely given up on their mortgage. Broken glass crunched under his shoes as he walked through the kitchen and into the garage. He punched the button, and the double-door began its rise, protesting with squeaks and groans.

He pulled the car into the garage and waited until the metal door finished complaining about being closed again. He gently lifted the girl and patted her on the back. Rebecca's head flopped on his shoulder, and a dribble of drool stained his shirt. The pink teddy bear lay face down in the front seat, thrown there before he had taped her hands behind her. She hadn't liked the toy. It bothered him that she seemed to be angry. Couldn't she understand he was her deliverer?

Once inside, Levi found a bedroom and placed Rebecca on top of the faded white bedspread. He removed the tape from her wrists and massaged the red marks circling her thin arms. A musty towel from the bathroom served as a pillow, and he slid the thin cloth under her head. His heartbeat accelerated, and he licked his lips. He'd never done this. There'll be some splatter. Have to be careful. It was something different. A treat.

He opened the box and pulled the gloves onto his hands. She still slept. Innocent. Oblivious. He placed the scissors next to her. No nicks on these blades. Still shiny. New. Like her. He dragged a finger across her forehead. A river of adrenaline flowed. He tapped his feet. Stared. Her chest rose and fell. Up and down. So fast. He sat on the bed next to her small body. Staring. His gloved fingertips lingered on his mouth.

He sighed, almost regretting what had to be done. Almost. Had to be just right. No mistakes. Gloves. Scissors. He scanned the box one last time. Clairol Nice 'N Easy #117. Natural Medium Golden Brown.

Twenty-five minutes later, he carried her still-sleeping form to the bathroom and rinsed her hair. Rebecca stirred twice but didn't wake. Did he give her too much sleepy medicine? After towel drying the newly darkened and shorter curls, he placed her back in the bed, pulling the covers to her shoulders.

Tomorrow would be a long day. There was a slim chance they could make it to their destination, but lots of variables stood in the way of the nineteen-hour journey. Drive too fast and risk getting stopped. Drive too slow and risk bringing unwanted attention. Use the interstate or stay on back roads? Each came with hazards. He'd let the Spirit guide him. And if he didn't like the Spirit's choice, well, he'd cross that bridge when he came to it.

After closing the bedroom door, he wrapped a mothy blanket around himself and stretched out on the worn carpet. How long do little girls sleep? It didn't matter. When she woke, they'd get back on the road. He wasn't in a hurry, and, truth be told, he enjoyed her company. Given the opportunity, there was no question she'd like him too. Sadly, at least for her, she didn't have that kind of time. Levi yawned and closed his eyes.

Sleep well, Rebecca.

......

Morning came five hours later, a bit after midnight. Levi woke to Rebecca's low whimpers and waited for his anger to subside before speaking. Best not to scare her.

"What's the matter, honey?" he asked.

A tiny voice in the darkness answered. "I want my mama."

"I told you I was taking you to see her."

"That's what you said yesterday. My mama told me to stay away from strangers. You're a stranger. I'm 'posed to stay away."

"Oh, that's not true, Rebecca. What's my name? Remember?"

After a moment, "Levi."

"That's right, honey. And if you know my name, then I'm not a stranger. Isn't that right?"

"Why couldn't Grandma come?"

"She wanted to, but she's really busy. She knew I would take good care of you. That's why she called me to come get you."

"Call her."

Levi sighed and ran a hand over his beard stubble. "Call who?"

"My mama. Call my mama."

"I can't call her now. She's working on a very important case. Tell you what. I'll make a deal with you. If you'll behave, we'll call her in a little while. Do you remember her phone number?"

"Uh-huh. She makes me say it all the time so I won't forget."

"Oh," he said, "what a wonderful mommy you have. My mother was ... how do I put this? Well, she's in heaven now."

"How do you know?"

A burning sensation rose through Levi, and he dabbed his forehead, erasing droplets of sweat. "Well, Rebecca, when good people die, they go to heaven."

"One time I wrote on the wall with crayons, and Grandma got mad at me. Really it was a bunch of times."

He cleared his throat. "I'm sure your grandma didn't stay mad."

"She said I had to tell Jesus I was sorry."

"And did you?"

"Uh-huh, but Grandma still spanked me. I pretended it hurt, but it didn't really. She doesn't spank very hard. My hair smells funny."

Levi stood, yawning and stretching. "You ready to go? We can get some breakfast in a while."

"Are we going to see my mama?"

"Soon, Rebecca. Very soon."

......

Traffic on Interstate 40 was sparse, with eighteen-wheelers

being the majority of vehicles. No cops so far. One uneventful stop at a rest area near Crossville, then back on the road. Rebecca sat quietly in the back seat, holding the pink teddy bear.

Levi glanced in the mirror. "Getting hungry?"

"Are we there yet? I'm tired of being in the car."

"Umm, no, we're not there yet. You want something to eat?"

"Do they have chicken nuggets?"

"That's what you want for breakfast? Chicken nuggets?"

"And fwench fwies, and apple juice, and a toy."

Does McDonald's have that stuff at three-thirty in the morning? "What do you want if they don't have chicken nuggets?"

"Nothing." Her bottom lip jutted out, and the bear went flying into the front seat.

Levi flexed his fingers on the steering wheel and glanced at the bear. "We don't throw things, Rebecca. If you can't behave, I'm going to have to put you back on the floor like yesterday."

"I'm telling my mama. You're mean."

Mean? What did he do? "Oh, honey, I'm not mean. Tell you what. I have to stop and get gas. How about we call your mama then? Does that sound okay?"

She nodded, but the lip remained extended.

"And when we call her, you be sure and tell her how mean I am, okay? She'll think that's funny."

Levi took the next exit and pulled into a truck stop. He topped off the fuel tank, then cautioned Rebecca to stay in the car.

"I have to go pay for the gas. If you get out of the car, we're not going to call your mom, understand?"

She nodded, and he checked to make sure the child locks on the door were flipped on. He jogged into the store and grabbed a prepaid phone, a pack of powdered white donuts, chocolate milk, sunglasses, and a baseball cap. The sleepy older lady at the register did her best to smile at him but only managed to stop frowning.

Back in the car, Levi opened the phone and activated it. "You ready, Rebecca? You can only talk for a second, okay?"

She leaned forward in her seat and reached for the phone.

"Just a second, honey. What's her phone number?"

The girl recited the digits in an e-i-e-i-o lilt.

Moments later, a tired voice answered. "Hello?"

Levi licked his lips and pounded a fist on his leg. He wanted to scream. To run around the parking lot in a victory lap. I win. Do you hear me? I win! Deep breath. "Hello, Agent Keeley."

A pause before she responded. "Who is this?"

She knows. Oh yes, she knows. So delightful. "In forty-five seconds, I'm going to turn off this phone. You'll never find it or trace it. Choose your words carefully. I'll be listening. Don't say anything that would make me angry. I have such big plans." He handed the phone to Rebecca.

"Hi, mama. Levi is mean. He says—"

"Shh. It's okay, baby," Maggie said. "Mommy loves you, sweetie. I'll see you soon, okay?"

"Today?" Rebecca asked.

"I hope so, baby. Are you okay? He didn't—"

"Bzzzzz," Levi said. "I'm sorry, but your time is up. Your country thanks you for your sacrifice, Agent Keeley. Such a sweet young girl."

He switched off the phone and removed the battery. That was fun. He glanced back at Rebecca and rubbed his hands together. Usually, fun things are sinful. But not this. Oh no, not this. After all, wasn't every good and perfect gift from God? Hadn't He provided Abraham with the perfect sacrifice? A last-minute switcheroo. A ram in exchange for Isaac. How fortunate. But there would be no sheep or goat or bull or anything else to save the child this time. He would take her to the wilderness. To the site he'd prepared. Offer the sacrifice. Gladly.

Rebecca had to die.

40

Jeremy fumbled for the phone, groaning as sharp pains zig-zagged up his leg. Four a.m. Something's happened. "Maggie."

"He called me. I talked to Rebecca."

No quiver in her voice. No sign of fear. That would come later when this was over. "Is she okay?"

"Sounded like it."

The "for now" went unspoken. "Get a trace on the call?" he asked.

"Not enough time and the caller ID was blocked. I wrote down everything they said. Jeremy, she called him Levi. What do you think that means?"

He stumbled out of bed and flipped the switch on the coffee maker. "Levi, Levite. Maybe it's his way of associating himself with that guy in Judges. I don't know. Maybe it's more. Did you turn the info over to the team?"

"Not yet. I called you first. They're next."

"Did Rebecca say anything else?"

She sniffled before answering. "She said he was mean."

"I'm sorry, Maggie." FBI protocol said he should sympathize. Tell her he understood. But he couldn't. He'd lost his daughter long ago, but not like this.

"Jeremy, he said my country thanks me for my sacrifice."

He rubbed a hand across his face stubble, letting the anger build. His chest ached. Her pain palpable. What should he say? What did she want him to say?

Maggie broke the silence. "You on the email loop yet?"

"Yeah. Wasn't easy to talk him into it, but Bailey got me set up last night. I'm officially a consultant again. No power, but at least I know what's going on."

"No new hits on his ATM?"

"Not yet. There's an agent on-site at the bank in Mexico, monitoring the account. As soon as Talbot uses his card, we'll know. Every FBI office in the country is aware of the situation. When he pops up, we'll be ready."

A sigh flowed through the phone. "So we keep waiting."

"Maggie, we're not waiting. We're going after Talbot with everything we've got. His and Rebecca's photos will be on every morning news broadcast. There's an AMBER Alert in virtually every state east of the Mississippi, and it's set to expand at noon if needed."

"Yeah, I know. But, it still feels like waiting. I can't sleep, can't eat. My mind keeps running through these horrible scenarios. And I haven't even begun to process my mom's death. Jeremy, I don't know what to do."

How could he respond to that? Tell her the truth? He felt the same way? That he'd do anything to get Rebecca back? Anger and pain flashed to rage. Talbot would pay with his life. It was Afghanistan all over again in so many ways. This time, though, he had a chance to save his family. And to punish the one responsible.

"Maggie, get the information to the team. See if there's anything they can do about tracking down the phone Talbot used.

I'm heading into the office. The task force is meeting at eight. If anything shakes loose, you'll be the first to hear it."

"Thank you, Jeremy. I know you're doing everything you can."

"It's not just for you. Got to complete my collection. I still don't have my picture of a giraffe. The elephant and hippo keep asking about it."

Another sniffle. "I'll remind her as soon as I see her."

"You do that."

A quiet minute. No speaking. Just being there.

"Sweetie, I have to go."

She cleared her throat. "I know. Go. Call me if anything happens. Bye."

Jeremy gazed at the phone, so much left unsaid. "Goodbye, Maggie," he whispered.

41

Passing through Nashville would be chancy, but taking the southern route through Louisiana meant adding hours to the trip. Time he might not have.

"Rebecca," Levi said, "you still want those chicken nuggets?"

"I need to potty."

He tapped his finger on the dash and glanced in the mirror. Flecks of powdered donut dotted her lips, and a chocolate milk stain covered her shirt. "Tell you what. We'll find a store and get you some new clothes. We don't want your mom to see those dirty ones, do we? Then we'll get something to eat. Before you know it, we'll be there."

"Can I pick the clothes?"

"Sure you can. If you behave and don't talk to strangers."

She squinted and worked her jaw back and forth. "I need new shoes too. These are dirty."

"We'll get you a pair of pretty shoes too. But we have to shop fast. We don't want to keep your mother waiting."

Downtown Nashville popped up on the horizon, and traffic thickened. Levi pulled on the orange Tennessee ball cap he'd purchased at the truck stop and checked his reflection. The oversized sunglasses hid what the hat didn't. His nose and mouth were visible, but unless he wore a bandanna or mask, it was the best he could do. Three fiery scratches flowed from his cheek to neck, courtesy of dear old Grandma.

"There's a McDonald's," Rebecca said, pointing out her window.

Levi switched on his blinker and took the exit. "Good eye, honey. And there's a Walmart across the street. We can kill two birds with one stone."

Her bottom lip assumed its projected position. "I don't want to kill a bird."

He laughed and spun his head around for a quick peek at the girl. "We're not going to kill anything. It's just something people say."

She crossed her arms and glared at him. "They shouldn't say that. It's not nice. We're 'posed to take care of animals."

How sweet. Take care of the animals. All except the chicken nuggets. He pulled into the McDonald's parking lot, stopped, and turned around to face his passenger. "Remember, no talking to strangers. Potty, then we'll grab a bite to eat and go get you some clothes. Make it fast. Mommy's waiting."

She nodded, and he stepped out of the vehicle and opened her door. She jumped out, and Levi extended his hand. Rebecca looked at him for a moment before placing her hand in his. He squeezed softly, her smooth skin and small fingers engulfed in his palm. His heart raced, and his tongue darted across dry lips. He glanced down and smiled at her.

Rebecca looked up, grinned, and tugged him into the restaurant.

......

The meeting started ten minutes early. No light banter this

morning. Dead serious faces stared back at Jeremy, united in their purpose. Find Rebecca no matter the cost.

"Okay," Director Bailey said. "Let's get right to it. Cody Talbot made contact with Agent Keeley early this morning. The call was brief, but the girl was still alive at that time. Details are in your packets. We'll get to assignments in a moment, but first I've asked Jeremy Winter to share his thoughts. For those of you who don't know him, Mr. Winter was with the Bureau for many years. I've asked him to join us as a consultant due to his wealth of experience in dealing with serial killers. He's already quite familiar with this case. Use him as an asset, but"—he cut his eyes at Jeremy—"remember his authority is restricted to consulting only."

Jeremy stepped forward and inclined his head. "Thank you, Deputy Director Bailey. Time is of the essence. Talbot's slipping. Becoming less predictable. Rebecca Keeley doesn't fit his pattern. He's made this personal. The good news is he'll make mistakes, but he's also far more volatile. Anything could set him off. When we find him, the girl's safety is the priority. If he feels cornered, he'll ..." Jeremy cleared his throat. "He'll kill her. No confrontations until we know she's safe."

The others in the meeting room murmured their agreement. At least two dozen personnel had joined the team, and Jeremy knew every one of them would do anything to save Rebecca. Any child in danger was unacceptable, but when it was a fellow agent's daughter, things got ratcheted to a new level.

Bailey motioned to the seated agents. "Don't forget. We are sworn to uphold the law. When we find Talbot, we follow the book. You get the girl back, and then you get him. It's not our job to administer justice. Winter is right. Talbot's made this personal. He'll make mistakes. So will you if you let your emotions take over. Are we clear on that?"

A few of the agents nodded, while others avoided eye contact. Jeremy did neither. The FBI's rules didn't apply to him. Wouldn't make a difference even if they did.

"Who's coordinating the public hotline?" Jeremy asked.

An agent in the back, top button open and tie hanging loose, motioned. "Special Agent Perkins. I'm on it. We're getting swamped with calls from all over the country. Thousands so far. The girl's photo's been on all the morning programs. We're using local PD to chase down what we can, but nothing solid yet. Without a vehicle description, it's tough. Anybody who spots a guy with a red-headed little girl picks up the phone."

"Keep on it," Jeremy said. "Don't assume she's still a redhead."

The director leaned forward. "Any update on the scene at Agent Keeley's house?"

"I've got that, sir," a female agent said. "Cause of death for her mother was strangulation. Human tissue under her nails, most likely Talbot's. No sign of forced entry. We've located a dollar store that thinks he bought some stuff there that morning. Their security camera is pretty rough, though. The VCR tape is being analyzed, and we've got the receipts. If there's any—"

An expletive echoed around the room, its point of origin in the back. "Hold on," Agent Perkins said, one finger held up to emphasize his point. "Yeah ... yeah ... you sure? Okay, stand by."

Jeremy strode toward him, his pace matching his accelerating heartbeat. "Got something?"

"Could be. Several calls came in around forty-five minutes ago, all clustered around a Walmart in, get this, Nashville. One of the callers said the guy had scratches on his face."

Nashville? Why would he risk going there again? "That's flimsy, but get the local guys out there," Jeremy said.

"There's more," Agent Perkins said. "A woman called from the same Walmart. Said she'd seen the news this morning, and there was a man and child who kind of resembled the photos on TV. The girl's hair was shorter and dark brown. The woman said she almost didn't call because she heard the girl talking to the man. She called him Levi."

This time the profanity came from the front. Director Bailey stood and pointed at Jeremy. "Get on the jet with the response team. Everyone else, shift all focus to Nashville and surrounding areas. I want copies of that store's surveillance footage here within the hour. Every person in there gets interviewed. Find out where Claire Lawson is and make sure she's protected. Reissue the AMBER Alert in Tennessee and all surrounding states. You, call the local ..."

Jeremy sprinted from the room, dialing Maggie as he ran. "We've got a sighting in Nashville," he said. "Not confirmed but highly likely."

"Rebecca?"

"Still with him. Her hair's been cut and dyed, but witnesses said she seemed unharmed and acted normally. We'll have the surveillance video here soon. They might want you to come in to confirm it's her."

"Won't be a problem," she said. "I'm in my office."

"Maggie, you're supposed to stay away from the case. You know the regulations."

"Would you? Besides, I'm catching up on old paperwork. And if I happen to overhear things, well, that's not my fault, is it?"

He stepped into the elevator, grinned, and rolled his eyes.

"You rolled your eyes, didn't you?" Maggie asked.

"Got to go," he said. "I'll call you when I land."

......

Levi traced his fingers over the scratches on his face, applying the makeup he'd purchased at Walmart. Interstate 40 toward Little Rock needed paving, and the rhythmic bouncing of the vehicle complicated his attempts at covering the wound. The CoverGirl Concealer turned red scratches into dark brown streaks. A glance in the mirror muddied his decision.

"Hey, Rebecca. Does this look okay?" He turned toward the back seat, letting her get a good look.

Her face scrunched into a frown. "Are we there yet?"

"Soon. We'll be there soon."

"That's what you said—"

Levi slammed his hand against the steering wheel. "I know what I said. I've had just about enough. Shut up and sit there. If you say another word ..."

Flashing blue lights on the eastbound side caught his attention. He checked his speedometer. Not speeding. Avoid eye contact. The white sedan made a U-turn, crossed the median, and accelerated, growing larger in the rearview mirror.

Everything's in the trunk. Can't get to my tools. "Rebecca, keep your mouth shut. You hear me?"

A whimper for a response.

Not now God. We're so close. Let me do this. *For You.*

The Arkansas State Police vehicle swerved around him, sped into the distance, and pulled over an 18-wheeler. Levi slowed and moved into the left lane, giving the officer a wide berth as he passed.

Ten minutes later, he exited the interstate, stopped in the parking lot of a decaying Stuckey's, and grabbed the duct tape from the trunk.

42

Four black SUVs pulled to the plane at Nashville International Airport. The SWAT team loaded their gear in three of them and rode to the FBI office to await developments. Jeremy rode in the fourth, escorted by a local agent.

He nodded at the driver. "Jeremy Winter. Anything new?"

The agent accelerated onto I-40 West and flipped on the SUV's flashing blue lights. "Ron Preston. Positive ID on Talbot and the girl. The area around the store's on complete lockdown. Roadblocks, dogs, the works, but no sign of the suspect or the child. They're probably long gone."

"We get a description of their vehicle?"

Agent Preston shook his head. "Not yet. It appears they walked to Walmart from across the street. Probably the McDonald's. We're going through the video now, but their exterior cameras are all focused on the drive-through. The inside cameras will tell us if they were there, but not much else."

"What did he buy?"

Preston leaned on his horn, encouraging the driver ahead of them to get over. "Unbelievable. Forty-five in the left lane. Sorry. I don't know what he bought. They'll have that for us when we get there."

"The APB been updated?"

The agent nodded. "Yep. Talbot had on sunglasses and a University of Tennessee hat, light shirt, and blue jeans. A couple of nasty looking scratches on his face too."

No question where Maggie got her toughness. "Claire Lawson?"

"On vacation up around Gatlinburg. Local PD's been informed, and we've got two agents camped outside her door. We offered to bring her into protective custody, but she refused."

Jeremy stared out his window, massaging his forehead and running through scenarios. Talbot wouldn't stay in one place too long. Not if he realized how close the FBI was to finding him. Nashville still doesn't make sense, especially if Claire Lawson wasn't here. He's got to be passing through. Jeremy pulled the phone from his pocket and dialed Maggie.

"About time," she said. "You landed twenty minutes ago."

"Sorry. Just getting caught up. Did you see the video?"

"It's them, Jeremy. Rebecca looked okay, but her hair has been cut and dyed. Her clothes were a mess, but she smiled and talked to him. She didn't seem scared, at least that's what I keep telling myself."

"That's good, Maggie. If Rebecca doesn't see him as a threat ..."

"Then she didn't see him kill Mom."

"Exactly. We'll be at the Walmart in ..." He glanced at the driver, who held up five fingers. "We'll be there in five minutes. Keep your phone nearby. I'll call as soon as I know anything."

Agent Preston exited the interstate and veered around the line of stopped vehicles. Police cars blocked all traffic, and an officer waved their SUV into the turning lane. As they pulled into the store's parking lot, Jeremy scanned the surroundings. Fast food restaurants across the street, two banks next door, strip mall down the road. Each location had at least one law enforcement automobile out front. Good. Too late, but good.

Emergency vehicles surrounded the two store entrances, forcing them to park a distance away. Helicopters swirled overhead, and half a dozen vans with satellite dishes lined the perimeter of the lot. Jeremy jogged toward the store, weaving through barricades and crime scene tape. An oversized white bus, "Mobile Command Center" emblazoned on its side and antennas covering its roof, sat immediately outside one entrance. Jeremy headed toward the blue-striped vehicle.

The officer stationed outside the bus reviewed Jeremy's identification and allowed him inside. A bank of laptops, radios, phones, and monitors lined the left wall, with rows of cabinets along the right. The bus had a dusty, electrical aroma, accented by a white tabletop fan oscillating in the corner. Three men sat at the counter working on the computers while a woman moved from station to station. Jeremy approached her and introduced himself.

"I'm Special Agent Amanda Truett," she said. "The rest of these folks are all Nashville PD."

"What's the current situation?" Jeremy asked. "I understand we have a positive ID on Talbot and Rebecca. Any luck identifying their vehicle?"

"Not yet. We've got footage from the restaurants and the banks, in addition to the store video. None of the cameras cover the road. Local detectives are working their way down the street, hoping we'll turn up something. But if they got back on the interstate from here, we're not going to find anything."

"If they ate across the street—"

"Got it covered," Agent Truett said. "Local news and radio put out bulletins asking anyone who ate there today to contact us. Honestly, if Talbot has any inkling of what's going on here, he's changed vehicles at least once by now."

Jeremy rubbed his eyes, stifling a yawn in spite of his adrenaline. "Any good news?"

"Well, we know what he bought," she said. "The store manager matched up the receipt to the video. Here's the list."

Girl's shirts, pants, and shoes. Snacks. CoverGirl makeup. Duct tape. Rope. Chef's knife set. Bleach. Toys. And flowers.

Jeremy leaned against the counter and closed his eyes. His stomach churned and spewed acid toward his throat. He'd been doing this too long to stop his imagination from covering the possibilities.

"Thoughts on this?" he asked.

"The makeup's to hide the scratches," Agent Truett said. "Everything else ... well, I don't know why he'd be worried about her clothes considering the other stuff he bought."

He placed the paper on the countertop and scanned the list again, his hands planted in his pockets. He closed his eyes and ran through the items. Talbot's intentions seemed clear. His destination did not. Where? The location would be intentional, not random. If he'd wanted, Talbot could have killed Rebecca anywhere, but he had something special planned for her.

He opened his eyes, turned to Agent Truett, and pointed at the laptops. "Pull up a map on one of those. And a Bible."

......

Levi merged back onto Interstate 30 and set the cruise control. Texarkana sat thirty minutes behind them, their destination still almost nine hours ahead. Stopping wasn't an option now that the girl was uncooperative.

He slurped the last of the strawberry shake, making sure Rebecca heard the noise, then reached back and lifted the blanket off her. She winced as the light invaded her darkness.

"That shake sure was good," he said. "Too bad you didn't want one."

She muttered and hummed, doing her best to protest.

"Oh, I'm sorry. I forgot. I taped your mouth shut, didn't I? And why did Uncle Levi do that? Because you wouldn't behave, remember?"

Rebecca stared at him, her eyes puffy and red.

"Do you need to use the bucket again?" he asked.

She shook her head.

"Nighty-night then. Don't worry, honey. This will all end soon." He winked at her and dragged the blanket back over her body. "Uncle Levi loves you, Rebecca."

Loves you to death.

43

Activity at the mobile command center wound down. The store would remain closed until tomorrow, but traffic now flowed normally. The roadblocks had been lifted, and the SWAT team continued waiting.

Jeremy scanned the displayed map again. Which route would Talbot take? He squeezed the phone against his ear. "They're not here, Maggie," he said. "No sightings and half of Nashville is looking for them. I'm sorry."

The silence on the phone dragged on for almost a minute before he spoke again. "Maggie?"

She cleared her throat. "Yeah, I'm here. Just thinking. Any luck getting a vehicle description?"

"They found several customers at the McDonald's who remember them. Depending on which one you want to believe, Talbot was either driving a red Ford minivan, a black Chevy pickup truck, or a metallic gold Mercedes-Benz."

"Not exactly helpful," she said.

He tapped the screen in front of him. "Maggie, I think he's going home."

"What? Why? How do you know that?"

"At the end of the Bible story, the Levite took the girl home. Talbot can take the interstate most of the way there. I can't be sure, but I believe that's where he's taking Rebecca. We've notified Highway Patrol in Arkansas and Texas to be on the lookout for vehicles with out-of-state tags."

"Jeremy," Maggie said, "the Bible says the Levite cut the woman into pieces when he got her home. If that's what—"

"Hey, no more of that. I'm going to Pleasant View. They've got enough agents here to handle the scene and respond if Talbot does happen to show up nearby. The SWAT team's staying here too. The Bureau's not going to move them on my hunch."

"A hunch or a belief?"

Good question. "A weak belief or a strong hunch. I'm not sure," he said.

"I'm going too," Maggie said.

"No chance. You know the policy. Besides, if Talbot doesn't go home, you'll be stuck in the middle of nowhere. Stay there. If anything breaks, I'll call."

"Sure thing," she said.

"You're checking flights, aren't you?"

"What? Our connection's dropping. I'll try to call you later."

"Listen to me, Maggie. Stay there. If I have to call Director Bailey and tell him to put surveillance on you, I will. You're in no condition to make good decisions. Let me handle it. Okay?"

She sighed, and her voice dropped to a whisper. "I can't stand this. Just sitting here, bouncing between hope and terror. It's torture."

"I'm catching a flight to El Paso and driving over to Pleasant View. Nothing direct, so it'll take me seven or eight hours to get there. I'll put a call into the sheriff's office and have them keep an eye out until I arrive."

"That's a long time to—"

"Yeah, but if Pleasant View is where Talbot's headed, he won't get there much faster. The jet's staying in Nashville with the SWAT team, so they'll be able to move quickly when he hits another ATM. He's got to be low on funds."

"I hope you're right," she said.

The sound on the other end grew muffled, and he brushed a hand under both eyes, wishing he could reach through the phone. "Maggie, don't cover the phone. It's okay."

But he knew it wasn't all right. How could it be with Rebecca still missing? He listened to her crying, pictured her face, fought back his own tears.

"You'd better get going," she said.

"I love you, Maggie. Rebecca too. I'll call you when I get to El Paso." He slipped the phone into his pocket and took several breaths to compose himself.

Special Agent Truett walked to him and stood close. "Just got an anonymous phone call. Thought you might be interested."

Jeremy's heart raced. "Somebody spot Talbot?"

She glanced around before answering. "No. But in the next few minutes, a couple of US Marshals are going to be here … looking for you."

He ground his teeth together and shook his head. "Cronfeld. Not now. Anonymous call, you said?"

Truett half-smiled. "Yeah, Director Bailey didn't want you to know it was him. The info's legit."

"Okay, I've got to—"

"My car's right here," she said. "Let's go."

......

Jeremy switched on his cell phone shortly before landing in El Paso. The flight attendant shook her head and started to speak but stopped when she saw his expression.

Fifteen voicemails and at least as many text messages. Something's happened. The first text came in an hour ago from Director

Bailey. Jeremy read the note and inhaled sharply. "Talbot used ATM in Sweetwater TX. 3 hrs from his home."

He dialed his phone and glanced out the window. On the ground within a few minutes.

"Sir," the flight attendant said. "You need to wait—"

Jeremy flashed his consultant's ID, "FBI" prominently displayed across the top. The phone rang several times before Director Bailey answered.

"Winter," he said, "how far away from Pleasant View are you?"

"Landing in El Paso now, and it's three hours from there. I'll make it in close to two. Is the team on the way?"

"The jet's headed for Fort Stockton. They'll be there about the same time. Every available agent from El Paso left about an hour ago. Between them and the sheriff, Talbot's place will be pretty well covered."

The plane touched down, and Jeremy grabbed his bag and unfastened his seat belt. "Make sure they don't spook him. Do we have eyes on the roads into town?"

"Limited. Local PD is doing what they can, but without knowing what kind of vehicle they're looking for, it's a shot in the dark. Too many roads and not enough manpower. The county sheriff is camped out near Talbot's place, so we'll know when he shows up."

The plane taxied toward the gate, and Jeremy stood and moved toward the exit. He ignored the looks from the other passengers. "Make sure the locals don't put the girl in any danger. Unless her life's in immediate peril, they stand by."

Bailey cleared his throat and didn't respond.

Jeremy clenched a fist. "Sorry, sir. I meant to say if you could ask your people–"

"Already done. I'm coordinating from here until we get agents on the scene. If Talbot is in Pleasant View, do whatever you have to do to protect the girl, but by the book. Clear?"

"The girl's my priority, sir. Talbot is secondary, but I can promise you, if he's there, I'll eliminate the threat."

"Look, I know this is personal for you. Don't make your situation worse."

Jeremy's stomach fluttered. "Sir?"

"Certain people would love to be able to point fingers when this is over. Don't give them the opportunity. We're not vigilantes."

The flight attendant pivoted the door open and extended her arm, motioning Jeremy off the plane. He nodded and arched his eyebrows, the closest he could manage to a non-verbal apology.

"Yes, sir," he said. "I know what I have to do."

"The gift..."

44

Levi stared out the window. Distant headlights grew large before morphing into fading taillights. Lots of cars out so early in the morning. From his vantage point, he couldn't make out any details, but it didn't matter. He knew who they were and why they were there. To stop him from doing what had to be done. God's enemies are out in force.

The sun will be up soon. Better get some sleep. Lots to do today, but everything'll be ready by late afternoon. He walked to the girl, curled in a corner. Sleeping again. He knelt and placed his face inches from hers. Her warm breath blew across him. A strand of hair dangled across her forehead. He pushed it back, careful not to wake her.

I brought you a flower, little one. When you wake, we'll play a game. I used to play it with my mom. She always loved me. Every time. But then I figured it out. She cheated, you know? Her love wasn't real.

Not like mine, Rebecca. For you.

You'll prove my love. My obedience. You'll thank me in heaven. I promise.

Until then, sleep well, my precious Rebecca.

He stretched out on his side, watching her. His eyelids drooped. He needed to rest. No more mistakes.

Forgiveness is near.

A bedtime song for you, Rebecca. One of my favorites.

Time is now fleeting, the moments are passing,
Passing from you and from me;
Shadows are gathering, deathbeds are coming,
Coming for you and for me.
Come home, come home,
You who are weary, come home;
Earnestly, tenderly, Jesus is calling,
Calling, O sinner, come home!

......

"It doesn't make sense," Jeremy said. "He should have been here hours ago unless something scared him off." It was already mid-afternoon, and his headache gave no indication it was going anywhere. He'd run through this a dozen times in the last hour. The evidence always ended up here, where Talbot grew up.

"I'm telling you," the sheriff said, "nobody's come near the house. I've been here all night. If a car had come this way, I'd have seen it, even if the vehicle stopped and turned around."

Jeremy scratched his cheek and surveyed the landscape. The officer was right. If anyone had driven down this road, they'd have been spotted. Talbot's home was empty.

The SWAT team parked less than a mile away. Its assortment of borrowed vehicles was spread among a cluster of trees. At least a dozen other FBI agents and law enforcement officers were within a five-mile radius, waiting for the signal to go. Three deputies from the sheriff's office patrolled Pleasant View. All surrounding counties remained on full alert.

Where is he? Jeremy returned to his vehicle and closed the

door, needing a quiet space to think. Nothing here, so we have to assume he's not coming home. We missed something. He's close, but—

A tap-tap-tap on his window broke the thought, and he glanced up, then smiled. Jeremy motioned to the passenger door and waited until the intruder sat beside him.

"Pastor Grayson. Didn't expect to see you out here. You must be pretty persuasive to get through this far."

The old man reached over and shook hands. "Son, never under-estimate the power of the Lord. Or your Miss Keeley."

"Excuse me?"

The preacher grinned. "Agent Keeley gave me her card when we met. I'm a little behind on current events, but when I found out what had happened with her family, I called to see if I could help. She said to find you, so here I am."

"Maggie got you past all the officers?"

"She can be quite persuasive herself. Now, son, how can I help you?"

Jeremy sighed and twisted the stiffness from his neck. "I'm sure Talbot was headed home. We know he was in Sweetwater. No way he's coming so close to Pleasant View unless that's his destination. Doesn't make sense."

Grayson patted Jeremy's knee. "Son, has anything Cody's done made sense? He's a troubled young man, but he's not stupid."

"I get that. Even if he was coming home, one sniff of all the activity in the area could have scared him off. But I thought, well …"

"What? You thought what?"

Jeremy closed his eyes and pressed back against the headrest. "I thought this was it. Levi Talbot's grand finale. Kill the girl, thumb his nose at the FBI, and fade away. It seemed to fit. The location, the victim, the Bible story, the supplies. It just seemed to fit."

The pastor scratched a bushy eyebrow. "Levi?"

"That's what he calls himself. Or at least that's what he told

Rebecca his name was. We're assuming it's to associate himself with the Levite in the story."

"Ah, Israel's priestly tribe. And the supplies?"

"Bought at a store outside Nashville. Knives, bleach, rope, that kind of stuff." Jeremy's stomach churned. "Talbot's probably got some sort of ritual planned."

"Forgive me for asking, but why the bleach?"

"My guess is he's using it to clean up the location of the crime. Maybe leave some sort of message."

"Yes, but why? Cody, uh, Levi knows you're on to him, right? Why bother trying to hide anything?"

Jeremy's mind filled with possibilities, but the old man had a point. What if they were looking at this all wrong? You cleaned up when you wanted to hide evidence. Talbot would have no need to conceal anything. In fact, the opposite was true. He wanted everyone to know what he'd done. So why—

He jerked his head toward the pastor. "Grayson, everything about this is different. All the other victims were killed in their homes, but not Rebecca. Talbot's traveled halfway across the country with her. That's a huge risk. Why take the chance unless he has something planned? Something special. Something that couldn't be done just anywhere. The Levites were priests, right? What kinds of ceremonies would they perform?"

The old man's hand trembled as he massaged his whiskers. "The Lord ordained quite a few, actually. There's Passover, when Moses led the Israelites from Egypt. And then there's, let's see, the Festival of Trumpets. I think that one was about—"

Jeremy patted Grayson's hand, then opened an Internet search on his phone. "Pastor, hold on a second. Slow connection, but I should have the info in a min ... here we go. Passover, Unleavened Bread, First Fruits, umm, this one. Day of Atonement. What's that?"

"Oh, it's later in the year, September I think."

"Understood, but what is it? Day of atonement for what?"

The pastor swept his hand toward the personnel milling around outside. "Not what. Who. For them and you and me. It's the one day the chief priest was allowed into the Holy of Holies to offer a ..." The life seemed to seep from Grayson, his bony, wrinkled face losing what little color it had.

Jeremy flexed his fingers and reached over, placing a hand on Grayson's arm. "It's okay, Pastor. I need to know."

The old man nodded once. "The chief priest offered a blood sacrifice to God. A sin offering for the nation. Two goats. He killed one and sprinkled its blood on the ark of the covenant. The tablets with the Ten Commandments were in the ark, so the goat's blood ritually covered God's law, appeasing His wrath."

Jeremy nodded. "And the other goat?"

"Turned loose. The priest laid his hands on the animal and confessed Israel's sins and rebellion. Then the goat was led to the wilderness and released, carrying the sins of the nation with it. But surely you don't think Cody believes—"

"That he's a high priest? Who knows? Either way, he'll use it as justification for another murder."

"Is it possible," Grayson said, "that he intends to use the girl as the scapegoat? The one that's set free?"

"Doubtful. Talbot's shown no hesitation to kill, and every desire to stay alive. If he is reenacting this atonement thing, where would he do it?"

"Well, now there's the problem. God told the Israelites sacrifices could only be done in locations He specified. And the last place he allowed them was in Solomon's Temple. The Romans destroyed that in 70 AD."

"So," Jeremy said, "he'll have to make his own."

The old man shook his head. "Don't see how he could. The temple was a huge complex, surrounded by walls and only one way in. The Holy of Holies was only one part of a much larger space."

"Anything like that around here? Something he could use?"

The pastor sat silent, save for the slight wheeze of his breathing. "I'm sorry, son. Nothing I can think of."

"Okay. I appreciate the help. I need to update the team. You want a ride back to town? I don't think anything's going to happen here, at least not anytime soon. I thought I'd drive around Pleasant View and talk to the deputies there. Maybe get some dinner later."

"Actually, if you could just take me down the road a piece, there's a crowd of folks there. I'm sure one of them can take me home."

"No problem. Wait here. This won't take long."

Jeremy shared the information with the other law enforcement officers and confirmed roadblocks had been set up throughout the county. Three government helicopters patrolled the outlying areas and watched for any vehicles attempting to bypass the checkpoints. Within hours, a grid search would start in Pleasant View, with agents going door to door. For now, there was nothing to do but keep looking.

He returned to the car and drove toward town, stopping at the security perimeter. A crowd of several dozen locals was clustered, some sitting on tailgates, others playing cards or talking.

"I appreciate your help, Grayson. If you think of anything that might help—"

"I've got your number. I'll be spending some time on my knees tonight for you, Rebecca, and Cody."

"Go heavy on the Rebecca prayers. The rest of us have had our chance."

Several new wrinkles appeared on the pastor's forehead. "When this is over, come see me, and we'll have a chat. I'll throw in a steak dinner. My treat."

Jeremy extended his hand. "Porterhouse, medium well."

The pastor clasped his hands around Jeremy's, squeezing tightly. "God bless you, son. Now, if you'll excuse me, I think I'll walk around and see what I can do about some of the drinking that's going on out there."

Grayson stepped out of the vehicle, and several dark bottles sailed through the air, away from the crowd and oncoming pastor. After a quick wave, he headed toward town, the sun low in his windshield. Riding off into the sunset. Talbot? Or me? Both?

Please, God. Not Rebecca.

45

Orange-tinged clouds settled on the horizon, waiting for dusk to cover the region. Jeremy slowed as he passed the pockmarked sign welcoming visitors to Pleasant View. Maybe he should do a little target practice. Work out some aggression. Better to save the pent-up anger, though. He already had plans on how to spend it.

He crested the hill and pulled to the side of the road. His finger tapped the dash, and he stared at the collection of dingy shops and homes. Cody wouldn't be there. A small town, half-dead, and Talbot wouldn't take the chance. Strangers were easy to spot, and with all the police activity, it was far too dangerous. People would be on edge. Shoot first, ask questions later. There had to be somewhere else. Someplace Talbot could take the girl and not be disturbed.

The flashing lights of a distant helicopter crept across the horizon. Soon the chopper would switch on its thermal imaging and begin searching for warm bodies on a cool night. Literally, a shot in the dark. The question was, would they find one heat source or two?

Truth is, the good guy doesn't always win. Not like the movies when the hero rides in on a white horse to save—

The movies. Jeremy whipped his head around and stared at the outline on the small hill to his left. An old drive-in theater. Fence around the lot and building. One way in. No lights. No signs of life.

He pulled his Glock from the holster and held the weapon in his lap, then switched off the car's lights and cruised toward the theater. He slowed to a crawl as he neared the old movie house. Backup was three, maybe four minutes away at the most, but he wouldn't call until he surveyed the location. If Talbot and Rebecca were there, a fleet of approaching vehicles would spook him. Best if Jeremy scouted it out first. And if he caught Talbot alone, so much the better.

A quarter-moon barely spit out enough light to allow Jeremy to maneuver through the parking area. Metal posts peppered the lot, their tinny speakers long since gone. He idled down a row until he came to a gap, then veered toward the squat building in the back, stopping a short distance away.

He turned off the engine, hunched forward, and scanned the darkness around the crumbling structure. No sign that anyone had been there for years. No vehicles parked nearby. Deathly quiet.

......

Deathly quiet, Levi thought. As it should be.

All is in order.

The ritual bathing done. Shoes removed. High priest garments on.

Safe.

He brushed aside the curtain and entered the room. The candles cast dancing shadows across the walls. Across the Ark of the Covenant. And across the girl.

The Lord would meet him here.

After the sacrifice.

After the atonement.

After the blood.

......

Jeremy grabbed his flashlight and stepped out of the vehicle, closing his door far enough to turn off the interior light. As he neared the building, more details emerged. A large window, surprisingly not broken, covered most of the right side. A pair of glass doors at the end. Concession stand. To the left, a short tower stood silhouetted against the star-dotted sky. Projection room. He paused, allowing his vision to further adjust to the dim light.

Movement to the right. He dropped to a knee and pointed his Glock. Nothing. Whatever it had been, it was too small to be a person. Bird, rat, armadillo, but not Talbot or Rebecca.

Jeremy moved to the double doors, running his hand down the gap between them. The left door jutted slightly, and he tugged on the handle. The hinge creaked, and he froze. Listening. Nothing. He waited a moment. Eyes narrowed, head tilted. Something. Over there. Another animal? Wait. Listen. Nothing.

He counted ten heartbeats, then pulled the door again, opening it far enough to turn sideways and squeeze through.

Dirt, sand, and trash covered the floor of the concessions area. Stealth would be difficult. He paused again, letting his senses work. At the opposite end of the room, a thin vertical strip of light. Moon reflecting on the windows? An odor of rotten cardboard and old dirt permeated the air, with just a touch of ... what?

Smoke and bleach.

He pointed his weapon at the strip of light and scanned the room. Too dark to tell much. Piles of rubble lined the walls and counters, dark gray mounds against a jet-black background. Turn on the flashlight? Too dangerous.

One deep breath. Mind clear. Shove the emotion down to his

chest. The grinding of debris under his shoes sounded deafening as he moved toward the light, his pistol pointing the way. Three slow steps. Stop. Listen. Scan. Three more steps. Repeat.

Repeat.

Repeat.

The flickering glow was close enough to touch. The sliver of brightness squeezed between the wall to his left and the one in front. He brushed his fingers along the light and froze. It wasn't a wall before him. Fabric. Bed sheets? A curtain.

Jeremy pushed the cloth mere centimeters, enough to allow him to see beyond. He leaned toward the gap, taking in the scene before him.

Several candles sat on boxes throughout the space, sputtering and casting eerie shadows on the walls. In the front of the room sat a cooler, now painted gold, flanked by stuffed toy angels. His Ark of the Covenant.

Off to the left, standing behind a heavy wooden table, a man dressed head to toe in white. Talbot. The murderer's eyes were closed, and he swayed slightly as his hands passed over the form on the table. Rebecca, pale, not moving. *No.*

Jeremy held his breath and eased into the room. No clean shot from here. Too dangerous with Rebecca between them. If he could get a step or two closer—

"No," Talbot screamed. "You can't come in here. He'll kill you. Get out!"

"Can't do that, Cody."

"My name is Levi. Levi! Can't you see? You have to go. Now!"

Jeremy took half a step. "Sure, Levi. Whatever you say. Just let me have the girl, and we'll go away. I promise."

Talbot reached beside Rebecca and grabbed a knife. "I'll kill her. I swear."

So she's still alive. "I know what's going on here ... Cody."

"Stop calling me that. Your gun. Lay it on the floor, and kick it over here."

"I don't think—"

Levi pressed the knife against Rebecca's throat. "Do it now."

I don't need my gun to kill you. Jeremy held out his left hand and squatted. "Okay. Easy. Here. I'm dropping the gun." He placed the Glock on the floor and kicked the pistol toward the table. The weapon slid to a stop at Cody's feet.

The blade stayed against the girl's neck. "Now get out. Get out, or I'll kill her."

"How come I'm not dead?"

Talbot squinted and shifted his stance. "What?"

Jeremy shuffled a few inches closer. "When I came in here, you said he'd kill me. Who's he?"

"God. This is his room. You're not a priest. You can't come in here, or he'll kill you."

"Huh. And yet, here I am. Don't you wonder why that is … Cody?"

Talbot pointed the knife at Jeremy. "I told you. Levi."

"Nope. Not anymore. How do you think I knew where you were? Who do you think sent me?"

"Sent you? Doesn't matter. If God is for me, who can be against me?"

Jeremy extended his hands, palms up, and slid closer. "See, that's the thing, Cody. God's not for you. He gave up. Said you weren't worth it. Too many mistakes. That's why I'm here."

Talbot brushed the back of his hand across his lips. "Liar! You just … just stay back."

"It's true, Cody. You know it is. Want to know why he gave up on you? You broke one of his commandments."

"He told me to. Sacrifice them, he said. All I did was obey. You can't trick me with—"

Jeremy shook his head and frowned. "Wrong commandment. Ever hear the one about honoring your mother and father?"

Talbot swallowed hard and swung the knife back and forth. "What? I took care of my mother until the day she died."

"What about after she died? Man, you should've seen her body. The way the birds pecked at her flesh and the scavengers chewed on guts. Not pretty. You didn't treat her with respect, Cody. I can show you. I've got the pictures on my phone."

"Shut up! I'll finish this and then he'll take me back. He always takes me back."

"Wonder what she said when she got to heaven? I mean, her own son killing her, then leaving her body for the birds and wolves. Imagine that was quite the conversation with God, don't you?"

Talbot's eyes widened. "I didn't have a choice. He knows that. She was sick. She was gonna die anyway."

Jeremy scooted another few inches. Six feet, maybe a little less, to Rebecca. "Did he tell you to kill her, Cody?"

"She was a threat. Putting everything in danger." He licked his lips and blinked rapidly.

Another few inches. "It's over. His judgment is final. You know that. He sent me to end this, one way or the other."

"No! I can still kill the girl."

"Sure you can. And do you know what'll happen if you do that? Your sins, Cody, all of them, poured out here. God's wrath filling this room. And when I'm done with you? After what you did to your mother, oh, the Lord's got something special planned for your body. And when there's nothing left but bones? Guess where I'm supposed to take them?"

Talbot's breaths came fast now, his eyes fixated on Jeremy. "Back to—"

"That's right. The hole under your bedroom. You remember? Back where your mom would lock you up while she did … things. I'll drop you there and leave you for the scorpions and snakes. You kill that girl, that's your eternity." Almost close enough to—

Cody screamed and raised the knife.

Jeremy grabbed Rebecca's arm and yanked her off the table nanoseconds before the blade dug into the wood. The girl moaned as Jeremy spun her body onto the ground behind him. He turned in time to see Cody lunging over the table toward them, his knife flailing wildly.

Jeremy stood his ground, shielding Rebecca from the attack. His attacker crashed into him, buckling Jeremy's left leg. Both men went down, and Jeremy grunted as the blade sliced his shoulder. He grabbed at Cody's wrists and used the attack's momentum to propel himself on top of his assailant.

Cody bucked and thrashed, kicked and screamed, desperate.

Jeremy used his weight advantage to wear down his opponent and wait for his opportunity. His shoulder throbbed, and blood soaked his shirt. Can't risk passing out. Not while Talbot's alive. When the chance came, he didn't hesitate. Chin pressed toward neck. Teeth clenched. Frown and, just like he was sneezing, he drove his forehead into Cody's nose.

Talbot gasped in pain, allowing Jeremy time to shift into a sitting position and use his knees to pin his foe's arms to the ground. The ex-FBI agent pried the knife from Cody's hand and threw it across the room. This fight was finished.

But Jeremy wasn't. His fist plowed into Talbot's left cheekbone three times before the man slipped into unconsciousness. Jeremy stood and moved to Rebecca, checked her pulse, and grabbed his phone. He dialed Director Bailey, reported his location, and requested an ambulance for Rebecca and himself.

"What about Talbot?" Bailey asked.

Jeremy stared at the man lying a few feet away. Cody stirred as he began to come to. "Sorry, sir. Talbot's dead. I had to shoot him."

He hung up the phone, retrieved his pistol, moved to the prone figure, and prodded him several times with his foot. "Wake up. Time to meet God."

Cody's eyes cracked open, and he turned his head. Blood still flowed from his nose, and the red marks covering his face were already changing to blackish-purple.

Jeremy squatted, grabbed Talbot's chin, and turned the man's face toward him. He waved the Glock inches above Talbot. "See this? It's more than you deserve. A quick death."

He placed the weapon near Cody's temple. "Give my best to your mom."

A whimper from behind him. "Mister Jeremy?"

That beautiful voice.

He shoved Talbot's head to the side and pressed the pistol just above the man's ear. One squeeze of the trigger. End him.

"Mister Jeremy, my arm hurts."

He glanced over his shoulder. "I know it does, sweetheart. I'll be there in just a second. Cover your ears, okay? And close your eyes. There's going to be a loud—"

"Can we go see Mama now?"

Talbot moaned, then smiled. Blood coated his teeth and dribbled from his mouth. "Too weak. He'll find another." A cough wracked his body. "Thy will be done."

One squeeze of the trigger and it would all be over.

He peeked over his shoulder again. Rebecca lay there, watching and waiting.

One squeeze of the trigger and he'd lose her.

"No," Jeremy said. "Too strong." He eased the pistol back into its holster and moved to Rebecca. "Ready to go home?"

She nodded and tried to sit up.

Sirens screamed toward the theater, and Jeremy glanced again at Talbot before sitting and gently helping the little girl into his lap. He wrapped his arms around her, careful not to squeeze too tightly. "Some people are coming to take care of you. They'll get you fixed right up. I promise."

She smashed her face against his chest. "You're not going to leave me, are you?"

He nuzzled his nose in her hair and whispered. "Never."

EPILOGUE

Jeremy placed his arm on the back of the sofa so Rebecca could lean against him. They each had slings, matching colors of course, and Maggie had insisted he stay in the spare bedroom while his knife wound healed. She said that taking care of two kids wasn't much more trouble than taking care of one. The swelling in his left leg was better and the bruises somewhat faded, but the doctors told him to get used to the stiffness and pray it didn't get worse. Oh, and invest in a good cane.

"Whatcha want to watch now?" he asked.

Rebecca looked up and shook her finger. "You're not supposed to have your feet on the coffee table."

He wiggled his socked toes. "I'm not? Who says?"

"Mama says we don't do that."

"Well then, I guess I'd better sit up straight, huh? And if I'm going to do that ..." He poked a finger in the little girl's side, laughing as she erupted in a fit of giggles.

Maggie came into the room and covered her mouth to hide her smile. "What's going on in here? You two are supposed to be resting."

Jeremy raised his hand. "She started it."

"Uh-uh. He did. His feet were on the table."

He poked her again. "Tattletale."

Maggie sat on the couch and grabbed the TV remote. "If I have to send you both to your rooms, I will."

"Yes, ma'am," Jeremy said.

"Yes, ma'am," Rebecca echoed.

Maggie opened the DVR menu on the TV. "Did you watch it yet?"

"Nope," he said. "Told you I wouldn't watch it without you."

She pressed a button, and the network's news ditty started playing as their logo swept across the screen. The anchorman positioned his hands on the desk and stared into the camera. "We start tonight with breaking news out of Colorado. A startling confrontation at a town hall event hosted by presidential candidate Senator Diane Morgans. Let's go live to Jackie Molson."

The view shifted to a woman standing in front of a small building. "Chaos in Colorado Springs today as Senator Diane Morgans, mere weeks away from her party's national convention and an almost certain nomination, held an open question-and-answer session. Nothing unusual about that. She's hosted dozens of these meetings. This session, though, has her campaign in crisis mode. Let's take a look at the video."

An image of a library's interior zoomed onto the TV screen. A hundred or so people sat in chairs facing the senator and other dignitaries. A line of people stood behind a microphone in the center aisle, waiting their turn to speak. A young man with a ponytail asked a question about the senator's commitment to environmental issues and received a somewhat generic response. Sporadic applause spread across the crowd as the next questioner approached the microphone.

A woman in jeans and a long sleeve yellow T-shirt tucked her shoulder length black hair behind her ears before holding the mic.

Jeremy leaned forward. "It's her."

The woman cleared her throat. "Senator Morgans, thank you for this opportunity."

The candidate smiled and nodded. "You're quite welcome. I enjoy getting out and meeting people. Hearing what they have to say about the issues."

"Yes. I wonder if you would address the accusations that your husband is a war criminal?"

Loud murmurs and a few boos filled the room, and the senator motioned for silence. "I have heard those rumors and can unequiv-ocally state that there is no truth to them whatsoever. My husband served with distinction, and I'm proud of him, as I am of all the men and women who serve our nation."

Applause resonated through the room, and an elderly man approached the microphone.

The dark-haired woman didn't move. "So you don't believe your husband murdered innocent Afghan civilians?"

A few more boos and a couple of shouts for the woman to sit down and shut up.

The senator's smile was wider than ever. "No, I don't. There is absolutely no evidence to support that rumor. None. Now, you've had your turn. Please allow someone else to have theirs."

The woman nodded and took a deep breath. "Thank you, Sena-tor. My name is Homa Nezam, and I am an Afghani immigrant. I was there when your husband murdered those people. I watched as he shot unarmed civilians in the head."

The room exploded into motion as reporters maneuvered for position. Camera flashes surrounded the Afghan woman. The senator no longer smiled.

Maggie turned the TV off. "Well, I guess this just got real interesting."

Jeremy chuckled. "That's an understatement. Cronfeld's got to be going nuts."

"Surprised you haven't heard from him yet."

"Nah. His wife's got him reined in, for now at least. They're too busy trying to handle Homa."

"Think she's in any danger?"

He shook his head. "Don't see how. She's pretty much surrounded by press day and night. Making the talk show circuit too. If anything were to happen to her, the whole country would suspect Morgans."

"So it's over?"

Jeremy stretched his legs and placed his feet on the coffee table. "Doubt it. No matter how this all turns out, they're going to want payback."

Rebecca glanced at her mother before sliding down the couch far enough that her feet could rest on the edge of the table.

"You two are a bad influence on each other," Maggie said.

"Yeah?" Jeremy said. He nudged Rebecca. "She started it."

Maggie rolled her eyes, sighed, and scooted closer to her daughter. "Bad influences," she repeated, before planting her feet next to Jeremy's.

SNEAK PEEK

A PEEK AT CHAPTER ONE OF WINTER'S
FURY, THE NEXT BOOK IN THE JEREMY
WINTER SERIES.

S hane Kingston pulled the closet door shut, shoved a couple of
old towels against the light-leaking gap at the bottom, then
scooted until his back pressed against the wall. Dress shirts, each
ironed and hanging with its matching tie, brushed his face and he
pushed them toward the other end, down where the polished
shoes rested in their cubbyholes, and the creased pants waited on
their wooden hangers.

Outside, the TV blared commercial-free recordings of *The Jerry
Springer Show* just loud enough for the on-screen ruckus to creep
through the door. Indistinct voices talked and screamed in a never-
ending cycle of confrontation.

Most of the day was booked, with a funeral starting soon and
then off to his second-shift job at the call center. Adulting left little
time for play. Better get right to it. He closed his eyes as they
adjusted to the lack of light. With darkness came peace.

His hand inched along the baseboard until he found what he
sought, right where he'd left it yesterday. Hard plastic, nearly a
foot tall with pop-out wings, buttons for lasers, and a broken

retractable helmet. No batteries, of course. Buzz Lightyear never spoke. Never zapped anyone. Never went to infinity and beyond.

But his day would come.

Too dangerous to make a sound now. There could be no noise from the closet until the yelling on the other side of the door stopped.

Shane hunched over Buzz, took a deep breath, pressed the button to extend the toy's wings, and flew him in slow, gentle figure eights before bringing him to a soft landing in his lap. Buzz always enjoyed his flights and kept his toothy grin, a stark contrast to Shane's pounding heart and beading sweat. The space ranger's right wing broke off years ago, probably kicked or thrown in the final confrontation between Shane's parents. After that, Mom was gone. Dad was happy. And Shane grew. Accepted the inevitable. Embraced it.

Jerry Springer's guests continued their screaming while the studio audience roared their approval, and Shane scooted lower until he was lying on his side, his back to the door. He popped Buzz's wings back into their retracted position and placed him on the floor so they faced one another. They couldn't see each other. Couldn't talk either. But it didn't make any difference.

Shane chuckled. What would a psychiatrist have to say about this routine? Lots, most of it probably correct. No question he had issues, but what thirty-three-year-old over-educated under-employed man didn't? You deal with what you've got. Maybe not in a way society approves of, but at least in a way that is productive, efficient, and creative.

He sighed, put Buzz back in the corner, and checked his phone. The funeral began in an hour. Such a waste of time. He didn't want to go but felt obligated. The widow, Brenda Clancy, was one of his employees, and he needed to represent the company and her coworkers. No doubt she was still traumatized. Her husband's death had been especially brutal. Words like *grisly* and *gruesome* came to mind. Rumor had it a firefighter threw up at the scene. A horrible, painful accident.

Just the way Shane planned it.

Read the rest of the story FREE on Kindle Unlimited!

AUTHOR'S NOTE

Thank you for reading *Dead of Winter*. I hope you've enjoyed the second novel in the Jeremy Winter series.

I'd greatly appreciate it if you'd take the time to leave a review of the book online when you get the chance. Other than buying their work, the best thing you can do for an author is write a short review.

There's more to come from Jeremy Winter. If you want to be among the first to know the latest news (and maybe win a free book), you can subscribe on my website, www.tomthreadgill.com. I send out a once-a-month-when-I-remember-to-do-it email with things like publishing dates and special offers. I promise not to spam you or give your email address to anyone else.

Made in United States
North Haven, CT
22 June 2024

53919677R00202